The Melrose Secret

The Melrose Secret

A Novel

William Bain

iUniverse, Inc.
New York Lincoln Shanghai

The Melrose Secret

iUniverse books may be ordered through booksellers or by contacting:

iUniverse
2021 Pine Lake Road, Suite 100
Lincoln, NE 68512
www.iuniverse.com
1-800-Authors (1-800-288-4677)

ISBN: 978-0-595-45458-7 (pbk)
ISBN: 978-0-595-69500-3 (cloth)
ISBN: 978-0-595-89770-4 (ebk)

Printed in the United States of America

For Eleanor, my wife, my one true love.

Acknowledgments

I want to thank Linda Bain and Dawn Govan, who helped to format my early manuscript. My thanks also go to Eleanor Bain, who provided constructive comments and helped me to recall the places we have visited, and which provide the background for many of the scenes in the novel.

Finally, a belated thanks to my late mother, Christina Bain who, from my earliest years, inculcated in me a love of reading and books.

Prologue

June 24, 1998. Melrose Abbey, Scotland

A large crowd had gathered at the Abbey grounds in the south of Scotland to watch the ceremony that would accompany the re-burial of the embalmed heart of King Robert the Bruce. Two years earlier, the heart had been found in a leaden casket during an archaeological "dig" in the Abbey Chapter House. Now, Donald Dewar, the Secretary of State for Scotland, would officiate at the final interment of the heart of the famed fourteenth century king who had freed Scotland from English rule.

Andy McPhee, a tour guide for Historic Scotland (the agency which supervised the ruins of the once-magnificent Abbey) watched as everyone followed Donald Dewar on a leisurely walk around the Abbey grounds. The hole where the lead casket lay was near Andy—it would shortly be covered by a stone plinth that would be cemented in place once the dedication ceremony ended.

Andy's boss had asked him to stay near the plinth. *As if anyone would steal an embalmed heart*, he thought.

A distinguished-looking gentleman detached himself from the crowd that surrounded Dewar. He walked past Andy with an erect military bearing. He stopped at the plinth, and removed a silver box from his pocket. Almost reverentially, he knelt and placed it in the hole beside the embalmed heart. Andy watched, as he was curious as to what had happened. When the elderly man rose and walked back to join Dewar, Andy casually walked over to the hole.

The silver box was nestled beside the lead casket. Andy saw the words *Capillus Jesu* inscribed on the box. He wondered what he should do, but his thoughts were interrupted as Dewar and the crowd approached for the dedication ceremony.

Andy stood to the side as Dewar spoke movingly about the debt Scotland owed to King Robert the Bruce who had defeated the army of England's King Edward II at Bannockburn in 1314. Dewar proceeded to say how proud he was that the king's descendant, Sir Jock Bruce, was present that day for the ceremony. He pointed to the elderly man that Andy had seen put the silver box in the hole. Sir Jock smiled, evidently proud of his ancestor, but his smile said more—it seemed to indicate that he had a secret.

A few weeks later, Andy left the church that he attended infrequently. He paused to speak to the priest as a thought had come into his mind. "Father," he said, "what does *Capillus Jesu* mean?"

"My, my, Andy; where did you get that?" the priest asked.

Andy dissembled. "Oh," he mumbled, "I read it in a book some time ago."

"It means the hair of Christ, or Jesus' hair," the priest said before moving to speak to a young woman.

CHAPTER 1

Some years later.

The Air Canada Airbus began its descent into Glasgow Airport. Seated in 1A in business class, Alan Bruce looked out of the window towards the Lowlands hills, merging to the west into the Highland mountains. Following the ribbon of the River Clyde, sparkling in the early morning sun, his eye was drawn to what appeared to be a pimple from five thousand feet. In reality, as he knew, it was Dumbarton Rock, the ancient promontory some three hundred feet high, at the confluence of the River Clyde and the River Leven, and on top of which sat Dumbarton Castle. In the hills above lay Bruce House, where he would soon see his grandfather, Sir Jock Bruce.

Alan smiled at the thought of seeing his grandfather, who had called him unexpectedly the previous day at his law office in Toronto. He was concerned about Jock's news regarding his health; but equally, he was intrigued by the mysterious secret that Jock felt he needed to tell him. In his mind he replayed the conversation the previous day with his grandfather. Sir Jock had said: "Today Alan, I had a visit from an American evangelist: fellow by the name of Mark Varley. He's with Jackson Ford's 'Crusade for Christ' in Edinburgh. Somehow—can't think how—he's got wind of a Bruce family secret and I need to tell you about it before I turn up my toes."

Alan had replied that he didn't expect that to happen for a long time. But he was surprised by Jock's response. "Well, that's part of my reason for calling. My doctors have found something—probably should expect it at age eighty-three—and I really do need to see you as soon as possible." Quite concerned now, Alan had cancelled his appointments and arranged an immediate flight from Toronto.

His thoughts were interrupted by the plane bumping down in Glasgow Airport. Jamie Robb was waiting for him as he came into the arrivals concourse. He hadn't changed much over the years. Even in his sixties, he still retained that strong military bearing he had acquired as a Sergeant Major in the Scots Guards, where he had served with Colonel Jock Bruce on many assignments. Now he was Sir Jock's driver and general handyman.

"Good to see you, Jamie," Alan said, holding out his hand for a firm handshake.

"And it's good to see you, Mr Alan. The Colonel is anxious to see you as soon as possible. He seems a bit upset about something, but he keeps his own counsel so I don't really know what is happening."

"Well Jamie, I hope to find out soon."

The dark blue Jaguar, with Jamie at the wheel, glided along the M8 motorway from the airport and over the Erskine Bridge, a graceful arch spanning the River Clyde, and moved west down the A82 to Dumbarton. Just short of the town, Jamie turned right at the hamlet of Milton and drove up the winding hill road. Bruce House nestled in the Kilpatrick Hills high above Dumbarton. It had been built by one of the Bruces centuries earlier, and its crenellated stone walls and imposing tower looked ready to withstand any siege. The covered entrance way to the main door was guarded by two stone lions, whose stern faces seemed destined to turn away anyone with sinister intentions. A short distance from the main entrance, a stone bridge traversed a cascading waterfall, which noisily splashed down the hill towards the River Clyde. To the south, a decorative lily pond provided a picturesque view from Sir Jock's library, with its twin bay windows.

Jamie stopped the car at the front entrance. As Alan opened the car door his grandfather appeared and shook his hand. Sir Jock looked at his grandson. Alan was well over six feet tall, with dark wavy hair, blue eyes, and an athletic build. "Welcome Alan. So glad you made it, and in such a timely fashion," he said.

Alan looked at him with affection. It had been a year since he had last seen Sir Jock. In that time his grandfather had become slightly stooped and although his hair was thinner and white, his moustache was still neatly trimmed. He still had the commanding presence of a military officer; his red and blue Guards tie showed his pride in his old regiment.

"Come in Alan," Sir Jock said, putting a paternal arm around his grandson's shoulder. "Have you eaten? It's breakfast time and Mrs Doig is anxious to feed you."

Alan smiled as they entered the hall. It was so familiar: nothing ever seemed to change. The panelled walls bore the portraits of many of the Bruce clan, and the Bruce tartan shield, with cross swords beneath, hung on the west wall. Instead of the formal dining room, Sir Jock led the way to the sun room, just off the kitchen, where Mrs Doig stood by the stove, ready to cook a full breakfast.

"Typical Scottish breakfast, Alan?" Sir Jock asked with a smile, certain of his answer.

"Well, no. My arteries wouldn't stand it. Can I have coffee, toast, and some fruit?"

"Ach! You'll no' get through the day without a good breakfast," Mrs Doig said. "You Canadians just don't know what's good for you."

"Perhaps, Mrs Doig, but I'll try it my way, even if it's only for today," Alan replied.

When Mrs Doig had left, Alan turned to his grandfather. "So Grandad, what's the news about your health?"

"Well it seems that I have a fast-growing cancer. My doctors found something when I had a check-up. And I'm not willing to go through surgery, radiation therapy, and chemotherapy. Not at my age. I've had a good life and intend to enjoy what is left of it."

Alan knew that once Sir Jock had reached the decision, he was unlikely to change his mind. Nevertheless, he decided to try. "Would it help to get a second opinion?" he asked.

Sir Jock snorted. "Second opinion? Facts are facts, Alan. Opinions are for politicians."

Alan shook his head. He wasn't going to change his grandfather's decision. "Well, in that case why don't you tell me about the Bruce secret. What's going on?"

"It's a long story Alan," Sir Jock replied. "But it's necessary to give you the background so that you will appreciate what has happened in the last few days. Perhaps we should move to the library. We'll be more private there and Mrs Doig can remove our breakfast dishes."

Alan glanced out of the library window at the lily pads floating on a large pond. Beyond that, he noticed that the ancient rhododendron bushes, cascading down the hillside, were already heavy with massive pink and purple blossoms. The view was both unexpected and relaxing, reminding him that Spring came earlier in Scotland than in Canada.

Comfortable chairs were arranged around a stone fireplace in which a welcoming log fire crackled and sparked. Weak early morning sunlight shone through a wall of windows, illuminating the well-stocked oak book-shelves encircling the rest of the room. Scattered Persian rugs covered the old oak floor.

"Why don't you sit there Alan?" Sir Jock pointed to a dark blue armchair on one side of the fire. "Get comfortable, because I've a lot to tell you."

Sir Jock sat opposite him. "As I told you when I called yesterday, it seems that an evangelical group from Alabama has somehow found out about a secret we Bruces have kept in the family for centuries. That simply emphasized my need to pass it on to you; and I'm delighted you were able to fly over at such short notice."

"Grandad, I'm always happy to see you. But the news about your health has been a shock."

Jock's hand rubbed his chin. "I'm sorry about that, Alan, but it can't be helped. I hope you are prepared for another surprise."

Alan looked with curiosity at the older man. "I hope so, Grandad. Why don't you tell me what it is?"

"Very well," Jock began. "This is an unlikely story I have to tell you. You're bound to be sceptical, Alan: I was for a while; but now I'm convinced. You see, we have had a lock of Jesus' hair in the possession of the Bruce family since the fourteenth century."

Alan looked at him and shook his head. "Are you sure that's not just an old wives' tale, Grandad?"

Jock shook his head. "I understand why you would think that. I'd always been a bit sceptical too, but when I looked into its provenance and finally got some scientific proof of its age, I became convinced."

"Go on then: tell me more."

"Oh, I will. Believe me. However, the key fact that made me phone you, Alan, is that a religious group in the States has learned of the existence of the hair, and I think they want to get their hands on it."

"That sounds crazy."

"Maybe, but that is why I wanted to see you. When I die you will take over my place in the family, and will have to keep, or pass on, the secret about that hair."

Alan sat back in the armchair and crossed his legs. "I'm getting comfortable Grandad." He smiled at the old man. "Why don't you begin?"

Sir Jock looked at the crackling fire and shook his head slowly, as if concentrating his thoughts. He gave a weary smile. "Let me begin with a bit of family history. No doubt you'll have heard some of this before from your father, but, it's best that I put it in perspective."

Alan sat back in the armchair and nodded for his grandfather to begin.

Sir Jock looked at his young grandson. "We need to begin this part in the fourteenth century. Strangely enough, the story begins not far from here. What I have to tell you is in the historical records. It was the year 1329 and the records show that our ancestor, King Robert the Bruce, who had unified Scotland as an independent nation, was dying. He was at his mansion in Cardross, just outside Dumbarton. Bruce knew that he had little time left, so he summoned the leaders of Scotland and told them of a vow he had made to God, that after he had made Scotland secure, he would make a pilgrimage to fight against the enemies of Christ. Obviously, the king knew that this was not going to be possible, so he asked the nobles to select someone to carry his heart to the Holy Land. They chose Sir James Douglas who had been Bruce's closest ally in the fight to free Scotland from rule by the English monarch, Edward II. Douglas was a strong personality and had gained a reputation as a fearless fighter.

Bruce died at his home in June 1329. His heart was embalmed and placed in a casket of silver and enamel, which Douglas carried with him on a chain about his neck. The following Spring in 1330, Douglas sailed from Berwick, intending to take the heart to the Holy Sepulchre in Jerusalem. He took with him about thirty-five soldiers, including six knights, who had been companions in many battles. Douglas and his force stopped firstly in Flanders."

"Why did Douglas stop in Flanders?" Alan interrupted Jock.

"I'm not sure. Probably to add to his force, for mercenaries were always willing to fight in a war, provided there was a good reward. In any event," Sir Jock continued, "from there he sailed to Seville in Spain. He was welcomed by Alfonso XI, King of Castile and Leon. Alfonso needed help to fight against the Moors of Granada, and Douglas' military reputation was well known. Since he had given himself seven years to fulfill his promise to Bruce, Douglas was content to help."

A knowing smile passed over Jock's face, and he nodded his head, reliving past experiences. "As an old soldier myself, I'm sure Douglas thought that a campaign against the Moors would be good experience for his planned journey to Jerusalem. But whatever the reason, tradition shows that Alfonso gave Douglas command of a division of his army. In a first encounter with the Moorish army outside the town of Teba de Ardales, Douglas forgot his usual caution. Along with ten companions, he charged after a band of fleeing Moors. As they caught up, the Saracens suddenly turned and encircled Douglas and his men. Seeing that he could not escape, history tells us that Douglas took the casket with Bruce's heart from his neck and flung it forward, saying: 'Forward brave heart, as ever thou were wont to do, and Douglas will follow thee!'"

Sir Jock's eyes twinkled. "Of course, you understand that we Scots love our traditions, but I must admit I've always wondered how anyone knew what Douglas said in the heat of battle! In any event," he continued, "when Douglas was found, there were many dead Moors around him and Bruce's casket was by his side."

"A good story, Grandad," Alan said after a moment, "and I always enjoy these tales. But what is its relevance to Jesus?"

Sir Jock paused and took a deep breath. "Here is where my story deviates from the publicly known history. What I have to tell you comes from a secret passed down from father to son in the Bruce family since that time, over 675 years ago."

"And so, you are going to pass that secret to me, is that it?" Alan asked.

"Why yes," Sir Jock stared at him. "I didn't have time to tell your father before he died in that climbing accident. Now I need to tell you, before it's too late."

He looked down at the floor for a moment, deep in thought, and his eyes twinkled as his gaze swept over Alan's face, before continuing.

"When King Alfonso learned of Douglas' courage and his sad death, he called the remaining Scottish knights to meet him in his palace. Alfonso spoke to Sir William Cathcart, and told him of his sorrow at the death of Douglas. He said that the casket with Bruce's heart had been recovered on the battlefield, and this he gave to Cathcart, who brought it back to Scotland for burial at Melrose Abbey.

Alfonso then went into his personal chamber and spoke to Sir William Keith. He gave him a letter to the family of King Robert and a silver casket, which he asked Keith to deliver to Bruce's heir, the young King David. That casket, with Jesus' hair inside, was interred with Bruce's heart at Melrose in 1998."

Jock sipped from his coffee. "But I'm getting ahead of myself," he said. "I took some of the hair and have kept it with me." He put his coffee cup down, and slowly loosened the buttons at the top of his shirt. He looked intently at Alan's expression, as he withdrew a gold locket on a gold chain from around his neck. He held it forward. "This is the locket Alan, and in it is a lock of Jesus' hair."

Alan looked at the old man with affection. He did not want to disturb Sir Jock's story, but could not contain his scepticism.

"It's a good story, Grandad, but I'm a lawyer, trained to examine evidence and to look for proof. As much as I would like to believe you," he searched for the right words, not wanting to cause offence, but could not contain an outburst. "Damn it! It's not believable! I'm sorry, I know this is important to you, but without some proof, how can I accept this as anything more than a piece of family folklore?"

Sir Jock laughed. “I thought you’d say that,” he said. “Didn’t expect any less from you, my boy! Yes, there is some evidence, maybe even ‘proof’ as you call it—you’ll have to decide for yourself.”

Jock looked at his watch. “My goodness, it’s almost noon. You must be exhausted after your flight and a five-hour time change. Why don’t you have a few hours’ sleep and we’ll continue over dinner this evening?”

“Sounds like a plan.” Alan slowly rose from the armchair, stretched and yawned. He did indeed feel tired and now he had a lot to think about. “Am I in my usual room?”

“Oh yes. First-right at the top of the stairs,” Sir Jock said. “We’ll have a pre-dinner drink at 6.30 here in the library and I’ll show you what proof I have. By the way, we’ll be joined by a rather charming young American doctor who has been doing some research for me. Her name is Kate Harris.”

CHAPTER 2

Charismatic preachers are rare, particularly those who go on "Crusades for Christ." The Reverend Billy Graham had done this for many years, but it had been decades since Edinburgh had seen anything to match the fervour which Billy Graham had inspired in the 1950s and later.

The Reverend Jackson Ford was no Billy Graham, but he was good nonetheless—no doubt about it. From his base in Montgomery, Alabama, he had built a large band of followers with his "televangelism", using the power of TV and the charisma of his personality, to preach the love of Jesus Christ, with an implied promise of salvation.

The Usher Hall had been selected as a good venue for the Crusade. It was the concert hall for the Royal Scottish National Orchestra, and normally seated 2300 people in its comfortable red seats. Tonight, however, another five hundred stood at the rear of the stalls and balconies watching the grand spectacle unfolding on the platform stage.

Ford stood in the centre, robed in white, with a lectern before him for his notes. Behind him were banks of seats stretching upward and accommodating rows of choristers, wearing bright blue robes. A magnificent organ filled the entire wall behind them, its pipes rising majestically in copper columns, stretching to the roof of the building. Ford felt very at home in such a theatrical environment. The massed choir had sung the hymns with passion and fervor. The audience was spellbound by his oratorical skills and evident commitment to Christ.

Jackson Ford was now coming to the end of his sermon at the Usher Hall. "Friends," he said, "I ask the Lord to bless you and fill you with his holy spirit, and draw us to Christ Jesus that we might also draw closer to those we love, and closer to those who love us. Deepen our wisdom, increase our compassion, and renew us in this season of restoration. In Jesus' name, Amen."

"Amen," came the answering response from his audience, an audience whose reactions were already being beamed live back to audiences watching the crusade on their TV screens at homes across North America.

Jackson Ford was indeed an impressive figure. Tall, with a mane of white hair, his green eyes sparkled with energy and compassion. His face was long and angular, with cheek bones that captured the TV cameras. He had started life as a minister in the Baptist Church in Montgomery, before the spell of his preaching, and advice from more mercenary colleagues, had drawn him into the world of televangelism. Yet he was not like some, whose careers had become mired in scandal and excessive wealth. Not that Jackson eschewed wealth: he just did not need extravagance. One Rolls-Royce was sufficient; and he did not have a private plane.

It was time for Mark Varley, Ford's right-hand man, to make the pitch for money. Varley was a financial brain. He had an MBA from Harvard, and early in his career he had established a number of entrepreneurial companies with a partner who had, in his words, "robbed me blind." Afterwards, he swore never to be poor again. With a wink at Providence, as Varley put it, he had encountered Jackson Ford soon after, and had seen the opportunity to create substantial wealth to help Jackson with his evangelism, and also to enrich himself. He had done well, and was now a multi-millionaire thanks to his "Reverse Tithing" concept, whereby his contract with Ford allowed him to retain 10% of all revenues. Yet he still had hunger for more. His commitment to Christianity was shallow: it was a means to fulfill his ambition for wealth..

Varley carefully placed his glasses over his dark brown eyes as he rose and looked over the audience. "The work of Jesus is demanding," he said. "We travel widely spreading the Word. We rely on help from people like you here this evening in the famed Usher Hall." He paused and looked straight into the TV cameras before continuing as he pointed, "and also on all of you out there watching us from your corner of the world. Please give generously, by calling the number on your screen."

Again Varley looked over the audience. "And for you here this evening in Edinburgh, please feel free to come forward and speak to our counsellors who are waiting on the stage behind me, to advise you on your problems and aspirations."

Seated in the audience, Andy McPhee looked at his wife Jenny. He had reluctantly agreed to come with her to the crusade—not because he shared the religious fervour that she had found after having recovered from a devastating heart attack. Andy had another reason, and one he hoped would earn him some money. He worked as a guide for Historic Scotland. Based at Melrose Abbey, his job was almost a sinecure, since there was really not much to do in the ruined abbey. There were no movable objects people could steal, only the remains of a once powerful abbey, which had long since fallen into disrepair. Of course, there was the plinth marking the site where the heart of King Robert the Bruce had been buried in 1998.

Andy had been there that day. He had seen an elderly white-haired man with a proud military bearing, place a silver box beside the casket containing King Robert's heart. Andy had not thought about this event for years, not until Jenny had persuaded him to come to the Rev Jackson Ford's "Crusade for Christ." That triggered a thought: back in 1998, when he had seen the words *Capillus Jesu* engraved on the silver box, he had asked his priest what the words meant. The priest had been curious why he'd been asked such a question, but had finally said that it meant "the hair of Jesus."

Andy was not a well-educated man; but he was wily, and now he wondered if he might make some money from this knowledge. In his crafty way, he thought that the American evangelists might be interested. And, of course, he would tell them, but for a cash payment.

Jenny reached the stairs leading to the stage, with Andy following closely. She was met by a young man who directed her to a desk where people were taking down particulars, especially credit card numbers, before directing the supplicants on towards Jackson Ford for a personal blessing.

While Jenny moved onwards, Andy searched out Mark Varley who was standing to one side.

"Mr Varley," he said: "I'm Andy McPhee."

"Good to meet you, Andy. Have you been blessed?"

"Well, I hope to be. That's why I wanted to speak to you. I have something you might want to know."

"Really?" Varley raised an eyebrow.

"Yes."

"And what would that be?"

"I know where you can find a relic containing the hair of Jesus."

Varley smiled condescendingly. "I hardly think that is possible," he sneered.

"Think what you like," Andy replied. "I know what I've seen with my own eyes. And I could let you know where to find it—for a suitable payment of course."

Varley was no fool. He had lived and worked with hucksters and knew the scams that they used. Yet there was something about the little red-haired Scot that rang true. He decided to learn more; but not here.

"Andy," he said, "as you can see we are very busy at present. Why don't you give me your phone number and I'll call you tomorrow?"

"Okay," Andy wrote his number on a card, gave it to Varley and looked to find his wife. Jenny had just been blessed by Ford, and was also looking for him. They met at the stairs going down from the stage.

The next day, Andy's phone rang at his small house in Melrose. It was Mark Varley.

"Andy," Varley said, "I have been thinking about what you told me. Candidly, it's hard to believe. And I wouldn't do anything without proof. But if you can provide that, then of course we can talk about an appropriate payment for you. Can you do that? Give me proof?"

Andy, of course, did not have proof. But he knew what he had seen; and the fact that Sir Jock Bruce had placed the object under the plinth gave him a feeling that it might be enough to convince the American that it could be true. So he said to Varley, "Proof? That really is a matter of faith, isn't it? Isn't that what your Jackson Ford says?"

"Well, yes. But faith, in this case, is a two-way street, Andy. I need to have faith that what you're telling me is true. And if it is, well then you can have faith that I'll make sure you get your just reward."

Andy grunted, "Aye, well, how do we get to that point?"

"Why don't we meet? Tell me where you are, and I'll meet you there."

Andy did not want Varley to know where he lived. And he did not want to Jenny to become involved either. "I can meet you at your hotel, if you like," he said.

"Fine, let's do that. I'm at the Caledonian Hilton, at the West End of Princes Street. Ask for me at reception when you arrive. Is 11 o'clock good for you?"

"Yes, that's fine," Andy replied.

They met in Varley's suite overlooking the view to the Castle and Princes Street. The Caledonian Hotel is part of the establishment in Edinburgh. Situated at the West End of Princes Street, its massive sandstone façade is one of total grandeur. Its rooms are well furnished and Varley's suite was quite opulent. Andy was impressed. Anyone who could afford to stay at the Caledonian should be able to pay a lot for what he had to offer.

"Well Andy," Varley began, "tell me about your fantastic story."

Until he could see some actual money on the table Andy had decided to give only a bare outline. "Fantastic, eh?" he said. "Aye, I suppose it may seem that way to you. However, I know what I know; and I know what I've seen."

"Go on."

"I know where you can find a silver box that contains Jesus' hair."

"Yes: you told me that when we met at the Usher Hall. I really need more information." Varley paused and stared at Andy. "Or do you just want to give me the box in return for some money?"

Andy returned the stare. "No, that's not what I had in mind, because the box can't easily be retrieved. Although I could," he hurried on, "but I'd need some payment before I tell you more."

"How much? What did you have in mind?"

Andy looked at the floor, apparently deep in thought, although he had already decided last night how much he was going to ask for. "Well, I think to start, one thousand pounds."

"One thousand pounds?" Varley laughed. "And what do I get in return?"

"Well, I can give you the name of the nobleman who had the box, and who buried it. Beyond that, it will need more than one thousand pounds, much more, to tell you where the box is."

Varley knew that Andy was out of his depth. He could smell a scam. And yet, in a strange way, this didn't quite seem like one. "Tell you what, Andy. I'll give you five hundred pounds now, and the rest when I have a chance to meet with the nobleman. Fair enough?"

Andy thought for a moment: five hundred pounds was better than nothing. And there could be more, much more, to come. Yet he decided to negotiate. "Seven hundred and fifty pounds, and I'll tell you."

Varley knew he had Andy. "No, five hundred pounds it is. And if you don't want that, we'll drop the whole thing."

Andy was trapped. With a show of reluctance he agreed. "Fine, for now. But I'll want more once you speak to him."

"And the name is?"

"It's Sir Jock Bruce, the descendant of King Robert the Bruce."

"And where can I find this 'Sir Jock Bruce'?"

Andy shook his head. "I don't know for sure, but I think he comes from the West of Scotland, somewhere near Glasgow.

With that, Varley produced an envelope containing five hundred pounds, the figure he had earlier decided to pay, and gave it to Andy. "I'll get back to you once I've verified this with Sir Jock Bruce," he said. "By the way," he continued, as Andy rose to leave, "One thing puzzles me. How do you know the box you saw being buried contained hair from Jesus?"

"It had an inscription on it, in Latin, *Capillus Jesu.* That means 'the hair of Jesus, if you know Latin."

When Andy had left, Varley's mind ran over what he would do if he could recover the box with the inscription *Capillus Jesu.* Even if it were false, the possibility of fabricating a story around it could have major commercial possibilities; and if it were true, then the sky was the limit. He couldn't begin to imagine how much money he could raise for Jackson Ford's cause; and one-tenth of it would be his! Varley picked up the phone and dialled Ford's room.

Jackson Ford's strong baritone voice said "Hello."

"Jackson, It's Mark. I have something I need to talk to you about."

"Come right up, Mark."

Varley took the wide carpeted stairs, not wanting to wait for the elevator. Slightly out of breath, he knocked at Ford's door.

"Mark, come in. What's the rush?" Ford looked at him with concern.

"Jackson," he gasped a few times, catching his breath, "I've come across something interesting. It sounds incredible, I know, but it could be important for the Crusade, and for the future of the mission."

"Sit down, Mark. Take your time."

Varley sat on a well-padded armchair beside the window. Jackson sat across from him and crossed his legs. He raised an eyebrow questioningly.

Varley began. He told Ford that the previous evening, at the Usher Hall, he had been approached by a man whom he had later met because of the story he had to tell. "In a nutshell, Jackson, he told me that he knew where a box was buried, containing the hair of Jesus."

"Incredible." Ford shook his head. "Did you believe him?"

"I'm not sure. I guess I'm as sceptical as the next person. And I can also smell a scam a mile off, but I didn't get any bad odour from this guy. I think he believes what he told me."

Ford looked across at Varley. He knew his background, and also knew that the main reason he had employed Varley was because of his financial ability—the skills to generate money for Ford's cause; it certainly wasn't because he thought of Varley as a convinced and committed Christian.

"So, what did you agree with this fellow?" he asked.

"Not much, really. I negotiated a payment of five hundred pounds to get the name of the Scottish noble who apparently buried the box with the words *Capillus Jesu* on it."

Ford's eyes opened wide. "The hair of Jesus Christ!" he exclaimed.

"Yes, that's what he said."

"And who is that person?"

"Someone called Sir Jock Bruce."

"Have you contacted him?"

"Not yet. I'll try to speak to him, if you agree."

Jackson nodded in agreement. "Why not," he said, "it would be interesting to get his side of the story."

As Varley stood to leave, Ford's phone rang. He answered it and said, "Please ask him to come to my room." He looked at Varley. "That was the front desk. They let me know that Dr Jim Cameron has arrived."

"Who is he?" Varley enquired.

"I met him last night, and asked him to come to see me. He was on the team with Professor Ian Wilmut—you know, the scientist who cloned Dolly the sheep?"

"I seem to remember something about that."

"Yes, he told me a little about it. They succeeded in taking some DNA from the egg of one sheep and fusing it with mammary cells from another, that eventually came to produce an embryo, which was then implanted into the uterus of another sheep. In time it produced Dolly."

Ford shook his head. "Amazing what science can do with DNA, isn't it?"

A thought entered Varley's head. Could DNA be extracted from the supposed hair of Jesus? And, if so, could cloning be a possibility?

* * * *

When he returned to his room it did not take long for Varley to find Sir Jock Bruce's phone number, using British Telecom's enquiry service. It was a 01389 number, which he discovered was in Dumbarton. Further enquiry showed that this was a small town to the west of Glasgow, and about sixty miles from Edinburgh. Varley picked up his phone and rang the number.

A woman's voice answered. "Bruce House."

"Hello," he said," I would like to speak to Sir Jock Bruce."

"Is he expecting to hear from you?"

"No, but I think he will be interested in hearing from me."

"You're an American, aren't you?" Mrs Doig said.

"Yes. My name is Mark Varley. I'm in Scotland with the Reverend Jackson Ford's Crusade for Christ."

"I don't think Sir Jock is particularly interested," she said.

"Perhaps not. But I really do think he will wish to speak to me."

"Very well, I'll see if he is available."

After a pause, Varley heard a cultured Scottish voice, quite different in its tone and accent from what he had been recently hearing in the streets of Edinburgh.

"Bruce," it said, brusquely.

"Sir Jock," Varley started, "my name is Mark Varley ..."

Bruce interrupted. "That I know, Mrs Doig has told me about you and your Crusade."

"Well," Varley continued, "I would really like to talk to you, but not about the Crusade."

"If not that, then what?" Sir Jock barked down the phone, impatient about being bothered by an evangelist from America.

"*Capillus Jesu,*" Varley said.

There was a lengthy pause. "What on earth are you talking about?" Bruce asked, trying not to reveal anxiety. But Varley knew from the delay, and the tone of voice, that he had struck home.

"I think you may know, Sir Jock," Varley said. "The hair of Jesus Christ. That's what I'm talking about. I would really like to meet you. Perhaps we'd find that we might have some common interest in that box."

Bruce almost dropped the phone. The box? Did he mean the casket? What on earth could this stranger know about the casket? But he did have the inscription correct. He licked his lips while he thought, then decided he should meet the American.

"Not sure I can help you, old boy," he said, "but if you care to drop in this afternoon, I'll be glad to see you for a few minutes. Where are you now?" he asked.

Varley replied that he was in Edinburgh.

"In that case, it will only take about an hour to get here." Sir Jock gave him directions and agreed to meet him at 3:00 p.m..

As Varley put down the phone he smiled. So Andy had been right. That was five hundred pounds well spent, and who knew how much more would follow, but not for Andy: Varley was not that altruistic. He could see huge gains for himself and, of course, for the Crusade.

Varley had the Caledonian Hotel concierge arrange the rental of a Mercedes from one of the agencies in Edinburgh. When it arrived at the hotel at noon, it came with clear directions about the route from Edinburgh to Dumbarton.

Varley followed the M8 from Edinburgh, through Glasgow's busiest streets, and passed Glasgow Airport on his right. A few miles later he took the lane for Erskine Bridge. From there, he took the A82 for Crianlarich, a distance off in the Highlands and, as directed, he slowed as he approached the hamlet of Milton. He saw the road to his right, and negotiated the traffic with a quick turn on to the road leading up to the hills, on which the Bruce estate rambled for eighty acres.

After a steep uphill climb, he saw the stone pillars with a sign: "Bruce House, private property." He was expected, so he drove on. The road wound alongside rhododendron bushes, covered with masses of large red, purple, and white flowers. As he turned into the drive leading to Bruce House, which looked to him like a small castle, he saw a man of military appearance with grey hair, standing beside a large dark blue Jaguar, parked outside the entrance to the stone building.

Varley stopped and parked beside the Jaguar. He got out and extended his hand. "Sir Jock," he said, "I'm Mark Varley."

"I'm no' Sir Jock," Jamie Robb replied. "I'm Jamie, his driver. But I know that the colonel is expecting you." With that Jamie turned and led Varley into the reception room of the house. "Wait here," he said gruffly. I'll let Sir Jock know you've arrived."

In a moment he returned and led Varley into the library, where Jock sat behind his desk. He rose to meet him. "Mr Varley, I'm Jock Bruce."

"Pleased to meet you, Sir Jock. Thank you for seeing me."

"Well, I don't have much time. I have to be in Helensburgh to meet some friends for dinner."

"Well, then, I'll get right to the point," Varley said. "May I sit down?"

Bruce motioned towards a chair in front of his desk, then sat back down magisterially.

Varley continued "I wanted to speak to you about a box you buried, and on which the words *Capillus Jesu* appear."

"Yes, yes: you said that on the phone. Don't know where you got that hare-brained idea from. Really don't."

Varley could sense Jock's prevarication. "Well, Sir Jock, I hardly think we would be having this discussion unless there were some truth behind it," he said.

Jock looked at him, wondering how on earth Varley had the information. He had told no one, and could not begin to grasp how the American knew about the casket and its inscription. "Well, let's—for the moment—imagine that there is some truth to what you say. What would it mean to you?"

Varley looked at the old man, gauging how he might react to a financial offer. "Well, if there is indeed a box of that description, you can imagine that my boss, the Reverend Jackson Ford, would like to have it. Even if it doesn't contain the hair of Jesus, it would be an attractive artefact for our evangelical movement."

"What on earth do you mean?"

"Sir Jock, it takes a lot of money to run Ford's worldwide campaign. I am his chief fundraiser, and with that box many people would want to become involved."

"So they would give you money?"

"That's right. We rely on people's gifts."

Sir Jock calculated: perhaps he could still sell the information about the casket, while still leaving it buried beside Bruce's heart. He knew that on his death, his estate would face huge death duty taxes under Britain's punitive tax system. And he did not want his heir, Alan Bruce, to have to sell the estate with all its historic significance to the family, in order to pay these taxes.

Jock looked for a moment at Varley. "I assume you would be willing to pay for this information," he said.

"Correct."

"What did you have in mind?"

Varley hesitated for a moment. "It would depend on what we might be able to do with the hair."

"What do you mean?" Jock raised an eyebrow.

"Have you heard of Dolly the sheep?" he asked.

"Of course. It was a clone. Didn't live too long, as I recall."

"Really?" That was news to Varley.

"So how does that relate to your story about Jesus' hair?"

Varley smiled enigmatically. "I don't know. I really don't."

Jamie Robb entered the room after knocking discreetly on the door. "Colonel," he said, "there has been an accident at the factory, and the police have asked if you can go there immediately. I have the car ready."

Jock stood up from behind his desk. His family had a factory outside Dumbarton that manufactured electrical components. He went outside the library to speak in private to Jamie Robb. "Mr Varley," he said on his return, "you must excuse me. Perhaps we can continue this discussion tomorrow."

"That would be OK," Varley said. In Jock's absence he had placed a small radio transmitter bug on his phone. He wanted to be sure to hear what Jock Bruce said, for he was sure that Bruce would speak to someone about his visit.

CHAPTER 3

Kate Harris sat in the first-class lounge of British Airways at Heathrow airport. Her flight from Boston had been delayed, and she had missed her planned connection to Glasgow. She would have to wait until 5:30 p.m to catch the shuttle service to Glasgow airport, meaning that she would be late for her 6:30 p.m. appointment with Sir Jock Bruce.

"Damn," she thought, "Jock is always a bit of a stickler for timekeeping, but I'm sure he'll understand."

As she took her cell phone from her handbag, she noticed a well-dressed middle-aged man staring at her. She smiled before dialling Bruce House. She was used to men looking at her. Kate was five foot eight with chestnut brown, shoulder-length hair. Slim, with a model-like figure and blue eyes, she knew that nature had given her an advantage. Best of all, she was intelligent. At school in Boston she had been advanced several grades, so that by the age of twenty-one she had a bachelor and master's degrees from Harvard in cellular biology. She had first met Sir Jock eleven years earlier, in 1996, when she had been in Edinburgh completing a PhD in biology under the world-renowned Professor John Brownlee. Now in her mid-thirties, people always seemed puzzled that she had not married. Kate herself was unsure of the reason. Perhaps she intimidated men: or maybe she had just not met the right one.

The phone rang at Bruce House and she heard: "Bruce House. This is Jamie Robb."

"Hello, Jamie," she responded, "it's Kate, Kate Harris. I just wanted to let you know that my flight was delayed getting in from Boston. I'm at Heathrow, booked on the 5:30 shuttle to Glasgow, which is due there around 6:50, so I'm going to be a bit late for dinner."

"That's no problem, Dr. Harris. I was about to leave to meet you off the 4:30 flight; I'll certainly be there when you arrive in a few hours' time." He paused, as a thought came to mind. "I will also let the colonel know."

"Thank you, Jamie," Kate replied. "I'll look for you. Bye."

Alan had slept for only a few hours. Feeling in need of some exercise he put on his running gear and let himself quietly out of a back door. The weather was bright and sunny with a slight breeze rippling the lily pond. He ran past the pond and over the stone bridge that spanned the waterfall and stream one hundred feet below. He paused for a moment on the bridge, leaning over the parapet to watch the waterfall cascade down the hillside, its spray sparkling in the sun. It was never-changing he thought, reflecting on memories of years ago, when he had stood on the bridge with his parents. He sighed at these thoughts. He jogged deliberately up a winding track into the craggy hills above Bruce House. It was a tough climb, but worthwhile. At the peak of the crags, he turned and could see the River Clyde flowing in a silver ribbon out to the sea. At Dumbarton Castle it met the River Leven, which drained from Loch Lomond, four miles away.

Alan moved on relentlessly, his mind wrestling with the facts, or legends, which his grandfather had imparted to him earlier. He loved Jock; but he seriously wondered if the old fellow was getting into his dotage, with the story about the lock of Jesus' hair.

Alan looked at his watch: 5:00 p.m.. He turned back towards Bruce House, which sat lower down the hillside, like a small castle guarding an ancient clan's history.

Alan showered and shaved after his run. He selected a fresh blue shirt and a Gucci tie to wear with his blue blazer and tan trousers. He knew that his grandfather would expect him to be smart for his dinner, particularly since there would be another guest. He found Jock in his library.

"Alan, did you sleep?"

"For a few hours, then I went for a run up to the Long Crags."

"Great," Jock smiled. "Gone are the days when I could do that." He looked at Alan. "A drink before dinner? Dr Harris's flight is delayed. Jamie has gone to meet her and she should be here in less than an hour."

"Thanks, a gin and tonic would hit the spot. But I can help myself."

"Go ahead. While you are there, I'll have two fingers of Dalwhinnie."

Alan poured the amber malt whisky into a crystal glass and handed it to Sir Jock. "Cheers," he said, touching his glass with Sir Jock's.

"Good health," Jock replied, taking an appreciative sip of the single malt. "I suppose you've been thinking about the news I gave you earlier?"

"Couldn't get it out of my head," Alan replied, "But, frankly, I'm sceptical."

"Thought you might say that," Sir Jock replied. "Can't say I blame you, but there is some evidence, hopefully proof, as you lawyers might see it."

Sir Jock took another sip of the Dalwhinnie. "Great stuff, single malt. Perhaps you might try one later. For now, let me show you something." He went across the room to a large desk beside the window and unlocked a drawer. He withdrew an envelope and removed several sheets of paper.

"Can you read Latin?" he asked Alan.

"Well every lawyer knows some Latin, and we use all sorts of Latin tags. Some say we use it to impress or bamboozle our clients. But read it? No."

"I thought that might be the case," Jock said with a smile. "So you'll be pleased to know that I have an English translation of the original letter from King Alfonso XI of Castile and Leon to King David II, Robert the Bruce's son and heir." He moved across the library to Alan. "Here," he said, "read this and perhaps things will become clear. By the way, if you need to check the translation the original document is in the vaults of the head office of the Bank of Scotland in Edinburgh."

Alan took the pages from his grandfather and began to read:

To his Majesty King David II of Scotland, Greetings.

I, Alfonso, King of Castile and Leon, convey to you my fraternal wishes for peace and good health.

By these presents, I send you the casket in which the heart of your father, the great King Robert the Bruce of Scotland, is embalmed. This was found beneath the body of the brave Sir James Douglas, who perished in conflict with the Saracen army at Castile. May God have mercy on his soul.

I learned from Sir James that it was the last wish of your dear father that his heart should be taken to the Holy Land. Sadly, this will not now occur.

Having given careful thought to this matter I have been guided by the Holy Spirit to reach a decision which pains me. Yet it is right that I follow this Holy Guidance. Accordingly, with the heart of King Robert, I am also sending you a Blessed silver casket in which will be found locks of hair from our Saviour, Jesus Christ. In this way, I believe that your father's heart and the hair of our Saviour may be together, bringing some fulfilment of your father's wish to be close to his Saviour's presence.

It is my wish that the casket with your father's heart, and the Blessed Casket be buried together in a sacred place in hallowed ground.

Some may question the veracity of my statements regarding the casket. To dispel doubt therefore, I will now advise you of its provenance,

Before Jesus was crucified, a crown of thorns was placed on his head. The thorns cut deeply into him. After his death, a Roman centurion, one Tiberius Gaius, was stricken with remorse at what had happened to our Saviour. He recovered the crown of thorns. On it he found clumps of hair, matted with the blood of our Lord and Redeemer. He removed the hair and, days later, he placed it in a small metal box on which he had inscribed: "The Hair of Jesus." No one knows definitively what happened thereafter until 325 AD, when the Empress Helena, the mother of Constantine, who is known as the first Christian Emperor, made a pilgrimage to Palestine. There, she had a divinely sent vision that she should visit Jerusalem. On her arrival she endeavoured to find the spot where the sacred body of Christ had been crucified. In time, she discovered that a statue of Venus had been erected over the site of the crucifixion. In this way, any Christian attempting to worship Christ would be seen to worship Venus at that site.

Empress Helena caused the statue of Venus to be torn down. Underneath the rubble, excavations discovered three Crosses. She wanted to identify the cross on which our Dear Lord had suffered. On one Cross a board was found on which Pilate had placed an inscription written in Greek, Latin and Hebrew.

Giving thanks for her discovery, Empress Helena knelt to pray. At the side of that Cross she found a small metal box, on which was inscribed, in Latin, "The Hair of Jesus."

It is this box which I now send you. How did it come into my possession? Again let me assure you of its provenance. In 381 AD a Spanish nun, named Egeria, made a pilgrimage to the Holy Land. She was gone for three years. During that time she visited many sites including the site that had been discovered by the Empress Helena. Egeria was a great healer, famed for her use of medicine to help those in need. One of these was the grandson of Empress Helena, to whom she had entrusted the silver box with the hair of Jesus.

In gratitude for his recovery, he gave the box to Egeria, and it returned with her to Spain. After her death, it was revered as a Holy Relic in the Convent of the Nuns of the Sacred Blood in Grenada. The convent was attacked by the Saracens, but, in a fierce battle, my forces relieved it.

In gratitude for this miracle, for which the nuns had prayed, I was given the box.

I recount this narrative at length, so that you may be assured of the true nature of the box and its contents.

May the Blessings of our Lord be and remain with you and your family forever.

Given By the Hand of

Alfonso XI

King of Castile and Leon

In the Year of Our Lord, 1331

Alan put down the documents and looked at Jock. "Incredible," he said. "It's a good tale. But how can you be sure that the hair is that of Jesus? It could belong to anyone."

"Not anyone," Sir Jock said with a slight smile. "Here is where science comes in. We know for a fact that the hair is two thousand years old."

"Really? How?"

"That's part of the reason for asking Kate Harris to come here. By the way, she doesn't know the story about the provenance of the hair, only that it is ancient."

They were interrupted by Mrs. Doig to let them know that Kate had arrived. Sir Jock gave a broad smile as he left the library, to return in a moment with a woman whose looks grabbed Alan's attention. He guessed she was about his age: early to mid-thirties.

"Kate," Sir Jock said, "meet my grandson Alan. He's a lawyer in Toronto."

Kate gave a dazzling smile as Alan jumped to his feet. "Pleased to meet you," she said.

"It's my pleasure. Can I get you a drink before dinner?"

"I think I'll wait if you don't mind," Kate said." It's been a long day and I'd like to shower and freshen up before dinner." She turned to Sir Jock, "Am I in the guest room?"

"Mrs. Doig has everything ready for you. We'll see you in the dining room at 7.30."

Kate's arrival in the dining room took Alan's breath away. She had changed into a simple emerald green silk dress, enhanced by a pearl necklace and matching earrings. He helped her to a chair across the table from him, with Jock seated at the head of the table, presiding like a Scots Guard Colonel at a formal mess dinner.

The meal was excellent. Mrs. Doig was an accomplished chef, and Sir Jock selected his best claret from the cellar to complement the rare Angus roast beef.

Over dinner the talk was light and witty. Alan spoke about his recent visit to New York, where he had seen the musical "Spamalot," the Monty Python spoof, which he felt was good fun.

Kate had not seen it, but the topic led to a discussion about the comedy of Monty Python, which even Jock knew and enjoyed.

As the coffee was served, Sir Jock suggested that they should move to his library. "It will be more private there, and there are a few things we should discuss."

When they were settled in the library, with Kate and Alan seated on matching armchairs on either side of the stone fireplace, Sir Jock poured himself a malt whisky.

Alan and Kate declined his offer of port, and savoured their coffees.

"Kate," Jock began, "I'm so glad you could come today, particularly since Alan is also here. I've been telling him some of the history of the Bruces." He looked at Alan with an appraising glance, "Even thought he was born in Scotland, he's lived in Canada since he was three, so despite frequent visits with his parents, I'm never sure that he knows enough for someone who will succeed me as head of the clan."

Jock took a sip from his malt whisky.

Alan said, "But he has been telling me a lot of history today, believe me!"

Kate looked at the two men. One, old, yet in control: the other, younger, attractive, intelligent, and obviously fond of his grandfather.

"This sounds like a story I'd like to hear," she said.

"Quite so, quite so," Jock grunted. "But first, Kate, can you confirm the results of the tests on the hair I gave you?" He turned to Alan. "Forgot to tell you earlier. I gave a few strands of hair to Kate. I asked her, as a scientist, to determine the age, if possible." He looked at Kate. "Well, my dear, what do you have to say?"

Kate looked at Alan and rose from her chair. She reached into her handbag and withdrew an envelope containing a report, and a clear packet containing several pieces of hair. "Well, to begin," she said, "when Jock and I first met it was in Edinburgh, eleven years ago. I was working on my PhD at Edinburgh University. At that time, archaeologists had unearthed an object at Melrose Abbey said to contain the heart of your ancestor, King Robert the Bruce." She paused, remembering that occasion. "I guess I assumed that the hair you gave me, Jock, was from King Robert." She gazed at Jock, scanning his face for signs of the disappointment she felt she was about to offer. Kate looked at Sir Jock with moisture in her eyes. "I think I could use one of your malts now," she said.

Taking a sip from the glass, she looked at the two men. "Here is what I found," she said. "The hair cannot be from Robert the Bruce. He died in the fourteenth century, in 1329 to be precise, nearly 680 years ago. Yet this hair is much older."

"Really?" Jock said raising an eyebrow. "How can you be so sure?"

"Well, I went to several scientists I know, all of whom are at the forefront of research on radiocarbon dating of ancient objects and …"

Alan interrupted, with a mischievous glance "What's radiocarbon dating? Sounds like a weird kind of matchmaking service."

"Hardly," she said. "It's a method that uses the rate of decay of the radioactive carbon isotope formed in the upper atmosphere as a result of cosmic radiation upon nitrogen 14. All of us, animals and plants, absorb carbon during our lifetimes. When we die, the radiocarbon steadily decays; and knowing the annual rate of decay, scientists can establish, within a reasonable margin of error, the age of the specimen."

Kate paused, and looked at Alan over her glass. "So far so good?"

"I think so. Please continue."

"Right," Kate nodded. "Well, as I said, when a living organism, animal or plant, dies, the metabolic function of carbon intake also stops. Radioactive carbon is not replenished. There is only decay. Using a newish technique, accelerator mass spectrometry, scientists can measure a specimen's precise radiocarbon date, even with a small sample."

Kate looked at Jock. "You'll probably be interested to note that this technique was used to date the Shroud of Turin and the Dead Sea Scrolls."

"Really," Jock frowned, "so it's reliable?"

"The best scientific method we have," Kate said. She paused, waiting for the next question.

"So, what have you found out about the hair's age?" he asked

"As I said," Kate continued, "the hair is certainly not from the fourteenth century. In fact, the report says it is roughly two thousand years old."

Alan looked at Jock. "Food for thought Alan?"

"Well, it certainly embellishes your earlier story," Alan replied.

"So, it's an earlier Bruce than King Robert?" Kate asked.

Jock shook his head. "Well, no, that's hardly likely. I believe it is the hair of someone from the Mediterranean area."

Kate laughed. "Really? Who from the Mediterranean was around Britain two thousand years ago?" She paused then answered her own question. "Well, if I had to guess, from my flimsy knowledge of history, could it have been someone like Julius Caesar? I seem to recall he invaded in 55 BC."

Jock finished his whisky and blinked several times before deciding he could trust Kate.

"Not Julius Caesar; but another J.C." he said.

"My God," Kate's eyes widened. "You don't mean Jesus Christ?"

"That's precisely who I mean," Jock replied.

Jock stood in front of Kate. "Obviously you are right to be sceptical. I've already begun to tell Alan the story. Best that I bring you up to date also, before I piece things together for both of you."

Alan threw up a hand. "Grandad, this is all very intriguing, but where do we go from here? What else can you say?"

Jock sat down and looked at the two young people in whom he was confiding things he, and generations of Bruces before him, had kept secret.

"Before I go on, Kate, it's important that I let you know about the provenance of the hair."

He quickly recounted the story about Douglas and King Alfonso. He produced a copy of Alfonso's letter and held it towards Kate. "Alan has read this. You should too. But, to save time, let me say that the letter recounts how the hair of Jesus was found, and how it came into the possession of the Bruce family."

"Okay." Kate said, "I'll read this later. Why don't you continue?"

Jock smiled. "Thought you might agree. What is it you Americans say, 'cut to the chase?'"

"Near enough," Kate nodded.

"Well, to continue," Jock said. "an important event took place in 1996. Kate has already mentioned her impression of that. Let me give you both a little more background. In the summer of 1996, a team of archaeologists began excavations at Melrose Abbey, where Bruce's heart was reputed to have been buried after its return from Spain in 1331. Digging under the old Chapter House floor, they unearthed a lead container. Knowing of the history, they sent the container to Historic Scotland in Edinburgh. That agency was anxious to establish whether, indeed, there was a heart in it, and if it was Bruce's."

"That's where I come in," Kate explained. "That's when we first met."

"Yes," Jock agreed. "You were part of Professor Brownlee's team."

"I remember it well," Kate said, "I was a young student then, very much in awe of the Professor, and intrigued with the legend and history of Robert the Bruce."

"Quite so," Jock nodded. "Well, Kate, as you remember, the staff at Historic Scotland were puzzled about what to do. They thought about x-raying the container to determine what was in it. However, it was made of lead and x-rays could not penetrate. The Scottish Office contacted me, as the putative heir, to confirm whether I would agree to their opening the container. At that point I told them that I wanted to be there, and would give a decision when I saw the container."

"So I drove through to the offices of Historic Scotland at South Gyle in Edinburgh. They had assembled a team, including Professor Brownlee, which is where Kate and I first met. Strange to say, the Historic Scotland office at South Gyle is in an industrial estate. Hardly the place for an event of this importance. In any event that was my view at the time."

Jock paused and looked out at the lily pond with a smile on his face. "When I first saw the container I was quite emotional. For in it, if correct, was the heart of my famous ancestor." He looked back at Alan, "I think you might have felt the same way, Alan."

"The container was of lead, and to help the investigation, I agreed that a small hole could be drilled in it to establish what it contained. Historic Scotland's team drilled a hole and inserted a fiber optic cable."

"Yes," Kate exclaimed, "I remember that. But when we looked inside, we had a surprise."

"Quite so," Jock agreed "for what we saw was another casket. So, of course, I agreed that the outer casket should be opened. The staff of Historic Scotland took a hacksaw and carefully cut off the base of the lead container. It was quite a spectacle: there were so many people around, including the media. By the way: some interesting photographs appeared in the Edinburgh papers. They showed the casket." He paused: "You can see the newspaper clippings later, if you wish." Jock moved away from the window and sat down between Kate and Alan, facing the log fire.

"When the end was cut off the lead casket, we saw that it contained a small cone-shaped lead container. It was about ten inches high, with a base of about four inches and with a flat top about one and a half inches in diameter. It was pitted with age, but otherwise it seemed to be in good condition." Jock glanced over at his guests, "Alan, Kate, are you sure you don't want another drink?"

"I think coffee will do for me," Kate said.

Alan nodded. "Me too."

When they had filled their cups and Jock grudgingly accepted a coffee rather than another Scotch, he continued. "Kate, do you remember seeing the brass plaque on the cone-shaped container?"

She looked up, in thought. "Yes. Although I can't recall what it said."

"I do" Jock replied. It was engraved with the words: 'The enclosed casket containing a heart was found beneath Chapter House floor, March 1921, by His Majesty's Office of Works'."

"Don't know why I remember that so well," he said. "But of course I do! It's part of my history!" He looked down and shook his head slightly. "Well, having established that there was a heart inside, and knowing that there was only one heart reputed to have been buried at Melrose, that seemed conclusive."

"To everyone but you," Kate interrupted.

"Correct," Jock agreed. "That's when I asked Brownlee to help."

Kate stood. "Maybe I can recount that part, Alan. Jock seemed determined to establish that it was, indeed, Bruce's heart. So, with his agreement, we drilled a small hole in the container and extracted a small specimen for analysis. We used radiocarbon dating, admittedly not as sophisticated as what we have today. However, it suggested that the specimen was between 650 and 700 years old, which would fit the timeframe for Robert the Bruce."

"So that's the proof?" Alan asked.

"Only part of it," Jock said.

"Yes. We did a DNA test," Kate interjected. "We took a sample from Jock and compared it with the DNA in the specimen. It was conclusive. The heart indeed was that of Robert the Bruce."

Alan finished his coffee. "Fascinating," he said. He turned to his grandfather. "But I thought King Alfonso directed that the hair he sent should be buried with King Robert's heart?"

"True," Jock said, "but I'm afraid not all of our ancestors were reliable." He smiled as a thought crossed his mind. "When Alfonso's letter and the hair came to Scotland in 1331, Bruce's son David, the future King David, was only a child. His mother, Elizabeth de Burgh, had been Robert the Bruce's second wife. She decided to retain the hair, so that it might bring protection to the family. In that way, it has been passed down the family through the years."

Alan rose from his chair and faced Jock. "But you told me that the hair was buried with the king's heart."

Jock nodded. "It is. Now it is."

"I sense you have more to tell us." Alan smiled.

"Of course! Allow an old man the luxury of telling the story in his own way." Jock walked to the side table and poured himself two fingers of Scotch from a crystal decanter, before continuing. "I'm not a terribly religious man, but having kept the hair for a large part of my life, I began to feel that I should meet the wishes of King Alfonso before I died. There was almost a two-year gap between the discovery of Bruce's heart and its re-internment at Melrose Abbey. People began asking questions about the delay."

Jock went to his desk, and from a drawer he produced several newspapers. "See here," he said, "this is an article from the Herald newspaper on January 16, 1998. The article was headed 'Relics return demanded. Bruce's heart still in Capital.' The story noted that in the summer of 1996, the lead casket containing the heart of Bruce was dug up in the grounds of Melrose Abbey. Historic Scotland promised that it would be returned after laboratory tests. But eighteen months later, the casket was still in an Edinburgh laboratory. A spokesman for Historic Scotland blamed the delay on a competition to design an appropriate memorial stone for the burial site, as well as extended excavations to delve into the history of the Abbey Chapterhouse."

Jock waved the newspaper article. "Typical PR spin," he grunted. "There's a little bit of truth, and a lot of bullshit, if you'll pardon me Kate!" He continued, "What really happened is that I had extensive discussions with the late Donald Dewar who headed the government in Scotland. Dewar was a sensible man, a lawyer by background, and a patriotic Scot. So when I told him that I wanted a private part of the Bruce family history buried alongside Bruce's heart, he understood. However, it took some time to work through the bureaucracy in the Scottish office. But when they eventually agreed, I had already decided that the silver casket, which had originally come to us from King Alfonso, should be buried alongside the heart. In this way I have sought to keep Alfonso's wish."

Alan looked at Jock. "But you told me that you had Jesus' hair in a gold locket round your neck."

Kate nodded in agreement. "And if the hair was buried with the heart, what did you give me for testing?"

Jock laughed. "Well, I told you that I met Alfonso's wish. But I'm a Bruce, and I felt that King David's mother, Elizabeth, would have also wanted us to keep some of the hair. For protection, you understand!" He laughed. "We Bruces can be crafty, you know!"

Kate looked at Jock with an inquiring frown.

"You look puzzled, Kate. What I gave you was some of the hair I had kept in the locket Alan just mentioned."

Alan smiled. "You surprise me, Grandad. I didn't know you could be so devious."

"Couldn't have put it better," Kate agreed.

"In any event," Jock continued, "I felt I had met Alfonso's wish, admittedly almost seven centuries later. So, when the heart was reburied, in a private moment granted to me by Donald Dewar, I inserted the silver casket in the opening beside the lead casket with Bruce's heart. It lies there to this day. It is covered with a stone plinth on which is carved the words: 'A noble heart may have nane ease gif freedom failye'."

"Obviously that reflects Bruce's influence in freeing Scotland from rule by England. Donald Dewar unveiled the plinth at Melrose Abbey in June 1998, on the anniversary of Bruce's defeat of Edward II of England at Bannockburn in 1314."

Jock stretched his legs and stood up. "And now you're both up to date," he said. "It's getting late and I'm afraid that this old body needs some sleep. There's more to tell, of course, but it will have to wait until tomorrow I'm afraid." With that he rose, bade them both goodnight, and left.

When Jock had left the library, Alan turned to Kate. "I know it's late for Grandad, but it's only four in the afternoon Toronto time."

"Same as Boston," she replied.

"Would you like to see a bit more of this part of Scotland?" he asked with a smile. "Can't say I know a lot, but there are some places my Dad and Mum used to take me. I thought a short drive might help us to talk."

Kate looked at him. He really was quite attractive; and over dinner, he had shown a sense of humour and was obviously intelligent. She rose from her chair. "I think that would be a good idea," she said. "Give me a moment while I get a sweater. I know how quickly the evenings cool in Scotland." While Kate went upstairs, Alan found Jamie and persuaded him to let him have the keys to the Jaguar.

"Okay, Mr Alan but be careful. Our roads are quite winding; and remember to drive on the left side," Jamie said, as he handed over his precious keys.

"No problem, Jamie. I've driven here many times before."

Kate arrived as Alan drew the Jaguar up to the front door. She looked stunning. She had thrown a dark green mohair stole loosely over her shoulders. It set off her emerald green dress and chestnut brown hair. He helped her into the car, and then took off down the winding road to the A82. He found he could not make a right turn, so he had to turn left for a mile and circle back at a roundabout, before setting off westwards past Dumbarton towards Balloch, at the entrance to Loch Lomond. In Balloch he turned right, and in the late evening sun Kate smiled as she saw the rolling countryside flash past.

"Where are we going?" she asked.

"I thought we'd go to a charming little spot that my parents used to visit. It's not far."

At Drymen, a quaint little hamlet with several hotels and pubs with white-washed walls, still busy with people sitting outside with their drinks, Alan turned down a switchback country road with tall stands of trees on both sides. On the left, Kate saw glimpses of the glittering waters of Loch Lomond. He slowed as he saw the sign for Balmaha. "Here we are," he said: "this really is a magical little spot." It was just a collection of a few houses, a pub, and a small hotel with a busy restaurant. He drove down to a deserted pier that jutted out into Loch Lomond.

"I can remember fishing from here with my Dad."

"Did you catch anything?"

"A couple of trout, as I recall. But most of all, I remember this as a place of tranquillity where I could have time to think, without the bustle of city life. The pier has changed a bit since then."

He looked at the ruins of the wooden pier that mouldered beneath the new metal mesh deck on which they stood. Kate sat on a square metal bollard and looked out over the waters of Loch Lomond. A number of small boats were moored in the Bay. Ahead lay a densely wooded island, its tree clad hills reflected in the Loch's calm waters. She heard a plop as a fish jumped in the water below the pier.

"Yes, I can see how you might find peace here," she murmured. "What happened to your parents, if you don't mind my asking?"

Alan's teeth clenched. He looked at the sky and sighed. "They are both dead. Dad died in a climbing accident in the Swiss Alps, ten years ago. He was a native Scot who emigrated to Canada and became a top banker. Mum was Canadian, an academic—social sciences—and she was killed in a plane crash three years ago."

"I'm so sorry," Kate said, putting a hand on his shoulder.

"Thank you. I still miss them." Alan shrugged his shoulders. "What is it they say: 'life goes on;' I guess that's true." He sighed. "But coming here brings back happy memories for me."

"I can see why."

Alan turned to Kate. "You know, today has been a bit of a shock for me. Hearing about Grandad's illness and his short life expectancy has been difficult. And then this news. Could it really be Jesus' hair?"

Kate looked at him sympathetically. "Well, the carbon dating for the hair does suggest that it is two-thousand years old, give or take a few years. So it is possible, even if not probable."

Alan glanced at Kate, and then looked out to the nearby island. It was a pleasure to be with such a pretty and intelligent woman. He threw his hands in the air. "And then there's this story about a silver casket, buried with the heart of Robert the Bruce; and the silver locket Grandad has. What do you make of that?"

"What do I make of that?" Kate retorted. "I'm a scientist. I'm trained to deal with evidence and facts."

"Much like a lawyer," Alan smiled.

She smiled back, "I guess that's so," she replied. "And if we are looking at evidence, I now have proof about the age of the hair." She blinked as a thought occurred. "I suppose if we had the silver casket that Jock said he buried under the plinth we could date that. It would be one more proof."

"Yes," Alan nodded in agreement. "It would confirm that part of the story."

"But we can't just go and dig up the plinth at Melrose," Kate said. "Or could we?" she added mischievously.

"No, that's not on." Alan paused. "Wait a minute. The silver casket came with a letter from King Alfonso. What Grandad has is an English translation. The original is in his deposit box at the Bank of Scotland in Edinburgh."

"So why don't we get that?"

"It's an idea. If we can establish its provenance, from the fourteenth century, it would begin to make sense of the story." He turned to Kate. "If I can get the Alfonso letter can you have it dated?"

"Yes, and maybe even translated. Much as I trust Jock, if we are ever going to make sense of this, I would like to be sure that the English translation he has is a faithful one."

"Agreed," Alan said. "Perhaps I should go to Edinburgh tomorrow."

"Would you mind if I tagged along?"

Alan looked at her. "That would be great, although maybe we should hold off for a day until Grandad tells us more about his meeting with that American evangelist."

With the sun going down behind the mountains they became aware of a large full moon which cast a golden path over the water leading to the island they had been facing.

'I guess it's time to go," Kate said with a sigh.

"I guess so; I've enjoyed the opportunity to talk to you, Kate."

"Me too. Let's see what we can discover tomorrow."

They returned to the car. Alan drove carefully, remembering Jamie's admonition to keep to the left, something he had to concentrate on for his first day in Scotland, as he knew from experience.

When they reached Bruce House Alan got out and opened Kate's door. He held out a hand and was rewarded with a gleaming smile as Kate slid her shapely legs out of the car.

"Goodnight Alan," she smiled.

"Goodnight, Kate," he said and kissed her lightly on the cheek.

She looked at him for a moment, appraisingly, then turned and walked swiftly into Bruce House. Alan parked the Jaguar in the garage, leaving the keys on a hook beside a desk that Jamie had informed him was his workplace. With much to think about, he went to his room and slept soundly. Tomorrow he would need to hear more about Jock's meeting with the American evangelist.

CHAPTER 4

As he left Bruce House, Varley called the Caledonian Hilton Hotel in Edinburgh on his cell phone. He told Ford that he needed to be away for a day or two, and Ford agreed, for the next day was a rest day for the Crusade. Varley spoke to the concierge, and asked for his advice about where he should stay for the night.

"Where are you?" the concierge asked.

"In Dumbarton."

"Dumbarton?" he said. "Hmm. I've had some guests who have stayed at Cameron House on Loch Lomond. It's only a few miles away."

"Perfect," Varley responded. "Please make a reservation for me. For one night only. I'll be back in Edinburgh tomorrow."

Having received directions, Varley took the highway to Balloch. He followed the signs to Cameron House. A right turn, a brief circling of a small roundabout, and he entered the tree-lined grounds of Cameron House. Loch Lomond, Britain's largest lake, lay straight ahead. The road curved to the right, and he saw a fairy-tale-like sandstone castle, with modern extensions. He stopped at the main entrance, and a kilted Scot came forward to greet him and offered to park his car.

Inside Cameron House, Varley was taken by a young porter to his room. It had a bay window, looking out to the sparkling waters of Loch Lomond with its mountain, Ben Lomond, rising to a flat peak across the Loch. The view was breathtaking, but Varley had no eyes for it. He pulled a receiver from his case and stood it on the table beside the window, while he waited expectantly for news from the bug he had placed in Sir Jock's library. He ordered a gin and tonic from room service and settled down in a large plaid-covered armchair to await a transmission. It didn't take long.

Sir Jock's voice rang out: "Alan, how are you?"

Varley listened carefully as Sir Jock spoke about his illness. His eyes widened with satisfaction as Jock spoke about "… the secret handed down from generation to generation of Bruces." As he listened to the rest of the story, every sense in his body told him that he might be on to something; something really important. He decided to have dinner in his room and wait for more information from the bug in Sir Jock's library. There were a few local calls after that, but nothing of interest to Varley. He suspected that nothing of interest would occur until Alan Bruce arrived the following morning, so he went downstairs to the hotel bar, after placing a recording device next to the receiver.

As he suspected, nothing happened until 9:00 the next morning when he heard Jock speaking to Alan. "Why don't you sit there Alan? Get comfortable, because I have a lot to tell you …"

Varley listened intently as Jock ran through the family history of the Bruces. His eyes widened as Jock spoke about the locket around his neck, in which some of the hair of Jesus was encapsulated.

Varley thought that Andy, the little red-haired Scot must have fabricated the story about the burial of a silver box in order to extract money from him. Though it was only five hundred pounds, Varley was not amused. He would get back at Andy later. His musings were interrupted by Jock's next words. "We'll have a pre-dinner drink here in the library, Alan. At that time, I'll show you the proof I have …"

Proof? Varley's mouth tightened as he thought. If there was proof that would verify the hair's provenance, then recovery of the locket from Sir Jock, or the mythical box that Andy had spoken about, would make this an historic discovery. Moreover, it would make him wealthy beyond his wildest dreams. He decided to stay on at Cameron House, and phoned Jackson Ford in Edinburgh to let him know that he needed another day to complete his enquiries.

Around 6:30 p.m. the bug picked up the conversation in the library at Bruce House. He heard Jock tell Alan about the letter from King Alfonso, the original of which was in his safety deposit box at the Bank of Scotland Head Office in Edinburgh. He pursed his lips as he heard Jock say that the hair had been dated as roughly two thousand years old. This was good news. It would help his story; and fund-raising would be simple. Everyone would want to come and see the relic with the hair of Jesus.

Varley heard Kate Harris arrive, and when the Bruces decided to leave the library for dinner he decided to take a break. He booked a private table by the window overlooking Loch Lomond, and went downstairs for an excellent meal.

Afterwards, he lingered in the Cameron House bar for a late night Scotch, confident that his tape recorder would pick up any discussion from the library at Bruce House. When he went to his room he was surprised to find that the recorder had stopped. "Damn it! A dead battery!" he cursed. He found a new battery and inserted it before re-winding to where he had stopped before dinner.

After a few clicks, he heard Jock say, "Kate, I am so glad you could come today …" He listened as the conversation progressed and Jock asked, "Kate can you confirm the results of the tests on the hair I gave you?"

At that point the recording stopped. But Varley had enough: he now knew that Jock Bruce believed the hair he had in the locket was two thousand years old, which suggested that it might conceivably indeed be the hair of Jesus. And Sir Jock had reacted when he had mentioned a silver box that Andy McPhee had seen Sir Jock bury. Although Varley did not yet know the site of that burial, he had enough. He would return to Bruce House, and see if he could persuade Sir Jock to sell the locket and the Alfonso letter, which provided proof of the hair's provenance. he was sure that Jackson Ford would approve.

Varley rang Bruce House after breakfast next day. Mrs Doig answered. "Bruce House. This is Mrs Doig." she said in her lilting voice.

"Mrs Doig, my name is Mark Varley. I met with Sir Jock yesterday and I wondered if I might speak to him."

"Just a wee minute," Mrs Doig said. "I'll see if he's around."

"Jock Bruce," was the next voice he heard. "Mr Varley: I hoped you might call. Where are you?"

"At Cameron House. I suppose you know it?"

Jock chuckled. "Know it well. Often have dinner there with friends."

"I wondered if we might meet, to continue our discussion from yesterday?"

"Should be fine," Jock retorted. "Can you make it here by two this afternoon?"

"I'll be there. See you at two." Varley hung up. How much should he offer Bruce, he wondered? He really wanted to get the gold locket from the old man, as well as the translated letter from King Alfonso. It would be even better if he could get the original from the Bank of Scotland vault in Edinburgh. First, though, he had to see what deal he could make with Sir Jock.

Back at Bruce House, Jock sat in the sun room having a mid-morning coffee. Alan had not appeared for breakfast. He had taken a black coffee and had gone for a run in the hills. He returned as Jock was finishing his coffee. Kate sat opposite him. She had slept late, and was having a coffee and some toast.

"Alan, why don't you come down after you've changed and join us?" Jock asked.

Kate looked up from the morning paper, which she had been attempting to read over Jock's conversation. She was not a morning person, and really needed time to come around. Time with a morning paper always helped her to focus on the day ahead.

Alan looked at Kate and Jock. "Thanks, Grandad. I'll have a quick shower and change. See you in a bit." When Alan returned, he sat across the table from Kate, poured himself a black coffee and said: "It was really refreshing being out in the hills this morning. I saw a deer and lots of rabbits."

Jock grunted. "Damn rabbits. Thought we got rid of them with myxomatosis, but that was fifty years ago when I was about your age."

Kate looked up. "Myxomatosis?"

"Yes, I think it was some sort of virus that killed them off. Stopped them eating up our vegetable garden. But they're back. Life goes on, I guess."

Alan smiled at his grandfather's reminiscence, which he recalled hearing before. To stop a long journey down Memory Lane, he said, "Grandad, I thought I might go to Edinburgh today. I'd like to see the original of the Alfonso letter if you don't mind."

"Mind? Why should I mind? All this will be yours soon enough. It's best that you set your mind at ease about its provenance." He raised an eyebrow. "That's what you want to do, isn't it?"

"Well, yes. Verifying what it says, and hopefully dating it, would be another piece in the jigsaw. Not that I don't believe you, Grandad," he added hurriedly.

Kate sensed a little tension rising in Jock. "I think what Alan wants to do is only reasonable." She smiled at Jock. "He's a lawyer, trained to get evidence and to examine it for relevance. Much like me, as a scientist."

Jock knew that Kate was humouring him. He looked at her sternly, but after a moment he smiled, and reached for her hand. "Young lady, you are not only intelligent, but extremely charming."

Kate patted his hand. "Thank you Jock."

Alan interjected. "Grandad, could you give me a letter authorising me to open your safety deposit box in Edinburgh?"

"Of course, I'll do that in a moment. By the way, that Varley fellow I mentioned to you yesterday phoned while you were out. I've arranged to see him at two this afternoon. I'll make sure he doesn't take the matter any further. I'll let you know the result when I see you later tonight. And now," he sighed, and carefully loosened his tie, unbuttoned the top two buttons on his shirt, and carefully removed a chain on which dangled a small gold locket—the locket that he said contained some of the hair from Jesus.

"Alan," Jock looked straight at his grandson, "I think you should take this, it will be yours in a few months anyway, as my heir, and I hope it will protect you from harm." He paused, and Alan saw a tear fashion in his grandfather's eyes. "It certainly," he continued, "hasn't harmed me!"

Alan reached across to his grandfather and took the locket in his hands. The gold was a dull colour, and on its face he could see the Bruce clan crest, a lion standing erect with the Latin motto *Faimus* inscribed. Alan knew from past stories that this translated as "We have been." Alan looked with love at the old man and with a choke in his voice, he said, "thank you, Grandad, this means a lot to me."

"Good. Now let me get a letter for you to take to the Bank of Scotland." Jock rose and went to his desk in the library.

In his absence, Alan looked at Kate. "Are you sure you want to come to Edinburgh today?"

Kate looked at him. He was wearing a blue blazer, a checked shirt, and a bright yellow tie, perhaps to lighten his sombre attitude. He really was quite charming, if a bit reserved.

"Of course," she smiled. "Edinburgh is an old love of mine. I spent a few years there, at Edinburgh University, and I always enjoy going back. You don't mind, do you?" She looked at him flirtatiously.

Alan blushed. Mind? He would give almost anything to have her with him. "I'd be delighted," he said. "Perhaps we can leave within the next hour. That way, I can buy you lunch at a nice restaurant I know in Edinburgh."

Kate agreed and went to her room to "freshen up" as she put it. While she was gone, Jock returned and handed Alan a letter. "This should allow you access to the safety deposit box. But, to be sure, I phoned Hamish McColl, the manager. He should be expecting you."

Kate came downstairs. She had changed, and now wore a blue pantsuit, with a blue, white, and yellow Hermes silk scarf worn jauntily over her shoulders. "Ready when you are Alan."

"Right," he said, "I'll just get the keys from Jamie. See you outside."

Kate gave Jock a hug. "Take care of yourself, Jock. I expect we'll be back around dinner time this evening."

Jock held her for a moment. "Thank you Kate. I'll see what Mrs. Doig can prepare for dinner. Bye for now, my dear."

Kate found Alan standing with the car door held open for her. "Thank you, kind sir." She smiled and slid into the front seat. Alan got into the driver's seat, and with a quick acceleration the Jaguar purred down the driveway, setting out on the one hour drive to Edinburgh some sixty miles away.

* * * *

Varley drew up at the entrance to Bruce House just before two o'clock. He rang the doorbell and Jamie let him in. For some reason, he had taken an instant dislike to the American whom he had first met the previous day. Varley gave what he called his "A-Plus Smile," often used on television, exhorting people to pledge to Jackson Ford's cause.

"Mr Varley," Jamie greeted him truculently.

"That's right: Mark Varley."

"Fine, follow me." Jamie led Varley into the library, where Sir Jock sat magisterially behind his large desk. He did not get up, but motioned to Varley to sit down.

"Mr. Varley, I've been thinking about our brief conversation yesterday. Do forgive me, for I'm an old man, and I'm afraid my attention wandered a bit when you mentioned a box with hair. Indeed, it made me recall that my late wife kept several locks of her hair in a silver and enamel box. It was a keepsake. I had it for years after Molly passed away, and finally gave it to my son in Canada."

Jock shook his head as if recalling events, and said, "and then Bob, my son, died. So I've no idea where that box is now."

Varley raised an eyebrow. He felt he was in for a hard negotiation. He didn't believe a word Jock had said.

"What a tragedy." Varley said with a slight smile. "But, leaving that aside, I really do think we have something more important to discuss."

"What do you mean?"

"Sir Jock, when I was here yesterday about the box with the Latin inscription, you couldn't conceal your surprise. It was obvious to me. So, why don't we get down to brass tacks? I'm willing to offer you a substantial sum to know where I can find that box."

Jock decided to play this out. "What did you have in mind, assuming there is such a box?"

"How does fifty thousand pounds sound?"

"Not interested."

"So, you admit there is such a box?"

"Not at all! I was playing along with your so-called assumption, just to see what kind of fool you are!"

Varley scowled. He was not going to let this old guy call him a fool. Angrily, he blurted out, "A fool? You think I'm a fool? OK then, if I'm a fool let's see how you react to this. What about the gold locket you wear and the letter from King Alfonso?"

Jock shot back in his chair. How on earth had this creature got to know about the locket and the letter?

"What?" he spluttered.

"You know, the letter from King Alfonso and the gold locket round your neck, in which you say there is some of Jesus' hair," Varley sneered.

"How on earth do you know all this?" he asked, feeling trapped.

Varley leant across the desk, and carefully removed the bug he had inserted in the phone the previous day. He held it up mockingly before Jock's eyes. "This is how I know. I heard every word you said to your grandson yesterday." He put the bug into his pocket and continued, "So we both know that I can't be fooled. Why don't we just sit quietly and discuss terms for your sale of the locket and the letter?"

Jock's eyes widened indignantly. "You, sir, are contemptible," he snarled. "I would like you to leave."

"Not so quick, old man. I know this has been a shock to you. I apologize for the mike. But really, what does it matter? You have something I believe you might be willing to sell; and I, believe it or not, am a willing buyer." He threw out a hand magnanimously. "If fifty thousand pounds isn't enough, how about one hundred thousand pounds?"

Jock's face reddened and his blood pressure rose. "If I had the things you mentioned, Mr. Varley, you are absolutely the last man on earth," he paused to regain his breath because the stress and exertion were affecting him, "believe me," he continued, "you are absolutely the last man alive I would sell such things to."

"I don't think you have any choice Sir Jock. For if you don't sell to me, I'll let the newspapers know, and they will make your life hell."

"Hell?" Jock asked. "That's where I hope you finish up."

"Not for a while. So, why don't we both calm down and try to negotiate a deal?"

Jock rose from his chair and pointed to the door. "Out!" he said. "Now! Get out!"

Varley leaned across the desk, with his fists clenched in anger, but did not move towards the door.

Losing his temper, Jock slapped Varley across the face.

Varley reeled back. "You old bastard!" he cried, and punched Jock in the chest. Jock collapsed with a soft "Aah!" as a sigh came from his lips. He slumped in his chair. His eyes rolled, and then his head fell forward and struck the desk.

Varley tried to catch Jock, but only succeeded in straightening him in his chair, where his head lolled backwards. Quickly Varley moved around the desk. He felt for a pulse, but there was none. Jock was dead.

Varley ran his fingers round Jock's collar, searching for the locket. It wasn't there! He searched through Jock's pockets, but again without success. He opened the desk drawers but could not find what he wanted. However, in the bottom left drawer he came across a large envelope. Opening it he saw a heading: "To His Majesty, King David II of Scotland.

"*Greetings....* ."

It was the Alfonso letter. At least he had something to show for his efforts. Now, if he could find the silver box that Andy McPhee had mentioned, things would start to fall into place. Very carefully, Varley closed the desk drawers. He straightened the body of Jock, so that the old man seemed to be asleep in his chair. Moving to the door, he said in a loud voice. "Thank you for your time, Sir Jock, goodbye."

On the way out, he saw Jamie working in the garage and nodded to him. He started his car and set out on the journey back to Edinburgh. Once there, he would call Bruno Conti in New York.

CHAPTER 5

Alan and Kate had time to chat on the drive to Edinburgh. Crossing the Erskine Bridge, which elegantly spans the River Clyde, they joined the M8 motorway, which would take them through Glasgow and on to Edinburgh.

Kate said, "Do you have any siblings, Alan?"

"No. How about you?"

"I have two older sisters back in the States; both married, with kids. The traditional thing, you know." She turned to face Alan. "And I guess you're not even married?"

"How did you know?"

"Ah, that's a woman's secret," she said with a twinkle in her eye.

"Okay, then, I guess you're not married."

"Can you tell?"

"No" he laughed, "men are not very good at that sort of thing."

Kate smiled and said, "Well it's not for the lack of offers: just never the right one."

Alan blinked, and tried to concentrate on the traffic. There was much more lane discipline on the roads here than in Canada, where the motorways often resembled racing tracks with cars weaving across lanes. In Scotland, he knew he had to stay in one lane, and move out only to pass.

"You sound as if you've lived your life," was all he could think to say, thinking as he did so that it was rather lame.

"Don't we all?" Kate replied. "Actually, Alan, I only believe in a serious relationship. Of these I've had only two; and once I was engaged. But it didn't work out."

Alan was quiet. He had to concentrate on the traffic, which was slowing as they neared Glasgow, but he was also unsure about what to say next.

They were both quiet for a few minutes until the traffic eased, and they were through the Glasgow city core and out on the motorway to Edinburgh.

Kate looked out of the window and, in a quiet voice, said, "Tell me more about Alan Bruce."

"Not too much to tell. I was born in Scotland, left here when I was young when my parents went to Canada to live. I grew up in Toronto, went to the University of Toronto for my undergrad and law degrees."

Kate turned towards him. "And what do you do for fun?"

"Fun? The usual I guess. A bit of golf, skiing in winter. I used to play football; quarterback for the U of T, but that's a long time ago now."

"I see," Kate said. "And I suppose there have been lots of fair ladies in your life?"

"Not all fair," Alan smiled, "some were brunettes."

Kate laughed. "That's not what I meant!"

"I know what you meant." He looked at her. "I'm not attached, if that's what you mean."

"Attached?" Kate enquired. "That sounds very legal."

"It's not. I am not engaged or anything like that. Mind you, there have been lots of girlfriends, just never the right one. I have never yet felt the need to settle down."

"So, you are still sowing your oats?" Kate said, with a mischievous smile.

"No more than most people," Alan replied. "I just remember what a splendid marriage my Mum and Dad had: they fitted together so well; they were foils for each other in a way, but complementary, if you know what I mean."

"I think I do," Kate said thoughtfully. She changed the subject. "What sort of law practice do you have?"

"Well, I used to be a partner in a big Toronto law firm. There, I specialized in health law. It's an expanding field, as Canada begins to get away from a highly socialised system of health care. But a few months ago, I got tired of the rat race, always a need to get thousands of billable hours to keep up with expectations. So I quit, and set up my own small practice. Life is much better now: I'm more in control." He paused. "Sorry, I guess I got carried away speaking about myself."

"No problem. I feel I know you better for that."

They chatted about the weather and Edinburgh, and in no time they were on the outskirts of Scotland's capital city. Alan took a turn on to Queensferry Road, and followed the signs to Leith, the port of Edinburgh. It had been some time since he last visited, but he remembered that there were a number of excellent seafood restaurants. He saw the signs to the Royal yacht Britannia, which had once sailed the seas with the Queen and Royal family, but was now moored in Leith as a tourist attraction. He drove on to a narrow cobbled street and stopped outside "The Shore" restaurant.

"Here we are," he said. "It's not too fancy, just excellent seafood." He looked at Kate. "I forgot to ask. I hope you like seafood?"

"It's one of my favourites."

After an enjoyable lunch and relaxed conversation, Alan drove up Leith Walk, the major road leading to Edinburgh's city centre. Reaching Princes Street, he made a right turn, and followed the one-way street signs that led north towards St. Andrew Square, and from there he followed the signs for The Mound.

The Bank of Scotland head office is situated on The Mound, the winding street that rises from Princes Street towards the High Street, overlooked by the craggy cliffs of Edinburgh Castle. Alan found a short term parking spot on Saint Giles Street, around a corner from the head office building. Locking the car, he and Kate crossed to the imposing main entrance. As he entered the main marble-floored banking hall, a uniformed attendant approached.

"May I help you, sir?" he enquired.

"Thank you," Alan said, "I would like to speak to Mr. McColl, the manager. I'm Alan Bruce. My grandfather, Sir Jock Bruce arranged an appointment earlier today."

"Let me see if he is available," the attendant said, as he led them to a cluster of chairs and left. In a few minutes he returned. "Mr. McColl's secretary will be here in a minute," he said.

A young woman arrived and chatted to them as she led them to the executive offices on the first floor. She took them into Hamish McColl's office, a spacious room with solid wood furniture. A large window looked out over Princes Street, and Alan recognized the tall tower of the Scott Monument to the right.

Hamish McColl stood behind his desk to greet them. He was of medium height, with thinning grey hair and thick glasses,. He wore a very traditional banker's suit, dark blue with a thin pinstripe. "Mr. Bruce," he shook Alan's hand and turned to Kate, "and this is?"

Alan introduced Kate. "This is Dr. Kate Harris, a family friend."

"I see. Well, please sit down." He motioned to chairs facing his desk. McColl gave a brief banker's smile and said, "What can I do for you?"

Alan gave him the letter from Jock. McColl scanned it quickly, and looked at Alan.

"And how is Sir Jock?"

"To tell the truth," Alan said, "his health is deteriorating, so he has asked me to retrieve a personal item from his safety deposit box."

"I see," McColl nodded sympathetically. "Jock probably didn't tell you, but this is the head office of the Bank of Scotland. As such, we stopped operating the usual branch banking services a few years ago." He smiled. "But Jock, and the Bruce family are long-time clients, so as a special favour to Jock, and a few others like him, I decided to retain some safety deposit services here for as long as they live."

He coughed and said, "Please give Sir Jock my best wishes. Now if you can show me the key, I'll get someone to take you to the vaults."

Fortunately, Alan had remembered to ask Jock for the key before he had left Bruce House. He took it from his pocket. McColl looked at the number on it, went to his desk where he compared it with the serial numbers from his file on Sir Jock, and also checked Sir Jock's signature on the letter against the documentation on the bank's personal file.

"That seems to be in order," he said. "Please come with me." He led them to the elevator, and asked his assistant to take them to the basement level, where the vaults lay.

When the elevator reached the basement they were led to a glass door where a young man with red hair and wearing what seemed to be the standard blue pinstripe suit, greeted them.

"Mr. Bruce," he said, "I am Andrew Barr. Mr. McColl asked me to help you." He opened the glass door and went to a desk in the corner of the room. "May I see your key, and the letter of introduction?"

Alan smiled. He knew bankers were thorough at checking identification but couldn't resist a teasing comment.

"Here you are." He gave Barr the key and the letter from Sir Jock. "You do know that these were already checked by your boss, Mr. McColl?"

"Yes," Barr answered in his lilting Edinburgh accent, "but I'm responsible for the vaults. It's my neck on the line if anything goes wrong."

Barr checked the key's number against the records on the computer terminal on his desk.

"Right," he said, "that checks out. Box A238: that's one of the big ones. Please sign this card."

He gave Alan a card that had been signed and dated by Sir Jock each time he had opened his box. Alan signed the card and returned it to Barr, who rose and motioned Alan and Kate to follow him. He entered a code in a wall, and a steel door slid open.

They entered the vaults, which were lined with steel safety deposit boxes, ranging in size from small boxes to large containers. Barr went to box A238 and inserted Jock's key. He then took a key from a chain attached to his belt and inserted it in a slot. He turned both keys, and withdrew a large deposit box. Turning, he led Alan and Kate to a private room, with a table and straight-backed chairs. He set the box on the table, told Alan to ring when he was ready, and left.

Alan sat facing the box. With some anticipation he lifted the lid. Inside lay a number of documents and medals from Jock's army service. At the bottom he found a large sealed envelope on which someone had written "The Alfonso letter." Opening the seal on the envelope, he pulled out a padded covering, below which he saw an ornate document. It was highlighted with blue, red, and purple ornamentation at the start of each sentence. Alan sighed. So this was the Alfonso letter.

Kate leant across to look. "Is that the original letter?"

"I think it must be." Alan noted that the Latin script included "Alfonso XI Rex and Davidus II Rex", which seemed to confirm its origins. He looked at Kate. "My Latin isn't good enough to confirm the translation Jock showed us; but it seems to be genuine." He carefully put the letter back in the padded covering and inserted both into the envelope. He stood. "We'll take this with us. Perhaps you can find someone among your academic friends to translate it. And you can also try to date it as being from the fourteenth century."

"Right," Kate nodded, "but aren't you concerned at the questions that might arise when someone translates it? Their curiosity might create problems."

Alan frowned. He hadn't thought about that. "I guess that might be a problem." He thought for a moment and then said, "perhaps you might give only the first and last pages for translation. That might conceal the part about the box with the hair from Jesus, and allow us to confirm the validity of the translation of those parts of the document. I guess we then have to take the rest on trust."

Kate pursed her lips. "Well, that's better than nothing. But surely we would need to have the full document translated?"

"Here's an idea: why not get several people to translate, give them a page each so no one will know the full story?"

"It might work, but it makes my task harder. I'll just have to put out feelers and see how many independent Latin scholars I can find. And, I think I would have to make sure they were not all in the same city. I don't want them comparing notes. That would only help someone to put it all together."

"Good idea," Alan nodded his agreement. "And will you also manage to date the manuscript?"

"That should be the easiest part," Kate agreed.

Alan rang the bell, and Andrew Barr entered. He took the safety deposit box from Alan, inserted it in slot A238, and then returned Jock's key to Alan. Barr then led them to the elevator and pressed the button for the ground floor. "I hope you enjoy your stay in Edinburgh." he said.

As they left the bank, Kate took the cell phone from her handbag and also pulled out a small address book. She searched for a number and dialled.

"Who are you calling?" Alan asked.

"I thought I'd see if Professor Brownlee is in his office. He'll be able to help with the dating, and also probably with the translation. He is well plugged into the academic community and will know who to contact." The phone rang. Kate spoke to Professor Brownlee, who agreed to see her in an hour's time.

"Perhaps we can grab a coffee somewhere before we see him," Alan said. "Can I borrow your phone? I'd better let Grandad know we may be late getting home." He dialled Bruce House.

Mrs. Doig answered. She was crying.

Chapter 6

Varley made good time on the M8 to Edinburgh. Pity about the old man's death, but he was probably overdue for a heart attack He thought that might prove to be the cause of the old guy's death. One punch would not have killed any fit person, he thought, trying to minimize the pangs of guilt he began to feel. But he was not truly remorseful. The thought of getting possession of the relic containing the hair of Jesus appealed to his entrepreneurial mind. He—and the Ford organization—could make a fortune from the relic, even if the hair was not that of Jesus. People believe what they want to believe.

Approaching the western outskirts of Edinburgh, traffic became heavy. Varley was impatient. He wanted to get to his room so he could phone Bruno Conti in New York. He suspected he would need Conti's "muscle" to help him with Andy McPhee.

The Mercedes screeched to a halt outside the Caledonian Hilton hotel. The doorman wearing a dark blue coat with gold trim and matching top hat, approached. Varley told him to park the car and to leave the keys with the concierge.

The doorman handed him a printed receipt and said, "Just call the concierge when you need it back, sir"

Varley crossed the lobby's marble floor, with a multi-coloured circular carpet set into its base. He nodded to the concierge in his dark blue uniform coat behind the desk to his right and crossed to the glass fronted elevators, to the side of the reception desk. It was now 5:30 p.m. in Edinburgh, which was 12:30 p.m. in New York. Conti ought to be in his office. Reaching his room, Varley searched through his address book and rang Conti's number.

In New York it was almost time for lunch. Conti had a reservation at his favorite Italian restaurant. His phone rang.

"Bruno? It's Mark Varley."

"Mark, how are you? More important, where are you?" Conti knew that Varley traveled frequently with Jackson Ford.

"I'm in Edinburgh, Scotland," he added.

"I know where Edinburgh is," Conti grunted.

"Good. I'm going to need some help from you."

"Another collection problem?" Conti asked. In the past, Varley had used him to collect what he called "difficult accounts." These were usually pledges made by people who, after a while, had decided not to make all the payments pledged. Often a visit from Conti who "prayed" with the people in a muscular way did the trick! Conti was built like a middleweight boxer. He had black hair, dark brown eyes, and almost no neck. His appearance alone usually managed to compel people to meet their pledges.

"It's not quite a collection problem," Varley replied. "But I think your powers of persuasion might come in useful. So, Bruno, here's what I need. I'd like you to catch a plane to Edinburgh tonight. Call and let me know the details and I'll meet you at Edinburgh airport, when you arrive tomorrow."

Conti snorted, "Hold on, Mark, I can't reshape my life just like that."

"Oh Bruno, I think you will! I'll make it worth your time, believe me."

Bruno glared at the phone. He knew that Varley was a good client; furthermore there was nothing in his diary that couldn't wait for a few days. "OK, Mark, I'll see what I can do. Where can I call you?"

Varley gave him the number of his hotel and hung up. Now he would have to see Jackson Ford. It was time to bring the evangelist up to date. He rang Ford's room, and arranged to see him in ten minutes' time. Next, he looked at the envelope with the Alfonso letter he had removed from Jock Bruce's desk drawer. He took time reading it and whistled in anticipation of the use he could make of its contents. This could be a real money-maker for him, and for Ford, of course.

Jackson Ford opened his door when Varley knocked. He looked questioningly and said, "Mark, I missed you last night."

"It couldn't be helped, Jackson. I was on the west coast of Scotland to try to get to the bottom of the story I told you about; you know—the casket with Jesus' hair."

Ford smiled benignly, "And I suppose you've come to show me the hair?" he said.

"Not quite, but I do have proof that the hair exists." Varley gave Ford the envelope with the English translation of the Alfonso letter. "Why don't you read this, Jackson? It might convince you that there is some substance to the story I told you."

Ford took the envelope, sat down in an armchair, and began to read. He shook his head in sorrow as he read about the crucifixion, and nodded as he read about Constantine. He looked at Varley.

"Well, Constantine certainly existed. He was important in helping to endorse Christ's role as our Saviour." He continued to read, occasionally looking up at Varley. When he had finished, he put the letter down on a side table.

"A remarkable story. Indeed, if it's true, it could be an astounding discovery." His eyes misted in thought. "Just think, if we had something of Jesus', what a difference that could make."

"Yes," Varley nodded his agreement. "It would increase our cash flow and make your crusades even more important."

"There is that, though that's not what I meant."

Varley continued, "Jackson, I've been thinking about Dolly the sheep, the cloned animal you told me about. Wouldn't it be remarkable if we could clone Jesus?"

"Clone Jesus?" Ford shook his head. "That would be blasphemy!"

"Why? Surely it could happen only if it were God's will?"

Ford thought for a moment then reached for the Bible that was never far from him. He turned to the Gospel of Matthew and looked for a reference. He slapped his knee as he found it, and handed the Bible to Varley. "Look there," he said. "The Lord promised to return, but did not specify when the Second Coming would occur."

Varley saw that Ford had opened the Bible at Matthew, chapter 24, and was pointing to Verses 42 to 44. He read it aloud.

"Watch therefore, for ye know not what hour your Lord will come. But know this, that if the good man of the house had known in what watch the thief would come, he would have watched and would not have suffered his house to be broken up. Therefore be ye also ready. For in such an hour as ye think not the son of man cometh."

Varley put down the Bible and looked at the evangelist. "So, this might be possible, Jackson?"

"I don't know. How can anyone know?" Jackson Ford rose from his chair and paced across the room. He looked out of the window towards the towering presence of Edinburgh Castle, then turned back to Varley. "Could this be a test, Mark? Are we to be the instrument for the Lord's return?"

Varley was quiet.

Ford continued, in a rhetorical outburst: "Could it be that we are being asked to be an agent of the Resurrection? Dear Lord," he sank to his knees in prayer, "guide me in this moment so that I may be aware of your wishes. Free me from doubt, if doubt should not exist. Make me sensitive to your will. Amen." Ford rose and looked at Varley. "Mark, I don't understand how cloning works. Do you?"

"I have only a very superficial understanding of it, Jackson."

"Right, so before we do anything, I will call Dr Jim Cameron, the scientist who worked on the team that cloned Dolly the sheep. He told me a little bit about the process a couple of nights ago. I'm afraid I didn't listen very carefully, because science is not really a great interest of mine. "But now," he shook his head, "now I will have to learn more about it."

Varley stood. "I'd like to meet Dr. Cameron," he said.

"I'll let you know when I arrange it. By the way, Mark, how are you going to get the box with Jesus' hair?"

Varley smiled. "I'll meet again with the Scot who spoke to me, and then we'll try to arrange a deal."

"Fine, Mark, keep me in touch."

Varley left and returned to his room. The phone rang. It was Bruno Conti, who had arranged a flight to Heathrow and an onward connection to Edinburgh. He would arrive at mid-morning the next day.

Varley put down the phone and looked for the phone number for Andy McPhee. It was time to get the silver casket with the hair.

Chapter 7

Alan listened to Mrs. Doig's sobbing. "What on earth's the matter Mrs. Doig?" he asked.

"It's Sir Jock. He's dead."

"What? How did that happen?" Alan was puzzled. His grandfather had seemed to be in good health when he had left Bruce House only a few short hours earlier.

"It was a heart attack, I think."

"A heart attack?"

"Well, that's what the doctor said."

"Mrs. Doig, I'm puzzled. Grandad seemed to be fine when I left."

"I know, I know. He had a visitor, an American, a Mr. Varley, who arrived around two o'clock. He left about half an hour later, and when I went into the library with Sir Jock's afternoon tea, at three, I found him in his chair behind his desk. I thought at first he was sleeping. But he didn't reply when I spoke to him. I went behind the desk and saw that he wasn't breathing. So I thought it must have been a heart attack."

"Did you call a doctor right away?"

"Of course. Jamie also came in and tried to revive him, but the CPR didn't work." She sobbed again. "And then an ambulance arrived and took him to Vale of Leven Hospital. They tried to revive him too, but it didn't work." She sobbed, and repeated, "It didn't work. My goodness, Mr. Alan, what are we going to do without Sir Jock?"

Alan was in shock: Jock was dead. It was too quick, even though his grandfather had told him that he only had a few months to live. However, perhaps it was a blessing: Jock wouldn't have to suffer the pain of terminal cancer. He tried to reassure Mrs. Doig.

"I'll leave Edinburgh now," he said, "and I should get to Bruce House in about two hours."

"Thank you, Mr. Alan. We need you here."

Kate looked anxiously at Alan. She had heard the conversation and had tears in her eyes, for she had grown fond of Jock. "Is it true?" she asked. "Is Jock really dead?"

Alan's eyes filled with tears. He couldn't yet believe that the sturdy spirit of Jock was no more. "I'm afraid it does seem to be true, Kate." He shook his head thoughtfully, "and now I'm going to have to return to Bruce House."

"I'll come with you Alan."

He thought for a moment. "Kate, I appreciate that, but since you've already arranged to see Professor Brownlee, why don't I drop you there, so you can start the testing, and then catch a train to Glasgow later on? If you call Bruce House, I'll get Jamie to meet you at the railway station in Glasgow."

Kate looked at him for a moment. "Well, if that's what you want, OK. I'll go and see the Prof. But I do want to get back to Bruce House this evening."

They drove south, crossing the High Street that led up to Edinburgh Castle, and continued over the George IV Bridge to Teviot Place. Kate pointed to a building that was part of the University of Edinburgh Medical School.

"Just drop me there, Alan. I know where to find the Prof." She turned and reached out to hug him. "I am so sorry, Alan. I really loved Jock."

Alan tried to hold back tears. "Thank you, Kate. He was all I had left in the world."

"I know, Alan," she hugged him again, and gave him a brief kiss on the cheek. "He was very special." She opened the car door. "Drive carefully. "I'll get the ball rolling with the Prof. and I'll be sure to get back to be with you at Bruce House later tonight."

Alan waved a hand, put the car into gear, and set off. Two hours later, he drew up at Bruce House, where Jamie met him.

"We are all so sorry about Sir Jock," he said gruffly.

"Thanks, Jamie. It's been a real shock to me, as I'm sure it has been to you and Mrs. Doig."

"Aye, that it has."

"Where is my grandfather's body?"

"As far as I know, it will be at the Vale of Leven Hospital until we can arrange for the funeral. Do you know how to get there?"

Alan shook his head, and Jamie gave him directions.

"Thanks, Jamie, I'll go there right now." With that, Alan got back into the Jaguar and drove to the old rundown hospital in the nearby town of Alexandria, near Balloch and Loch Lomond. Once there, Alan asked to see the duty doctor, who turned out to be a young Englishwoman. He enquired about his grandfather and was taken to the morgue. He saw Jock's body and broke down in tears. The doctor touched his arm.

"If it's any help, Mr. Bruce, he didn't suffer."

"So you're sure it was a heart attack?"

"Almost certainly. It had the classic signs; but the only way we could be sure would be with a post mortem. Do you want to authorize that?"

"No, my grandfather had terminal cancer. He didn't have long to live anyway, and I don't want to put him through that indignity."

"Fine." the doctor said. "No doubt you will make arrangements for his body to be collected."

Alan hadn't yet thought that far ahead. "Of course," he said, "I'll be in touch tomorrow."

* * * *

Back in Edinburgh, Kate walked through the entrance to the medical school on Teviot Place. She crossed the courtyard, with the well-remembered stone buildings on all four sides, and entered Door Three, which lay straight ahead. It led to Biology Teaching, where she knew she would find Professor Brownlee in his office, which she remembered so well. She knocked on the door and smiled when she entered and saw that his desk was still cluttered with research papers. Brownlee had not changed much in the last eight or nine years since Kate had studied with him. His bushy hair was now quite white, and he still had glasses perched at the end of his nose. She could almost swear that he was wearing the same herringbone tweed sports jacket that she recalled from the past. He got up as Kate entered.

"Dr. Harris. Kate, how are you?"

"I'm fine, Professor."

"What brings you to Edinburgh?"

"Well, it's quite complicated. Let's just say that I've been visiting friends, and since I was in Edinburgh today I thought I would try to see you. It's been a long time."

"Yes, it has, Kate." Brownlee poured himself a coffee from a pot bubbling in a corner of his office. "Would you care for a cup?" he enquired.

Kate knew from past experience that the coffee she was usually served in Scotland was a pale imitation of what she was used to in America.

"No. Thanks anyway," she said.

Brownlee sipped his coffee. "I can tell there is more to this visit than just a renewal of our acquaintance. Am I right?"

Kate smiled. Trust the Prof. to get right to the point. "Well yes, there is," she agreed. "I have been given part of a document that purports to be from fourteenth century Spain. I have been asked to see if I can verify its age."

"That shouldn't be too difficult with carbon dating and spectroscopy."

"I know, I've done that before in Boston, but I don't have access to facilities in Scotland."

"I can probably help. Do you have the document with you?"

Kate pulled out the first page of the Alfonso letter and handed it to Brownlee.

"Hmm!" he said, "it does look old, and it's in Latin." He read, "To his Majesty King David II of Scotland, Greetings. I, Alfonso, King of Castile and Leon ..."

Kate interrupted him. "You can read Latin?"

"Of course. It was mandatory in Scotland when I was at school. In fact, it was difficult to get into university without at least some Latin." He looked at Kate. "Would you like me to go on?"

Kate nodded her agreement, and noted that Brownlee's translation echoed what she recalled from having read Jock's English translation only yesterday, in Bruce House.

Brownlee stopped at the end of the page he had been given, and looked across at Kate. "This seems to be an historic document," he said. "Where did you get it?"

Kate told him about Sir Jock Bruce, and how he had given the document to his grandson Alan, to be dated and translated. She explained that she and Alan had been in Edinburgh when he had learned of Jock's death only an hour ago, and had returned to Bruce House.

Brownlee adjusted his glasses, which kept sliding down his nose. "I see. Sorry to hear about Jock Bruce's death. He was a fine, indeed distinguished, Scot. A proud descendant of Robert the Bruce." He lifted the page, "So you want it dated?"

"Yes, if you can."

"I'll do more than that. I'll speak to Harry Morton at the School of Modern Languages. He may be able to help identify the inks used in the document. That would help to confirm that it is, indeed, of Spanish origin."

"Thank you, Professor," Kate stood. "Do you have any idea how long this might take?"

"Allow a few days, Kate. Give me a number where I can reach you, and I'll call you when the information is ready."

Kate left, stopped a taxi, and went to Waverley Station, the main railway station in Edinburgh and phoned Bruce House to arrange for Jamie to pick her up from the Queen Street Station in Glasgow in just over an hour.

Later, when Kate reached Bruce House, she found Alan pacing outside waiting for her arrival. She rushed to him and, seeing the sorrow in his eyes, gave him a brief hug. They were both devastated at the loss of Jock. Kate looked up at Alan. "How are you?" she asked.

"About as well as might be expected," he said, then shrugged. "That's a lie, I am really down. Jock meant everything to me. I'm still puzzled about why he had the sudden heart attack." He thought for a moment, then turned and walked through the door into Bruce House. He called for Jamie and Mrs. Doig to join him in the library with Kate.

When they arrived, Alan poured a drink for everyone. "This has been a shocking day," he said, "and if you are feeling like me, a 'wee snifter', as my grandad used to say, may help to relax you."

Alan sipped the single malt, which he knew was an acquired taste. He looked at Mrs. Doig. "Tell me again how you found Sir Jock."

Mrs. Doig repeated the story she had told him few hours earlier when he had learned the news in Edinburgh.

"And you say that this Varley fellow had left only half an hour earlier?"

"Well, yes," Mrs. Doig said hesitatingly. "I heard him call out, 'Goodbye and thank you Sir Jock.'"

"Did you hear any reply?" Alan asked.

"No," she paused and wrinkled her brows in thought, "no, I can't say I did."

Jamie jumped in. "I saw Varley leave. It must have been about 2.30. Then, at around three, Mrs. Doig called me into the library. That's where we found Sir Jock. I tried to revive him. I've had some training in CPR, but it didn't work out." He shook his head, "I'm sorry."

"Don't be, Jamie," Alan replied, "I'm sure you did everything possible."

"Aye, I did," Jamie said. He frowned, deep furrows on his face. "I never liked the look of that Varley. There was something sleazy about him, for an evangelist.

If I thought he'd done anything to harm Sir Jock I would strangle him!" he growled.

Alan looked thoughtful. Varley had been after the hair. That much, Sir Jock had made clear to him. But he couldn't have got it. Alan touched the gold locket in his pocket. He took another sip of the Scotch; it was beginning to taste better. Alan rose suddenly and went to Jock's desk. He opened the bottom left drawer where Jock had kept the Alfonso letter. It wasn't there. Quickly he opened the other drawers. Nothing! He turned to Kate.

"The letter is missing! Varley must have taken it!"

CHAPTER 8

Andy answered Varley's call on the second ring.

"Hello," he said, "This is Andy McPhee."

"Hi Andy! This is Mark Varley."

"Mr. Varley, what can I do for you?"

"Ah! Andy, isn't it what can I do for you?" he teased. "I have been to see Sir Jock Bruce. We had a pleasant chat, but he denied knowing anything about a silver box. So Andy, I thought you might want to repay the five hundred pounds I gave you."

"Not a chance. We had a deal. I gave you Sir Jock's name, didn't I?"

"Of course you did; but now I need to know where I can find the box."

"That will cost a lot more than five hundred pounds," Andy replied.

"I see." Varley hesitated, thinking over his next move. "Why don't we meet to discuss the matter?"

There was a pause, while Andy thought about what to do. He really didn't want Varley near Melrose Abbey until he had extracted money—a lot of money—from him. On the other hand, why should he make a journey into Edinburgh: why not do it closer to home? "Fine," he replied. "Can you come to Melrose?"

"Where is that?"

"It's about an hour's drive south of Edinburgh. I can meet you at Burts Hotel in the town square. You can't miss it; it's a white-washed building."

"Sounds good to me," Varley replied. "How about tomorrow, around six o'clock?"

When Andy agreed, Varley hung up the phone. He would take Conti with him as a persuader, should McPhee prove to be recalcitrant.

Varley rang down to room service for a large gin and tonic. Before it arrived his phone rang and he heard Jackson Ford say, "Mark, I wonder if you could come up to my room? I have Dr Jim Cameron with me. What he has to say will no doubt be interesting and educational for both of us."

Varley waited until his gin and tonic had arrived, and drank it greedily. Then he went to Ford's room.

Dr Jim Cameron was an intense individual. Of average build, his shoulders were slightly hunched, as if he had spent most of his life crouched over laboratory instruments. His jacket lapels were spotted with what appeared to be food stains, and his tartan tie was slightly loose around his neck. Varley shook his hand and sat down on a chair beside Jackson Ford. Cameron sat opposite, with a wine glass in his hand.

"Mark, Dr Cameron and I have decided to share a nice claret. Do you want some?" Varley took a glass from the table, and poured the red wine into it.

Jackson Ford looked at Cameron. "Dr Cameron, or may I call you Jim?" he asked with a charismatic smile.

"Of course," Cameron replied, "let's not to be too formal."

"Good. I was fascinated the other evening when you told me about how Professor Wilmut's team had cloned Dolly the sheep. But I'm afraid the technique you described was beyond my scientific grasp. I did mention it to Mark here, and we both thought that in the interests of understanding more about what appears to be a miracle we should try to learn some of the details from you."

Cameron put down his wine glass. "Oh, it wasn't a miracle. More like hard work and determination to follow through on the science."

"I see. Tell me more, please." Jackson Ford smiled appreciatively, his charm evident.

Cameron took a deep breath before continuing. "It was in 1997 that Wilmut's team finally had success. We took an unfertilized egg from a female sheep, a ewe, and then we removed its nucleus. As you may know, the nucleus of a cell contains its DNA. So, when you remove the nucleus you also remove the egg's DNA." He looked at Ford and Varley to confirm that they were following his tale. "The next step was to take mammary cells from another ewe. We treated the mammary cells, and then placed one cell next to the egg, minus the nucleus, which we had removed from the first ewe. When pulses of electricity were sent through the two cells, they fused into a single cell. At that time, the egg cell had the nucleus of the mammary cell, including its DNA."

"Clear so far?" he asked.

Jackson nodded.

"Next," Cameron continued, "we sent more electricity through the fused single cell." His eyes widened, remembering the moment. "Then, it began to divide. It was just like what occurs in nature. We let the embryo develop for several days before implanting it into the uterus of a black-faced sheep. And then, hey presto! Months later Dolly was born, an exact replica, or clone, of the sheep from which we had taken the mammary cells."

There was silence for a moment: "What a remarkable event. Where is Dolly now?" Ford asked.

"She's dead. She had a shorter than normal lifespan, something scientists are trying to understand. Part of the reason is probably that the cells we took from the sheep used in the experiment were from a mature animal. So, the cells had aged, and although Dolly chronologically was a newborn, her cells were several years old. That might explain her short lifespan."

"The Lord works in mysterious ways," Ford murmured. He bowed his head then looked at Cameron. "We are but putty in His hands."

Varley decided to broach the subject of human cloning. "Jim," he began, "this is fascinating stuff. It could mean a lot for people if, for example, they could clone a child who had died prematurely."

"There are ethical problems with that, Mark." Ford looked gravely at him.

"Quite so, I understand that. Even so, I'm wondering if it is possible to clone a human being."

Ford gave him a knowing glance: he, too, was interested in what Cameron had to say.

Cameron sighed, "I'm not sure that human cloning is possible. Mind you, a few years ago a sect called the Raelians claimed to have cloned a baby they called Eve. They said she had been born to a 31-year-old woman in the United States. But there's never been any proof of that. No one has seen the girl, and to all intents and purposes the Raelians have disappeared from the radar screen."

"So that's it?" Varley asked.

"Not quite. Have you heard of Dr Severino Antinori?"

"No."

"He's an Italian doctor who has been in the news recently for having treated women for infertility. He's had remarkable success, even with women over the age of sixty."

"My goodness," Ford exclaimed, "that's unnatural!"

"Perhaps, but it's what he does. In any event," Cameron continued, "in the late 1990s Dr Antinori announced that he would embark on cloning a human being. Then, I think it was in 2002, he announced that he had implanted a clone into a woman who was expected to give birth in January 2003."

"And did she?" Varley asked.

"I don't think so. Certainly there is no scientific proof."

"Where is Antinori now?"

"I'm not sure: I imagine he's somewhere in Italy."

Jackson Ford stood, and held out his hand. "Jim, this has been a distinct pleasure for Mark and me. You have no idea just how educational it has been. Unfortunately, I am pushed for time: I have to prepare for my final sermon at the Crusade later this evening. I hope you will excuse me."

"Of course." Cameron rose to leave. Ford went to the door with him and said: "I would be honoured if you would be my guest this evening at my Crusade."

This was the last thing Cameron wanted to do. "I'd love to come, but I have a dinner appointment with colleagues," he excused himself.

Ford nodded, "I see. Well, Jim: I hope we will meet again." He shook Cameron's hand as he left.

When the door closed, Ford looked enquiringly at Varley and raised an eyebrow. "Was that useful?"

"You have no idea just how useful," Varley said. "When I get the box, and the hair, I may want to visit Dr Antinori."

"And when might you get this box?" Ford asked

"Perhaps tomorrow: I'm meeting my contact in Melrose. It's a small town about an hour south of here."

CHAPTER 9

Alan looked at Mrs. Doig. "Varley?" he asked, his cheeks reddening with anger. "Do you know where I can find him?"

Mrs. Doig looked at Jamie, but when he didn't respond she said, "I'm not sure. I think he's with the Crusade in Edinburgh, you know, the one with Jackson Ford, the American evangelist?"

"I'll find him then," Alan growled. "But first I'll have to make arrangements for Grandad's funeral."

Jamie finally spoke up. "Sir Alan," he said, "I think you'll find that Sir Jock made all the arrangements in advance with his solicitor in Edinburgh. A few weeks ago, he told me that if anything happened to him, I should look in the envelope in the top right drawer of his desk and follow the instructions."

Alan looked at Jamie, puzzled at what he had heard. "You said, Sir Alan. What on earth do you mean?"

Jamie looked down and frowned. "Oh, I thought you knew. Sir Jock was a baronet, and on his death the title passes to his male heir."

"Really?" Alan muttered. "Well, I'll find out about that later." He went to the old desk, and opened the right top drawer. In it he found an envelope on which Jock had written: "To be opened in the event of my death."

He slit the envelope and pulled out a sheet of paper on which Jock had written: "Whoever opens this envelope should contact my solicitor in Edinburgh, Mr. Cameron Learmonth of 45 Albyn Place. Mr. Learmonth is an old friend, and has full instructions regarding my will and my wishes with regard to my funeral arrangements."

"Damn! Damn! Damn!" Alan shouted. "Why did this happen when I wasn't here?"

Kate moved to him and touched his arm. "Alan, it couldn't be helped. Jock's time was limited, as you know."

He held her hand for a moment. "I know," he said with a choke in his voice. "Thank you, Kate." He gave a deep sigh and turned to the staff. "Mrs. Doig, Jamie, thank you for everything you have done for Sir Jock in the past. I won't forget, believe me." He picked up the phone. "Now, if you'll excuse me, I'd better call Mr. Cameron Learmonth in Edinburgh."

Kate also went to leave, but Alan motioned her to remain.

Having reached Learmonth's office and explained to the receptionist who he was, and the reason for his call, Alan had to wait less than a minute before the solicitor's cultured voice boomed down the phone.

"Sir Alan, I'm so distressed to hear about the passing of my old comrade, Jock Bruce. We served together as young officers many years ago before I decided to practise law." He paused. "Now, tell me what happened?"

Alan replied that Jock had apparently suffered a heart attack.

Learmonth grunted. "Not the worst way to go. Certainly better than a lingering, probably painful, end from cancer, which Jock would have been facing." He sighed before continuing. "In any event, Jock has left me clear instructions regarding his funeral arrangements. With your permission, of course, Sir Alan, I shall follow these exactly as he decreed."

"That would be perfect," Alan said. "But you keep referring to me as Sir Alan. I don't quite understand why."

"It's really very simple. Sir Jock was a baronet. It's an hereditary title, though technically it is not an order of knighthood. However, like knights, baronets are entitled to be called Sir. The only other benefit, as I recall, is that a baronet is entitled to have a pall supported by two men as principal mourners and four others assisting at his funeral." Learmonth glanced at Jock's instructions and gave a brief smile. "Jock didn't mention that. I imagine that was not his style."

Alan rolled his eyes and looked at Kate. "For the time being, Mr. Learmonth, please refer to me as Alan, or Mr. Bruce. We Canadians are not all that impressed by titles, although I do appreciate the significance, believe me. And I would be grateful if you could make the necessary arrangements for the funeral."

"It will all be taken care of Sir … Mr. Bruce. And when might I see you to review the will?"

Alan though for a moment. "I can be in Edinburgh tomorrow."

"Fine. May I expect you at 2:00 p.m.?"

"That would be excellent." Alan hung up the phone and turned to Kate. "Learmonth will take care of the funeral arrangements, and I'm going to see him tomorrow in Edinburgh." He looked at the floor in thought, then stared at Kate. "Will you come with me?"

"Of course, Sir Alan," she said with a mischievous smile

Next, Alan rang directory enquiries to obtain the number for the Ford Campaign in Edinburgh. When he was put through he spoke to a young woman, explaining that he need to speak urgently to Mark Varley. He learned that Mr. Varley was not available, but might be contacted at the Caledonian Hilton Hotel. He rang that number and asked for Mr.Varley's room. There was no reply, so he left a message. "Mr. Varley, this is Alan Bruce, the grandson of Sir Jock Bruce, whom you saw earlier today. My grandfather has asked me to speak to you. I'll be in Edinburgh tomorrow and will call to arrange a meeting."

CHAPTER 10

Varley parked his car at Edinburgh airport and went into the arrivals area. It was not long before he saw Bruno Conti. He had travelled light, with only a small carry-on case.

"Bruno," Varley said, "good to see you."

"Mark," he sighed, "I'm exhausted. I couldn't sleep on the flight to London; arrived at 6:30 a.m. and then had to wait nearly three hours for the flight to Edinburgh."

Varley looked at Conti. He had not shaved, looked badly in need of a shower and a change of clothes. "No problem, Bruno. I'll get you to our hotel in twenty minutes. Then you can sleep for a few hours before we need to go for a drive to Melrose."

"Melrose? Where or what is that?" Conti growled.

"It's a small town just south of Edinburgh, where we will meet someone whom I might need you to talk to."

"Work him over, you mean!"

"Whatever—hopefully that won't be necessary." Having said that, Varley led Conti to his car and gave him a quick briefing on the situation, telling him only what he would need to know. As he moved into the traffic bound for the centre of Edinburgh, Varley glanced at Conti, whose head had slumped forward onto his shoulders with eyes tightly closed. "Wake up Bruno," he growled, "I need to give you some background."

Conti's head jerked up and his eyes blinked. "Sorry Mark, I just need some shut-eye."

"OK, but here's what you need to know. I've met a guy here, and he has something I, and Jackson Ford, need to get. He's been very cagey about giving me the information I need, and I think he may be trying to gouge me rather than negotiate. So, my old buddy, that's why you are here," Varley paused and smiled as he looked at Conti, "for back-up," he said. "Capisce?"

Conti smiled: "That I can do."

Varley drew up outside the hotel, asked the doorman to park the car, and led Conti to the reception desk. When Conti had his room key-card, Varley told him that he should grab a few hours sleep and meet him in the lobby at 4:00 p.m. They would then drive to Melrose.

Varley took the elevator to his room then rang Jackson Ford and asked to see him. Ford was available, so Varley went immediately to his room.

"Jackson," he began, "I think we need to talk about what I can offer my contact for the box that he said he had seen. I think it's worth a lot. What do you think?"

Jackson Ford beamed a smile that he often used to charm people. "Mark, I think it's probably priceless." He shook his white mane of hair. "But, as you know, there are limits to what we can pay."

"I know, I know," Varley replied, "but I need to have a ballpark figure."

Ford crossed his legs and picked up the Alfonso letter, which Varley had stolen from Sir Jock's desk. He tapped it with his hand. "I've been re-reading this letter. It's not the original, but I assume it is a fair translation. It mentions the Empress Helena of Constantine, who is a known historic figure. One can't, of course, confirm the story about finding the cross on which Jesus was crucified, but assuming that is true, the question remains, how did the hair get to Spain?" Ford rubbed his eyes. "Thanks to Google, I have been able to confirm that a Spanish nun by the name of Egeria, the name used in the letter, did indeed visit the Holy Land in the fourth century, and I have confirmed that King Alfonso did fight the invading Moors. So," he paused, "I'm inclined to believe it. I have faith, Mark." He repeated: "I have faith." His eyes glowed with rapture. "This is meant to be, Mark. I can feel it."

Varley knew Ford well: the old preacher sometimes got carried away with his own eloquence. However, he was often a shrewd judge of people and situations. How else would his Crusade have thrived financially?

Varley decided it was time to make some hard-nosed calculations of the financial benefits that might come from having the box with the hair of Jesus. "Jackson," he began, "assuming we can acquire the box, what use could we make of it?"

"Use? Use?" Ford asked. "Well, of course, I should be compelled to reveal it to the world. That, I'm sure, is what God would wish."

"And that would help us to bring more people to Christ?" Varley asked.

"Naturally, that is my goal. That is what I am called to do."

Varley nodded his head. "And so," he continued, "we would attract more people, more pledges?"

Ford nodded in agreement. "More people certainly. The financial side, Mark, is your responsibility, but I'm sure you can calculate what it might mean."

Varley sat quietly calculating the financial benefits that they might gain from exposing the box to the world. His eyes widened as his mental calculations began to tax even his brain. He went to a desk in Ford's room and picked up a calculator. "Let's see Jackson," he said, "I can do a rough calculation. From experience, we know that direct-mail normally gives a 10 per cent response rate. Face-to-face, we can get as high as 50 per cent, but that's hard work and time consuming. An appeal from you on TV could get a 20 per cent response rate. And with the box, Jesus' hair, and the story you have to tell, we might get as high as 30 per cent response. So, with an audience of 1 million—and that might be achievable with the right advance publicity—we might get up to 30 per cent."

Ford was getting enthused. "Go on, Mark, this is getting interesting."

"Well, if we assume a $100 pledge that would yield $30 million."

Ford's eyes widened. "$30 million! Just think what we could do for the Lord with that." Varley did. It meant $3 million to him, given his tithing arrangements.

"So," Varley continued, "we could make a reasonably generous offer to my informant?"

"Do what you think, is necessary, Mark. Just get me that box."

After his meeting with Jackson Ford, Varley met Conti in the hotel lobby at four o'clock.

"Sleep well Bruno?" he asked.

Conti looked more relaxed after a few hours sleep. "Yes," he replied. He had changed into a chocolate brown sports jacket, with tan pants and a gold shirt with a dark blue patterned tie.

"Good. You're looking better," Varley said, "although your clothing looks more like the Bronx than Edinburgh."

"What did you expect? You give me a couple of hours to catch a plane and you expect Beau Brummel?"

"No, it's OK, Bruno. I guess I've been too long in this conservative city."

They had a coffee together in the hotel before driving to Melrose. They arrived at 5.30 PM and parked in the small square, opposite Burts Hotel, easily recognizable as the white building Andy McPhee had described.

"Bruno, perhaps it would be better if I met alone with my friend Andy. I'll see if I can cut a deal with him. If not, I'll let you know, and we can go from there."

"I'll just sit in the car, close my eyes and wait for you."

"OK, I'll be back as soon as we've had dinner."

"Dinner? It feels like lunchtime."

"I know, it's the jet lag. We're five hours ahead of New York time in Scotland."

"Well, if you don't mind, I may see if I can grab a sandwich or a hot dog while I'm waiting."

"Not too many hot dogs in Scotland, Bruno. You are more likely to get fish and chips."

"Whatever," Bruno said. "I'll find something."

Varley left the car and walked toward the white-washed Burts hotel, an attractive building with window boxes filled with colourful red geraniums. He walked past a small reception desk on the left, past the lounge bar on the right, and took a left turn down a corridor, at the end of which he saw the dining room. It had several tables draped with white tablecloths and the walls were covered in a dark blue striped wallpaper. In the centre of the room was a large circular table on which sat a stone urn filled with a dried flower arrangement. Varley sniffed—some of it looked like dried thistles. He selected a table in the corner next to a window overlooking a rose garden. Through the open window he smelled the scent of lavender.

He did not have long to wait. Just before six o'clock Andy got out of an old blue Ford, which he parked two slots away from where Bruno Conti sat impassively. Andy entered the hotel and Varley rose to greet him as he came into the dining room. "Andy, good to see you again."

"Mr. Varley," Andy shook Mark's hand and sat down opposite him.

"Perhaps we can discuss business over dinner Andy."

"Aye. That would be fine." Andy replied.

The waiter brought the menus and asked if they would like a drink before dinner.

Varley ordered his usual gin and tonic, while Andy chose a pint of McEwans draught beer.

They chose their meals and while waiting for the food to arrive, Varley took a long sip of his drink and looked across at Andy who had obviously dressed for the occasion in a dark blue suit with a white shirt and a Melrose Rugby football club tie. "Well Andy," he began, "I hope we can reach agreement on your letting me know where that silver box is."

Andy looked at him and took a long drink from his beer. "Didn't Sir Jock Bruce tell you?" he asked.

Varley shrugged his shoulders. "I wasn't able to see him. Besides, you know where it is. So that's why I am here."

Andy looked at him slyly. "Oh I see, just like that, you expect me to tell you? Remember, Mr. Varley you bargained with me to get Sir Jock's name, and didn't pay what I wanted. Well this time I need to get what I want, or else I will not help you."

"Really, Andy," Varley smiled. "I'm not here to quibble over a few pounds. Just let me know what your figure is and we can probably agree it quite quickly."

Andy scowled. He had been prepared for a lengthy bargaining session and was not sure how to react. He took another drink of beer. The meal arrived and as Varley started to eat, Andy said, "So what's your offer, Mr. Varley?"

"Offer? What do you want?"

"I reckon this is worth a lot to you and Mr. Ford," he said. A thought came into his head and he smirked. "Maybe I should get bids from some other churches as well."

"Why would you do that? I've already said that we will meet your price."

Andy decided to ask for what he felt would be a ridiculously high price. "OK. Fifty thousand pounds!"

"Fifty thousand pounds? That's a lot of money Andy."

"Aye, I ken that it is. But that's my figure." he said with determination.

Varley paused: this little guy was beginning to annoy him, but he needed to know where he could find the casket. "OK, Andy, I agree," he said. "When do you want the money? I can give you a cheque for part of it, with another once we retrieve the box."

Andy was not sure how to respond. Cheques could always be cancelled, whereas cash was tangible, something he could put into the bank and be secure that it existed. "I'll need cash," he said.

"Cash, Andy? Come on Andy, do you really think I have fifty thousand pounds cash on me?"

"No, but I'm sure that you can get it."

"Rest assured I can. But if and when I do, I will need to see the box before I give you the money."

"That's not the deal, Mr. Varley; the deal is that I show you where it is. After that it's your job to retrieve it."

Varley thought for a moment. What was it that McPhee had said when he had met him in Edinburgh? Oh yes, he had said that he had seen Sir Jock Bruce bury the box. "You'll show me where it's buried?" he asked. "That's the deal?"

"Indeed, Mr. Varley as you put it, that is the deal."

Varley sat back in his chair and stared at Andy. The little man was really annoying him now. Didn't he understand that the value lay in Varley being able to retrieve the box? He gave a slight shake of his head, then reached a decision. "Right, then I'll need to get back to Edinburgh to collect the money. I could be back tomorrow morning. Just let me know where to meet."

"I'm working at the Abbey tomorrow," Andy blurted out, before realising that he had given a clue to where the casket was buried. He paused and thought. "Tell you what," he continued, "why don't we meet here at the same time tomorrow? You show me the cash, and I'll take you to the site."

Varley agreed. They finished their meal, shook hands, and Andy left while Varley paid the bill.

He saw Andy drive away before he crossed to his car where Conti looked inquiringly at him.

"Did you see that guy who just drove away?" Varley asked.

"The little red-haired guy?"

"Yes; he's the one."

"I got him. No problem."

"Well he seems to work at the abbey. I'd like you to go there tomorrow morning, take a tour and see what's going on. I'll book you a room overnight at the Burts hotel across the road. It's quite comfortable."

"What about you, Mark, are you staying here?"

"No, I need to go back to Edinburgh to get some cash from the bank to pay off McPhee. I'll be back tomorrow afternoon. Let's meet at your hotel at four o'clock."

Mark saw Conti checked into Burts hotel, and returned to Edinburgh. He met with Ford and told him about the need for fifty thousand pounds. Ford gasped at the amount, but signed a cheque for Mark to cash next morning when the bank opened.

Next morning, while Mark Varley was meeting with the Bank of Scotland manager, who was curious about the need for so much cash, Conti made his way to Melrose Abbey. He paid the adult admittance fee of four pounds fifty, and waited for a guide to show him and about ten other people around the ruins. Before long, a short red-haired guy appeared. It was Andy McPhee.

"Please gather round, folks," he said, "and I'll tell you a little bit about the history of Melrose Abbey. Then you'll have lots of time to explore on your own." The visitors stood in a semicircle in front of Andy. He looked at them. As usual, he thought, most were American: he could tell them from their clothes, particularly the stocky fellow in the colourful brown jacket and gold shirt. "Let me begin in the twelfth century." Andy said. "It was in 1131, that King David I of Scotland got the Cistercian monks to build a new abbey. There had been an earlier one, which had been founded by St Aidan in the seventh century, but that's about four miles away from this site. In 1385, King Richard II of England's army came here and burned down the abbey because he was annoyed at the Scots raiding his country ..."

"Sheep stealing you mean?" said an English voice.

"Perhaps. In any event, the abbey was rebuilt. What you see here today is the ruins of that abbey." Andy pointed to the walls of the abbey which towered majestically above them. "As you go around look carefully at the carvings in the stone. It really is quite remarkable. Some of it is very well preserved. You might see carved images of the coronation of the Virgin, a number of saints—St. Andrew, St. Paul, St. Peter, and St. Thomas, as well as mythical dragons and gargoyles. If you look on the lintel of the Bell Stair, you might see an inscription: 'Be helde to ye hande'...."

"And what is that in the Queen's English?" interrupted the tiresome English voice.

Andy looked at her with disdain. "It means 'keep beholden to, or keep in mind, the end, your salvation.'" He continued: "Talking of the end, there is a legend that Melrose has a demonic connection ..."

"Demonic? What do you mean?" asked the Englishwoman.

"Well, the legend is that a thirteenth century wizard named Michael Scott is buried here, along with his magic books. He prophesied that he would die as a result of a stone falling on his head."

"And did he?" the English voice enquired.

"That's the legend," Andy replied, "and speaking of burials, we also have on the grounds a stone plinth, marking the spot where the heart of King Robert the Bruce is buried. You'll see it as you wander around. It's just off the East Processional. It's marked with a stone."

"Only his heart is buried there?" Bruno asked.

"Yes, it's a long story. His body is buried at Dunfermline. He asked that his heart be taken on a crusade to the Holy Land, after his death. Unfortunately, the knights taking it there made a detour to Spain to fight the Moors and were killed. The heart was brought back to Scotland, and buried under the Chapter House, where it lay for centuries, until it was unearthed during archaeological excavations, first in 1921 and again in 1996. It was identified and reburied here in 1998, by the Minister for Scotland. Robert the Bruce's descendant, Sir Jock Bruce, also attended the ceremony. And now, if you would like to view the abbey, please take your time. I'll be here to answer any questions."

The crowd dispersed. Bruno followed, not particularly interested in anything except the site where Bruce's heart was buried. The guide had mentioned that Sir Jock Bruce had attended the ceremony in 1998. Perhaps that might be the clue to what Varley was looking for.

He found a stone plinth beneath which Robert the Bruce's heart lay. The stone was inscribed with a carved heart and what appeared to be a multiplication cross, but which he later learned was the cross of St. Andrew, the patron Saint of Scotland. The plinth was about six to nine inches high and about a foot in diameter. It was surrounded by a small metal rail about four inches high, which formed a square about three feet by three feet. The base of the stone plinth was surrounded by pebbles within the square formed by the metal rails.

Conti was sure that below it lay a concrete base into which the stone was set. He bent and read the inscription on the plinth:

A NOBLE HART MAY HAVE NANE EASE GIF FREEDOM FAILYE.

He rolled his eyes. Couldn't these Scots write plain English? He'd ask the guide for a translation if he saw him on the way out. Meantime, he thought he would return to the hotel and call Mark Varley. He answered the phone, after two rings.

"Mark, it's Bruno.

"Hi Bruno: what's going on?"

"Well I've been to Melrose Abbey. The little red-haired guy you pointed out to me yesterday is a tour guide there."

"Really?"

"Yup! And the heart of King Robert the Bruce is buried there. He said that Sir Jock Bruce was there when it was buried."

"Now that's interesting," Varley replied. "Very interesting indeed. I'll see you at 4 o'clock, Bruno." Varley hung up. He thought for a moment, and then smiled broadly. Perhaps the silver box was buried near Robert the Bruce's heart. He intended to find out in a few hours.

CHAPTER 11

Next morning, Alan and Kate drove to Edinburgh, where Alan had an appointment with Cameron Learmonth, Sir Jock's solicitor, at two o'clock. Kate had phoned Professor Brownlee, who expected to have some news for her about the carbon dating of the first page of the Alfonso letter she had left with him.

Alan drove Kate to the professor's office in the Edinburgh Medical School at Teviot Place. They agreed to keep in contact, and Alan said he would return in the late afternoon, after having met Cameron Learmonth.

Kate got out of the car and looked at him with concern. "Alan, you will call me if you need to talk, after you've met Mr. Learmonth, won't you?"

"Of course, but I plan on seeing this Mr. Varley first, if possible. My appointment with Learmonth isn't until two this afternoon."

Kate smiled. "Oh, then if I'm finished with the Prof. before two, would you like me to meet you at Mr. Learmonth's office?"

Alan nodded. "That would probably be a good idea; but if you're ready before two, give me a call, and if I'm finished with Varley, perhaps we can meet for lunch before seeing Learmonth."

Kate agreed and turned towards the professor's building. Alan watched her trim figure as she left; her brown hair bobbing gently on her shoulders as she walked. Alan started the engine and turned the Jaguar towards Princes Street. He had difficulty in finding a parking spot for the car, but finally discovered a parking garage at Castle Terrace, under the crags of Edinburgh Castle. He locked the Jaguar and walked down Lothian Road to the Caledonian Hilton hotel. At the front desk he asked for Mr Varley's room. The hotel receptionist looked at him. "We do not give out room numbers," she said.

"Well can you dial his room and let me speak to him?"

"Certainly, sir." She rang Varley's room and handed the phone to Alan when Varley replied.

"Mr. Varley," Alan said, "this is Alan Bruce, Sir Jock Bruce's grandson. I left a message last night asking if we might meet. I'm downstairs in the lobby."

Varley frowned at the phone. What did this mean? Had he been connected with Sir Jock's death? He answered: "I'm not sure what you want to talk about. I'm really rather busy; we are running a very active Crusade, you know."

"I won't take long," Alan said, "but it really is important, to you as well as to me, that we meet."

Varley hesitated. There really was no possible connection between his visit and Sir Jock's death. However, to avoid a meeting might only encourage any suspicions that Alan Bruce might hold.

"OK," he said," I can probably spare fifteen minutes. I'll meet you in the lobby in five minutes' time."

Alan put down the phone and walked through the small waiting area to a room behind the front desk. It faced Chalmers restaurant, the hotel's brasserie. In a few minutes the elevator door opened and a tall black-haired man stepped out. He glanced to his right, and Alan rose to meet him. Varley was smartly dressed in a blue suit with a matching blue shirt and red tie.

Alan looked at him. "Mr. Varley?" he enquired.

"Yes, I'm Mark Varley, I suppose you are Alan Bruce?"

"That's correct. Can we find a quiet corner to talk?"

Varley led the way to a table in the next room, larger than the first and with a grand piano as its focal point. They found a quiet corner, and sat in chairs facing each other across a small table.

Varley ordered coffee for them before turning his attention to Alan. "This all seems very puzzling Mr. Bruce; what is it that you want to discuss?"

Alan looked at him, trying to control his growing anger. "Discuss?" he asked. "It's more than that. My grandfather died after you had met him yesterday, and a document is missing from his desk."

Varley looked straight at Alan. "Sir Jock is dead?" he asked. "Why, that seems incredible. He seemed very healthy when I left. I am sorry. Please accept my condolences."

Alan pursed his lips. "Thank you. I have to ask, did my grandfather seem ill before you left?"

Varley felt he could answer honestly. Sir Jock had been dead, not ill. "No I can't say that he was ill."

Alan looked at him, sensing that Varley was not being completely frank. "I see." He paused and looked straight into Varley's eyes. "They tell me it was a heart attack. Are you quite sure he was alive when you left?"

Varley rose. "I hope you're not accusing me of harming Sir Jock in any way."

"No, please sit down."

With a show of reluctance, Varley sat in the chair.

Alan continued. "But I'm afraid, Mr. Varley, I have to ask you about a document which is missing from my grandfather's desk."

Varley frowned. He had not expected that anyone would have missed the Alfonso letter, at least not so quickly. He decided to play out the discussion, to emphasize his honest acquisition of the letter. "Document?" he asked. "What sort of document are you talking about?"

Alan knew then that Varley had the letter. "Oh, I think you know, Mr. Varley. A document purporting to be a letter from a Spanish King."

Varley gave a short laugh. "You mean the Alfonso letter?" He smiled. "I told Sir Jock that someone at our Crusade had told me a strange story about Sir Jock and a silver casket. When we met he laughed at the outrageous fabrication and gave me the letter. He said it was one of many that had been in circulation, and that he had other copies. He told me to keep it as a memento of my visit to Scotland, a land of fables."

Alan put his coffee cup down with a bang. "I don't believe a word of that," he said.

Varley looked at him carefully. "Frankly, I don't care what you believe: I've told you what happened."

"In that case, I don't suppose you have any objection to returning the letter to me?"

"You seem to be making a fuss about a few sheets of paper."

"To you maybe, but it was my grandfather's, and I'm his heir. It should be mine."

Varley thought for a moment. He could have a confrontation with Bruce or seek a solution. He decided that a compromise would be the better solution. "OK, if it's so important, I'll return it to you. Where should I send it?"

Alan was not going to be fobbed off. For all he knew, Varley would return to America with the letter, and he would never be able to recover it. He stuck out his chin in confrontational mode.

"Send it? No need to send it. I'll take it with me today."

Varley smiled. He had already made photocopies. "Well if that's what you want, let me go to my room and get it for you." He rose and returned a few minutes later and handed an envelope to Alan. "There you are, Mr. Bruce. I'm afraid you don't have the charm and grace of your grandfather."

Alan accepted the envelope, knowing as he did so that Varley had probably already made copies—why else would he have been so agreeable? "Thank you," he said and left the hotel without shaking Varley's outstretched hand.

Meanwhile, Kate had found Professor Brownlee. He was not in his office when she arrived, so his secretary directed her to his laboratory, which Kate knew well from her PhD studies in Edinburgh ten years earlier. She found Brownlee perched on the arm of a chair with his glasses sitting on top of his head. He was reading aloud from a sheet of paper. "... and so beyond doubt ..." He looked up in surprise. "Kate, I didn't expect you this early. I was just reading the report I have received from Harry Morton—you know, the chap I said I would ask to look at the manuscript." He looked at Kate for a moment. "He's the Professor of Modern Languages here. I think I told you."

"Yes, I remember the name. What does he have to say?"

"Well, it's a bit complicated, but there's no doubt that the manuscript is genuine. It's Spanish."

"How was that confirmed?"

Brownlee looked at the report he'd received from Harry Morton. "Let's see." He read aloud. "We made a Raman microscopy study of the pigmentation used in the historiated initials. The predominant red pigment is cinnabar mercury sulphide, probably extracted and refined from local sources. The black lettering is lamp black. Some of the blue and purple pigmentation is from agurite, known to be plentiful in the Grenada area of Spain. The earliest established usage of this pigment is around 1300 AD. Furthermore, King Alfonso XI is known to have used this palette of pigments in other manuscripts, several of which are in the Prado Museum in Madrid ..."

Brownlee looked at Kate. "It does seem to be genuine."

"That's interesting," Kate replied. "Do you also have carbon dating of the document?"

"Kate, Kate," Brownlee shook his head. "You always were impatient."

Kate laughed, "Forgive me. I'm just anxious to have it confirmed."

"Well, I will put your mind at ease. It appears to date from the first half of the fourteenth century. That's the best I can do, I'm afraid."

Kate hugged him, and Brownlee blushed. "That's a perfect thank you" he said with a smile.

As Kate rose to leave, a man with a wrinkled sports jacket and grease-stained tie entered.

Brownlee introduced him. "Kate, this is Dr Jim Cameron. He's quite famous. He was part of the team that cloned Dolly the sheep."

"Dolly the sheep?" Kate said. "Oh yes, I remember, that was quite a success, wasn't it?"

"Yes," Cameron said, "we had a breakthrough." He looked at her. "You're American, aren't you?"

"Is my accent so obvious?" Kate smiled.

"There seem to be a lot of your countrymen around just now." Cameron said. "Maybe it's to do with Jackson Ford's Crusade. Are you involved with that?"

"Goodness, no." Kate said. "That's not my interest. Why do you ask?"

Cameron looked at her. "Well, only yesterday, Mr. Ford himself asked me to meet him to tell him about cloning. He and his assistant, a Mr. Varley, seemed to be very interested."

Kate raised her eyebrows. "Really? I wonder why?"

"Ah, that I don't know. Perhaps it's to do with the moral issues involved."

"Hmm," Kate murmured. "That might be right." Having said that she knew that Ford and Varley probably had other plans. She thanked Professor Brownlee and Jim Cameron, and left with the report from Harry Morton. Outside the Medical School, she found a taxi and asked to be taken to the Caledonian Hilton Hotel. She dialled Alan's cell phone and told him that she was on her way to the hotel with good news.

"Fine," Alan replied. "I'll meet you there. I've finished my meeting with Varley, and I'm just across Princes Street. I've been walking, trying to make up my mind about Varley and his plans."

As he was speaking, the traffic lights changed, and he crossed the street, arriving at the hotel as a taxi drew up. Kate stepped out and hugged him.

Without thinking, he kissed her lightly on the cheek. She looked up in surprise, "Sir Alan" she smiled, "this is so sudden."

Alan blushed. "Sorry, I guess I am a bit excited."

"With me?" She raised an eyebrow provocatively.

"No—I mean …" he blushed slightly, "well, let's put it this way. I've had an interesting talk with Varley. He's up to no good."

"Shouldn't we go somewhere private to talk about it?" Kate asked.

"Of course. There's an old pub on Rose Street—Ma Scott's. My dad took me there years ago. He used to go there as a young man with his rugby team. It's not far."

They turned to cross Princes Street just as Varley emerged from the hotel. He watched as they disappeared into the crowds milling on the busy street.

As they sipped on draught beers, Kate told Alan about her meeting with Professor Brownlee, which appeared to confirm the fourteenth century provenance of the Alfonso letter.

Kate said, "Something rather strange happened just before I left the Prof. Dr Jim Cameron appeared, and Brownlee said he had been part of the team that cloned Dolly the sheep. You remember that, of course?"

Alan thought for a moment. "It sounds familiar."

"It was the first cloning of a mammal."

"So why does that strike you as strange?"

"That's not what I mean. Cameron said that he had been invited to speak to Jackson Ford and Varley about cloning."

"Really?" Alan said. "So that's what they intend to do. My grandad was right. They're going to try to clone Jesus, if they can get hold of the casket buried with Bruce's heart." Alan touched the locket in his jacket pocket. It might prove important in foiling Ford's plans.

They finished their drinks and took a short walk downhill to Albyn Place. Cameron Learmonth's office was in a distinguished Georgian building in the New Town, an architectural feature of Edinburgh's past glory, and reckoned to be the best assembly of Georgian architecture in Britain.

Cameron Learmonth's office was spacious with twelve-foot ceilings and a large bay window looking out over mature gardens. He was of medium height with white thinning hair, parted on the left side, and a bristling military moustache. His three-piece blue pinstriped suit was emphasized by a sparkling white shirt, on which his Guards regimental tie stood out. A white handkerchief flopped from his breast pocket. He stood as they entered the room.

"Sir Alan," he said, "I'm so sorry to hear the news about my old friend Jock. He was quite a few years older, but one forgets chronology at times." He turned to Kate. "And this is?" he enquired.

"This is Dr Kate Harris; she was a friend of my grandfather and is now mine." Kate raised an eyebrow, and stared at him. A blush flashed across Alan's face.

"I mean she is now my friend, also."

Learmonth sensed a bond between the two younger people, but wisely said nothing to that effect. "Please be seated." He motioned Alan and Kate to sit on high-backed chairs facing his large oak desk, remarkable for the few papers on its gleaming surface.

"Would you like tea or coffee?" he asked. They declined the offer. "Well, then, Sir Alan."

"Please call me Alan, or Mr. Bruce," Alan said. "I don't think I'll ever use that title."

Learmonth frowned. "It's a grand old title; it shouldn't be lost. A baronetcy is one of the titles that passes down through the generations."

"I know, perhaps I just need time to get used to it."

"Well then," Learmonth continued. "I had invited you here to tell you about your grandfather's will. Frankly, I prefer to do this in private, if Dr Harris could excuse us."

Kate rose, but Alan motioned her to sit and said. "I have no objections to Kate being here, Mr. Learmonth, so perhaps you can begin."

Learmonth frowned. This was bad form, he thought, but if his client insisted he would comply. "Very well," he said, opening a drawer and withdrawing a large sealed envelope. He found a silver dirk, which he used to slit it open, before pulling out several sheets of paper, holding them up for inspection. "Here is Sir Jock's last will. He made it only a few months ago, when he first learned that his days were numbered. We had dinner that evening at my club," he reminisced, "a splendid affair, and the last time I saw my old friend." A tear showed in his eye before he shook his head and continued. "Please forgive an old man. I don't usually get sentimental about clients."

"I understand," Alan said. "I'm a lawyer also, in Toronto."

"Then you do know how I feel."

Alan nodded, but he wanted Learmonth to get to the point.

Kate looked at the two men, and shook her head. No wonder lawyers were criticised.

The old lawyer read the will to refresh his memory, and then looked directly at Alan.

"It's all very simple," he said. "You are the sole heir. Sir Jock has left everything to you, including his business, the land, and Bruce House in Dumbarton, and a number of stocks he held. There's also a fairly substantial bank balance, and investments and properties throughout the country. That's the good news. The bad news, and I am afraid there always is bad news, with a rapacious government constantly anxious to extract taxes from us, is that there will be substantial taxes to pay. Nevertheless, Alan, you will be a very wealthy man."

Alan sat quietly, deep in thought. What would this mean to his life in Toronto? He could hardly sell Bruce House. It was a family trust, he felt. Yet he did not see himself living permanently in Scotland. "Thank you, Mr. Learmonth," was as much as he felt able to say. "I really think I need time to let this all sink in.

My life is in Toronto, and I don't know what I should do about the Bruce House estate."

Kate interjected: "Alan, you don't have to decide now. Take your time."

"Quite wise, young lady." Learmonth nodded. "My advice, Alan, is to take time to get over the shock of Sir Jock's death. It will take us a considerable time to settle the duties and taxes payable, and to wind up Jock's tax affairs. When all that has been completed you will have a more certain assessment of your financial position. That will allow you time to clarify your thoughts about Bruce House, and no doubt other matters," he added, looking appreciatively at Kate.

"Thank you, that's good advice, Mr. Learmonth. Now perhaps we can discuss the funeral arrangements."

Learmonth had already arranged everything. The funeral service, as Jock had stipulated, would be held in Edinburgh's St. Giles Cathedral, on the High Street near the castle. He would then be buried in a family vault in Edinburgh.

Alan thanked Learmonth and arranged to meet him in three days' time at St. Giles. As he and Kate stood to leave, Learmonth said. "Just a moment, Alan. I almost forgot. Jock contacted me just before he died and sent me a letter." He rummaged in his desk. "Here it is." He looked at it with curiosity. "I really don't know what's inside. Jock directed me to give it to his heir—that's you of course, Alan—exactly one year after his death." He put the envelope back into his desk drawer and gave a slight smile. "It's a puzzle, isn't it? Not Jock's usual style, but he must have had a reason."

"I wonder what it is," Alan murmured.

CHAPTER 12

Varley's phone rang as he was having lunch in his room. It was Conti.

"Mark, howya doin', buddy?"

"Bruno: I'm okay, what's up?"

"I've been thinking. If we need to dig up something that is buried, why don't you bring a couple of spades with you?" He paused before adding, "come to think about it, maybe a pickaxe, sledgehammer, and a hammer and chisel might be a good idea. Just in case we need to break through some stone or concrete."

"Good idea, Bruno, I'll pick them up on my way to Melrose this afternoon. See you at your hotel around four." Varley put down the phone and sipped his coffee. It began to seem probable that the silver casket might actually be buried at Melrose Abbey. That was where Andy McPhee worked: it was where Robert the Bruce's heart was buried; so there was already a connection with Sir Jock Bruce. Finishing his lunch, Varley, decided it was time to go to the bank and collect the fifty thousand pounds. He took a taxi to the Bank of Scotland branch office on the Mound. Before coming to Scotland he had opened an account there to cover the expenses of the Crusade. Now with the pledges that had poured in from Scotland and the rest of the UK, several million pounds lay in a high interest account awaiting transfer to the States, as soon as a favourable currency rate could be obtained.

At the bank, Varley asked to see the manager. He did not want to be bothered with dealing through a teller at one of the bank's counters. She would have been nonplussed at the request for fifty thousand pounds in cash.

After a short delay, he was taken to the manager's office. There, Janet Scott greeted him. "Mr. Varley, it's a pleasure to see you, how is the Crusade doing?"

"It's very effective Miss Scott. We are helping to transform people's lives with the good news about Christ."

Janet Scott looked at Varley, gauging his sincerity. She gave a quick smile. "Yes, and if I may say so, you are also transforming your account with us. That, I'm sure, is also good news."

"Well, of course. We need money to help us do our work, Miss Scott."

"Of course, of course." Janet Scott looked at Varley. "And is there something in particular I can do for you today?"

"Well, yes." Varley gave her the cheque for fifty thousand pounds which Jackson Ford had signed.

"I would like cash."

Janet Scott blinked, "Dear me, Mr. Varley. That is a lot of cash to carry around."

"Don't I know it? However, we have a number of payments we need to make, and a lot of people want to have cash. They don't want to wait for a cheque to clear, or in some cases they don't even have bank accounts."

"I see." Janet Scott found this was very unusual; still Varley was entitled to get his money "How would you like the money?" she asked.

Varley had not thought that through; he did not want to carry a sack full of money around. "Why not give it to me in large denominations, say one hundred pound notes?"

Janet Scott's eyebrows rose. She didn't think most people would be used to receiving payment in such large bills. There was something not quite right, but she was a banker, not a policeman. "Just a moment, Mr. Varley." She picked up the phone and gave instructions.

Five minutes later, an assistant brought in a large manila envelope. Janet Scott counted out fifty thousand pounds in the red Bank of Scotland one hundred pound notes, which Varley checked, before signing a receipt for the cash.

"Thank you, Miss Scott," he said, shook hands and left. He got a taxi back to the Caledonian Hotel and took the money to his room.

Ford rang him shortly afterwards. "Mark, I've been thinking. Can you come to my room?"

Varley found Ford pacing up and down. "Mark, I'm excited at what we might be able to do once you get that casket," he began. "It could be a sign that I am being called, even more clearly, to do God's will." His eyes flashed upwards as he turned to Mark and stopped pacing. "You know, Mark, it really is imperative that you acquire this relic; and if the hair said to be inside is really that of our

Lord …" He sighed deeply, "dear me, I hesitate to think of what we are meant to do. I shall pray for guidance."

Varley listened silently. He was used to Ford's outbursts. "I hope to get the casket within the next twenty-four hours," he said. "I've been to the bank, and got cash to pay my informant."

"Good, good," Ford nodded his agreement. "See me as soon as you have it."

En route to Melrose, Varley stopped at a small hardware store and purchased two spades, a sledgehammer, a pickaxe, a hammer, and two strong chisels, as well as two sets of gardening gloves. The latter was a last-minute thought as much for protection of his carefully manicured hands as for avoiding fingerprints, although, with second thoughts, he believed that might prove to be important.

He reached Melrose Abbey just after four o'clock. Conti was standing outside Burts Hotel. "Hi! Bruno. I have the tools in the car."

"Great, I don't know what we will need, but since you mentioned that something was buried, I thought we should be prepared."

They went into the hotel and ordered a beer, before sitting in a quiet corner of the bar. Varley suggested that Conti should go to Melrose Abbey and conceal himself, so that he would be available to help, should McPhee prove to be difficult about identifying the site where the casket was buried. Having said that, Varley acknowledged that he didn't know for sure where the casket was. If it wasn't at the Abbey, he would return and collect Conti, and then the two of them would go to the site that McPhee showed him.

"Okay, Mark, but how do I get to the Abbey?"

"I will drive you there, then come back, to meet McPhee at six."

It was only a short drive to Melrose Abbey, where Conti got out of the car. The Abbey was quiet. It closed for tours at 6:30 p.m., but there was no one around. He lit a cigarette and paid the admission fee for a second day, before taking off into a distant part of the grounds. Later, he would move to the Abbey itself, and conceal himself in the old stairway until everyone left.

Back at Burts Hotel, Varley sat at the bar waiting for McPhee's arrival. He was sipping a gin and tonic as Andy arrived, flushed in anticipation of receiving fifty thousand pounds.

"Would you like a drink, Andy?" Varley enquired.

"Aye, a pint of McEwans would go down well."

Varley got the order from the bar, and sat down across the small table from Andy.

"Well, Andy," he began. "This is your big day."

"My big day?"

"Yes, the big pay-off."

Andy took a long drink of his beer. "So you have the money?"

"That is what we agreed, yes. Fifty thousand pounds."

Andy licked his lips in anticipation. "Where is it?"

Varley tapped a briefcase by his side.

"Well, let me see it."

"Not yet, Andy. It wouldn't be wise. Too many people might see you."

Andy nodded in agreement. He really didn't want anyone knowing about his sudden windfall. He would keep the money hidden, perhaps move away and buy a new house and car. Or else gradually start to increase his standard of living, so that no one would suspect him. He looked at Varley. "Well, what do you suggest?"

"Let's see … Tell you what Andy. Take me to the site where I can get the casket and I'll give you the money."

Andy licked his lips. "Right, that's what I agreed. I'll show you, and that's it!"

Varley sensed that Andy was not going to help him retrieve the casket. But that didn't matter. Once there at the site he would get the casket despite any objections from Andy, so he said, "Right, Andy. Why don't you take me to the site?"

Andy told Varley to follow his car. Varley took his time finishing his gin and tonic, and paid the bill, all the time watching Andy's car which idled across the road. He left the hotel and started his car, and followed Andy for the short distance to Melrose Abbey. They parked their cars. It was now well after 7:00 p.m. and the grounds were deserted. Andy motioned Varley to follow him, unlocked the door leading through to the Abbey, and led him across the grass to the side of the ruined church before stopping at the plinth beneath which Bruce's heart had been interred.

"Before we go any further, Mr. Varley, let me see the money."

Varley opened the briefcase. Andy gasped as he saw the Bank of Scotland notes. He reached in a hand and ruffled the corners of the banknotes, smiling as he heard the sound of money vibrate softly in the night air. "I will need to count it, of course," he said. "I need to make sure there's fifty thousand pounds in the bag."

"Don't you trust me, Andy?"

"Almost; but not quite."

"Well, wait a minute Andy, you still haven't shown me precisely where I can get the casket."

"Get? My agreement was to show you the site." He pointed at the plinth and laughed. "There it is. It's buried under the plinth. That's the deal! Now let me have the money!"

Varley pulled back the briefcase as Andy tried to grasp it from him.

"Hold on," Varley said, "I need to get the casket."

"That's your problem Varley. I've kept my side of the deal. Give me the money!"

Varley pushed him away. "You'll get the money when I get the casket," he shouted. "I'm going to get a spade, so we can dig it up."

"You can't do that!" Andy screamed. "It would be sacrilege to disturb the Bruce's heart."

"Sacrilege?" Varley sneered, "You know nothing about sacrilege. It's only a relic. We won't take the heart, I assure you." Out of the corner of his eye Varley saw Bruno Conti approach behind Andy. He held a large stone in his hands, part of the Abbey's structure, which he had picked up from under one of the arches.

Andy grabbed Varley's jacket and shook him violently. "Give me the money Varley, it's mine!"

Varley pushed him away and he staggered backwards as Conti advanced. Conti lifted the stone and hit Andy's head. Andy's body crumpled as his skull was fractured by the impact. He fell and struck his head on the plinth.

Varley bent down. There was no pulse. Andy was dead.

Conti said, "I thought you needed help."

"Well yes, but you didn't have to kill him."

Conti shrugged. "An accident. I heard him scream about fifty thousand pounds, and I figured that if you gave him that, he would let everyone know that it was you who disturbed the site. So I guess it had to happen."

Varley was stunned. Two deaths already in pursuit of the casket and the hair of Jesus. Both had been accidents. He was sure that Sir Jock's death certainly was; and as he thought about Andy, he realised that the little Scot might have blackmailed him for more money once the casket had been unearthed. He sighed deeply. Although he knew he had a hair trigger temper, he didn't think he was normally violent. But Jock and Andy had tested his patience. Whatever, it was done. Now it was time to get the casket. First though, they needed to find a place to dispose of Andy's body.

Conti suddenly had an idea—something he'd noticed on his tour. The Abbey grounds were shielded with stone walls about eight feet high. Beyond that stood the Commendator's house, which had been the home of the Abbot and was now a museum. A mill lade, carrying water from the River Tweed a quarter of a mile away, ran past the Commendator's house. It emptied into a main drain, or sewer, which had been used to flush the latrines at the east of the property. Conti took control.

"Grab his feet," he said. Together they picked up Andy's lifeless body and carried it over to the latrine pit, about eight feet deep, and with stone walls. They lifted Andy's body over the guard rails, a metal fence about three feet high, and with a heave they tossed it down into the green and stagnant waters at the bottom. There was a splash as Andy's body hit the water. Conti said: "Great place for that little shit!" He laughed as another thought crossed his mind. "Only yesterday, this guy told a story about a legend. Some wizard died here hundreds of years ago. He was hit by a falling stone."

"How ironic!" Varley said. "Now, let's get the tools we need. They're in the trunk of my car." While Conti fetched the tools, Varley examined the plinth. It was made of stone, set in concrete. It was about one foot in diameter, and was surrounded by a border of small gravel stones. On its surface there was a carved heart, entwined in Scotland's national flag, the x-shape of St. Andrew's Cross. He wondered how best to open the plinth. Conti arrived with the spades, the sledgehammer, the pick axe, and the hammer and chisels. He threw them down beside Varley. "Where do we start?" he asked.

"Don't know. I'm still thinking about it." Varley said, picking up the gardening gloves he had bought earlier. He offered a pair to Conti.

Conti shook his head. "I ain't planning to plant anything here." He picked up a spade. "Why don't we see if we can dig down and pull the thing up?" he asked.

"Be my guest," Varley motioned to him.

Conti dug into the gravel, making a shallow channel around the plinth. It seemed to go deeper. He dug down for another foot and hit concrete. He stopped and wiped his forehead. "Looks like it's been concreted into a pad below the surface," he said.

Varley thought about this development and said, "OK. Stop that. Let's see if we can get in through the top." He picked up a chisel and began to bang it into it the plinth with a hammer. Several flakes of stone fell off, but the plinth didn't budge. He went round the rim, tapping away, trying to break any seal that might be there. It still didn't move.

"Let's try this," Conti said, picking up the pickaxe. He raised it above his head, and brought the point down with a muscular whack on the top surface of the plinth. It cracked. He hit it again and the plinth began to splinter. He lifted the pickaxe for a third strike, but Varley shouted "Stop!" Conti dropped the pickaxe.

"You might damage the casket. Let me try this." Varley picked up a chisel, inserted it in the cracks on top of the plinth and began to tap it gently, first on one side, then on another. After a minute he saw the plinth separate. He put down the tools and pulled the plinth apart. Below was a layer of concrete. Conti picked up the sledgehammer and with a few blows caused it to crack. He used the point of the pickaxe to lever the concrete apart. In a moment Varley glimpsed a lead casket. That would be Bruce's heart. Nestled beside it lay a silver and enamel casket. He gently lifted it out and blew at the dirt which had fallen on it from the fractured plinth and concrete. He turned it in his hand and saw the words in Latin: *Capillus Jesu*. This was it! The hair of Jesus Christ—just as foretold in King Alfonso's letter! Varley felt ethereal: he held history in his hands!

Conti looked at him strangely. "That's it? That's what you were going to pay fifty thousand pounds for?"

Varley nodded, deep in thought. "Yes, Bruno. That's it. It's what we wanted." He looked around. "Now we ought to vamoose. We don't want to be found here."

Darkness had fallen as they reached the car. Conti put the tools in the trunk, and they drove off through the quiet streets of Melrose. Varley stopped the car at a bridge some miles beyond the town and Conti went to the trunk, removed the tools, and threw them into the river below.

Reaching Edinburgh, Varley took Conti back to the Caledonian Hotel, where he checked out. Varley drove him to Edinburgh Airport to catch the last shuttle flight to London, where Bruno would spend the night before catching a morning flight to New York. Varley did not want Conti staying around, and Bruno didn't mind. On the flight to New York he smiled and patted the briefcase by his side: it contained fifty thousand pounds, or nearly ninety thousand dollars. Not bad for a couple of days' work, he thought!

Back at the hotel, Varley went to Ford's room. It was now almost 11:00 p.m. and Ford was ready for bed. He had exhausted himself with an energetic and apocalyptic performance at the Crusade earlier in the Usher Hall. He was in his dressing gown and blue pyjamas; but he was anxious to learn about whether Varley had been successful. He knew right away that it had gone well. "Mark, from your demeanour I assume you have good news for me so late at night."

Varley nodded. "Yes, indeed, Jackson. I think the Lord is with us." He reached into his briefcase and held out the casket.

Ford fell to his knees, as he took the casket into his hands. "The hair of Jesus. The hair of Jesus," he repeated. "We are blessed, Mark. Truly blessed." He pointed to Mark to kneel, bowed his head and said: "Dear Lord, we are indeed blessed to receive this living proof of your being, your life and your resurrection. Guide us in knowing how we should use this to spread your word. In Jesus name, Amen."

"Amen," Varley repeated.

"Have you opened the box?" Ford demanded.

"No," Varley shook his head. "I just wanted to deliver it to you."

"I wonder if we should?" Ford pondered. He closed his eyes in silent prayer. His eyes opened and rolled upwards. "Not yet, I think, Mark. We will wait until we return to Montgomery. There, I will know how to reveal it to the world."

Chapter 13

Jock's funeral took place three days later at St Giles Cathedral, the famed church on Edinburgh's High Street, which had been so important in the Reformation led by John Knox in Scotland. The cathedral was packed, for Jock was well-known and had many friends. It was a moving ceremony in which Jock's service to his country was eulogized by those who had known of the many contributions he had made to his native land. Afterwards there was a private burial service. Alan was glad to have Kate by his side, and others such as Jamie and Mrs. Doig, who had worked faithfully for Jock for many years. Alan had reserved separate rooms at the Caledonian Hotel for Kate and himself. Jamie drove Mrs. Doig back to Bruce House, where Alan told them to expect to see him within a few days.

He and Kate sat in a corner booth of the bar and Alan ordered drinks. Kate looked at him with concern.

"It's been a hard day for you, Alan."

"Well yes," he sighed, "I think you know by now that I was very fond of Jock." He blinked rapidly as his eyes misted. "He was one of a kind; one of the old school, I guess."

"He was, Alan, a real gentleman." Kate touched his hand and smiled. "Mind you, I think there was a bit of a rascal in the old boy. He must have been a real catch when he was young."

"Thanks Kate." Alan sipped his whisky and smiled. "And now, it's up to me to continue the Bruce name and traditions. That's going to be a challenge." Kate laughed to brighten his mood.

"Oh, come on, Alan, or do I need to call you Sir Alan now?"

It worked. Alan remembered an old line from his early dating years. He smiled and his mouth showed a wry sense of humour."Call me what you like. Just call me!"

"That's a line I've heard before," Kate laughed. "Is it built into male DNA?"

"No idea. But it usually works—at least for me."

"Well that's good to know. I didn't think you were at all the depressive sort. My prescription, for what it's worth, is that you should get on with your life, and make sure that you match Jock's achievements."

"I guess you're right, Kate," Alan sighed, "I've been getting a bit depressed lately." He held her hand. "But being with you helps me; it really does." He smiled. "Why don't we have a nice dinner together? I feel like unwinding tonight."

"Suits me," Kate said, smiling back at him.

"Hold on, I'll ask the concierge to make a reservation."

Alan left to speak to the concierge. When he gave his name, the concierge said, "Mr. Bruce, there is an urgent message for you here." He passed the written message to Alan. It was from Inspector Dawson of the Lothians and Borders Police, who asked him to call as soon as possible. Alan asked the clerk behind the front desk for a phone, and was directed to one in the lobby. He dialled the number he had been given and asked for Inspector Dawson.

"This is Dawson," said the voice. "Who is this?"

"Inspector Dawson, I'm Alan Bruce of the Bruce family, Sir Jock Bruce's grandson."

"Mr. Bruce, thank you for calling. I was in touch with Historic Scotland's office in Edinburgh about a crime committed last night at Melrose Abbey. They asked me to advise you, as you are the heir to Sir Jock Bruce. I called Bruce House, and a Mrs. Doig told me I could contact you at the Caledonian Hotel."

"Yes?" Alan asked. He had never been to Melrose Abbey, and did not immediately make the connection with Bruce's heart.

"Well sir, I'm afraid that someone has smashed the plinth that protected Bruce's heart."

"Has the heart been removed?" Alan asked.

"No, that's the strange part. It's still there in the lead casket that Historic Scotland said we would find there. The plinth itself is smashed. It's in several pieces now, but I guess that can be replaced." Dawson paused. "I was wondering, sir, if you have any idea why this could have happened?"

"I've not a clue, Inspector. I have been busy over the last few days, with the funeral for my grandfather."

"Aye, I heard about that," Dawson said. "Sir Jock was a credit to Scotland."

"Do you have any idea why this happened, Inspector?" Alan asked.

"Not yet, sir. However, there is one other matter. We also found a dead body. It was the body of one of the guides—a chap by the name of Andy McPhee. Do you know him, Mr. Bruce?"

"No, never heard of him. In fact, I've never even been to Melrose." Alan paused. "Tell me Inspector, how did he die?"

"We're not sure. He was found at the bottom of the latrine pit, so he may have slipped. No one understands why he would be there at night after the grounds were closed to tourists. He was found some distance away from the plinth, so that might just be a coincidence. We'll find out from a post-mortem." Dawson cleared his throat. "If you should come across any information, Mr. Bruce, you will phone me?"

"Of course, Inspector. I'm as anxious as you to find the people behind this."

Alan hung up the phone. Varley! It had to have been him; Jock had told Alan that Varley knew that the casket had been buried, but not where. So it would seem that he must have found out and retrieved the casket. The Inspector had said that the lead casket was lying on its own, so whoever had cracked open the plinth had been looking for the silver casket, and apart from Jock, Kate and himself, only Varley seemed to be aware of its existence.

Alan returned to the bar where Kate sat nursing her drink. She looked at him questioningly. "My goodness, Alan, that took a long time to make a dinner reservation."

"Reservation?" Alan groaned. "I forgot. Something else has happened, Kate." He told her about the phone call from Inspector Dawson.

"So, Varley has the casket and the hair." Kate said. "Do you think he will go so far as to try cloning?"

"I wouldn't put anything past him, Kate. It must have been him." Alan rose. "I'll see the concierge about a dinner reservation. I won't forget this time," he said as Kate smiled back at him. He crossed the lobby and spoke again to the concierge, who reserved a table for them for dinner at The Witchery near Edinburgh Castle. Alan started to walk back to the bar, but paused as he saw Mark Varley step out from the elevator. He moved towards Varley and said, "Mr. Varley. Can I have a word with you?"

Varley turned and blinked. Alan Bruce was the last person he wanted to see. "What is it Mr. Bruce? I'm in a hurry."

"Oh. I just wanted to ask if you had been to Melrose Abbey."

Varley's lips tensed involuntarily. How on earth had word got to Bruce so quickly he thought? Aloud, he said, "Melrose Abbey? Where's that?"

"I think you know, Varley. I reckon you've been there and broken into the plinth where Robert the Bruce's heart was interred."

"You're raising your voice, Bruce." Varley snapped. "I've no idea what you're talking about."

"I think you do, Varley. You threatened my grandfather: in fact, I wouldn't be surprised if somehow, you caused his heart attack."

"That's slander."

"Not if it's true."

"Well, do you want to repeat it even louder, so everyone can hear? That would help my case," Varley snapped at him as hotel staff looked on anxiously.

Alan calmed down. As a lawyer he knew he had no proof, only a strong suspicion. "I think you're lying, Varley," he said quietly, "and if I find you had anything to do with the break-in at Melrose Abbey I'll find you."

"And what?" Varley interrupted. "Find me, and join our Crusade?"

"No. That's the last thing on my mind, but I'll be watching you, and if you have what I suspect you have, I will make life tough for you wherever you are." Alan looked at him with fists clenched.

Varley decided it was time to end the confrontation. "Excuse me, Bruce," he said and deliberately bumped him as he passed.

Alan reacted quickly and turned to punch him, but felt a restraining hand. It was Kate.

"Don't Alan." She looked at him with concern. "It's not worth a brawl. I heard what was said, so calm down. You don't need to be so aggressive. Let's sit in the bar for a while." She took his hand and led him away. At the bar she turned to face him. "So," she said, "after all that, did you remember to make a dinner reservation?"

Dinner at The Witchery proved to be a pleasant relief. The restaurant itself was located in a sixteenth century building on the High Street, not far from Edinburgh Castle. The receptionist checked their reservation, and then led them into a long narrow room with rich wine-coloured banquettes lining the walls providing seating for those who wanted to face into the room. They were led to a corner table covered in a white linen tablecloth with white napkins bound with red ribbons. Three candles flickered on the table, augmenting the soft light provided by wall sconces.

Kate gasped as she saw a large papier-mâché bust of the devil in a niche in the wall, in the centre of the room. She looked at the polished wooden ceiling, which was decorated with sprites and what appeared to be astrological signs. "Quite spectacular," she murmured.

"As are you," Alan said with appreciation. Kate was stunning in a dark blue dress, close-fitting at the waist and with a hint of cleavage.

"Thank you," Kate said, smiling.

A tall young waiter appeared. His white shirt, black waistcoat and red bow tie matched the décor. He gave them the menu and then left. When he returned, Alan ordered The Witchery fish soup, while Kate had a starter of char-grilled gateaux of Mediterranean vegetables. They agreed to share a main course, a platter of Scottish seafood with a half lobster. Alan selected a white burgundy to help wash it down.

With the opulent red seating and the soft flickering candle light, not to mention the succulent food, Alan began to relax after the day's stress, and he and Kate laughed together, as they each told stories about their past.

They left The Witchery hand in hand. It was a fine warm evening, so they decided to take a leisurely walk down the hill to Princes Street then back to the Caledonian hotel, where they took the elevator to the fourth floor. Kate stopped outside her room, leaned back and gazed up at Alan.

"Thank you Alan; it's been a marvellous evening. I can't remember when I last enjoyed a dinner more." Alan bent down and kissed her. She responded with passion, and they were locked in the embrace for about thirty seconds before Kate drew back.

"Wow!' she said, "that certainly is one way to end the evening."

"I can think of another," Alan said with a knowing smile.

"No idea what you're talking about," said Kate, opening the door to her room. She turned to him. "Perhaps you'd better come in and let me know what's on your mind."

After breakfast the next morning, they took the Jaguar back to Bruce House. They were both happy. It had been a passionate evening, and Alan had not left Kate's room until early morning when he went to his room to shower and shave.

They reached Bruce House around lunchtime. Mrs. Doig welcomed them with a plate of her home-made Scotch broth and a salad. Afterwards, Alan took Kate by the hand.

"Let's take a walk," he said. They walked over the stone bridge to the west of Bruce House, stopping for a moment to gaze at the waterfall far below. They followed the track leading on to the moors above Bruce House. Nothing was said for a few minutes as they each enjoyed the views over the River Clyde, leading out to the Firth of Clyde some miles away. Alan stopped as he reached a gate in the fence. He leaned against it and turned to Kate.

"This has been a hectic few days Kate, and very eventful for me. I don't know how you feel about it. I'm afraid you've inadvertently got caught up in the Bruce family's affairs, probably more than you would have wanted to." Kate reached out and held his hand.

"I can't pretend that there haven't been some surprises, Alan. Far more than I anticipated when I agreed to help Jock establish the age of the hair he gave me. What's happened since then—Jock's death, the vandalism at Melrose Abbey, and the mystery surrounding Varley, is way beyond anything I could possibly have imagined."

"I could echo that. It's been strange, almost as if we are part of a bigger picture."

"Oh don't get carried away, Alan; events happen! Sometimes what we think of as coincidences don't deserve a second thought. They don't have any valid statistical relationship with each other."

"Absolutely: I agree. But a happy coincidence, Kate has been my getting to know you better."

"In the biblical sense, you mean?" Kate laughed.

"No," he blushed slightly, and a wry smile flickered across his face. "Well, yes, that too. But I really don't want it to end here."

"Well, I do need to return to Boston tomorrow. I only took a week's vacation and I have classes to teach next week."

"I know, and I really need to get back to Toronto soon, or I'll lose all my clients. But I really want to keep in touch with you, Kate. Boston's only an hour and a half's flight from Toronto, so I was wondering if you'd like to visit Toronto, say next weekend, so we can continue to get to know each other better?"

Kate looked at him teasingly. "Or you could come to Boston. Maybe on alternate weekends?"

Alan laughed and reached for her. She was everything he desired. He kissed her passionately, knowing that she was the one good thing that had arisen from his visit to Scotland.

The next day he drove Kate to Glasgow airport. They embraced for a minute then her flight was called and she disappeared with a wave and a blown kiss, having agreed to visit Alan in Toronto in a week's time.

Alan drove back to Bruce House and saw Jamie and Mrs. Doig, who were naturally concerned about their future employment. Alan assured them that they would continue to work for him, maintaining Bruce House and its grounds. He told them that he expected to return to Scotland in a few weeks' time.

Alan sat behind Jock's desk: all this was now his, although he would have to wait some time before he could know the extent of the net wealth he had inherited. As Cameron Learmonth had mentioned, even with the death duty taxes, Alan would be wealthy. Perhaps he might spend more time in future at Bruce House and reduce his legal practice in Toronto. Subconsciously, his hand moved to the left desk drawer in which Jock had kept the English translation of the Alfonso letter. He pulled the drawer open; it was still empty. The sight of it reminded him of Varley. He took Inspector Dawson's phone number from his pocket and on an impulse he dialled. He was directed to Dawson's extension by a receptionist.

"Inspector Dawson," he said, "this is Alan Bruce. I was wondering if you had made any progress in identifying who destroyed the plinth at the Abbey."

"Mr. Bruce: interesting you should call. No, we have not made much progress there, I'm afraid. We've been rather busy trying to find out what happened to poor Andy McPhee."

"The guide?"

"Yes. Apparently he was seen having dinner several nights ago with an American gentleman in Burts hotel. Then, the following evening, they had a drink in the bar. That was the night he died."

"Do you have a description of the American?" Alan enquired.

"He was about six feet tall with black hair and was well-dressed."

Varley, Alan thought: it was probably him. Aloud he said, "Funnily enough, I met someone like that in Edinburgh yesterday. His name is Mark Varley and he is with Jackson Ford's Crusade"

"Varley?" Dawson said. "Well, perhaps I'll check that out, although it could be a coincidence. I'm sure there are hundreds of Americans in Scotland right now who might match that description."

"Only trying to help, Inspector," Alan said. "My main concern is to find out who damaged the plinth."

"Rest assured, Mr. Bruce, we will contact you whenever we have any information. And thank you for the name of Mr. Varley; we will try to speak to him."

The next morning, Jamie drove Alan to the airport and he got a British Airways shuttle to London, where he transferred to an Air Canada flight to Toronto. Alan settled back in a comfortable business class seat and relaxed. Little did he realise that life was about to become so much more complicated for him.

CHAPTER 14

Two days after Jackson Ford, Mark Varley, and their team had returned to Montgomery, Alabama, they met in Ford's office in the expansive Church building complex, from which Ford delivered his weekly TV programme. Ford sat in a comfortable armchair; he was in a good mood and his eyes glowed with an inner fervour. He was obviously anxious to speak to Varley.

"Mark, sit down. How are you? Are you over the jet lag yet?"

Varley looked at the evangelist. He knew Ford's mercurial temperament; obviously Jackson was on a high.

"I'm fine, Jackson, a couple of days R & R have helped." He paused, and then added with a smile, "and knowing how successful the Edinburgh Crusade was certainly helps." He sat down opposite Ford, crossed his legs and continued: "The first accounts I've looked at show that we made a profit, sorry a surplus, of about $10 million." (He knew that Ford did not like to be reminded of the financial success of his Crusade, not when his thoughts were on the spiritual side). Varley gestured with a sweeping motion of his hand. "Mind you, the final figures could be slightly different, but all in all, a remarkable Crusade." He smiled and thought: not bad at all. My share is $1 million.

"I'm sure that's good news, Mark," Ford replied, standing. "We need money to continue the Lord's work." He started to pace back and forth, "but most of all, we have the casket with our Lord's hair. That is a blessing we have been given from the Crusade in Scotland." He stopped and turned to Varley. "I have seen it, Mark. I have seen Jesus' hair," he said, with a brief sob of emotion.

Varley looked at him. "You mean you opened the casket?"

"Yes, yes, of course. I prayed constantly, and knew it was time to do so. It's remarkable Mark, really, really remarkable. His hair, several locks of it." Ford threw his hands in the air. "Who could believe it? After two thousand years we have visible proof of our Lord."

"What does it look like?" Varley said, also getting to his feet.

"Look like? It's hair, Mark; a dark colour, black or dark brown, but it is his, of that I am sure."

"I hope it's in a safe place."

"Yes, of course it is." Ford nodded his head. "I've sealed the casket in my safety deposit box at the bank. It will stay there until we decide how to bring forth to the world, this good—nay this great and happy news." Ford was now getting carried away with his own eloquence, Varley thought.

"So when might that be?" he asked.

"When?" Ford looked thoughtful. He sat down and motioned Varley to follow. "That's what we need to talk about Mark. We need to make maximum use of the casket and the hair, so that we may fulfil the Lord's expectation of us. I thought we should discuss that."

Varley had already considered a plan. It would have two phases. The first would involve Jackson Ford revealing the existence of the casket on his weekly television programme. One week later, he would show the casket itself. And then? Well, that would be a decision Ford would need to make. But if he did agree to proceed with cloning, the sky would be the limit for the interest that might be created worldwide. And, if the cloning attempt was successful, Varley did not even try to assess what might happen. It would be a new world; perhaps in every sense.

Varley knew that it was time to advise Ford of the plan. "Here's an outline of what I have in mind, Jackson. We'll get great media coverage if we can build up some suspense before you show the casket on TV."

"Suspense?"

"Yes. What I suggest is that you use one of your sermons, perhaps in a week's time, to review the success of the Edinburgh Crusade. You know—so many thousand people who came forward to commit themselves to Christ—then towards the end, you describe how you received word about the casket." Varley frowned. "I'm not sure we want to say that we paid money for it. That might raise questions in people's minds." And, Varley thought to himself, it might also raise questions in the minds of the police, about the shattered plinth and the dead body at Melrose Abbey. He continued. "So, we will need to build a good story, one that will be believable."

"Believable?" Ford snorted. "What can be more believable than the casket with Jesus' hair?"

"I know Jackson. You and I believe that, but there will be many sceptics, so we need to have a bullet-proof story."

"Well, we have the Alfonso letter. Surely that provides a trail that demonstrates its provenance?"

"Good point, Jackson, I had overlooked the letter, although since it's an English translation people may question its authenticity. We'll need to have a story to explain that."

"Why can't we get the original Alfonso letter?" Ford asked plaintively.

"I don't know how to do that. The important thing is that we have the casket and the hair. We'll say that the original is lost, or that it will be revealed later: whatever it takes. The main story is the casket and the hair. That's what will get the public's attention."

"Right; and then what? Do we try to clone Jesus?" Ford asked.

"Jackson, that's your call. Personally I think we should. Think about the publicity; and if the cloning succeeded—well, then we would be in a new ballpark; a new world."

"A Brave New World," Ford chuckled.

"What?"

"It's the title of a book by Aldous Huxley. It's very old, from the 1930s, I think. He described a world in which people were bred to have different sets of genes. The cloning was done through what he called the Bokanovsky Process."

"You remember that?"

"Well, not quite. I've been doing some research on cloning. It isn't very simple. In fact, the cloning of primates seems to divide the scientific community. Some think it is impossible; others surmise that eventually science will find a way." Ford shook his head. "It will be the Lord's decision, if science succeeds. For the moment, Mark, we have to decide about whether we should try to clone Jesus." He paused and bowed his head in silent reflection, then looked straight at Varley with a light in his eyes. "You know what? I think I'll call Dr Jim Cameron. You remember him, the guy we met in Edinburgh?"

"The Dolly-the-sheep man?"

"That's him. Yes, yes; that's what I'll do."

Varley stood. "So can I take it Jackson, that you agree with at least the first phase of the plan? That you will start to reveal the existence of the casket in your TV programme, perhaps as early as next week?"

"Yes, yes: I'll begin to prepare my sermon; and Mark, perhaps you can make arrangements to leak some advance news that I will have an astounding revelation? That will certainly spark interest and begin to attract more viewers."

Mark Varley agreed to do so. As he left, Ford was dialling long distance to Edinburgh. Jim Cameron's phone rang.

"Dr. Cameron? This is Jackson Ford," he said in his deep baritone voice. "I hope I'm not disturbing you."

Disturbing? Cameron thought. What on earth did the American evangelist want?

"No, not at all," he replied.

"Well, then, I wanted to thank you for meeting me while I was in Edinburgh. Now that I am home in Montgomery, Alabama, I have had time to reflect on our discussion about cloning and I was wondering if you might give me some advice."

"Yes, of course: if I can."

"Well then, the question of cloning humans has come up in some of the issues I am asked to cover in my religious work. I know about the religious, moral, and indeed philosophical issues, but I am completely naïve about the medical and scientific issues, so that is where I need some help."

"I see," Cameron replied, "what exactly do you need to know?"

"Well, has anyone actually cloned a human being?"

Cameron chuckled. "Not to my knowledge. Mind you, there have been several claims to have done so."

"Really? Who made these claims?"

"Well, you may remember that a few years ago a sect called the Raelians claimed to have cloned the first human being. They said it was a baby girl they called Eve." He laughed, "Somewhat ironic, Eve. In any event, they said she had been born to a thirty-one-year-old woman in the United States, but there's never been any proof."

"The Raelians?" Ford asked. "Yes, I seem to have heard of them, but not recently. Is there anyone else, anyone with more credibility?"

"Well yes, in a manner of speaking. There is Dr. Severino Antinori, an Italian doctor."

"And has he been successful?"

"Well, he has said he had collaborated in the birth of a least three babies from cloned embryos. But, not unexpectedly, he didn't give details for legal and other reasons. You see, cloning of humans is banned in Europe, as indeed it is in the States. Excuse me for a moment Mr. Ford, I need to get some reference material."

There was a pause before Cameron continued. "Here it is. I knew I had kept the press cutting. It's from the Times of India. From July 30, 2003. It's an interview with Dr Antinori. Here's what it says: 'We have to learn to face reality. Assistive Reproductive Technology is progressing by leaps and bounds. We have to learn to move with the times, and make full use of our capabilities. Failures and abnormalities experienced in animal cloning will not happen in human cloning, because the techniques like ICSI (intracytoplasmic sperm injection) and IVF (*in vitro* fertilisation) are more suitable for humans. Also rigorous screening will be part of the entire exercise.' That's the end of the quote I have from the article." Cameron concluded.

Back in Montgomery, Ford nodded his head. "Jim, where could I find this Dr Antinori?"

"Let me see." There was a pause before Cameron continued. "He seems to be director of the International Associated Research Institute for Human Reproductive Infertility."

"Dear me. That's an impressive sounding organization: where might it be located?"

"I believe it's in Rome."

"Thank you Jim, that is very helpful. I do hope we can remain in contact. Meantime, God bless you." Ford now had the information he needed. He put down the phone and knelt in prayer for several minutes. He rose with a broad smile on his face. The decision was made. He would attempt to clone Jesus.

He rang Mark Varley's office, only to find that he was elsewhere in the building. He left his office and walked down the carpeted corridor, with prints of Old Masters on the walls. He found Varley in a conference room with four of the backroom staff, who usually handled publicity for his TV programme. The room was furnished with a large cherry wood conference table around which were deep green leather chairs.

"Jackson, this is a surprise.' Varley rose to greet him. "We're just beginning to prepare our approach to get the maximum publicity for your next programme."

"Well, go ahead," Ford replied, "I'll just listen in if you don't mind."

Varley nodded. "I've been telling the team that you will be making a revelation in your next sermon. And that will be followed in the next few weeks with your exposure of an ancient religious relic, one that will set the world talking."

"That's right," Ford nodded his agreement.

"So guys," Varley motioned to the two men and two women seated at the conference table, "we need to get maximum publicity. We need a large audience for next week's service, so that we can generate more commitments from people."

"Yes, indeed," Ford agreed. "The Lord calls us to do his work, and what I will say will reflect the message I have been called to deliver."

Varley assigned tasks to the group. Grace Christopherson, a young brunette, would approach the religious media. Tamara Volpine, an intern from the University of Alabama, would deal with the local media. It was left to Tom Prentice and Jerry Michaels to alert the national media. The story line was that everyone should watch the Jackson Ford TV service on the following Sunday, for news of a revelation of historic and religious importance.

The team set to work to flesh out the story, and news releases were to be prepared for approval by Ford and Varley, who left and went to Ford's office. There, Ford leaned on the edge of his desk. "Mark, I have been given a message, after prayer. It is to proceed with an attempt to clone Jesus." He told Varley of his telephone conversation with Dr Jim Cameron. "And so, Mark, I would like you to go to Rome and meet with Dr Antinori. Explore what can be done, then let me know." His voice rose. "We must follow the Lord's bidding. It is out of our hands."

"OK, Jackson: do you have an address or phone number?"

Ford shook his head. "No, but I know that he's in Rome at some Institute." He found a sheet of paper on his desk. "Here it is: the International Associated Research Institute for Human Reproductive Fertility."

"I guess I can get the phone number and address without too much difficulty. When do you want me to go to Rome, if I can make the arrangements?"

"As soon as possible, Mark. You've set the ball rolling with a team working on publicity. You can approve the news releases today, I expect. Then, if Antinori can see you, I think you should head to Rome right away. We need to know if cloning is possible, and how it will take place. I don't profess to fully understand the science. I'll leave it to you, Mark. Hire whoever you need and spend what is necessary. We have lots of money now. You mentioned the financial success of the Edinburgh Crusade; and we have more, much more: so money is not an issue. I want to know that cloning is possible and that we can do it. Then we will have a miracle, one everyone in the world will know about." His eyes opened wide. "The Second Coming of Christ."

It did not take long for Varley to find the phone number and address of Dr Antinori in Rome. He dialled long distance and was answered by a woman. "Do you speak English?" he asked.

"Why of course," came back the reply, in an Italian accent, "we are an international Institute you know."

"Good, I would like to speak to Dr Antinori."

"Is it about a fertility treatment, perhaps for your wife?"

"Not quite. I can explain if I speak to Dr Antinori."

"The doctor is away. Can someone else help?"

"Does he have an assistant?"

"Yes, Dr Sophia Vacca. I'll connect you."

There was a pause. Then Varley heard a woman's voice with an English accent, tinged with an Italian lilt. "This is Dr. Vacca."

"Dr Vacca, my name is Mark Varley. I'm calling from Montgomery, Alabama. I'm interested in learning about cloning."

"Do you have something in mind?" she asked.

"Well yes, but I will really need to speak to you or Dr Antinori in person."

"Antinori is away, and I am leaving the Institute to set up my own practice. You know of course that cloning is banned in Europe?"

"I've heard that; yes."

"So, I cannot continue my research here. I have other plans. Cloning is necessary and I can succeed."

"Really? That's very interesting," Varley said. "I would like to meet you, as soon as possible."

There was a pause before Dr Vacca said, "I'll be at a conference in London next week. I could meet you there." Varley heard the rustle of paper as Dr Vacca searched for her itinerary. "Yes, I will be staying at the Ritz Hotel, 150 Piccadilly. Do you know it?"

"No, but I'll make a reservation. What day is best for you?"

"Let's say Thursday. I have a break from conference on Thursday afternoon."

"Good, I'll make my travel arrangements. I look forward to meeting you, Dr. Vacca."

"Likewise, Mr. Varley. I'm sure you will not be flying to London unless you have a real need to find out more about cloning." Sophia Vacca smiled as she put the phone down. She had incurred substantial start-up costs for her new practice, and needed to recruit patients to help pay her bills.

Varley hung up the phone and asked his secretary to make arrangements for him to be in London by the following Wednesday, and to reserve a room for him for two nights at the Ritz Hotel. He wanted to arrive early to get over the six-hour time difference or jet lag, for his meeting on Thursday with Dr. Vacca.

CHAPTER 15

Varley walked down the corridor and entered Jackson Ford's room. Ford was on his knees, deep in silent prayer, but he sensed Varley's presence and said "Amen," before rising to his feet.

"Well I've done it, Jackson," Varley said, "I've been in touch with Antinori's office. He's away, but I've arranged to meet his colleague Dr Sophia Vacca in London next week." He told Ford of his conversation with the Italian doctor. Ford nodded in agreement.

"Good that's excellent work. Do what you can to make it happen. He looked at his watch. "My goodness," he said. "I hadn't realised it was so late. We have the reception at the Governor's mansion this evening at seven. Black tie."

The governor, Mike Malloy, was a friend of Jackson Ford. He was coming up to re-election and Varley knew that Malloy would be counting on a healthy political donation to his campaign from Ford. "I hadn't forgotten. I'll see you there later," he said.

At seven o'clock, Jackson Ford's Rolls-Royce drew up beside the Governor's Mansion on South Perry Street. The mansion was a charming white painted building with four Corinthian columns at the front entrance. A valet took the keys from Ford, who was greeted effusively by Governor Mike Malloy as he entered.

"Jackson, how are you?" the Governor boomed. Malloy was well over six feet in height with fair hair arranged strategically to cover his receding hairline. Like Ford, he was dressed smartly in dinner jacket and black tie. They shook hands, and Malloy took Ford by the arm, and led him through the crowd, introducing him where necessary, although Ford already knew most of those present. The

Montgomery social elite was quite exclusive, and Ford's fame assured him of attention.

Varley watched from a corner of the room, sipping from a mint julep. As the crowd mingled, Malloy ascended the central stairway and asked the crowd for a few minutes' silence.

"Thank you all for being here this evening, to honour the Reverend Jackson Ford. On behalf of all of us, Jackson, I just wanted to say how much we Alabamans appreciate what you have done, and are doing, to further the Lord's work.

"Amen." cried many voices. Malloy continued.

"In particular, we wanted to say 'thank you' for the success of your Edinburgh Crusade. It attracted a great deal of attention throughout the world, and, dare I say it, brought the great State of Alabama's name to the attention of many who knew nothing of our achievements and expertise. So, Jackson, after consultation with my political colleagues, we have decided to endow a Chair in New Testament Studies at the University of Alabama: 'The Jackson Ford Chair.'" Loud applause broke out, as Ford and Malloy shook hands. Malloy concluded: "And now, ladies and gentlemen, you will find dinner being served on the lawn at the rear of the Mansion."

While staff directed the guests to the large white tents set up outside in the warm night air, Malloy took Ford by the arm. "Old friend," he said, "perhaps we can have a quiet word before we join the others." He led Ford into the Governor's Board room, with ivory-coloured walls above matching wainscoting. A large dark wooden table was surrounded by elaborately-carved wooden chairs. Malloy sat in his chair, at the head of the table and signalled to Ford to sit to his left.

"Jackson," he said. "I really do appreciate what you've done. It is a great achievement and makes all of us in Alabama proud. The designation and endowment of $2 million for the Chair in your name, is a slight token of our regard for you."

"Well, thank you Mike. I am but a humble servant of our Lord."

"Quite so, I wish we could all be as diligent. However," he gestured with his right hand, "it is left to some of us to serve people in other ways."

"You mean politically?"

"Of course, Jackson." Malloy smiled. "Religion is your calling. Mine is to serve the people here on earth, helping to make their lives better." He shrugged his shoulders. "Sometimes we succeed. At other times, who is to know? However, like you, I need funds to maintain my ability to do so. Campaigns cost money, Jackson. Lots of money, and I am in need right now, with a major re-election campaign starting."

Ford smiled. Varley had warned him that this might happen tonight, as a '*quid pro quo*.' "Well, Mike, you can count on me for a generous donation." He paused. "Indeed, if my next few sermons attract the attention I think they will, it could well be a very generous donation."

Malloy's political antennae were alerted. What did Ford mean?

"Sounds interesting, Jackson. Care to tell me more?"

Ford told him that over the next few weeks, he would be alerting the world to the find he had made, an ancient relic related to Jesus. This was more than he had authorized in the news releases about his Sunday sermon, which were being issued that very evening to the media, but he trusted Malloy to keep his confidence. "Of course, Mike, I trust you to keep this to yourself. If my expectations are realised, we will bring even more attention to Alabama and hopefully more money from tourism."

Malloy nodded his agreement. "Your story is safe with me, Jackson. But I hope you will alert me to any developments. The state will always support you. And now, old friend, I think we should join our guests."

The news releases, stating that people should watch the Jackson Ford "Hour for Christ" on TV next Sunday, attracted little attention from most of the national media. They were used to groups that tried to get free publicity. However, reporter Cindy Ritcey of CNN wondered if it might be worth her while to attend. She did not have any other assignments and persuaded her director to send a cameraman with her, on condition that she secured a private interview with Jackson Ford, following the conclusion of his service.

The Jackson Ford team agreed. Publicity on CNN might help in their cause. Ford himself was not entirely happy at the agreement, and Varley felt it might be counterproductive. A skilled reporter could often probe, and unearth information that the interviewee wished to keep confidential. So, Ford and Varley decided on a slight change in their plans. If the issue of the provenance of the Jesus casket arose, Ford would mention that he had a letter from King Alfonso X1 of Spain, dated from the fourteenth century, that revealed the story. It would attract even bigger audiences for the following TV programmes, and, no doubt, more commitments and pledges.

The Church was packed on Sunday. People even stood at the back. The local media had bought into the news release, and had publicized the fact that the Reverend Ford would make a revelatory announcement.

Behind the pulpit, set up in the centre of a massive stage to accommodate the programme's TV crews, a one-hundred person choir, all robed in royal blue gowns, sat in eight rows of chairs. Ford, of course, was the central attraction.

Clad in pure white, he towered above the audience, his hair artfully arranged to make him look even more distinguished. He was in his element. It was show time!

The congregation sang the hymns with fervour and joined in the prayers. Then it was time for Ford's sermon.

Jackson Ford stood silently for a moment, looking right and left over the congregation, so that everyone present sensed that he or she, was, for a moment, the object of his attention. He raised his right hand.

"I have news from the Lord! Great news! I want to tell you a little, so that you, like me, can feel the uplifting presence of Jesus.

For the last few weeks, I and my team have been in Edinburgh, Scotland. Many of you may have seen the programmes broadcast live from that beautiful city. You will have seen many people, ordinary people, just like us, come forward and commit their lives to Jesus Christ. It was a miracle to behold."

Ford paused and again looked over the audience.

"All of you" he pointed at random, "are witness to the power of Christ, the power to change lives, the power to bring love, and care, and concern, into people's lives. That also happened in Edinburgh. Ordinary people, who had been living lives barren of hope, came forward. They made a commitment, and their lives changed. Through the power of Jesus, their lives changed, and we all must change as we await the return of Jesus. In Matthew 25 verse 13, we read. 'Watch, therefore for ye know neither the day nor the hour wherein the son of man cometh.' Consider this parable in Mark 13, verses 34 to 37. 'For the son of man is as a man taking a far journey, who left his house, and gave authority to his servants, and to every man his work, and commanded the porter to watch. Watch ye therefore: for ye know not when the master of the house cometh, at even, or at midnight, or at the cockcrowing, or in the morning: Lest coming suddenly he find you sleeping. And what I say unto you I say unto all, Watch.'"

Ford took a drink of water from the glass on the shelf below the pulpit.

"Watch," he repeated. "For Jesus will come. We do not know when—but we must be prepared. I was reminded of the need to be constantly vigilant, only last week in Scotland. 'We know not the day, nor the hour, when the son of man cometh.' Well, let me tell you my experience. Quite by surprise, I was told that there was a silver casket, which contains some hair from our dear Lord. Was I sceptical at first? Of course! However, we secured proof of its provenance. And the silver casket itself has been generously given to us by an anonymous donor. So, we have physical proof of the Lord's existence on this earth, and the promise of his return."

There were cries of "Hallelujah" from the congregation.

"Yes, Hallelujah!" Ford said. "And next week, I will bring the silver casket for all to see. And now, let us bow our heads in prayer."

Ford concluded the prayer. The choir sang the closing hymn, and Ford offered a benediction. The Jackson Ford Hour ended with Varley speaking to the TV audience about the need to make a commitment and to pledge funds to support the Crusades. "We have volunteers waiting to take your call. Please don't delay. Call now." A telephone number flashed on the screen as phones began ringing.

Ford strode through the central aisle, and shook hands with people, as the congregation left the Church. When all had left, Cindy Ritcey from CNN approached him with a microphone in her hand, and followed by a cameraman.

"Reverend Ford, I'm Cindy Ritcey of CNN. Your team promised me an exclusive interview."

Ford looked at the reporter. She was in her early thirties with short blonde hair and a wide smile. She wore a black suit with a white, open-necked blouse.

"Of course, Miss Ritcey. I'm happy to do so."

"Well, do you want to talk here, or somewhere private in the Church?"

Ford looked around. Many people who had left the Church were watching the TV crew, always a focus for people's curiosity. "Let's go inside," he said. Ford led Cindy and the cameraman to his office, and indicated that she should sit down in a chair opposite his desk. He settled comfortably into his large leather chair behind the desk.

"Miss Ritcey, what can I tell you?"

"Well, I'm curious about the revelation you made about the Jesus casket. Can we talk about that?"

"Certainly"

"Right." The CNN camera man adjusted his equipment, and nodded to Cindy. She turned to the camera.

"This is Cindy Ritcey of CNN. I'm with the Reverend Jackson Ford, who has just told his TV audience that he has a silver casket containing hair from the head of Jesus Christ." She turned to Ford: "Reverend Ford, tell us more. Where did you get this casket?"

Ford looked straight at the camera. "Well, Cindy, it came to my attention when I was on my Crusade in Scotland."

"Came to your attention? What does that mean?"

"It was brought to me in Edinburgh, during my Crusade for Christ."

"And who brought it to you?"

"That I can't reveal at present."

"OK. Well how do we know that it's for real?"

"I have seen documentation that is authentic."

"Can we see it?"

"Not yet. Perhaps later."

"Reverend Ford, unless you provide proof, people will suspect a hoax. It wouldn't be the first time."

Ford looked angrily at her. "It would be for me." He looked disdainful. "I don't subscribe to hoaxes or scams. This is the real thing."

"Even so," Cindy replied calmly, "and I don't doubt your word, sir, but there are many sceptics, people who will look for proof. Now, you said you had proof of its provenance: what does that mean?"

"It means that we have a letter from a fourteenth century King of Spain that gives the history of the casket. Furthermore, the hair has been carbon dated as being roughly two thousand years old."

Ford looked down at his desk, before looking up dramatically, with wide open eyes at the camera. "That is from the time of our Lord, Jesus Christ. It all makes sense."

"And when will we see the letter, and the report on carbon dating of the hair?"

"In due course, Cindy, in due course."

Cindy Ritcey had enough: a good story for CNN; an exclusive. She knew that the cable news business had very small audiences, so even small spikes in viewer ship were very important. They could amount to a couple of million people, and as CNN's audience ratings improved she thought that the story might capture a big percentage of air time over the next few weeks.

"Thank you, Reverend Ford." She turned the camera. "This is Cindy Ritcey from CNN in Montgomery, Alabama."

Ford escorted Cindy and the cameraman out of the Church. When he returned, he found Varley waiting.

"Well, the news is out, Mark, a little earlier than we planned."

"That's right, "Varley replied. "We'll just have to stall the media when they begin to contact us for more information. We've got a 'teaser' out there, and that should increase our audience figures next week. But Jackson, please don't say any more. We should just tell the media to watch next week, when we will give more information."

Phones began to ring. Other media had seen the CNN exclusive. They too wanted interviews.

CHAPTER 16

Alan Bruce picked up his phone on the second ring. His secretary announced that a Dr. Harris wanted to speak to him. He didn't normally work on Sunday, but he was making up for his absence in Scotland and had promised a key client that he would have the legal work completed for Monday.

"Hello, Kate," he said, "how are you?"

"Fine, Alan, have you been watching CNN?"

"No, I'm working on a legal issue for a client. He needs my review of the papers to be in his hands tomorrow morning. Why?"

"Well I've just seen an interview on CNN, in which Jackson Ford has revealed that he has a silver casket containing the hair of Jesus. In fact, CNN is calling it 'the Jesus casket'."

"My God: he's told people?"

"More than that, Alan. He's said he has a letter from a Spanish King proving its provenance, and that he has had the hair carbon dated as two thousand years old."

Alan sighed. What did Ford want to do with the hair, he wondered. He felt he knew: Ford was going to try to clone Jesus.

"Anything else?" he asked.

"Yes, CNN also showed a taping of his sermon. As far as I could see, it was based on the Second Coming of Jesus."

Alan groaned. "So he's going to do it!"

"So it would appear. What do you want to do?"

"I really don't know Kate, I need to think about it. Can I call you back?"

"Of course. Miss you, Alan."

"I miss you too. I'll try to see you next week. Bye."

Alan hung up the phone. He would finish his legal work, get the material ready for his client then turn his mind to Jackson Ford and Varley.

The following afternoon, Kate arrived unexpectedly at his office. Alan had just returned from a meeting with his client, a difficult meeting, covering a complicated contract between his client's company and a major hospital in Ontario. He had settled behind his desk with a large coffee when his secretary announced Kate, who swept into his office and gave him a kiss.

"Surprise, Alan!"

"My lord, Kate," he got to his feet. "It's great to see you; but how did you come to be in Toronto?"

"Come to be?" she smiled teasingly. "Is that the lawyer talk for 'why are you here?'"

Alan laughed. "More or less: do you want it in Latin?"

"No, thank you."

"Thank God for that. I couldn't do it."

Kate laughed with him. "To tell the truth, Alan, I have a few days to myself. I started to think about Jackson Ford and cloning. I've done a little research, and I thought I should come to see you face-to-face, so you have a better grasp of the topic. Besides which, I've been missing you."

"It's mutual, Kate. I've been missing you too." He pointed to two comfortable wing-back armchairs in a corner of his office. "Why don't we sit over there and you can fill me in, as they say."

Kate sat and crossed her legs. "Well, to begin at the beginning," she said, "you know about the birds and bees of course."

"Naturally," Alan replied. "That always has been of interest to me."

"Well let's see if I can provide you with cloning 101." Kate took a deep breath. "In essence, cloning is really quite simple. You have to take some cells from an individual—skin, for example."

Alan interrupted, "That includes hair, I guess."

"Of course. Hair is skin, if you like. Then, having those cells, you need an egg—from a female of course. You remove the genetic material from the egg—in scientific terms, the egg is enucleated. Then the nucleus of the cell from the skin, or hair, is placed in the enucleated egg. When that happens, the egg has the DNA of the donor cell and the egg is a genetic clone of the donor. Clear so far?"

"I think so." Alan nodded his agreement.

"Right. Next, a jolt of electricity is passed through the egg with DNA in it. That starts the egg dividing, just as it does normally in nature. If all goes well, a human embryo will begin to grow in a dish in a laboratory."

Alan sighed. "That sounds heartless."

"I guess you could say so. However, if the embryo does begin to grow after a few days and a number of cell divisions, it would be implanted into a woman's uterus. There, all being well, it would grow into a baby. Eventually a child would be born."

"So that's all it takes?" Alan asked.

"All?" Kate shook her head. "No wonder we scientists are so misunderstood. It's a great adventure, Alan. In a way, it's the great unknown. There's a lot of debate in the scientific world about whether cloning a human being is really possible."

"So, no one has ever done it? Clone a human, I mean."

Kate looked at him and frowned. "There's some debate about that," she said. "You may remember that a sect called the Raelians said they had cloned a baby girl some years ago, but they never produced her, and they seem to have disappeared off the map. More realistic claims have come from an Italian doctor—a Dr Antinori—who claims to have cloned or assisted in cloning several babies. Again, the babies have never been produced as proof. Antinori is, however, a very successful practitioner in helping women, previously thought to be infertile, to have babies. So he has some credibility."

Kate looked into Alan's eyes. "Am I boring you?" she asked.

"Not at all. It's fascinating."

"Okay then," Kate smiled, "here is the very latest. It's to do with another fertility expert, Dr. Panos Zavos. He's a reproductive scientist. In July 2006, the Archives of Andrology published a scientific paper he had written. In it he said he had copied the techniques from the cloning of Dolly the sheep, known as somatic cell nuclear transfer or SCNT. He took a man's skin cells and fused them inside three eggs taken from a woman's ovaries. These were given a burst of electricity to encourage them to develop as embryos. The paper said that after three days the embryos had reached the four cell stage and were transferred into the patient's uterus. However, two weeks later, blood tests showed the woman was not pregnant."

"So it didn't work," Alan said.

"That's right. But there's more. The paper said, and I quote: 'This is the first evidence of the creation and transfer of a cloned human being for reproductive purposes. Even though no pregnancy was established, human reproduction from SCNT may be possible and applicable in the future.' End of quote."

Alan looked thoughtfully at Kate and asked, "Do you think it is possible?"

"I'm not sure. There's no scientific proof that it has happened. But science is used to solving mysteries, and as a scientist I'd never say never. By the way," she added, "in that same month of July 2006, Dr. Zanos told a reporter that his paper had been submitted to the Archives of Andrology in 2005 and since that time he had transferred cloned human embryos to another five women. But none of these had resulted in pregnancies."

"Wasn't that the same with Professor Wilmut? Didn't he try it many times before Dolly the sheep appeared?"

"Hundreds I think. So, given time, I guess I would bet that human cloning will occur."

Alan stood. "In that case, Kate, we—you and I—need to talk about what we should do about Jackson Ford and Varley." He looked at her expectantly, almost pleadingly. "Can you stay in Toronto tonight?"

"I sure can. I came prepared." Kate smiled at him.

"Well, if you don't mind, you could stay with me." He took her hand.

Kate squeezed his hand. "Sounds like a plan. I have an overnight bag with me. It's with your secretary."

Alan told his secretary he would not be back until the next day and picked up Kate's case. Kate and he took the elevator from his office on the twenty-second floor of Commerce Court West, one of the large bank buildings in downtown Toronto, where many professional firms had their offices. Reaching the parking level, he led Kate to his car, a late model Mercedes. As it came up to the surface level and entered the traffic on Wellington Street, Alan said, "It will only take about fifteen minutes to get to my place."

He drove west along Lakeshore Boulevard, with Lake Ontario on his left. Two massive skyscrapers lay ahead. He pointed to the one closest to the lake. "That's Palace Place. I have an apartment on the twentieth floor."

"Looks interesting," Kate said, "I can hardly wait to see it."

Alan turned left off Lakeshore Boulevard and headed the car towards Lake Ontario. He passed Palace Pier, the twin tower to Palace Place, turned left into the underground parking and took the elevator to the twentieth floor.

Kate gasped as she entered his apartment. "What a beautiful view." She pointed to the floor to ceiling windows, outside of which the blue waters of Lake Ontario sparkled in the sunshine. To the left, she saw Toronto Island, which lay a short distance offshore from the downtown Toronto skyline. A small fleet of white-sailed yachts raced across the lake with colourful spinnakers billowing in the wind.

Alan pointed to the left. "That's downtown Toronto."

Kate looked in the direction Alan was indicating.

"I guess that big tower is the CN Tower everyone associates with Toronto."

"That's right. Supposed to be the tallest free-standing structure in the world, and nearby is the Sky Dome, now called the Rogers Centre, where the Toronto Blue Jays play baseball."

"Interesting," Kate murmured, not sure why Alan felt the need for a mini-travelogue: perhaps he was nervous. She looked at the interior of the apartment, interested to see what it said about Alan. Her eyes flickered with surprise, as she noted that it was smartly furnished with tasteful pictures on the walls, above a gleaming Brazilian cherry wood floor covered with several large silk rugs and an eclectic mix of furniture. It was a bit untidy, but not bad for a single guy.

"Did you choose all this?" she asked, raising an eyebrow.

"I cannot tell a lie," Alan grinned. "No, I had an interior designer."

"I thought so. It didn't seem like the traditional male apartment!"

"Yes," Alan laughed, "I'm not a Designer Guy. I needed help and I'm quite happy with the outcome. Mind you," he looked knowingly at her, "I did choose some furniture myself."

"Oh really, like what?"

He took her hand and led her from the living room into a large bedroom, which looked to the south over Lake Ontario. "There," he said pointing to a large king-sized bed. "That's all mine."

"Not tonight, it isn't." Kate replied.

"I hoped you'd say that." Alan leaned over and kissed her.

An hour later, having made sure that the king-sized bed could accommodate both of their needs, Kate showered and changed for dinner. Alan also showered and when he came back into the bedroom, Kate sat by a mirror applying her makeup. She wore a dark blue dress with a pearl necklace and matching earrings.

"Wow!" Alan whistled, "You look good enough to eat."

"Thank you." Kate smiled at him in the mirror. "But you can't get out of buying me dinner with mere compliments."

"Not my intention. When you're ready, join me in the living room and I'll make a nice gin and tonic for us. We can chat for a while: our reservation is not until eight o'clock."

Kate and Alan sat with their drinks in deep blue leather armchairs looking out over Lake Ontario.

"Kate, "Alan began, "I've been thinking about Jackson Ford and the hair, and cloning. From what you told me earlier, I now seriously believe that he will try to make a clone of Jesus."

Kate nodded in agreement. "I agree. All the signs are there."

"And quite honestly, I don't know what to do. Somehow he has obtained the casket that Jock buried at Melrose Abbey. I suspect that Mark Varley is behind it. So Ford, to be fair, may not know how it came into his hands. I could demand it from Ford, but I have no proof of ownership."

Kate interrupted, "But I was with you when Jock told you about it. Wouldn't that count?"

"It would help, but it isn't enough proof. Ford has the casket and I don't. Possession is important, and he'll probably have a good convincing story about how he got it."

"Well, what about the Alfonso letter? He doesn't have the original, only an English translation."

Alan nodded his head. "Good point, Kate. At some point, people will want to see the original, so I suppose I could reveal that. It might help. But again, if I were Ford I wouldn't care. I would still have the casket and the hair. I could stall the media and anyone else who might be interested, and go ahead with the cloning. If that succeeded, no one would care about the original letter. All the interest would switch to the birth of the baby."

"I suppose you're right. Does it really matter?" Kate said, taking a sip from her drink and sighing. Alan shook the ice in his glass, deep in thought.

"I don't really know, Kate. However my Bruce genes are offended by what has happened. Jock wanted to rectify what should have been done centuries ago, and have the casket interred with Robert the Bruce's heart. And, you know, I guess that's what I also would like to happen," his hand rubbed his eyes. "However, the reality is that no one in the world will now let this happen. This historic, religious relic really now belongs in a national museum, so it can be preserved for posterity."

"Hmm!" Kate murmured, "So what you are saying is that we leave Ford with the casket and the hair? He gets away with it? That doesn't seem fair to me."

"It isn't, Kate. It isn't." Alan finished his drink and put his glass down on a table "Got it!" he said.

"What?"

"Wait a minute." Alan disappeared into the bedroom and reappeared a few moments later. He sat beside Kate and showed her the gold locket. "This is the answer."

"The locket Jock gave you?"

"Yes. It also contains some of Jesus' hair."

"True—according to Jock. So what?"

"So," he paused, "maybe I should try to make a clone."

"You've got to be joking."

"No, I'm deadly serious. You see, if Ford succeeds, and I succeed, it will make the Jesus aspect seem farcical. Ford's plans for his clone would be destroyed. You can't have two of Jesus."

Kate's shoulders heaved with laughter. She wiped her eyes, careful not to smudge her makeup. She stopped laughing and looked at him.

"Are you really serious?"

"I think so." Alan's brows wrinkled in thought. "I should probably sleep on it; but it might be worth trying. After all, I have the original Alfonso letter, and both of us heard Jock talk about the locket."

"Yes, but as you said earlier that is not conclusive proof."

"No it isn't. But it's the best I can do for the moment." He rose. "Let's go to dinner. I want to enjoy having you in Toronto with me."

Dinner was at a small Italian restaurant about 10 minutes drive away. The restaurant was not too busy at 8:00 PM, so Alan and Kate had a quiet corner table. A pianist played softly in the background, and they had a delicious meal. Afterwards, with darkness falling, Alan drove back to his apartment at Palace Place. When they entered the apartment, he turned to Kate. "Let's do it," he said.

"Again?"

Alan laughed. "Well, perhaps later." He chuckled again. "No, certainly later. But what I meant is let's see if we can clone Jesus ourselves."

CHAPTER 17

Varley gave directions to the Crusade's PR staff. They were not to give any further information to the media. The message was: watch next Sunday's TV programme when more will be revealed.

This did not satisfy the more curious; and Cindy Ritcey of CNN sensed she was on to a real story, perhaps a really big story, so she began to phone religious leaders to get their views.

A spokesman for the Catholic Church, Monsignor Brendan O'Connell was first.

"So, Monsignor," Cindy began, "I assume you have heard about the Reverend Jackson Ford's claim that he has a casket, let's call it the Jesus Casket, containing hair from Jesus." She looked at the camera. "Do you believe that?"

Monsignor O'Connell frowned. "Well, it's difficult to believe such a claim. It seems unbelievable that a casket like this could have been in existence with no one knowing about it. And the story about the hair from our Saviour? Dear me, that's unlikely."

"So you're sceptical."

"I'm afraid so."

Cindy thought for a moment and decided to try a long shot. "Monsignor, Reverend Jackson Ford, in his sermon, spoke about the Second Coming of Jesus; could the casket have anything to do with that?"

"Again, very unlikely. I don't know what Reverend Ford was meaning. Perhaps he'll enlighten us in due course."

"Indeed. Thank you, Monsignor O'Connell."

Cindy turned to the camera. "That was Monsignor Brendan O'Connell of the Catholic Church. For CNN, this is Cindy Ritcey."

On the TV set in Ford's office, Jackson Ford and Mark Varley watched the interview.

"It's beginning to build up nicely, Mark," Ford said. "Next Sunday, I'll reveal more; perhaps even show the casket during my sermon."

Varley scowled. "Let's be careful, Jackson, we can't afford to have anything happen to it. After all, we need the hair if we are to try cloning, and I'd be afraid that someone might try to steal it."

Ford shook his head. "Don't worry about that. I'll speak to the Governor and get him to arrange for plenty of security on Sunday."

Varley relaxed slightly at this news. "Okay. By the way Jackson, I'm flying to London tomorrow to meet Dr Sophia Vacca. I should be back on Saturday in time for the Sunday programme." He looked into Ford's eyes, for confirmation. "I assume you have no problem with my speaking frankly to her?"

Ford seemed deep in thought. He was beginning to prepare his next sermon in his mind. He shrugged his shoulders. "Do what you have to do, Mark. If it is possible, I believe we should try the cloning."

The next day Varley caught the 2:00 p.m. Delta flight from Montgomery. It was going to be a long day. He would not reach London until 9:05 the next morning London time, or 3:05 a.m., his body time in Alabama.

The flight was uneventful. Varley had a first class seat and managed to sleep for a few hours. As he passed through Passport Control at Heathrow Airport a warning signal appeared on the Immigration Officer's computer screen. It advised that Inspector Dawson, of the Lothians and Borders police, should be contacted if Varley appeared in the UK. She looked at Varley. "How long do you expect to be staying, sir?" she asked.

"I guess a few days."

"And where will you be staying?"

"At the Ritz Hotel in London."

"Thank you, sir." She handed him his passport. When he had left, she e-mailed the information to Inspector Dawson in Scotland.

Varley took a black London cab from Heathrow Airport to the Ritz hotel in central London, about a forty-five-minute drive through heavily congested roads. He had a traditional English hotel room with chintz-covered chairs and bed covers and with a vase of red roses on a side table. He ordered room-service breakfast then called Dr Vacca's room. She was not there, so he left a message asking her to call his room when she was free.

At two o'clock, after Varley had slept for a few hours, his phone rang. It was Dr Vacca.

"Mr. Varley?" she asked.

"Yes, this is Mark Varley. Is that Dr. Vacca?"

"Yes, I am returning your call."

"Thank you for that. Well, as you can see, I am now in London. Can we meet as arranged?"

"Of course. I'll be in the lobby."

Varley brushed his hair and straightened his tie before catching the elevator to the ground floor. He looked around. A young woman with black hair arranged in a chignon stared questioningly at him. He walked over to her. "Dr Vacca?" he enquired.

Sophia Vacca, wearing a dove grey suit with a slim skirt, uncrossed her legs and slowly rose from the chair where she had been reading from a file. She was about six inches shorter than Varley's six-foot frame. "Yes, I'm Sophia Vacca." Varley shook her hand. Quite a looker, he thought.

"Let's find a quiet place to talk." he said, leading the way to a table in a corner of the lobby. He ordered coffee. "Dr.Vacca," he began, "I'm glad we have been able to meet so quickly after I called you in Rome."

She looked at him with appraising brown eyes.

"Well, it must be important for you to fly to London from—where did you fly from?"

"Montgomery, Alabama." Varley gestured with his hands apart. "You speak perfect English."

She smiled. "Well, it's the international language of science, and I did spend two years here in London, at Hammersmith Hospital. It has a first-class fertility and reproductive medicine programme."

"That explains it then. OK," he continued, "I'm interested in cloning. I imagine you are an expert."

"Not really. No one has been successful so far in cloning a human being. Some have come close, but so far," she paused, "how do you Americans put it, 'close, but no cigar?'"

Varley smiled. "That's the phrase."

"How much do you know, Mr Varley?"

"Well, I've learned a little about Dolly the sheep. A Dr. Jim Cameron, who was part of that team told us the story. He was the one who directed us to Dr Antinori."

"I see. Well let me tell you a little bit about the history so far." Dr. Vacca took a drink of coffee, and then recounted the trail of cloning from the Raelians to Dr Antinori and on to Dr Panos Zanos.

Varley listened with interest. "So, Dr.Zanos seems to have come close?"

"Yes, that seems to be so; but I believe I can do better. I intend to succeed. That is why I am setting up my own practice. I have left Rome."

A waiter appeared and asked if they wanted more coffee. Varley shook his head. "So, Dr. Vacca how do you intend to go about this? Why should you succeed?"

"First things first, Mr Varley. I have arranged to set up a laboratory on a motor yacht, which I have chartered for the next six months. It will operate in the Mediterranean, beyond any nation's jurisdiction, in international waters. You see, no country in Europe will allow human cloning. For that matter, neither will the United States."

"I didn't know that."

"It's a fact. In international waters, I can practice freely. It is there that I will develop an embryo that can safely be inserted into a woman's uterus. After that we are in God's hands. But I will succeed. I am determined."

Varley listened intently to Sophia Vacca's passion for her goal. He decided he would try to recruit her to his aim of cloning Jesus.

"Thank you, Dr. Vacca. That answers my first question, about how you would do it. But you haven't answered my second question. Why should you succeed?"

Dr Vacca's eyes narrowed and her mouth closed in a thin line. "That is my secret," she said. "I know what has gone wrong in the past. Quite simply, it has to do with proteins that are vital to having a fertilised egg divide properly. I have perfected a technique in the laboratory to get around that. More than that I will not say."

Varley sensed that the Italian doctor was getting angry. He had to defuse the situation, or lose the opportunity to hire her.

"Fine. OK." He threw his hands wide in a conciliatory gesture. "I understand that you have proprietary secrets. I'm not interested in that. What I want to do is to hire you to develop a clone."

"I'll need more information. Who is the donor. Is it you?"

"No." Varley looked around. "Look, I'd prefer to talk about this in private."

"All right, why don't you book a conference room at the hotel."

Varley wondered about going to his or her room, but sensed that Dr.Vacca wanted to keep the discussion at a professional level.

"OK, give me a minute." Varley left and spoke to the concierge. He returned with a key. "We can meet in this room on the first floor."

They sat at opposite ends of a small table in the private room. Dr Vacca took a notebook from her bag. "Tell me what you want, Mr. Varley. Who is the donor?"

Varley sighed. This was going to be difficult to explain.

"Well, it's a long story. There is no living donor as such. I have hair from a distant ancestor. That's what I hope you can use. You know, extract the DNA."

Dr Vacca threw down her pen. "Are you serious?" she demanded.

"Deadly serious. This would be the donor. I—we—want to develop a clone of him."

Vacca looked at him. "And how old is the donor? How old is the hair?"

"Several centuries."

"My God! You can't be serious!"

"Oh, I am. We are willing to pay very well for your services."

Dr. Vacca looked at him with a frown. "Oh you will have to pay a lot, believe me, if I decide to help." She thought for a moment. "Who is this person? He's not Hitler, or any tyrant like that?"

"Quite the opposite. In fact he is more of a saint."

"A saint!" Sophia Vacca shook her head. "You want to clone a saint? Are you a religious nut, as they call it, from the States?"

"No, I'm not a nut as you call it. But I am religious."

"Let me think about it." Dr Vacca rose.

Varley stood and took her arm. "Please sit down, Dr Vacca. I think we can work together on this. You seem to think you can succeed, where others have failed. I have faith in your expertise. But if you don't want to do it, I will speak to Dr Antinori, or find someone else. However, I have lots of money and I think you will find, on reflection, that this may be your opportunity for a major breakthrough."

Sophia Vacca glared at his hand on her arm. Varley quickly withdrew it.

"As I have said, Mr Varley, let me think about your proposition. I will call your room later." She turned and left. Back in her room her lips flickered in a tight smile. Varley had said he had lots of money. That should help pay her bills. In fact, she would ask for a large payment to test Varley's intentions. If he met her demands, her costs would be covered for the six months' rental of the motor yacht Nova Wisp in the Mediterranean.

Varley went to his room to await her call. Dr Vacca was not going to be a pushover. Still, she had not said "No."

* * * *

Back in the States, Cindy Ritcey had another interview on CNN. It was Governor Mike Malloy of Alabama.

"Governor Malloy," she began, "how do you feel about the fact that Reverend Jackson Ford says he has a casket containing hair from Jesus Christ?"

Governor Malloy looked straight into the camera, his media training working to his advantage. "Well, Cindy," he said, in his deep Alabama voice, "I think that is wonderful news for all of us, not just my fellow Alabamans."

"Do you believe Reverend Ford?"

"Jackson Ford is a highly believable person. He has devoted his life to Christ. He's just returned from a highly successful crusade in Edinburgh, Scotland."

"Yes, I know all that. Let me put it this way: if the Jesus casket exists, what do you think should happen to it?"

"Well it seems to have been given to Jackson. He is the one who should decide."

"But surely it is a relic, or could be, if true, a relic of historic and religious significance. Shouldn't it be on display somewhere, like in the Smithsonian in Washington?"

"Cindy, that may be so eventually. I'm sure that Jackson will do the right thing. Perhaps we may even want to retain it right here in Alabama," he said, thinking of the tourism dollars that the casket might attract to his state. Not a bad idea for someone running for re-election. Tourism meant jobs, and jobs meant votes. "Yes," he nodded his head "perhaps that might be Jackson Ford's intention."

Ford had been watching the interview on TV. He switched off, rang the governor's mansion, and left a message asking Governor Malloy to call him when convenient.

* * * *

Back in London, Varley's phone rang in his room at 8:00 p.m.. It was Dr Vacca.

"Mr Varley, can you meet me in the conference room—the same one as we had earlier today?"

"I'll be there in a few minutes." Varley quickly put on his tie and jacket, and took the elevator to the first floor conference room.

Dr. Vacca was seated at the table. Without any preliminaries, she said, "Mr. Varley, I have been thinking about the proposal you made earlier. Before I decide, I need a few more facts."

"Right, shoot."

"How old is this hair you have? You said several centuries. How many?"

Varley knew he had to be honest. "It's said to be about 20 centuries old."

"Mamma mia! Two thousand years! Do you realise how difficult that would be?"

"No, but I'm sure you're going to tell me."

"Yes, I am. I've been doing some research since we met earlier. It is possible to extract and sequence DNA from hair. A few years ago, a researcher at the University of Arizona reported in *Current Biology* that he had done this from twelve hair samples between 60,000 and 64,800 years old. This was thought to be impossible previously, since it was believed that the hair shaft contained only small amounts of DNA. It's much better to have the hair root." She paused, and looked at Varley. "Does your sample have hair roots?"

Varley thought for a moment. He hadn't yet seen the hair, but from Ford's description and the Alfonso letter, he assumed that some roots would be there. "I think, so," he replied.

Dr. Vacca gazed at him for a moment. "You think so. Don't you know?"

"Well, I'm fairly sure."

She waved a hand dismissively. "Well, we'll see in due course. In any event, the research seems to show that hydrophobic keratin in the hair—that's the protein polymer that gives hair its structure—protects it from water and degradation. So, it might be possible."

Varley smiled. "I take it then, that you are willing to try."

"Yes," Sophia Vacca nodded, "but it will be expensive. I would need at least $500,000 up front and a similar amount, if a successful pregnancy results."

Varley blinked. He had not expected such a high fee. But Jackson Ford had authorized him to proceed. "Agreed," Varley said. $1 million was nothing, if they could successfully clone Jesus.

"Right." Dr. Vacca nodded. "We have an agreement. I suppose you have a surrogate mother?"

Varley blinked. He'd assumed this would be part of the service. "No, I don't."

"Pah!" Dr. Vacca threw her hands in the air. "Don't you realise that I would need an egg from a woman's ovaries, so that I can develop an embryo? Then I will need a woman who will carry the baby until it is born."

Varley sighed. He was getting tired of being lectured by this woman. "Yes, I know about the birds and the bees doctor. That I understand. I will arrange that, if you tell me what you need."

"Right, Mr Varley, if you give me your address, I will send you, by fax or e-mail, full details of my requirements."

Varley gave her his business card with his contact details. She looked at his card.

"Montgomery, Alabama?"

"Yes, I am with the Jackson Ford Crusade for Christ."

"Hmm," Sophia Vacca thought for a moment. That probably explained his interest in a saint. Aloud she said. "Good. I will contact you again in a few days." She stood. "I will need five hundred thousand dollars transferred to my bank account before I begin. I will send you the details when I write." She shook Varley's hand and left.

Back in his hotel room Varley looked at his watch. It was 9:00 p.m, so he still had time to call Jackson Ford, for it was only 3:00 p.m. in Montgomery. He was put through to Ford's office and told him of his meeting with Dr Vacca.

"So it's a go.' Ford said.

"It seems to be. It's going to cost $1 million; half up front, half on pregnancy."

"That's okay. Money is not a problem. When will you be back?"

"I'll catch a flight tomorrow morning, and should be in Montgomery late afternoon. Jackson, for this to work, we need to find a surrogate mother."

"Let me think about that." Ford hung up.

Next morning Varley received a call from Inspector Dawson. He was in the Ritz hotel's lobby.

"Mr Varley, Inspector Dawson of the Lothians and Borders Police. I wonder if I might speak to you? I'm downstairs in the lobby."

Varley was taken aback. How did Dawson know that he was in London? Disguising his anxiety he said, "Of course, Inspector. I'll join you in a minute." When he put down the phone, he wondered if Dawson could make any connection between him and Melrose. He didn't think that was likely, and decided that he could bluff his way through any questions. Dawson rose to meet him as Varley exited the elevator.

"Good morning, sir. I assume you are Mr Mark Varley? I'm Peter Dawson, Inspector Dawson. Perhaps you'll recall that we spoke on the phone when you were in Edinburgh recently?"

"Yes, I do. Something to do with a place called Melrose, if I remember correctly."

"Yes, that's right. There was an act of vandalism at the site where an ancient king of Scotland's heart is interred, and also a dead body." He gazed intently at Varley. "Andy McPhee," he said.

Varley hoped to disguise any reaction. "Oh. And what has that to do with me?"

"I'm not sure it has, sir, but I'm pursuing inquiries. It seems that an American, by the name of Bruno Conti, stayed at Burts Hotel in Melrose on the night that the vandalism occurred. Do you know him?"

Varley blinked. "Doesn't seem familiar," he said.

"Really? Well, sir, the surprising thing is that his bill was paid by a credit card issued by the Crusade for Christ." Dawson looked straight into Varley's face. He knew that Varley was concealing information.

"Really?" Varley replied. "We had a lot of people working for us in Edinburgh. I didn't know all of them. But I sure don't recall a Conti working for the Ford crusade."

Dawson held his gaze for a moment. "Are you certain, sir?"

"Yes."

Dawson's eyebrows rose questioningly. "Perhaps, then, you can explain how a credit card from the Crusade was used."

Varley blinked rapidly, as he thought about an answer. "I really have no idea, Inspector. I imagine someone stole or duplicated one of our cards. We issued a lot to staff and helpers during the campaign in Edinburgh. If you like, I'll check on that when I get back to the States."

Dawson looked at him for a moment, displaying his disbelief, and then rose. "Thank you, sir. I would appreciate knowing the facts about that card." He started to walk away, then turned as if an afterthought had just occurred. "Oh. By the way, if you do happen to meet Mr. Conti will you let me know? Here's where you can contact me." He gave Varley his card and left.

* * * *

The next morning, after his interview with Cindy Ritcey of CNN, Governor Mike Malloy called Jackson Ford. "Hi, Jackson, Mike here, how are you?"

"Fine, Mike. I called earlier to see if you could arrange for extra police security at the Church on Sunday."

"No problem. Are you expecting trouble?"

"I hope not. I haven't decided yet whether to show the casket, but I don't want anything to happen to it."

"Of course not. By the way, I did an interview today with Cindy Ritcey of CNN."

"Yes: I saw it."

"So you know that she suggested that the relic should go to the Smithsonian?"

"Yes. But I liked your idea of keeping it here in Alabama. In fact, Mike, I would propose to build a shrine to accommodate it, if the State would support me."

"Well, you'll have my support, if I'm re-elected."

"Of course, Mike. That's what we want. In fact, I'm going to make a donation of a quarter of a million dollars for your campaign. Not sure how we deal with that legally, but perhaps you can get your advisors to contact my accountants first."

"That's mighty generous of you, Jackson. I'll let my people know. And you'll have the extra police on Sunday."

Varley and Ford met late the following day when he returned to Montgomery.

Ford paced up and down in his office, wrestling with a decision. "Mark, I've been thinking about the question of a mother. My first instinct was to find a Jewish virgin from the Holy Land, to replicate Mary. That seemed the obvious thing to do. Then, I began thinking about what God would want. The Bible is vague about how, and when, Jesus will return. Matthew said: 'Keep watch, because you do not know what day your Lord will come.'" He nodded, in agreement with his own train of thought. "So, I prayed for guidance. And I am, as yet, far from certain about what to do. However, it begins to seem that it may not be necessary to replicate a Jewish mother. For, as I understand the briefing on cloning from Jim Cameron, the mother matters very little. The clone carries virtually all of the genetic code of the original. On that basis, then, I think we could choose anyone, perhaps even a young virgin from our own flock."

Varley's eyes widened. "Do you have anyone in mind?" he asked.

"Of course not. The idea just came to me."

The jet lag from his flight from London was beginning to catch up. Varley yawned. "Jackson, I'm tired. Can we speak about this tomorrow?"

Ford agreed and Varley left. On his drive home he began to consider options to find an egg donor and a surrogate mother, knowing that both were necessary if his deal with Dr. Vacca was going to work.

CHAPTER 18

Kate looked with concern at Alan. "Son of a gun, I think you're serious."

Alan sat on the edge of an armchair. "Yes, I think I am. You see, Varley undoubtedly is the one who got the casket from the plinth at Melrose Abbey. Whether he smashed it himself or employed others doesn't really matter. He took something that belonged to my family, and was destined to be interred forever, beside Robert the Bruce's heart. So I'm offended."

Kate sat in the armchair and put her hand on Alan's knee. A Diana Krall CD played quietly in the background. "Well, that certainly makes your feelings clear! However, if you don't mind my saying so, I think you're getting a bit emotional about the whole thing."

"What do you mean?" Alan snapped. "I'm entitled to be annoyed. In fact, I still feel that maybe Varley's visit was a cause of Jock's heart attack."

"Even so, Alan, Jock didn't have long to live. He told you so."

"I know, I know." He rose, walked to the window, and gazed out at the lights twinkling over downtown Toronto. "I'm a pretty determined guy when my mind is made up, Kate. Probably part of my genes. Maybe that's why I was a quarterback at school. And now I really want to thwart Ford and Varley."

Kate walked to the window and stood beside him. "You realise, if you do that, you may bring a child into this world?"

Alan turned and held her hand. "Perhaps Kate, only perhaps: from what you've told me it has never been done. Cloning hasn't worked so far."

"Then why not assume that, even if Ford tries, he may not succeed?"

"That's too easy. He might. And heaven knows what he or Varley, whom I simply don't trust, will do with the cloned child."

"And so your answer is to clone a second child. How does that help?"

Alan sighed. "I'm not sure, but part of me says to go for it. There can't be two Jesuses, so Ford's claims will be laughed out of court, as the saying goes."

Kate gave an exasperated shrug and walked back to sit in an armchair. Soft jazz played quietly in the background. Both were quiet for a minute before Kate said, "and have you thought what you would do with the child?"

"Well, I could bring it up myself, or have it adopted."

"Alan Bruce, that is no way to bring a child into this world. Babies need a mother as well as a father."

Alan walked over and sat on the arm of the chair. "Maybe I'll need to find a mother," he said, leaning to kiss her neck.

"Well, I wouldn't want to be the so-called mother of a clone," she snapped angrily, pushing him away. "I still believe that the natural way of conceiving children is best."

Alan blinked, and bit his lip. He knew he should tell Kate his secret, but didn't know how to begin. Lost for words, he shrugged his shoulders.

Kate looked at him, waiting for a response to her outburst. "Well?" she said. "Don't you have anything to say?"

Alan shrugged, and turned away. He stood staring out of the window.

Kate sighed. She wondered what was going through Alan's mind.

Alan turned towards Kate. "Do you think we could talk about this some other time?" he asked. "Perhaps I'm reacting emotionally, and I don't want that to spoil our evening."

"Well, I'm afraid it has," she said. "I'm a bit surprised with your attitude, so I think I'll leave now, and catch a flight back to Boston." She stood, anger showing in her face.

Alan came forward and put his hands on her shoulders. "Don't do that Kate," he said. "I'm sorry if I've been a bit off-balance about this. But I don't want it to affect our relationship."

Kate looked at him, as her anger began to dissipate at his contrition. "Maybe we're both getting worked up over this whole thing. Besides, it's probably too late to catch a flight to Boston." She shook her head and slowly expelled her breath, trying to calm herself. "Why don't we just sleep on it?"

"Great idea." He took her hand and began to walk toward the bedroom.

Kate shook her head. "Sorry, Alan, but I'm not in the mood. You've upset me with your attitude. I need time on my own. I'll sleep on the couch here in the living room tonight."

Alan sighed, shook his head, and walked alone to his lonely bedroom.

The next morning, Alan rose early, and made coffee and toast for Kate. Both felt remorseful for their tiff the previous evening, and over breakfast each tried to let the other know, however subtly, that they should put the disagreement behind them. They were both more relaxed when Alan drove Kate to Pearson Airport in Toronto, where she caught an Air Canada flight to Boston. She promised to do some research on cloning and surrogacy, and to call Alan in a few days' time, when she had more information.

On the drive to his downtown Toronto office, Alan was deep in thought about his conversation the previous evening with Kate. Was he crazy, he wondered? Or did his plan make any sense?

He decided to await Kate's call before giving it further thought. He had a busy few days ahead of him. The lawyer for the hospital had made many amendments to the draft document he had sent them. There would be a series of meetings with his client and with the hospital's lawyers to try to finalize the deal. He would have to give his attention to that. His legal work paid his bills—quite successfully, he thought, given that he had cleared over seven hundred thousand dollars in the last fiscal year and was on track to do better this year. And there was also Jock's estate. What was it Cameron Learmonth had said? Oh yes: "it would be a significant inheritance." If he decided to proceed with cloning, he thought he would be able to pay any reasonable fees.

Back in Boston, Kate had two classes to teach and had to participate in a research forum. When she got back to her apartment it was 6:00 p.m.. She changed into jeans and a T-shirt and heated a pizza for dinner. Kate opened a bottle of Amarone and sat before her computer to refresh her memory about cloning and the key participants. She remembered the names of Dr. Severino Antinori and Dr. Panos Zavos, but surely there had to be others. She searched a number of databases and was beginning to despair when she came across an interview in an Italian paper with a Dr. Sophia Vacca. Kate knew very little Italian, but what jumped out at her was a telephone number in Rome. She looked at her watch. It was now 8:00 p.m. in Boston, or two o'clock the following morning in Rome. It was too late to call, but she made a note of the number and decided to rise early next morning to try to speak to this Dr Vacca.

Kate rose at 5.30 the next morning. It was still dark outside, but it would be close to noon in Rome. She dialed long-distance and listened to the clicking sound as a connection was made.

An Italian voice answered. Kate blinked as she heard the unfamiliar language.

"I'm sorry, I don't speak Italian. Do you understand English?"

"Naturally, we are an international centre."

"Good, thank you. May I speak to Dr. Vacca?"

"Dr. Vacca has left us."

"Do you have a number where I might reach her?"

"Momento." The line was quiet for a moment then Kate heard, "Dr. Vacca is now in France, in Villefranche. Here is the number."

"Thank you." Kate jotted down the number and dialled it moments later.

"*Bonjour*," she heard.

"*Bonjour. Je voudrais parler aux docteur Vacca.*"

"You are an American?"

Kate smiled. "Well, yes. Is my French accent so bad?"

She heard a laugh at the other end.

"Not too bad, but why don't we continue in English. This is Sophia Vacca."

Bingo! Kate thought.

"Dr. Vacca, my name is Dr. Kate Harris. I'm a biologist at Harvard. I'm interested in cloning and I was directed to you as an expert in the field."

"There are no experts, Dr. Harris. A number of us are explorers, no more, no less. But I do intend to clone a human being. I am confident I can succeed."

Kate thought to herself: this Dr. Vacca sounds like one feisty lady. "I'm glad to hear it," she said. "Could I meet you to explore a project?" She coughed. "Sorry, I guess that's the scientist in me. What I meant to say is that we—my partner and I—are anxious to talk to you about cloning a baby."

"Dr. Harris, I would be happy to meet with you. Presently, I am in Villefranche, in the south of France. Do you know it?"

"No."

"It's near Nice and Monaco. I'm busy for the next five days, but I could see you in Villefranche next week, say on Thursday or Friday."

"That sounds good, Dr. Vacca. Let me consult with my partner and I'll call you back later today."

"As you wish." Dr. Vacca hung up.

Kate looked at the phone and smiled. Dr. Vacca was going to be an interesting challenge. It was now after 6:00 a.m.. She rang Alan's apartment in Toronto. There was no reply, so she left a message asking him to call her. Kate went for her morning run, came back, showered, and had a coffee. It was now 8:00 a.m.. She called Alan's office. His secretary told her that Alan was at a client's office. Kate asked her to tell Alan that she had called.

Kate then went on to her computer to find out about surrogacy. She was astounded to find how many sites there were on the Internet devoted to the subject. She read as much as she could so she could discuss the mechanisms and the cost with Alan, if he should decide to proceed with the attempted cloning. This was always assuming that Dr. Vacca agreed, and felt that the DNA from the hair could be used.

Alan called at 10:00 a.m.. "Hi Kate. What's up?"

"What's up?" she asked. "Where have you been? Not in your apartment at 6:00 a.m.?" She laughed. "Just teasing, Alan."

"That's OK, we pulled an all-nighter on the file I'm working on. I got home at three, slept for a couple of hours, changed my clothes and was back at the opposition's offices by six. Looks like another full day ahead. How are you?"

"Oh, I'm OK. I have some news for you. I found a doctor who specializes in reproductive medicine. Her name is Dr. Sophia Vacca. She's Italian, now based in the South of France. We have a tentative appointment to meet her there, next Thursday or Friday."

Alan whistled. "Gee, you don't let the moss grow under your feet! France? Next Thursday?"

There was silence for a moment before Kate heard Alan say, "Kate, I have to go back into my meeting. I'll call you later. Bye."

Kate hung up the phone. She thought for a moment, re-dialled, and made a booking on a flight to Toronto for the following Saturday. Since her last visit she had found time to think about her relationship with Alan. He was quite different from Jack Onslow, to whom she had been engaged four years earlier. Jack had also been a scientist, and they had shared similar research interests. But he had not brought out the fun and sense of excitement she felt with Alan Bruce. Alan was a challenge and, at the same time, someone whose impulsive nature tended to bring out Kate's innate sense of adventure.

Alan worked another all-nighter and reached his apartment at 7:00 a.m.. Hopefully the file was closed. The hospital's lawyers intended to consult their client over changes to which the lawyers had agreed, and to meet Alan again, if necessary, on Monday. So, he had a free weekend. He slept for four hours, had a coffee, and dialled Kate's number in Boston. There was no reply, so he left a message then went for a run along the boardwalk, which stretched for miles along the shoreline of Lake Ontario. He crossed the delicate white arched bridge, which spanned the Humber River and ran along the track eastwards to Queen's Quay. He paused for a minute to watch the ferry boats sailing between the mainland in downtown Toronto and Toronto Island, a short distance across the harbour, then retraced his route to Palace Place. Back in his twentieth floor apartment, he had just left the shower when the phone rang. It was Kate.

"Alan, I'm at Toronto Airport. Do you want to collect me, or should I catch a cab?"

"That's wonderful, Kate. I'll be there in fifteen minutes."

When they returned to Palace Place, Alan made coffee. They sat in chairs in the corner beside the window that looked over the Humber River, and the white bridge spanning its banks. People walked, cycled and rollerbladed on the boardwalk. In the distance, flotillas of yachts with white sails straining in the wind, raced on the waters of Lake Ontario.

Kate looked at Alan. "I felt I had to see you. There's a lot I need to tell you, and I thought it would be better face-to face. Besides which, I was missing you."

Alan crossed his legs and stretched his arms in the air. "I'm sorry about last time, Kate. I hope we can get back on track again."

Kate gave him a stern look, then smiled. "Of course. Do you think I would have come back to Toronto if I was still mad at you?"

Alan face showed his relief. "That's great, Kate. I'm all yours. I'm just beginning to unwind after the last few days. I think we finally cracked the problem on that file I told you about."

"The one with the hospital contract?"

"Yes, that's the one."

"Well, I hope I don't wind you up again." She smiled, "still, I did think you should hear what I found out. I've been thinking about the argument we had last time I was in Toronto, and I just want you to know that I'm willing to help you find out about cloning, if only to put your concerns to rest." Impulsively, she leant over and kissed him. "Besides, I thought it would be fun to have a whole weekend with you."

"Go ahead: make my day." Alan laughed, seizing her around the waist and giving her a passionate kiss.

"Wow!" Kate said. "Save that for later. Here's what you need to know."

Briefly, Kate told of her discussion with Dr. Vacca, who was willing to meet them next week in France. Kate felt it was necessary to have a face-to-face meeting to determine the feasibility of cloning from the hair in the locket Jock had given Alan.

After a few minutes thought, Alan agreed.

"Okay, I think you're right Kate. It seems that is what we would need to do. I guess it's only by speaking to her that we can establish whether it is feasible. If it is, then fine, I think we might go ahead; if it's not, then that's even better, for then I'll know that Ford won't succeed."

"It would certainly help to set your mind at rest, if it can't be done." Kate replied.

"Yes, you know, that might be the best solution. But, if not, then I need to think my way through all the consequences of going ahead. You certainly gave me a lot to consider, with what you said a few nights ago."

"Okay," Kate said, "but there's more you should know. Surrogacy isn't cheap." Kate stood and went to her case: she pulled out a file, before walking back to sit opposite Alan. "Here's what I found out. First of all, surrogacy in total can cost up to fifty thousand dollars to pay for the surrogate mother, the egg donor, and agency fees: these are the people who help find an egg donor, and a woman who is willing to act as a surrogate mother. On top of that, there are hospital fees and medical fees, so it's not cheap."

"It sure doesn't seem to be," Alan said. "And I guess that is for a normal surrogacy, if that is how it might be described."

"I guess so, Alan. I've no idea what Dr. Vacca will charge. However, I think you have to be prepared to pay a lot, probably well into six figures."

Alan whistled. "Whew! I guess I hadn't really thought my way through that. I think I need another coffee." He went to the kitchen, returned with a coffee pot and refilled their cups.

They sat again by the window. Alan sipped his coffee, rubbed his chin thoughtfully, and said, "You know, Kate, I still think we need to explore it with Dr.Vacca. Can you go to France next week and meet her?"

"On my own?" Kate frowned. "Won't you want to be there?"

"Of course. That's what I meant. Will you be able to go with me? I'll buy the tickets," he added hurriedly, afraid that Kate might think him cheap."

"Let me see. I'll need to check my schedule." Kate went to her Blackberry and brought up her schedule. "It might be possible, Alan. I'll have to switch classes with someone; but if I can do that, we could leave on Wednesday, and be back next weekend." She looked at Alan. "How about you?"

Alan went to his desk and came back with his Blackberry. "Looks good. I've got two new associates, and provided we close the hospital deal on Monday, I should be free to fly out on Wednesday."

Kate went to the phone in the kitchen. "Mind if I call Dr. Vacca?"

Alan nodded his agreement.

Kate rang and spoke to Sophia Vacca who agreed that she could meet them the following Thursday at 3:00 PM.

"Where should we go in Villefranche? Where is your office, or clinic?" Kate asked. She smiled as Dr. Vacca told her and said goodbye. Kate turned to Alan, who had watched as the conversation unfolded. “It’s all set up. We’ll meet her next Thursday in Villefranche.”

“At her office?”

“No. On a ship. She’ll collect us at the harbour beside the Welcome Hotel.”

CHAPTER 19

When Varley arrived at his office the following morning, an e-mail from Dr Vacca was on his screen. He read it intently.

Mr Varley.

Based on our recent discussion, here is what I will require, if we are to proceed with the project:

1. *Transfer of $500,000 to my bank account in London at Coutts Bank: account VJA 693F. This will be my first payment for my professional services.*

2. *Receipt of the hair to determine the feasibility of DNA extraction.*

3. *Identification of an egg donor, if different from the mother. She will have to be placed on birth control pills to coordinate her cycle with the mother or surrogate mother. In addition, I will prescribe a medication to prevent premature release of eggs, and later, hormone injections to stimulate the ovaries and mature the eggs. Without going into further detail at this time, I shall need to have the egg donor in my care for approximately two weeks.*

4. *The surrogate mother, if that is your choice, must be between the ages of twenty and thirty-eight. Ideally she must already have borne one child. She must not smoke, use illegal drugs or over-indulge in alcohol.*

5. *On a successful achievement of pregnancy, a further payment of $500,000 will be paid by you.*

6. *If you can meet these requirements, please acknowledge without delay. I am prepared to begin the process on confirmation of your agreement, and receipt of funds in my bank account.*

7. *I am now based at Villefranche, in the South of France. When you are ready with the egg donor, and/or surrogate, you should advise me, so that we can arrange a date and time to meet here.*

Yours sincerely,

Dr. Sophia Vacca

Varley took off his glasses and rubbed his eyes. This broad was tough; she was calling the shots. He pressed "print" on his computer, and when the copy was made he walked along the corridor to Jackson Ford's office.

Ford was on the phone and he motioned Varley to come in and sit down. "Miss Ritcey," Ford said, "I can't tell you anything in advance about my sermon on Sunday. Why don't you come along and listen?" Ford's eyes blinked. He ran his fingers through his white hair. "An interview afterwards? I'll have to think about it," he said. "Now, Miss Ritcey, if you'll excuse me, I have people in my office who want to speak to me. Goodbye and God bless." Ford put down the phone and sighed. "The media are all over us Mark. What can we do?"

Varley swung his glasses by the leg. "Do? Nothing, Jackson. That's what we want: lots of publicity. It will attract more people to our cause, and give us the funds we need."

"But don't we run a risk? What if we become an object of ridicule?"

"Jackson, that is a constant problem for Christians. So much of the media is secular and left wing. They criticize Christians and sneer at us in a way that is annoying. They wouldn't attempt to do anything similar with Moslems or Jews. That would be racist. But it seems to me that Christians are sitting targets for those who have no faith, few morals, and a seeming determination to destroy the foundations of our society."

Ford clapped his hands. "Well said, Mark. I couldn't have done better."

Varley's tongue wet his lips. "I guess I got carried away."

"Not to worry." Ford pointed to the sheet of paper in Varley's hand. "What's that?"

Varley handed it to him. "It's from Dr. Vacca. This is what she needs." Ford quickly read the e-mail before putting it down on his desk.

"I guess this is more or less what we expected," he said. "It reminds me again about the need for a surrogate mother." Ford stood and started to pace around the office, as he often did while thinking. "I've been thinking and praying about it. You know, I now think it doesn't make much difference whose egg we use, within reason, or who carries the baby. Although, ideally, it should be a fine moral virgin. But nationality doesn't matter, not now."

"Okay, so do we advertise? I think that is done sometimes. I think there are agencies to find egg donors, or surrogate mothers."

"I'd prefer not to do that. Haven't we anyone in our own flock? We have lots of young females. Would anyone there be interested?" Ford sat down behind his desk and opened a directory of staff members and started to leaf through it. "My goodness," he said, "we have many young females working for the crusade. But I don't know which are married, single, engaged or," he smiled, "which are virgins."

"Not an obvious way of knowing that, Jackson," Varley said with a wry smile. "Tell you what, why not leave it with me and I'll try to make some discreet enquiries. Although," he shrugged, "I've no idea yet about how to deal with the virgin thing. I guess I'll need to be very diplomatic."

Varley returned to his office to find one of the publicity staff waiting for him. It was Grace Christopherson. Grace was in her mid-twenties and dressed in a long grey skirt topped with a white blouse buttoned to her neck. She waved a sheet of paper at him.

"Mr Varley, this is a list of all the media who want interviews with Reverend Ford."

Varley took the list. It seemed that not only the local media, but some national papers and TV channels, in addition to CNN, were showing interest. So far so good, he thought. He placed the paper on his desk.

"Thanks Grace, the answer is that we will not be doing any interviews before Sunday. After that we may talk to a few selected reporters."

"So that's what I should reply?"

"Yes." Grace went to the door and, as she opened it, Varley had a thought. "Grace, why don't you come back and sit down? I've something I want to talk to you about."

Grace took a chair by the side of Varley's desk and demurely crossed her legs as she sat, making sure to smooth the skirt over her knees.

Varley looked at her for a moment, and removed his glasses.

"Grace," he began, "if an opportunity came up to serve our Lord, would you be there?"

"Of course, Mr Varley, that is what I am doing as part of the crusade."

"I know, but supposing that Reverend Ford asked you to do something significant, something that would advance our cause, would you help?"

"Naturally. What do you have in mind?"

"Grace, this isn't easy for me to ask, but it's important to know if you meet the criteria for something of historic importance." Varley twirled his glasses and coughed. "Grace, please feel free to ignore my next question. It is somewhat personal and intrusive, but it's something I need to know. He looked down at his desk before gazing at her. "Grace, are you a virgin?"

Grace blushed, clasped her hands tightly together, and looked down.

"Of course, Mr. Varley. I'm saving myself for the right man."

"And if the right man was Jesus?"

"What do you mean?" Grace gasped.

"Grace, let's put it this way. The casket which Reverend Ford has contains DNA from Jesus' body. That might give us a chance to see if we can help bring about a Second Coming."

Grace's face went pale. "I don't see how that can happen."

"Frankly, Grace, it would be a miracle, a modern miracle, but it is something we feel we are called to attempt." He stood, came around the desk, and put a hand on Grace's shoulder. "Would you like to speak to the Reverend about it? It might help you to decide."

"I don't know," Grace responded, shaking her head. I really don't know, Mr Varley. I'll think about it."

"Of course. Sleep on it. Perhaps we can talk again tomorrow."

When Grace left, Varley dialled Ford's office and told him that he may have found a possible candidate, Grace Christopherson. The next day Grace called in sick, but said she expected to be at the service on Sunday.

The church was packed on Sunday. People had lined up outside for hours before the doors opened at 9:00 a.m.. Ushers led people to seats, making sure that a multicultural, gender-balanced congregation was positioned for best viewing by the Crusade's TV crew. Images were important for the Crusade's success. It couldn't just be a white male-dominated project.

A number of national TV crews had tried to get into the service, but Varley had given instructions that the only live television coverage would be on the Jackson Ford Crusade for Christ programme. On that basis, he had already doubled the advertising revenues, and would charge the national TV companies handsomely, if they wanted to buy any "clips" from Jackson's sermon.

Ford led the congregation through the early part of the service. The blue-gowned choir was inspired by the occasion. The congregation sang the hymns with fervour. Then it was time for Ford's sermon. This was the moment the congregation and a large TV audience had been anticipating.

Inside the church, Cindy Ritcey of CNN sat at the back of the congregation. Some reporters had tried to smuggle in recording devices, but had been stopped by the security staff, considerably enhanced by a large number of Alabama State police, the added security that Governor Mike Malloy had guaranteed to be there.

The congregation hushed as the Reverend Jackson Ford slowly climbed the steps to the pulpit at the front centre of the church. Behind him, the cameras panned over the choir, who looked intently towards Ford. He stood at the pulpit, a magnificent figure with his white hair, white robe and a gleam in his green eyes. He raised his hands in the air.

"Today the Lord is with us," he said.

"Hallelujah," rang out from many in the congregation.

Ford lowered his hands as the TV cameras zoomed in on his face. "Today," he continued, "I want to tell you about the mysteries of science, and the mysteries of Christianity. Too often, they are perceived to be in conflict. People say that they cannot be reconciled. Many are sceptical about this. It was always so, but perhaps the conflict today seems more intense. Let me give you a little history.

"In the sixteenth century, Copernicus suggested that the earth travelled around the sun. Today we accept that, but in his day, coming from a Catholic priest, such a suggestion was thought of as a sacrilege. Despite being a scientist, he had great faith and is known to have described God as 'the best and most orderly workman of all.'

"Next, I want to tell you about Galileo. He was a devout Catholic; there was little choice to be different in those days, and he argued that the Earth was not the centre of the universe. One quotation from him sticks in my memory. He said, 'There are two big books, the book of nature and the book of super nature, the Bible'.

"In the following century, the seventeenth century, Sir Isaac Newton formulated the laws of gravity. He said, 'Gravity explains the motions of the planets, but it cannot explain who set the planets in motion. God governs all things and knows all that is or can be done. The most beautiful system of the sun, planets, and comets could only proceed from the counsel and dominion of an intelligent

Being … this Being governs all things.' Newton was a great scientist, but he was also a leading Christian." Ford paused dramatically and raised his hands.

"In our lifetime, there are many examples. Let me choose just one: Stephen Hawking, the famous physicist. He has said science may solve the problem of 'how' the world began; but it cannot answer 'why' does the universe bother to exist. Let me tell you why. It was because God ordained it. Today science believes it has developed biological answers for how we came into existence, but it cannot tell us why. That is God's domain. So my friends," Ford gazed around the church and with a sweeping gesture of his hand included all present in his words, "I see the complementary role of science and Christianity. Science asks the question 'how' and Christianity asks the question 'why?' Many of you have come here today out of curiosity. You will have heard of my disclosure last week that we now possess a relic related to our lord Jesus Christ." He turned dramatically and pointed to several large screens behind him. At his signal the screens showed a silver box engraved with the words *Capillus Jesu.*

"This is a relic, this is a casket we have been given by the will of God. The caption reads 'The Hair of Jesus Christ.' In it, we did indeed find hair. It has been dated through well-established scientific tests. Without doubt, it is two thousand years old!"

The congregation gasped. Many wept and fell to their knees in prayer. Ford slowly looked over the congregation and wiped his eyes.

"So, my friends, science has helped us to answer the 'how'. It tells us the hair is two thousand years old. It is from the time of our Lord." His voice rose, and he shouted: "it is the Lord's!"

Ford took a drink of water from the glass on the pulpit. The congregation was silent, in anticipation of further news.

"Now, why did this come to us? No doubt you will ask that question. Is it related in any way to the Second Coming of Jesus?" Ford shook his head. "These are our human questions. Only God can provide the answers. In the name of our Lord, Amen."

"Amen." came from the congregation. People were talking to their companions about the news. At the back of the church, the TV reporters rushed outside to be the first to break the news to their own TV audiences.

As the service ended, people crowded around Ford. Many wanted to know where they could see or touch the casket. Varley and security staff shepherded Ford to his office, and assistant ministers waited at the exits to speak to the departing crowd.

Ford disrobed in his office and sat down with a sigh. Varley poured him a coffee. Ford's hand shook as he took it.

"Mark, I hope that was what we needed."

"Jackson, that was great!" Varley drank some coffee. "Do you want to speak to any of the TV reporters, or do you want me to handle it?"

Ford was weary, and emotionally drained. "Right now, Mark, I think I need to rest. "Why don't you talk to them?"

"Okay, I'll give them a brief statement I've already prepared. We've already made arrangements to sell them your sermon. That will get the message out on an even wider basis." Varley left, walked through the church and saw several TV crews waiting on the stairs outside. They swarmed towards him. "Who are you?" "Where's Jackson Ford?" "What's going on?" "Where is the casket?" came from several quarters. Varley held up his hands.

"Ladies and gentlemen, if you'll give me a chance I have a statement to make."

The reporters gathered round. Microphones were set up in front of Varley, and the cameramen focused on him. He took a sheet of paper from his pocket.

"My name is Mark Varley," he began, "I'm a senior member of the Reverend Ford's Crusade staff. He's asked me to make the following statement." He waited as the reporters and cameramen became silent.

"Today I have informed my congregation and TV audience that we have been given, by the will of God, a casket containing hair that we reliably believe to be that of Jesus Christ. The casket is silver, and measures about four inches long by one inch deep. In it there are strands of hair, which have been radiocarbon dated and verified as being two thousand years old, the era of our Lord Jesus Christ. In addition, we have been given a document dating from the fourteenth century, which verifies the provenance of the casket to the early years. The casket and hair are in a safe and secure place. The significance of this finding is a major part of our prayerful thoughts. We will do God's will, when we have been given guidance." Varley stopped and looked over the reporters. "Copies of the statement are here for you." A staff member distributed copies to the reporters. Varley turned to leave.

"Mr Varley, will you answer some questions?" a reporter asked.

Varley shook his head and walked back into the church. Alabama State troopers prevented reporters from following, as the door closed firmly behind him. He found Ford in his office; Grace Christopherson was with him. She had just arrived and had introduced herself to Ford.

"Of course, Grace," Ford was saying, "I know who you are. You are a treasured member of our flock." He pointed to a group of armchairs arranged around a large circular mahogany coffee table. "Why don't you sit down?" He looked at Varley. "Mark, come and join us."

Varley sat to the right of Grace, while Ford eased down into a chair facing the young woman, whose nervous gaze flicked from Ford to Varley.

"Would you like coffee or water, Grace?" Varley asked.

She shook her head.

Ford looked at her with a wide paternal smile. "Grace, I know that Mark has spoken to you about an opportunity to serve the Lord. Have you had time to think about it?"

Grace's eyes blinked rapidly. "It's not been out of my mind since Mr Varley—Mark—spoke to me. I didn't know what to think. Then …" she looked at Ford, "… then I listened to your sermon today about science and Christianity; about the 'hows' and the 'whys.'" Grace smoothed her skirt and pushed back a lock of dark hair that had fallen over her right eye. "Then it came to me: if God in his wisdom had caused the casket to be given to you, it must have been for a purpose. Only he knows why." Grace looked up with her eyes raised to the ceiling. "And so, Reverend Ford, I think it is my duty to help in whatever you have in mind."

Varley looked at Ford and smiled. Ford nodded his head. He reached over to Grace and asked her and Varley to join him in prayer. They all knelt. Ford thanked God for His guidance and asked for a blessing on Grace, and what they were about to do. Grace wept. She wept tears of relief, tears of joy; and she trembled, not knowing what lay ahead. But she had confidence in Jackson Ford.

Varley gave Grace a glass of water and poured more coffee for Ford and himself. When Grace had calmed down, he told her that she should go home and pack since he needed her to accompany him on a flight to France the next day, Monday. He told her to bring enough clothes for a month and added that all her costs would be fully covered. As well, he said that her salary was now doubled in recognition of her commitment. He promised to call her at home as soon as he had made the arrangements.

When Grace had left Ford said, "What now? Shouldn't you contact Dr. Vacca? We need to move quickly before Grace changes her mind, or before the media or other others decide to intervene. Lord knows, lots of people want to get their hands on the casket or hair."

Varley agreed and returned to his office. There he sent an e-mail to Dr. Vacca.

Dr. Vacca,

We accept all the conditions you have set out.

The first payment of $500,000 will be transferred electronically to your account at Coutts Bank in London first thing tomorrow (Monday) morning.

We have identified a suitable surrogate and a donor. She is twenty-five and of irreproachable character. We are prepared to travel immediately to Villefranche to meet you and to begin the process. I will bring the hair with me. Please advise, by return, if a meeting on Tuesday is suitable and provide details of where we can meet you.

Yours sincerely,

Mark Varley.

Varley pressed "send" and, while waiting for Dr Vacca's reply, decided to contact the Crusade's travel agency. He asked them to reserve two first-class flights to Villefranche, or the closest airport in France, with open dates to return. He wanted to leave on the following day, Monday.

Varley groaned when the travel agent replied. They would fly with Northwest Airlines, leaving at 4:25 PM. There would be two stops en route in Memphis, Tennessee, and in Amsterdam. They would not reach Nice, the nearest airport to Villefranche until 10:30 on Tuesday evening. Quickly he e-mailed Dr Vacca requesting that the meeting be on the Wednesday morning since he would not arrive until late on Tuesday evening.

He did not have to wait long before Dr Vacca's reply appeared on his screen.

Dear Mr Varley,

Thank you for agreeing to the conditions and terms set out in my previous e-mail.

Provided the $500,000 is in my bank account tomorrow, Monday, I shall meet you on Wednesday at 10:00 a.m. Please go to the Welcome Hotel in Villefranche. It is close to the harbour. Ask for Dr. Stefano Donadoni, who is one of my assistants. He will bring you to me.

Please ensure that the hair is hygienically sealed.

Yours sincerely,

Dr Sophia Vacca.

Varley sighed. It was going to be a long trip. He hoped Sophia Vacca would make it all worthwhile.

Chapter 20

The next morning, Kate and Alan went for a run along the boardwalk on the shore of Lake Ontario. They passed the butterfly pasture, planted with a rich profusion of colourful flowers, among which Monarchs, Red Admirals and other species of beautifully-coloured butterflies hovered for a moment before swooping into the air.

The early morning sun shone on the boardwalk, which was becoming busier as others began their daily routine: jogging, cycling, rollerblading or simply strolling with a dog.

Tired but elated by the exercise, they returned to Alan's apartment. Kate showered first while Alan made coffee and toast. Kate took the coffee and went and sat beside a small glass table in a corner by the window. When Alan returned from his shower, they drank in silence. As if a thought had suddenly come into his mind, Alan jumped up and switched on the flat panel TV set on the wall behind them. He helped Kate to turn her chair to watch.

"I thought we might see what's happening in Ford's world. It's Sunday; I wonder if he has said anything."

"Try CNN first, Alan," Kate said.

On CNN, Cindy Ritcey's face appeared on the screen, gazing into the camera. She said, "I'm here at the Church of Christ in Montgomery, Alabama, where the Reverend Jackson Ford has preached an astonishing sermon on science and Christianity. He said that the two could be reconciled. Then he dramatically showed pictures of a casket, which he said contained some hair from Jesus Christ."

CNN flashed the photographs on the screen. "He said that the hair had been dated as being two thousand years old, to the time of Jesus Christ. And later, we were told that the provenance of the casket had been proven." Cindy looked at her notes. "In his sermon, highlights of which you will see shortly, he also asked whether the casket and the hair were related in any way to the Second Coming of Jesus Christ."

The screen flashed to Jackson Ford, standing on the pulpit and saying, "… Are we meant to do something with the hair? Is it related in any way to the Second Coming of Jesus Christ?"

The camera switched back to Cindy Ritcey. "After the service, Mr. Ford was not available for an interview. However, one of his senior staff, Mark Varley, read a statement."

The camera showed Varley reading the statement before Cindy again appeared on the screen. "And so we are left with many questions. If the casket and the hair are real, what does Reverend Jackson Ford propose to do with them? And what did Mark Varley mean, by his comment about 'doing God's will, when we have been given guidance'?" She raised her eyebrows. "Could this, in fact be in any way related to the Second Coming? There's more to find out. We will keep you in touch with CNN. This is Cindy Ritcey in Montgomery, Alabama."

Alan snorted. "Trust CNN to sensationalize things."

Kate shook her head. "On the contrary, I think that seemed to be a fairly balanced report."

"Really?" Alan grunted. "What a difference for CNN."

"What do you mean?"

"Well, my impression is that CNN is interested in events only if they happen in America, or involve Americans. Otherwise the rest of the world doesn't exist. Americans tend to be isolationist."

Kate frowned. "Isn't that a generalization?"

Alan nodded. "Yes, I guess it is. Sorry."

Kate was riled. "Well, which channels do you watch? Where do you get your information?"

"Usually from CBC, the Canadian Broadcasting Corporation. But that is also a bit isolationist. It's Canadian news mainly, and it usually has a left wing slant, particularly on anything affecting the United States."

"So what do you do?"

"Well, I try to watch BBC Newsworld. It tells me about the world in a way that I don't get from CNN or CBC." He smiled. "But again it has a left-wing point of view."

Kate chuckled. "Another item of information. Sir Alan is a Cavalier, not a Roundhead."

Alan raised his eyebrows. "I didn't know you knew about that. The English Civil War, I mean."

"I'm a fount of information, Alan Bruce, as you will find out." She patted his cheek affectionately.

Alan reached for her and kissed her neck, then her lips.

Kate released herself. "Another piece of information: Cavaliers are randy."

Alan laughed. "Guilty as charged, doctor." He rose, deep in thought, and looked out of the window, then turned to Kate. "On a more serious note, it does begin to look like Ford is going to try cloning. Reading between the lines of his sermon and Varley's statement, I can't see any other explanation. I'd like to stop them."

"But if it is God's will…." Kate said mischievously.

"You know what? Alan interrupted, snapping his fingers. "Maybe I should call Inspector Dawson in Scotland."

Kate smiled provocatively and switched the TV channel to BBC Newsworld. "That was CNN for you, let's see what your precious BBC has to say."

They waited while the BBC announcer covered a story about famine in Darfur. Then Austin Moore, the BBC's anchor in Washington said, "In Montgomery, Alabama, a strange story has just emerged from an American evangelist, Jackson Ford. He claims to have discovered a casket containing hair from Jesus Christ. Over to our reporter Simon Locksley in Montgomery." The scene switched. Simon Locksley wore glasses and had thinning fair hair. He began. "We've just heard an interesting sermon from the Reverend Jackson Ford. He has spoken about the Second Coming of Jesus Christ, and he has mentioned that he now has in his possession, in a casket, some hair belonging to Jesus. He hasn't yet revealed what he intends to do with the hair, but obviously there is some speculation. More about that later. With me now I have Monsignor Brendan O'Connell of the Roman Catholic Church." The cameras switched to show a middle aged cleric with a round face and dark rimmed glasses. Locksley continued. "Monsignor O'Connell, what do you make of what's been said today?"

O'Connell blinked several times before saying, "Well, all I've seen so far are the news highlights of his sermon. It is difficult to know what Mr. Ford has in mind. The relic, if it exists, ought to be brought forward, so that its provenance can be tested, as well as the scientific proof that he says he has about the hair being two thousand years old."

"I see," Locksley said, before introducing an idea that had just occurred to him. "When the Reverend Ford spoke about the Second Coming and the hair, do you think he might have thought about cloning Jesus?"

Monsignor O'Connell gasped. "What an appalling idea. Even if it were possible to clone a human being, it would be wrong and immoral. The church is against cloning, it risks being a tragic parody of God's omnipotence. The Pope, when he was still Cardinal Joseph Ratzinger, rejected the idea of human cloning. He insisted that the sanctity of life is untouchable." O'Connell licked his lips. "In any event, our Lord is not a human being, as you and I are."

"Thank you, Monsignor O'Connell," Locksley smiled and the camera switched back to Kathy Kay in the BBC studio in Washington.

Alan switched off the TV and frowned. "Well it didn't take them long to suss out that Ford might want to try cloning." Alan stood and went to his desk, returning with a number written on a yellow pad. "I am going to call Inspector Dawson in Scotland."

When he dialed, he was told that Inspector Dawson was off duty for the weekend. "Well that's that. Dawson isn't there. Now I'm going to switch off about Ford and Varley. I'm all yours, Kate."

She smiled. "Well, it's about time Sir Alan. What now?"

"Now, I'm going to take you for a good lunch."

Alan drove south from Toronto to Niagara on the Lake, a charming small town, about sixty miles away, and only ten miles from Niagara Falls. The small town's main street was festooned with colorful flower boxes containing geraniums of all hues.

"This is the place for theatre," Alan said. "The Shaw Festival is held here every year, with plays by Shaw and others." With difficulty, they found a parking spot on the main street, which was thronged with tourists. Horse-drawn carriages clip-clopped slowly past, with their passengers enjoying the travelogue given by the driver.

"This is quite charming," Kate said.

"And there's more." Alan led her along the street and they walked down to the lake. He pointed out where the Niagara River entered into Lake Ontario. Just a short distance away they saw the shores of New York State. Hand in hand they strolled, as Alan led Kate to Queen's Landing Hotel, which sat on a hill overlooking a marina and the blue waters of Lake Ontario. He had booked a private table by the window for lunch. It was a buffet and Kate and Alan enjoyed an eclectic array of foods.

"Cheers," Alan said, toasting Kate as a waiter opened a half bottle of champagne.

"Cheers." She touched glasses. "What a wonderful place."

"I've always liked Niagara on the Lake," Alan said. "The theatre is really quite excellent, and it's a place that I often come to for relaxation."

"So, are you relaxed?"

"No, not entirely, to be honest. But let's just enjoy ourselves for the moment." He reached over and took Kate's hand. With a catch in his voice he said, "You know Kate, I love you, I really love you."

Kate blushed and lowered her head before looking into Alan's eyes. "Alan, we hardly know each other yet."

"What does it matter? I'm used to making decisions. That one wasn't hard. You're the most wonderful woman I've ever met."

Kate laughed. "Well, you do have good judgment, I give you that." She held his hand. "For what it's worth, Alan, I think I'm falling in love with you too."

After lunch, they wandered down to the marina, and watched children feeding the swans. Hand-in-hand they returned to Alan's car.

"There's more to see," he said. He drove along the Niagara Parkway towards Niagara Falls, and pointed to the vineyards which covered the fields and hillsides. He stopped at the Whirlpool, where the Niagara River made a right angle turn, as it sped from the Falls to disgorge into Lake Ontario. They took the cable car over the whirlpool, and laughed as they watched the swirling waters below. Alan put his arm around her waist, and she leaned back into his embrace.

They were both happy on the return journey to Toronto, listening to CDs of operatic music and soft jazz. Alan turned off the Queen Elizabeth Way as he approached the Toronto city boundary and went south towards his apartment.

Kate's cell phone rang. It was Dr. Vacca. Kate listened intently, nodded a few times in silent assent, then said, "I see, Dr. Vacca. I have to speak to my partner. May I call you tomorrow?" She obviously received a positive reply for she concluded: "Thank you, goodbye."

Alan glanced across at Kate and raised an eyebrow inquiringly.

"That was Dr. Vacca. She now has to change our appointment next week; she is suggesting a week's delay."

"Why?" Alan asked.

"I'm not sure. I think she probably has other patients to see first."

"Right. Well, let's check our schedules when we get to the apartment."

Checking proved to be relatively simple. Alan was almost certainly free, and Kate had two weeks without classes to teach. She agreed to call Dr. Vacca next day to confirm.

They sat in the wicker chairs, looking out over the lake. Allen had made gin and tonics, which he placed on the glass table. As Kate lifted her glass, Alan obviously reached a decision. Without drinking, he put his glass down and disappeared. A minute later he reappeared and knelt in front of Kate.

"Kate Harris, you are the best thing that has ever happened to me," he said, looking very serious. "You've changed my life. I love you. I love you dearly and deeply. I want to spend my life with you. So, Kate, will you marry me?" He held out a small blue box.

Kate looked at Alan with tears in her eyes. She opened the box. Inside was an engagement ring. It had a large emerald in the centre, surrounded by sparkling diamonds.

Kate held out her left hand, and Alan placed the ring carefully on the third finger before kissing her passionately. She responded for a moment before saying, "But I haven't said yes, yet."

Alan kissed her again. Kate put her arms around his neck, pulled him close and murmured, "Of course it's yes, Alan. I've heard of whirlwind romances, but I never expected it to happen to me. Sometimes I think the scientist in me is too analytical, but it's been different with you. You make me laugh, and bring out a side of me that I seem to have subdued for a long time. I guess I have been too wrapped up in my career." Tears glistened in her eyes, as she stared at Alan. "You know what, Alan Bruce? I love you very much."

"This calls for champagne," Alan said, and went to the kitchen, returning with a bottle of Dom Perignon and two champagne flutes. He twisted the bottle, holding the cork steady, and then pulled the cork out with a healthy "pop," before pouring champagne into the flutes.

"But what about the gin and tonics?" Kate asked pointing to the two glasses that Alan had poured previously.

"Plant food!" Alan said, and emptied them into a potted plant that sat nearby.

Kate admired the ring. "It's lovely Alan. Where did you get it?"

"Well, it was my mother's. If she were alive, I know she would be delighted that I'm getting such a wonderful wife." He looked anxiously at Kate. "You don't mind do you?" She laughed. "No, I think it's flattering." She turned the ring on her finger, watching as the light caught the diamonds. "It really is lovely." She looked at her watch and stood. "Darling, I have a plane to catch in two hours. After we celebrate a little, will you still be able to take me to the airport?"

"It's a deal," Alan said picking her up in his arms.

An hour later, Alan drove Kate to Pearson Airport, and stopped outside the departures area. Kate didn't want to let go, and held him as they kissed passionately. A security guard knocked on the car window and told Alan that he needed to move.

Reluctantly, Kate opened her door. "I'll call you tomorrow when I hear from Dr. Vacca," she said, "and we really need to plan to get together next weekend, either here or in Boston: probably Boston, for you really ought to meet my family."

Alan returned to Palace Place, feeling elated, but lonely without Kate. How his life had changed in a few short weeks, he thought. He sat by the window, planning his next day's meetings. More importantly, he began to think about how he would break the news to Inspector Dawson about Ford having possession of the casket that Jock had buried in Melrose Abbey.

CHAPTER 21

Varley and Grace Christopherson had a tiring flight from Montgomery. After two stops, they finally reached Nice in the South of France at 10.30 on Tuesday night. Varley's travel agent had arranged a limousine, which they found without difficulty. The driver stood in the arrivals area holding a sign: "Auto pour M. Varley." He took their luggage and led them to his car, a large black Mercedes.

"*Parlez-vous francais?*" he asked.

Varley shook his head. "No."

The driver was not surprised at the answer. He smiled: "Well, I will take you to the Hotel Welcome in Villefranche."

Twenty minutes later, they reached Villefranche. The town was built on a hillside, with ancient, red-tiled buildings, cascading down towards the Mediterranean, glistening in the light of a full moon. The Hotel Welcome was a peach-coloured building on the waterfront. A porter took their bags and led them into the small entrance foyer, where a bright eyed young woman looked at them from behind the front desk.

Varley introduced Grace and himself, and then the receptionist asked them to complete the reservation forms indicating their passport numbers. "Your reservation is for two nights, monsieur?" she asked.

"Yes," Varley said, "but it could be longer."

"That might be difficult, monsieur, we are always heavily booked."

"Oh, well, let's just see how it plays out," Varley grunted. He was tired and wanted to sleep.

The receptionist gave them the room keys and a porter took their bags.

"Goodnight Grace," Varley said. "Let's meet for breakfast at eight tomorrow morning."

Grace nodded. This was all a new experience for her. She had never been in France, and she was exhausted from the lengthy flights.

Varley opened the door in his room which led to the balcony, and sat outside, gazing over the harbour, where a variety of ships bobbed at anchor in the pale moonlight. It was peaceful and tranquil. Tomorrow, he might see Villefranche in a different light.

Next morning, Grace joined Varley in the small dining room for the continental breakfast. She poured some orange juice into her glass and took a roll, butter and some cheese from the table on which a selection of food was arranged.

Varley sat drinking coffee and signalled to Grace to sit with him. "Did you sleep well, Grace?" he asked.

"Yes, thank you. I was so tired, but now I feel quite rested."

"Great. When we finish breakfast, let's go for a walk. We don't have to meet until 10 o'clock."

It was 8:30 a.m. by the time they finished breakfast. They left the hotel and walked towards the seafront passing a large bust of Jean Cocteau on a raised dais.

"Cocteau," Grace read. "He was a famous poet, writer and film director."

"You're well-informed." Varley replied.

"Well, I read about his career at school: he was multi-talented."

They walked along the seafront. To the left, opposite the Mediterranean, they saw many restaurants, now closed, but obviously busy with tourists in the evening. Beyond the restaurant area, they entered a series of small cobbled passageways, leading up the hillside towards the main road. People were beginning to open cafes and shops ready for the day's activity. Villefranche had become a magnet for cruise ships, many of which anchored in the morning in the bay's deep waters, before sending thousands of tourists towards the town for a day's sightseeing.

They returned to the Hotel Welcome. As they entered the lobby, the receptionist at the front desk waved to Mr Varley. She pointed to a chair in the corner where a dark-haired man wearing jeans and a T-shirt, sat smoking. "You have someone who wishes to see you, Mr.Varley," she said.

Varley shook hands with Stefano Donadoni and introduced Grace.

"Please follow me," Donadoni said in his Italian-accented English. He led them to the small harbour surrounded on two sides by red-roofed buildings. Tenders for cruise ships were entering and leaving at regular intervals, while the passengers jostled for position to get off the tenders, so that they would have first choice of the taxis lined up at the dockside to take them to Nice, Monaco, Monte Carlo or the hillside artistic colony of Saint Paul de Vence.

Donadoni led them to a small boat, where a sailor helped them to board, and then manoeuvred the craft through the cruise ship tenders which were docking.

"It won't take long," Donadoni said, sensing that Grace was nervous. He pointed to a white motor yacht sitting at anchor two hundred yards out in the bay. "That's where we're going," he said, indicating a craft called the 'Nova Wisp.'

Varley looked at the ship. It was about one hundred and fifty feet long. "That's Dr. Vacca's?" he asked. "Not quite," Donadoni replied. "She is renting it for six months so she can continue to work."

"And you work with her?" Varley asked.

"Yes, I also am a doctor, a specialist in laboratory and reproductive medicine. A challenging job."

They reached the Nova Wisp, and a sailor helped them to board. Donadoni led them aft and knocked on a door before entering. Sophia Vacca sat behind a mahogany desk. She was impeccably groomed, with her dark hair once again in a chignon.

"Mr Varley," she said, "welcome. I have had the transfer confirmed with my bank. Now we should discuss the arrangements."

Dr Vacca turned to look at Grace. "And who is this?"

Varley introduced Grace.

Dr. Vacca looked at her appraisingly. "You are in good health?" she asked.

"Yes, I am," Grace replied.

"Well, we'll see about that. Stefano, take Miss Christopherson to the examination room. I will see her in a few minutes."

When they left, Sophia Vacca motioned to Varley to sit down. She leaned back in a chair behind her desk, and slowly crossed her legs. Her brown eyes stared at Varley. "Mr. Varley, I hope you realise what a major task you have asked me to perform. Cloning is difficult, if not almost impossible, at best; but to attempt it with hair from someone who lived two thousand years ago?" She raised an eyebrow. "I had to think for a long time before agreeing to even consider the task. God knows I love a challenge. But this is the most demanding thing I have ever tried to do." She shook her head, acknowledging the difficulty she faced. "However, I am a scientist and an explorer of the unknown. It is not in my nature to admit defeat and so," she raised her shoulders expressively, "I accept the challenge."

Varley sat quietly. Dr. Vacca continued.

"Now, this young woman, Grace Christopherson, is she to be the egg donor?"

"Well, yes, but she will also carry the child."

"Well that simplifies my task, but only slightly. Now does she meet the criteria I set out in my e-mail?"

Varley pulled out his copy of the e-mail and examined it for a moment. "Well yes," he said. "Grace meets all the criteria, except for the fact that she has never borne a child. She's still a virgin."

Dr. Vacca smiled. "A virgin? What a delightful find in a woman in her twenties."

Varley sat quietly while Dr Vaccca continued. "Perhaps you will let me see the hair."

Varley opened his briefcase and gave her a pouch in which Ford had inserted most, but not all, of the hair from the casket.

Dr. Vacca took it and shook her head. "That's it?"

"Yes, and we tried to provide hair with roots."

"Better than nothing, I suppose." Dr Vacca frowned. "I'll have to see what I can do with it. Unless I can extract DNA and sequence it, we will not be able to proceed. You understand that?"

Varley nodded.

"Right. Now I will examine Miss Christopherson. If she seems suitable, I intend to sail tomorrow evening to get into international waters. There I will attempt to clone the individual from two thousand years ago. A saint, you say?"

Sophia Vacca smiled. She suspected who the "saint" might be. But if it were true, and she succeeded, her fame would be world-wide. Her scientific pedigree would be enhanced. She looked at Varley, who sat quietly, considering what was passing through her mind. He suspected that Sophia Vacca might have gleaned some information from the TV programmes in America. Probably some of this information had been transferred to European screens.

Dr. Vacca continued, "If my examination of Miss Christopherson is successful—that is, if she appears to be a suitable candidate—I will want her to stay on board with me for at least two weeks."

"Do you have accommodation?"

"There is one guest cabin available at present. Nova Wisp has a crew of nine sailors. That is why my expenses are high." She stood. "Now, Mr Varley, perhaps you will allow Stefano to show you to the lounge. You can wait there until I complete my examination."

An hour later, Dr. Vacca entered the lounge. She sat on a sofa, across from Varley. "So far, so good," she said. "I think Grace Christopherson will be a good subject." She gazed at Varley for a moment, attempting to assess his understanding and motivation. "I take it you have explained what is going on to her?"

"She is well aware of it, and she wants to be involved."

"Very well, I shall have to have you sign a formal contract and an indemnity should anything go wrong. Miss Christopherson will also have to sign a similar document, acknowledging that she agrees to participate in a research project which could have adverse consequences." Dr. Vacca handed him some legal papers.

Varley glanced at them. "I'll need time to examine these."

"Naturally. I must know your answer by this time tomorrow. If it is positive, I plan to sail with Miss Christopherson, and begin the preparations." She stood. "And now, Mr. Varley, Stefano will take you ashore. Miss Christopherson is comfortable here. If you agree to the terms, perhaps you will bring her case from the hotel, when you return tomorrow."

Back in his room at the Hotel Welcome, Varley rang Ford's office in Montgomery. He was told that Ford was in a meeting with the Governor and would call as soon as he could.

Varley decided to spend the intervening time reviewing the documents that Dr. Vacca had given him. The agreement was quite clear, and the indemnity appeared not to be contentious. However, he decided he would ask Ford when he called, to have them reviewed by the Crusade's attorney as a matter of urgency, because he had to give a "yes" or a "no" to Dr. Vacca the next day.

Ford rang about an hour later. Varley told him about the meeting with Dr. Vacca and agreed to fax the legal agreement immediately, since Ford already had his attorney with him. The documents went through with only a slight delay, and Ford told him that the attorney was going to look at them immediately in an adjacent office.

"Mark," Ford continued, "my attorney was with me when I met with Mike Malloy. That meeting has just finished and you should know about it." Varley heard Ford take a deep breath before he said, "the Governor came to see me, because of political pressure he is getting. Indeed, the President has now become involved. He called Mike and asked if there was any truth to what he called the Jesus Casket." Ford groaned in disbelief. "It's truly amazing that this catch-phrase of the media has become adopted into political language. In any event, the President said that such a relic ought to be in the Smithsonian in Washington."

"Did you agree?"

"Of course not; and Mike saw my point. If we can keep the casket here in Montgomery, perhaps in a shrine in our church, we will bring hundreds of thousands of tourists to Alabama. Mike saw that by doing so, he could take credit for creating jobs here. Not an insignificant objective when he's moving into a re-election campaign."

"I can see that," Varley responded.

"So, Mike is going to call the President—fortunately, a Republican like himself—and explain the situation. He expects that the President, for political reasons, will need to make it public that he believes the casket should be in the Smithsonian. But Mike thinks he won't push it."

"Has Mike thought about any religious points of view, say from the Catholics? You heard what Brendan O'Connell had to say on CNN."

"Yes, Mike's aware of that. He thinks that if he speaks to the Bishop and perhaps proposes a multi-faith—Christian faith, that is—shrine, the Catholics won't make any noise."

"But what about the Vatican?"

"Mark, you know as well as I do that the Vatican will want the casket in Rome. But that won't work. The President could hardly agree to having it leave the States."

"I guess that's true, but I hope we can avoid getting caught up in a political or religious battle."

"Whatever God wills will be, Mark," Ford replied. There was a pause before he said, "Hold on a minute, Mark. John Clark, our attorney wants to speak to me." There was silence for a few minutes then Ford spoke again. "Mark, good news. John doesn't think there's anything to trouble us in the documents you faxed. You can sign them on behalf of the Crusade."

He thanked Ford and said he would call next day, when he had spoken to Dr. Vacca. Varley went to the bar and had a large bourbon on the rocks. So far, so good, he thought. Finishing his drink, he left the hotel and climbed up the hill to the Citadel, the sixteenth century fortress, which looked out over the harbour. In the distance he made out the white hull of Nova Wisp, and wondered how Grace was feeling.

In fact, Grace was confused. She had willingly agreed to help Ford, but when the extent of what she had to do had been revealed, she had been upset and anxious about her future. Ford and Varley had reassured her, and had promised to look after her for the rest of her life. So, she had prayed, and eventually it had come to her that she should do as Ford had asked. Now, here she was aboard Nova Wisp, with this Italian doctor who seemed very efficient, but a bit cold. Perhaps all researchers were like that, she thought. On the other hand, she had a luxurious suite with a bedroom, sitting-room and private bath, and a steward who looked after every need. Perhaps it would all work out.

Varley returned to the hotel and phoned Nova Wisp. He spoke to Dr. Vacca and said that the agreements had been reviewed and that he was authorized to sign them.

"Good," Sophia Vacca replied. "Please bring them with you when you come back to Nova Wisp tomorrow morning. Stefano will meet you in the lobby of your hotel at 10 tomorrow morning. And please don't forget to bring Miss Christopherson's case."

"Does that mean she is suitable?"

"I believe so. The next few weeks will give us an answer one way or another."

At 10 the next morning Varley met Donadoni in the lobby. As before, they took the small boat back to the Nova Wisp, where Varley met Grace and gave her the suitcase with her clothes.

"Are you OK?" he asked.

"I think so. It's a bit difficult to get my head around this, but I'm sure it is for the best. It's what Reverend Ford believes to be right, isn't it?"

Varley took her hand. "Of course, Grace." He looked into her eyes. "Is your accommodation comfortable?"

"It's perfect. Quite luxurious, in fact."

"Good. Well Dr. Vacca tells me she expects everything will work out. Please call me as often as you like. I expect to be back in a few weeks' time to collect you and take you back to Montgomery."

"A few weeks? It will take that long?"

"I'm not sure. I'll ask Dr.Vacca to talk to you. But don't worry: if you have any concerns just call me and I'll come back for you."

Varley left to see Dr. Vacca, convinced that Grace would settle down on board the ship. They met in her office, where she took the legal documents from him and confirmed that they had been signed. She signed a copy and gave it to him. "For your records," she said. "I hope you will not need the indemnity. Apart from that, my initial examination of Miss Christopherson shows she is very healthy. She is also at a point in her monthly cycle that means we should be able to proceed with harvesting eggs in a week or so."

"And then?"

"Ah, then! Then we will see if your Saint's hair can work magic. We need a miracle, Mr. Varley. I will do what I can. But as a Christian, I advise you to pray. I will call you when I have confirmed the viability of the DNA. That will be a discovery." She smiled. "After that, we will try for a miracle!"

CHAPTER 22

Alan's phone rang in his apartment at 6:00 a.m.. It was Inspector Dawson.

"Good morning Sir Alan. This is Inspector Peter Dawson of the Lothians and Borders police. I hope this is not too early for you."

Alan smiled. It was 11:00 a.m in Scotland, so certainly not too early for Dawson. He took the phone into the kitchen and started to brew his morning coffee. "No, Inspector, I needed a wake-up call."

"Oh! Sorry about that sir, but you did leave a message asking me to call you."

"Yes that's right. You see, I've been watching TV programmes here in North America, and I've seen that Jackson Ford, the televangelist who was in Edinburgh recently, claims to have a casket containing hair from Jesus Christ."

Dawson laughed. "Yes, it was on the BBC News last night. These Yankee evangelists will do anything for publicity."

"No, it's true," Alan said. There was a pause before Dawson replied in very sober tones.

"Really, what makes you say that?"

"It all goes back to what my grandfather, Sir Jock Bruce, told me shortly before he died." Alan recounted Jock's letter, telling of Bruce's heart being taken to Spain by Sir James Douglas, and being returned after Douglas' death by King Alfonso, along with the casket containing Jesus' hair.

"You see, Inspector," Alan continued, "this casket was supposed to have been buried with Bruce's heart at Melrose. But, for whatever reason, the Bruce family at that time decided to retain it. So it stayed in the family, handed down from generation to generation, until Sir Jock. Then Robert the Bruce's heart was found at Melrose Abbey in 1996, and re-interred there in 1998. Jock decided, with the agreement of Donald Dewar, to correct the decision reached many centuries before. Donald Dewar, you may remember, was the Secretary of State for Scotland at the time."

Dawson interrupted. "Yes, I once had a meeting with Donald Dewar: a fine man."

"Well," Alan continued, "Jock placed the casket beside Bruce's heart, just before the plinth was covered."

Dawson replied quickly. "So you are implying that Ford, or someone in his employment recovered that casket from the plinth?"

"Is there any other explanation?"

"I can't see one at present," Dawson replied.

"There's another thing, Inspector," Alan continued, "In the TV news here, there was a piece showing Jackson Ford's sermon, and also an earlier interview he had given on CNN. In that, he referred to having a letter from a Spanish king proving the provenance of the casket. Well, the letter he has is an English translation. His henchman, Mark Varley, took it, I believe, from my grandfather. I challenged him about this when I saw him in Edinburgh, and he returned it, or purported to do so, though I'm certain he must have made copies."

Dawson interrupted. "And where does that information lead?"

"Well without the original, they don't have real proof of the casket's provenance, do they?"

"I suppose not,' Dawson replied. "So, where is the original?"

"It's in a safe place in Edinburgh, Inspector."

There was silence, while Peter Dawson digested the importance of this news.

"Let me see if I have this straight, Sir Alan," he said. "Ford has the casket purportedly containing Jesus' hair, and that's in Montgomery, Alabama. He can't prove its provenance without the letter. And you have the original letter, or know where it is in Edinburgh. So you can prove the provenance, but you don't have the casket!"

"Well put, Inspector," Alan laughed. "It does begin to sound like a Catch-22. However, my point is that Ford has stolen the casket from its resting place at Melrose Abbey. I want it to be returned there, as my grandfather wished, and consistent with the stated intent of King Alfonso, so many centuries ago."

Dawson was silent for a moment. This was all becoming rather complicated. "I need to think about the next steps," he said, "and it would be helpful if you could provide proof that Sir Jock did actually bury the casket beside Bruce's heart. Otherwise, I'm afraid we are left with a simple case of vandalism of the plinth."

"I'll see what I can do, Inspector," Alan said. "Goodbye."

He went over the conversation, and realised that he had inadvertently credentialed Ford's story about the casket, by citing its provenance. So, if people began to learn that the relic was genuine, there was no way on earth that he would ever be able to have it re-buried at Melrose Abbey. Still, he would find a way to ensure that it came back to Scotland: the least he could do for his family, he felt.

Alan had an urgent meeting with the hospital's lawyers starting at 8:00 a.m.. When there was a break at 10:00 a.m., he called Bruce House. Jamie Robb answered.

"Jamie, this is Alan Bruce in Toronto."

"Aye, Sir Alan. How are you?"

"Fine, Jamie. I'm in a meeting right now, but I needed to ask a question. Did you ever hear Sir Jock speak about a silver casket?"

"No, he didn't speak about it. He kept it locked in his safe. I saw it there once."

"Good, and do you know what happened to it? It wasn't in the safe, you know, after Sir Jock's death."

"Well, I didnae steal it, if that's what you're suggesting!"

"No, no, of course not. Sir Jock told me what he had done with it. Did he tell you?"

"No, he was always very circumspect, if that's the word. He kept his business affairs private."

"And what about Mrs. Doig, would he have spoken to her?"

"Just a wee minute. Sarah's here. I'll ask her." He returned after a minute. "No, Sarah knows nothing about a silver box."

"Okay. Thanks Jamie. I hope to see you soon. Bye."

Alan frowned. It was going to be his word, and perhaps Kate's—for she had also been present when Jock told his story—against Ford's. All he had was hearsay evidence, apart from the letter. Ford, however, had the casket. He smiled. He had the locket with some of Jesus' hair. That might still be important in thwarting Ford.

* * * *

Kate was facing a busy day in Boston. She had classes to teach and a faculty meeting to attend. At 9:00 a.m. she dialled Dr. Vacca's phone in France. There was some static on the line before a voice said: "Nova Wisp."

"May I speak to Dr. Vacca?"

"This is Dr. Vacca."

"Dr Vacca, this is Dr. Kate Harris in Boston. I just wanted to confirm my meeting with you next week, that is on Thursday week."

"Yes," Sophia Vacca replied, "I should be back in Villefranche by then. If not, I'll call you forty-eight hours in advance. Stefano Donadoni, my assistant, will wait for you in the lobby of the Hotel Welcome at 10:00 a.m.."

The line went silent, Kate shook her head. Sophia Vacca might be a first-class researcher, but she had little business sense.

* * * *

In Edinburgh, Inspector Peter Dawson shook his head, as he spoke to colleagues at the front of the office. He was going off duty. "What a day," he said. "Remember the vandalism at Melrose Abbey? I just heard from Sir Alan Bruce in Toronto. He's the heir to Sir Jock Bruce, and he says he has a letter from a Spanish king in the fourteenth century, that proves that yon Jesus casket that they're talking about on TV is real!"

People laughed. "Aye" said one policeman, "and so is the Loch Ness Monster!"

Nearby, sat a BBC reporter, Harry Valentine, who had been waiting for an interview about a drug bust in Leith, Edinburgh's seaport. He sensed the makings of a story. He left and went to the BBC studios in SW Thistle Street Lane in Edinburgh. There he decided to call Alan Bruce in Toronto, prior to recording a piece on tape, which he hoped would be shown later.

* * * *

Kate spoke to Alan in the middle of the afternoon, and they made plans to fly to Villefranche on the following Tuesday.

"That's great, Alan. You'll arrange the flights?"

"Yes. Do you want to fly from Toronto or Boston?"

"Boston," she said, "and why don't you come here for the weekend. You can meet my family. After all," smiling as she said so, "I had met yours."

"That was only Jock."

"I know, but that's all the family you had, sadly."

Alan agreed to meet Kate in Boston for the weekend, before returning to the conference room. The final details of the contract with the hospital had been agreed. All that remained was to have the papers signed by the clients. He left and drove home. As he entered his apartment, the phone rang. It was BBC Scotland.

"Sir Alan Bruce?" the voice enquired. "My name is Harry Valentine. I am a reporter from BBC Scotland."

"Yes," Alan said wearily.

"I believe you have in your possession an original letter from a Spanish king which provides proof of what is being called the Jesus Casket. Is that correct?"

Alan put his hand over the phone and gasped. How had the BBC got to know about the Alfonso letter?

"Letter?" he asked. "What are you talking about?"

"Well, I believe you have such a letter, and that it's here in Edinburgh. Can you confirm that?"

Alan thought for a moment before deciding. "Yes I do have that letter. It's from King Alfonso XI of Castile and Leon."

"And that is the provenance of the casket that Reverend Jackson Ford says he has in his possession in Montgomery, Alabama?"

"That casket should be in Scotland. It's not Ford's. It belonged to my grandfather, Sir Jock Bruce."

"So how did Reverend Ford get possession of it?"

"You'd better ask him."

"Thank you, Sir Alan." Harry Valentine put down the phone. He definitely had a story to tell. He spoke to the director of BBC news and prepared his presentation, which would be shown on the BBC Newsworld TV channel around the world later that day.

Harry Valentine's story flashed on Alan's TV screen as he watched BBC Newsworld's 9:00 p.m. news report. He listened with growing astonishment as Valentine's report unfolded. Valentine was in his early thirties, with dark hair, a small moustache, and a long face with a prominent nose.

"This is Harry Valentine in Edinburgh. Today a new slant on the so called Jesus Casket that the American televangelist Jackson Ford says he has in Montgomery, Alabama. Earlier, the Reverend Jackson Ford said he had a letter from a Spanish king that proved the provenance of the casket. So far, apart from saying he received the casket while he was here in Edinburgh during his recent campaign, Ford has not released any further information. Neither has he shown the casket itself, only a photograph; and he has not produced the letter.

"Today, in an interview with Sir Alan Bruce, who lives in Toronto, and is the heir to the late Sir Jock Bruce, new facts emerged. Sir Alan Bruce says that the casket belonged to his grandfather, and that he has the original letter proving its provenance. In fact, he said that letter is in Edinburgh and that the casket should also be here. So who is right, Ford or Bruce? Furthermore, I believe an export licence would be required if the casket was to be exported from the UK." Valentine smiled and waved his right hand. "So far as I have been able to establish to date, no such export licence has been issued. That might mean that the Reverend Ford will be required to return the casket to Scotland. That would certainly make Alan Bruce, at least, happy."

Alan turned off the TV and chuckled. Yes, indeed, that would make him happy! On an impulse he rang Kate. She answered after two rings.

"I don't suppose you've seen the BBC Newsworld report just now?" he asked.

"No, I'm watching CNN. Why?"

When Alan told her, Kate laughed aloud. "Why that's just great. Ford will be on the hot seat tomorrow."

"Oh! You'll probably find out that CNN has caught up to the story by then," Alan said with mild sarcasm."

"Certainly it will. After all, it's about an American, and it's in America!" she replied, before laughing. "Game, set and match, Alan!"

Despite himself, Alan chuckled. "Right. You win. See you on Saturday. Love you."

Chapter 23

The white motor yacht, Nova Wisp, sailed serenely through the calm blue waters of the Mediterranean. In the distance, Grace Christopherson saw the rustic red roofs of Villefranche dwindling in size, until the land itself became a blur. She stood on the deck, watching white waves break over the ship's bow and then change into a luminescent path behind the ship, marking its path through the sea like a softly shining ribbon of white tying it to the distant shore.

Standing in the bright sunshine, Grace was filled with a sense of happiness. She had been orphaned at an early age, and with a modest education she had seized on the opportunity a year earlier to join Jackson Ford's Crusade for Christ. Already she had visited Scotland, and now she was in France, in the Mediterranean. In fact, she felt she was setting out on a great adventure. She wore a white blouse and white linen pants and had tied her hair with a green ribbon. For the first time in her life she glowed with a sense of purpose.

Sophia Vacca touched Grace's shoulder. "Miss Christopherson, please come with me."

Grace followed Dr. Vacca along the deck to a cabin at the rear of the ship. It had been converted into a doctor's examination room, with an examination couch and a wall-mounted blood-pressure cuff. Dr. Vacca sat down at a small desk and looked at Grace. "You do realise what we are going to do?"

Grace nodded.

"Tell me, in your own words."

Grace, bit her lip. "Well, I'm going to become a mother—a surrogate—at least that's what I've been told."

Dr. Vacca looked sternly at Grace. "And do you know the identity of the father?"

Grace shook her head. "No, not really. Reverend Ford told me that God would direct the process." She stared intently at the doctor. "If God is behind it, it must be the right thing to do."

Vacca sighed. The girl was really quite simple—she had to be; however, that was not her problem. She looked at Grace and said; "As a doctor, I have to advise you that there are risks associated with cloning."

"Cloning?" Grace asked. "I didn't know that's what you're going to do."

"Well, it is. There will be no father present to impregnate you in the normal way. We will use a donor's DNA to fertilize your eggs. Then it, or they, will be returned to your body to see if we can achieve pregnancy." She stopped and looked at Grace. "Do you agree to that?"

Grace looked down at her lap where her fingers were tightly clenched. She blinked a few times and then said in a soft voice. "Yes, that must be what Reverend Ford wishes. He is a good man, a prophet. I always follow his advice."

Dr. Vacca gave a soft sigh. "Very well, then. I need you to sign a consent form. It describes the process we will follow, and also outlines the specific risks or complications that might arise. You should not sign the form, or proceed with the process, unless you are completely satisfied. Do you understand?"

"Of course. If I have any questions, will you help me find answers?" Grace took the form and placed it on the examination couch.

"Yes, of course I will provide answers," Dr. Vacca reassured her and placed a pen down on the desk in front of Grace. "Now, I'll leave you to read the consent form. When I return, let me know if you have any reservations about proceeding. Ask me anything you're not sure of. I cannot proceed until you have signed the form." With that, Dr. Vacca stood, and left Grace alone. She returned a few minutes later. Grace had no questions; the consent form had been signed.

Dr. Vacca left Grace once more, and found Stefano Donadoni in the laboratory, which had been created in what had previously been a large lounge area. It was well equipped with a DNA sequencing machine, centrifuges and microscopes, all of which Dr Vacca had leased. Donadoni had several hairs with the roots attached and was beginning the attempt to extract DNA. He was looking for DNA in the hair root, for it contained the nuclear DNA that Dr. Vacca needed.

"Let me know when you have any results, Stefano," Sophia said before returning to see Grace. In a few days, provided Stefano had extracted the DNA by then, she would take several eggs from Grace's ovaries and remove the genetic material.

Then she would inject the cloned genetic material and pass an electric current through the dish in which they were held in the laboratory. She would then wait and see if a miracle of life could be created.

* * * *

Back in Montgomery, Varley returned to a media storm. Ford had hidden from the reporters calling for interviews. He was very relieved that Varley was back. Mark was the best person to deal with the likes of CNN and Cindy Ritcey.

Jackson Ford slumped in a large armchair in his office. He had shadows under his eyes and was not sleeping well. Varley was concerned, because Jackson Ford would have to be at his most commanding and authoritative if they were to benefit from the publicity that they had expected, although it was now proving to be a bit overwhelming.

"Jackson," Varley said, "you look exhausted. You need to rest. I'll take care of the media."

Ford nodded in appreciation and closed his eyes for a moment's thought. He sighed. "Sometimes, you know, Mark I wonder if we should have forgotten about the casket and about cloning. It's all getting a bit much. However ..." and he began to relax slightly: his shoulders visibly fell, and his hands were placed on the arm of the chair. "... However, that's my mere mortal reaction." He smiled. "When I pray, I feel that we are doing what is expected. If it weren't so, surely God would prevent the cloning."

Varley nodded his agreement. "Of course, Jackson. We will complete what we set out to do."

Ford stood and lifted a coffee decanter that stood at the side table.

"Coffee, Mark?" He poured coffee for them. "You've been travelling, Mark, so you may not have seen a report on BBC Newsworld last night. I don't watch that show myself, but it has created a bit of an uproar here in the States. Cindy Ritcey has been phoning for an interview to follow up on it, and the BBC now have a team here in Montgomery. They also want to speak to us."

Varley hadn't seen the BBC programme from the previous evening, but Ford had been given a tape of Harry Valentine's televised report, which they both watched in Ford's office. Varley scowled when he heard that Alan Bruce had said he had the *original* letter from King Alfonso, and that the casket should be returned to Scotland. When he heard Valentine's comment about the need for an export licence, he frowned.

"I didn't think about that. But then again we didn't know." Varley switched off the tape.

"What now, Mark?" Ford asked.

"I guess I'd better get our attorney to look into the export licence issue. After that, I'll deal with the media." Varley returned to his own office and rang John Clark, the Crusade's attorney, and advised him of the issue. Clark said he would get back to him in a few hours after he had checked on the export licence requirements. Varley's phone rang half an hour later. He picked up the receiver, expecting to hear John Clark. But instead it was Inspector Dawson in Scotland.

"Mr Varley, this is Inspector Peter Dawson in Edinburgh. Sir, we have been advised by Sir Alan Bruce that a silver casket that is alleged to be in your possession belongs to him."

"Preposterous! I received it from a person who wanted to help our Crusade."

"Really, sir? Would you care to let me know that person's name?"

"No. He wanted to be anonymous, and that's the commitment we made."

"And did this person tell you how he came to have the casket in his possession?"

"No, that was not a concern of mine," Varley said.

"Well, if I were to tell you that Sir Alan Bruce said that the silver casket had been buried at Melrose Abbey beside the heart of King Robert the Bruce, would that help your recollection?"

"Sounds like a fairytale."

"Perhaps," Dawson paused, "but you will no doubt recall that when we met I was investigating a death at Melrose Abbey, and the vandalism of a plinth where Robert the Bruce's heart had been interred?"

"Yeah, I remember you saying that."

"So, circumstantially, Sir Alan's tale might be true."

"Still seems like a fairytale to me," Varley replied.

Dawson changed tack. "By the way, Mr. Varley, do you have an export licence for the casket?'

Varley knew it was time to say "no comment."

"Inspector, I don't see that that is an issue I should discuss with you. Now if you'll excuse me, I have another call to answer."

Varley hung up, shaken by the fact that Alan Bruce had now started to go public about the letter and the casket. He hadn't expected that. As for the export licence, he hoped John Clark would give them an answer before too long.

Luckily, he did not have long to wait. Five minutes later, Clark called with good news. Although the UK had a system of export controls designed to prevent the export of items listed as "national treasures," the United States did not apparently subscribe to any international conventions.

"Furthermore," Clark said, "while an export licence was required for exports outside the UK of, and here I quote, '... archaeological material or any object more than fifty years old, found in UK soil or its territorial waters other than any object buried concealed for less than fifty years ...' close quote, in practice there were well documented cases of such material being exported without a licence. So, Mark," Clark concluded, "you have nothing to worry about with regard to the UK trying to get the casket back. They don't have sufficient grounds, as far as I can see."

Varley was very relieved. It could have been huge, but now it was one less problem to deal with, he thought.

After lunch, Ford asked Varley to join him in his office. Governor Mike Malloy was there, along with his chief of staff. They sat in dark blue leather chairs, around the cherry wood conference table. "Jackson," the Governor began in his formal style, "I wanted to talk to you about all the publicity you're getting *vis-à-vis* the casket." He spread his hands expressively. "What is it they say? All publicity is good publicity?" He laughed. "Simply not true for a politician. That's why I'm here, Jackson. Frankly, I'm getting heat from the opposition about the support I've given you. Now, I don't mind, that is part of political life, after all. But last night I'm told there was a programme on the BBC, now repeated on some of our local channels, that said you needed an export licence from the Brits for the casket, and you don't have that. Tell me that's not true."

Ford looked anxiously at Varley, who smiled. "Yes that's true, Governor."

"Then why are you smiling, damn it?" Malloy shouted, his hand striking the table angrily.

"Because our attorneys say we don't need one. The States doesn't recognize such things. As well, there have been lots of examples of the Brits letting items leave the country without a licence, so it's a red herring."

Ford looked relieved. Malloy's shoulders shook with laughter. "Son of a gun! That's great." he said, and pointed a finger at Varley. "Mark, you've got to let the media know without delay. It will get a monkey off my back for sure, and it will help your cause."

Not to mention your re-election, Ford thought.

When Malloy left, feeling happier than when he had arrived, Varley looked at the list of telephone calls. Cindy Ritcey of CNN had called seven times; and a guy by the name of Simon Locksley of the BBC had been almost as persistent. Varley decided the obvious answer was to hold a press conference, inviting all the media who wanted to attend, otherwise he would be caught up in an endless series of repetitive interviews, some of which might work in his favour, but more likely he would be caught saying slightly different things. He didn't want to dilute his message.

The press conference was set for 5:00 p.m.. His staff sent notices to the national and local media and arranged space in the conference hall adjacent to the church.

At five o'clock Varley entered. Five or six TV crews were present, as well as reporters from various newspapers. Varley put on his glasses and looked slowly over the reporters who were arranged in rows, below the level where he stood on a small stage behind a lectern.

"Ladies and gentlemen, my name is Mark Varley. I am the CEO of Jackson Ford's Crusade for Christ. I have a short statement to make. Then I will answer a few questions." He picked up a sheet of paper from the lectern in front of him, and said, "We in the Crusade have been advised that, last night, certain allegations were made on a TV programme by BBC's Newsworld, which challenged ownership of the casket mentioned in the Reverend Jackson Ford's service and programme last Sunday. These allegations are false. The casket was received by us from an anonymous donor. At the same time, the late Sir Jock Bruce freely gave me an English translation of a letter from King Alfonso XI of Leon and Castile to his ancestor, King David I of Scotland. In that letter King Alfonso asked that the casket, whose provenance he confirmed, should be interred beside King Robert's embalmed heart, in recognition of the great assistance that he, King Alfonso, had been given by King Robert's friend Sir James Douglas, who had been killed helping Alfonso fight the invading Moors in Spain. That was in 1331. Many years later, in 1996 to be specific, archaeologists unearthed a lead casket at Melrose Abbey in Scotland. After examination it was determined by an agency called Historic Scotland that the heart was most likely that of King Robert. It was apparently re-buried in a formal ceremony at Melrose Abbey in 1998. At no time, neither in 1996 nor in 1998, was there any reference to the silver casket mentioned in the BBC programme. In fact, it is now obvious that it had not been buried with King Robert's heart, as King Alfonso directed. What happened to it in the intervening years is not known. However, its provenance is proved by the letter from King Alfonso, and the casket itself is now here in safe hands in Montgomery."

Varley looked over the assembled media to whom copies of the statement were being circulated. Staff handed copies into the eager hands of reporters, who started to shout questions.

"Ladies and gentlemen," Varley said, raising his hands, "I said I will answer a few questions." He pointed to Cindy Ritcey of CNN, who jumped to her feet.

"Mr Varley," she began, "won't you tell us the name of the person who gave you the casket? It would help answer a lot of questions we have."

Varley smiled. "I've already said that the donor was anonymous and wishes to remain so. However, if he wants to come forward ..." He shrugged his shoulders.

"Mr Varley, I'm Simon Locksley of the BBC. Last night we heard from Sir Alan Bruce, who said that the casket belonged to his family, and specifically to his late grandfather, Sir Jock Bruce. Now would Sir Jock have given you the casket? Was he the anonymous donor?"

Varley smiled inwardly, but kept composed for the reporters. This was too good to be true, he thought. Aloud, he said, "As I've already mentioned, the donor wishes to be anonymous. I have no further comment on that subject."

Simon Locksley held up his hand. "One final question, Mr Varley. Do you hold an export licence for the casket?"

Varley shook his head. "No. It is not required in the United States." He looked at the reporters. "Thank you, that is all."

Returning to Ford's office, he noted that Jackson had been watching on the Crusade's close circuit TV. Ford jumped to his feet and shook Varley's hand. "Mark, that was magnificent. A tour de force. Congratulations."

"Thanks, Jackson. I hope it will help to curb the media frenzy. More importantly, it will be good publicity for your programme next Sunday." He lifted his chin aggressively. "What's more, since this started, our campaign donations are up by 15 per cent, so the public is really interested."

Ford's eyes widened. "Really? That's good, I'm sure; so long as they are beginning to make a commitment to Christ."

Varley laughed. "Of course. Once we have them by their wallets, their hearts and minds will follow!"

* * * *

The next day, Nova Wisp had reached international waters, at least twelve nautical miles from any country. It cruised slowly beneath the bright blue sky. In the distance, the white hull of a cruise ship steamed towards Naples, farther south down the Italian coast.

Stefano Donadoni sat in his laboratory, with Sophia Vacca. "Success," he said, "I have the DNA."

Dr. Vacca nodded. "Good. When I have extracted eggs from Miss Christopherson we will begin."

She left and took Grace to an adjacent room set up for an operation. Stefano Donadoni entered. Initially he had trained as an anaesthetist, but had later branched into laboratory medicine. Donadoni used the ultrasound to visualize Grace's ovaries, and smiled contentedly as the monitor displayed Grace's left ovary, where he saw fifteen fluid-filled sacs, each containing a single mature egg. Dr.Vacca nodded as she looked at the monitor and worked quickly, so that within thirty minutes she had the eggs she needed. Together, she and Donadoni returned to the laboratory, leaving Grace to recover. They worked as a team, having rehearsed the procedure many times while working together on experiments.

Over the next two days, they observed the dish in which the eggs lay and saw cell division taking place. On the third day, Dr. Vacca decided it was time. Grace was taken into the small operating room and given a sedative. The fertilised egg was injected into her uterus. Now the waiting began, to see if she would become pregnant. Dr. Vacca took regular blood test specimens from Grace, and Donadoni checked the hormone levels. At last he smiled. The pregnancy was confirmed.

Sophia Vacca rang Mark Varley's office in Montgomery.

"This is Dr. Sophia Vacca," she said when he answered. "The second instalment of five hundred thousand dollars is now due."

Varley gasped. "You mean you've done it? Grace is pregnant?"

"Yes, why else would I call you?"

"OK, OK, I understand. I'll get the five hundred thousand dollars wired to your account in London. When can I see Grace? I'd like to bring her home."

"I will call you again to let you know a date, just as soon as I receive confirmation of the bank transfer," she replied, before the line went dead in Varley's hands.

Elated, Varley rushed along the corridor to Ford's office, where Jackson sat with his fingers steepled as he began to compose his sermon for the following Sunday's service. He looked up in astonishment. Mark Varley did not usually rush anywhere, as his bulky body attested.

"Jackson, great news. Grace is pregnant. I just heard from Dr. Vacca."

Ford sank to his knees. "Please join me in a prayer of thanks, Mark," he said. "A new page will open once Grace returns to us."

CHAPTER 24

Kate met Alan on Saturday when he arrived at Logan airport. They kissed and held hands as they walked to her car. Kate flashed her engagement ring in front of Alan. "Everyone thinks it's wonderful," she said. "What a beautiful ring."

They reached her car. On the drive to her parents' home Kate gave Alan a pen picture of her family. "Dad—Bob—is an investment banker, so hopefully you'll have something in common with him."

"Give him my investments, you mean?"

Kate playfully slapped his knee. "Well, you could do worse!"

"And your mother?"

"Mom's an academic; a professor of English literature. She's a sweetheart; you'll like Beth. My sisters, Emma and Julia, are on the West Coast, so all you have to worry about at present are Mom and Dad."

Kate turned into a driveway. The old brick house stood in a wooded area, surrounded by a mature garden where beds of petunias, roses, and geraniums splashed colour over the green lawn. A large oak tree stood to one side of the house, and cast a shadow over the front porch, where Bob Harris stood casting an appraising eye over Alan. Bob was over six feet tall with dark grey hair and moustache. Alan, returning Bob's look, noted that Bob had blue eyes and a small gap between his front teeth. At Bob's side Beth Harris looked like an older version of Kate. Her hair was cut short, and her green eyes sparkled as she surveyed Alan, the young man who intended to marry her daughter.

They shook hands and entered the house. The front foyer was wide with dark-stained wood flooring and a Persian carpet. Beth led them into the living room, which had a large bay window at one end and a marble fireplace to the right. Pale ivory sofas faced the fireplace, and an eclectic selection of chairs was placed around the room.

"Would you like a drink, Alan?" Bob Harris asked.

"Well I suppose a gin and tonic would hit the spot," he replied.

"Right: good choice," Bob said and walked to a richly-lacquered cabinet to the side of the window, where he pulled out a bottle of Tanqueray gin.

Beth and Kate stood. "We'll get ice," they said and left.

Alan knew he had been left alone with Bob for a reason. Bob gave a knowing smile, and also disappeared into the kitchen. He returned in a moment, with a container of ice. "How many lumps?" he asked.

"Two, please. Any more kills the taste."

"Right." Bob Harris walked over and gave him a glass. They touched glasses, while Bob sat opposite Alan and took a sip of his drink. He smiled and said, "Beth and I are delighted at the news of your engagement, Alan. I've seldom seen Kate happier." He paused, and swirled the ice in his glass, before looking into Alan's eyes. "The girls have left us alone for a reason, I suppose. Having been through this twice before, with Kate's sisters, I guess this is the point where I'm supposed to ask if your intentions are honourable?"

Alan smiled. "Oh, I wouldn't go that far!" he replied. They both laughed, and Kate and Beth reappeared.

"He'll do!" Bob said, and Kate kissed her Dad.

The weekend was also another opportunity for Alan and Kate to find out more about each other. They explored the Quincy market with its myriad stalls selling food, especially lobster. Outside on the cobblestoned streets of the Faneuil Hall Market Place, they laughed at the antics of the jugglers, and swayed to the music of a steel band. Alan had never been there before and was enthralled by the place's energy and colour. They returned to the Harris house to find Beth Harris standing outside waiting for them and looking flustered.

"What's the matter, Mom?" Kate asked.

Beth shook her head. "I'm sure it's nothing, but Alan has been mentioned on CNN. They had an interview last night with someone called Mark Varley, and he said that Alan had a historic document that proved that this so-called Jesus casket, that's been in the news recently, is true." Beth looked at them with concern. "Is it true Alan?"

Kate and Alan looked at each other. Alan spoke. "Yes it's true, Beth. Let's go inside and I'll tell you the story."

Bob and Beth Harris sat silently on a sofa while Alan told them the history of the Alfonso letter and the casket, as it had been told to him by Jock. But he did not mention the gold locket Jock had given him.

"After that," he went on, "the plinth at Melrose abbey was vandalised—smashed—and in no time it came to light that Jackson Ford had the casket. However, I've no real way of proving that my grandfather actually put the casket in beside King Robert's heart, although I'm sure that it was."

"There's no doubt about the provenance of the casket," Kate joined in, "the letter makes the connections. But, you know, the most important thing is the hair. I've had it carbon-dated. It is roughly two thousand years old."

"So this story about Jesus' hair is true?" Beth asked, while her hand pulled nervously at her necklace.

"It would seem to be," Kate replied, smoothing her skirt over her knees.

"And," Alan interrupted, waving a hand in front of him, "we don't know what Ford or Varley intend to do with the hair." He shook his head. "All this talk of the Second Coming of Jesus makes me wonder about cloning. I'm not really sure what they'll do if they succeed."

Bob Harris stood. "Well, that's certainly one of the best and most intriguing topics for a dinner conversation I have heard in a long time." He looked at his watch. "I've a table for the four of us at my club in an hour's time. Perhaps we should allow the ladies to freshen up." When Beth and Kate had left, Bob looked at Alan and frowned.

"One thing troubles me about what you've said about the casket, Alan. On the TV news, showing a press conference with Mark Varley of the Jackson Ford crusade, he said that if the casket had been buried with the king's heart, as the letter from that Spanish King—Alfonso, or something like that—had directed, then why wasn't the casket found at the same time that the heart of Robert the Bruce was found, way back in 1996?"

Alan rubbed his chin. "Because back in the fourteenth century, my ancestors apparently decided to keep it. Then, many centuries later, my grandfather Jock decided to correct that omission. He placed the casket with the heart." Alan shook his head. "But I don't have proof—at least proof that would meet the requirements of a court."

The weekend went too quickly for Kate and Alan. They had an enjoyable time together, and before Alan kissed Kate goodbye at Logan airport on Sunday, he agreed to come back on Wednesday to catch a flight to Nice. From there they would go to Villefranche to meet Dr. Vacca.

Alan reached his apartment around 9:00 p.m.. The phone was ringing, and a flashing light indicated that he had messages waiting. The caller rang off before he reached the phone, so he dialled star 98 to get his messages. There were twenty, almost all from media who wanted an interview. He deleted these without replying, then rang Kate to let her know that he had arrived safely in Toronto, and that the media were pursuing him.

"Don't speak to them, Alan," was Kate's advice. "Try to keep a low profile. We don't want the media following us when we go to France."

Alan agreed and said goodnight. He went to his fridge, poured a cold beer into a glass and sat in the corner by the window. He ran his fingers through his dark hair, and put his feet up on the coffee table. What was he getting into, he wondered?

His thoughts were interrupted sharply by the ring of the phone. Probably the media, he thought; but on instinct, he rose, drink in hand, and walked to the kitchen. He looked at the screen on the phone. It was long-distance. The caller showed as Jackson Ford Crusade for Christ. He shook his head in disbelief. What could they possibly want? Curious, he lifted the receiver and said, "Hello."

Mark Varley answered.

CHAPTER 25

It was Sunday morning in Montgomery, Alabama. Outside the church, long lines of people waited to get in. The media was assembled in force, possibly even more than the previous week, Varley thought, as he looked out from Ford's office window, overlooking the parking area and the approach to the church. Ford seemed tranquil, almost mystical. In his hand he held the casket. It had been polished and now gleamed brightly, catching the rays of the sun shining in through the window behind him.

"This is the day, Mark, the day that the world will see the casket in which our Lord's hair has been preserved for all these many centuries." Ford's eyes sparkled, and his smile showed his sense of being part of destiny.

"The hair is in a safe place?" Mark Varley enquired.

"Why yes, apart from the hair you took when you visited Dr. Vacca."

"That was the hair we selected, mostly the hair with roots attached as she requested?"

Ford nodded his head.

"So, the rest is in the safe at the bank?" Varley asked.

"Yes, it should be secure there." Ford began to don his white robe before brushing his hair. He looked in a mirror on the wall to satisfy himself about his appearance. "And now, Mark, it is time for the service."

Varley left and took his place on the platform. The organist began to play the first hymn, and the blue-gowned choir, men and women of different ethnic back grounds, entered at the front entrance to the church and proceeded slowly down the aisle in two lines. The music swelled, and the voices of the choir rang out in a rolling harmony, which swept over the congregation, as they advanced towards the platform. At the rear came Jackson Ford. A spotlight caught him, a symbol of good and purity, suggested by his white robe and white hair. In his hand he carried a wooden box.

A murmur ran through the crowd. Was this the so called Jesus casket, people whispered? The Crusade's TV cameraman caught the scene for the millions watching the now-syndicated programme, arranged through Varley's negotiating skills.

The choir reached the platform and divided into two lines, one to the right and one to the left. They ascended the stairs and arranged themselves like a blanket of blue flowers in front of the rows of seats behind the pulpit, still singing the hymn. Jackson Ford took the right set of stairs, slowly walked across the platform and ascended the pulpit.

The hymn ended. The congregation sat rapt, expectant, not knowing what they were about to hear; but eager; curious about the box that Jackson Ford briefly held in the air before placing it before him on the lectern. He looked over the congregation, scanning to the left, then the right, to ensure that everyone present felt included, embraced by his gaze.

"What a showman!" Cindy Ritcey, seated at the back of the congregation, whispered to her neighbour.

"Don't knock it. He's a publicity machine," came the reply. "A natural."

Ford welcomed the congregation and led the prayers. The service followed the usual pattern of hymns, readings from the Bible and prayers, before it was time for Ford's sermon. The silence was complete in the church as everyone waited to hear Ford's words.

He lifted his hand and a spotlight shone on him, while the lights in the church dimmed. He was a messianic figure on TV.

"Today," he began, "my sermon is based on faith. Faith is the essence of Christianity. Our faith is based on facts. We know that the Bible is reliable in what it says. Our history is important." Ford raised his right hand dramatically. "Historians test the reliability of ancient accounts. They challenge and question. Quite rightly, they ask questions to help them reach conclusions to prove facts. Questions such as: can the listed events be corroborated from more than one source? During the many years since the initial event has the story been told accurately and without biased change? The New Testament passes all of these tests. The Bible itself was written over many years, by many different authors. They were kings and common folk, just like ourselves. The Bible was written in different languages—Hebrew, Aramaic, and Greek. It is a best-seller in the world. Why? Because of the truth it tells and the faith we have as Christians."

Ford went on to elaborate for another ten minutes, then paused and drank some water. His eyes scanned the congregation, so that everyone present felt that they, and they alone, were the object of his attention for a fleeting second. He lifted a wooden box and held it aloft. Dramatically, he lowered the box then, as the TV cameras zoomed in, he removed a silver casket. The congregation gasped. Ford held it silently, watching as a spotlight shone on its polished surface.

"*Capillus Jesu.*" Ford read the words engraved on the casket. "The Hair of Jesus Christ," he shouted, eyes wide open as if in rapture.

"Hallelujah!" cried many in the congregation.

Ford raised his right hand to command attention, while the casket remained tightly grasped in his left hand. "This casket was given to us during our crusade in Scotland. Its provenance is known. It came to Spain originally, having been found in the Holy Land by the Empress Helena, the mother of Constantine the Great, who helped to establish Christianity. It was kept for many centuries in a convent in Spain before King Alfonso sent it to Scotland to the young King David, the heir of King Robert the Bruce, a famous historic figure, who helped to free Scotland from domination by England. Its history since then is unclear, but what is certain is that it is genuine. It does contain hair, the hair of our Lord and Saviour. The letter verifying that, is indeed from the time of King Alfonso, whose letter gives details of the provenance of the hair. And the hair has been confirmed as being two thousand years old. It dates from the time of Jesus."

Ford paused dramatically and raised his hands in the air, before shouting. "It is the hair of Jesus Christ!"

People in the congregation fell to their knees in prayer. Shouts of "Hallelujah!" rang out through the church. At the rear, Cindy Ritcey shook her head.

"What a charlatan," she said.

"Yes," said her companion, "but a very effective charlatan."

Ford held his hands aloft, waiting for silence before continuing.

"Our faith is confirmed. Jesus is with us now and for ever. Amen."

As the service ended, the choir slowly moved through the aisle towards the front door, where they turned right towards the changing rooms; Jackson Ford followed behind them holding aloft the silver casket. He was followed by two Alabama State Troopers, who had been charged with ensuring its safety. Ford passed the casket to them, and they took it immediately into an ante-room where Varley met them. He took the casket and locked it in a safe. There it would lie until the troopers accompanied Ford to the bank where the manager had arranged to be present to see that the vaults were opened to secure the relic.

Ford shook hands with the departing congregation, many of whom wanted to see, touch, or hold the casket. To each, Ford's reply was concise. "Perhaps, in time."

The media began to line up for interviews, but Ford shook his head. No point in trying to upstage himself. His message was already out. However, that did not satisfy the media. The news programmes carried highlights from Ford's sermon, and many reporters began to question the provenance of the casket.

On CNN, Cindy Ritcey had a typical commentary.

"Today in Montgomery we heard again from Reverend Jackson Ford about the so-called Jesus casket. Last week he showed a photograph of the casket. Today, he went one better." The TV screen showed the moment when Ford had held up the casket in the church.

She continued. "So we saw the silver casket, said to have contained the hair of Jesus, but no hair was shown. Apparently it is being kept in a safe place. However, in his sermon, Reverend Ford said that there was proof of the hair being genuine. Seemingly, it all goes back to a Spanish King, Alfonso XI, who sent it to Scotland in the fourteenth century. Why he would do that is unanswered at present, because Mr. Ford won't speak to us directly."

"So," she smiled, "we're left with doubts in our minds. Jackson Ford in his sermon spoke about faith and about historical accuracy. Fine, here is my question to him: why don't you show us the *original* letter from King Alfonso, so we can judge for ourselves whether the provenance of the casket is correct? And, by the way, can you also provide proof of the dating of the hair? That also would perhaps help to convince those who are, at present, sceptical."

Ford and Varley sat together in Ford's office watching the news. "How can she say such things?" Ford scowled. He shook his head. "Where is the charity in the media?"

Varley shook his head, removed his glasses, and rubbed his eyes.

"It doesn't exist Jackson." he said, "However, you got the point across in your sermon about faith and history, so people like Cindy Ritcey will not trouble too many people. Not at present, anyway." He put his glasses on. "I think at some point we may have to get the hair dated. That will help convince the media, and the public, that it is genuine. Really, we are going on what I heard from Sir Jock Bruce" He frowned as he recalled his wire tap. "But, you know, it would help if we had the original letter from Alfonso."

"How could we get it? Ford asked anxiously. "Doesn't it belong to Alan Bruce?"

"Yes," Varley said. "Perhaps I should call him. We might be able to negotiate a deal." He dialled directory enquiries, and asked for the number for Alan Bruce in Toronto. He found there were twelve matching names and obtained all the numbers. It took seven calls before he was answered by the Alan Bruce he wanted. The conversation was brief and unproductive as far as he was concerned. Varley shook his head as Alan Bruce hung up on him. He sighed, removed his glasses and rubbed his eyes. He leaned back in his chair and put his feet on his desk deep in thought. Then he snapped his fingers, and smiled, before dialling a number from his private list. Bruno Conti answered from New York.

"Bruno, it's Mark Varley."

"Mark, you guys sure are getting lots of publicity, all on account of that box we dug up in Melrose."

"Yes I know. Don't say anything about that to anyone. I have already had calls from the police there. They suspect something about Andy McPhee, the guy whose head stopped that stone you dropped!"

Conti laughed loudly. "Yeah! What a pity he got in the way." He became more serious. "You haven't said anything to the police, have you?"

"No, I wouldn't do that Bruno. But now I need you to do something else for me. I want you to visit Alan Bruce in Toronto. He's a lawyer, has his own firm, at a place called Commerce Court. Here's what I want you to do ..."

CHAPTER 26

"Mr Bruce," the voice said, "This is Mark Varley in Montgomery, Alabama."

Alan looked in disbelief at the phone. What did Varley want, and how did he manage to get his number?

"What do you want, Varley?" he growled.

Mark Varley answered in a pleasant tone,. "I just wanted to have a talk with you, Alan."

"Don't Alan me! What do you want?"

"Well, if we have to move to business right away—okay, I would like to purchase the Alfonso letter from you. The original."

Alan laughed. "Not a chance. Why don't you give me back the casket, and we'll forget that we ever knew each other?"

"As you say, not a chance," Varley replied. "We have the casket and we're keeping it."

"And I'm keeping the original letter. So we are at an impasse."

"I'd prefer that we weren't, Bruce. What would it take to get you to change your mind? One hundred thousand dollars? Two hundred?"

"I don't bargain like that, Varley." Alan thought for a moment and then said, "Tell you what, Varley, return the casket to me, and I'll speak to Inspector Dawson in Scotland. He is anxious to find out how you managed to get the casket from the plinth containing King Robert's heart."

Varley laughed mockingly. "That old story again! Face it, Bruce, there's no proof that the casket was ever buried there, as it should have been, according to Alfonso's letter. It wasn't found in 1996, when the archaeologists supposedly discovered the heart, and no one saw it being buried with the heart in 1998, so your story is full of it. Politely, it's a fairy tale."

"No," Alan replied, "it's no fairy tale. You and I both know that, and I suspect that you were involved in vandalising the plinth at Melrose and stealing the casket."

Varley laughed, mockingly. "That's slander!"

"Not if it's the truth, as I've said to you before. Besides, I'm not repeating that to anyone—at present." Alan changed the subject. "What are you doing with the hair, Varley? I hear talk of cloning."

"Don't believe everything you hear," Varley said, then mischievously, he added, "but don't disbelieve it either."

Alan did not intend to let Varley gloat, so he added. "Two can play at that game."

Varley raised his eyebrows. Could it be that Alan Bruce had some of the hair from the casket? If so, what was he going to do with it?

"You mean you have some of the hair?"

"None of your business," Alan snapped, and hung up.

In Montgomery, Mark Varley stared at the phone for a moment before putting it down. This might be a potential complication. He didn't think for a minute that Alan Bruce would attempt cloning. It was an expensive and risky business, after all; but he couldn't take chance that Bruce would do so, and perhaps pre-empt or mock the sincere attempt the Crusade was making to clone Jesus. After thinking for a few minutes, he decided to call Bruno Conti.

*　*　*　*

The next day Alan had several meetings outside his office. He returned after lunch to find a heavy-set man with dark hair sitting in the reception area. He nodded at him and went down the corridor to his office. Donna, his secretary followed. "Mr Bruce, the gentleman in reception is a Mr Conti from New York. He would like to speak to you about a retainer to help his business."

"Give me a few minutes Donna. I've a few things to do. I'll buzz you when I'm ready."

Alan emptied the files from his case and called one of his associates to brief him on some of the information he had obtained at his meeting that morning with a client. There would have to be a few minor adjustments to the contract, but nothing serious. With that out of the way, Alan rang Donna and asked her to bring Mr Conti to his office.

Alan rose from his desk and looked at Bruno Conti, a well-dressed American with a friendly smile. They shook hands and Alan led him to a conversation area in his office where several chairs were arranged around a large coffee table. Donna asked Conti if he would like coffee, and disappeared to fetch it.

"Mr Conti," Alan said, "what can I do for you?"

Bruno Conti opened the buttons on his suit jacket, which was straining to contain his bulk. He smiled, quietly assessing Alan Bruce, for he'd learned over the years to gauge the mettle of opponents, many of whom later regretted underestimating his cunning, which lay beneath an apparently simple surface.

"Well, Mr Bruce," Conti began, "I'm involved in the arts business in New York. We deal with ancient paintings, manuscripts and such. Although we are not Sotheby's, we do have an exclusive set of clients who are always looking for priceless works." He handed Alan a business card which he had quickly printed in New York, after his call from Varley. Alan glanced at the card, noting that Bruno Conti described himself as a fine art dealer, based in New York. He gazed questioningly at Conti.

"I see, Mr Conti, and why do you need a lawyer, especially a lawyer in Canada?"

Bruno Conti opened his hands expressively. "We are always looking for business, no matter where the opportunity arises."

Alan began to smell a rat. "I see. And why me? I don't have any clients in the arts business."

Conti's eyes opened in mock astonishment. "Really? I was told that you might have an ancient manuscript for sale."

Alan realised his instincts had been correct "Who told you this? Mark Varley, by any chance?"

Conti gave a deep theatrical sigh. "I'm sure you realise I can't divulge the name of clients."

"No, but I can guess."

Donna entered with coffee, but Alan waved her away. "Well, you can tell Mr. Varley that the manuscript is not for sale, no matter what."

Conti puffed out his cheeks and let out a loud sigh. He looked calmly at Alan for a moment. "So you're not willing to negotiate a price?"

"No, I'm not!" Alan's voice rose in anger.

"Mr Bruce," Conti said, "I really hope you can be persuaded. It would be best for you."

Alan stood. "I think you should leave," he said, pointing to the door.

Slowly Conti stood and advanced to within a foot of Alan. "I'll leave for now," he said. He tapped his finger against Alan's chest. "But I'll be back. If you won't accept a reasonable offer, we'll have to find some other way to convince you, if you follow me."

"Don't try to threaten me," he said, striking Conti's hand. "The law deals very effectively with people like you in Canada."

Conti smiled and turned away. He paused at the door, then turned to face the obviously angry Alan. "There's no need to threaten me Mr. Bruce. But I if I were you I would think seriously about my offer. We will pay good money for the letter. One way or another we will get it." He left, nodding to Donna on the way out. "Thanks for the coffee," he said sarcastically.

Conti took the elevator to the ground floor of the Commerce Court office building. He looked around, and a slim young man with close-cropped black hair and a dark stubble on his face walked to meet him. Conti pointed to a corner area where several seats lay vacant. They sat, and Conti handed the young man a brochure that he had lifted while waiting in Alan Bruce's office. It showed a photograph of Alan Bruce. He pointed to it. "Fabio, I want you to follow this guy wherever he goes. His name is Alan Bruce. He's a lawyer, and his office is on the twenty-second floor. Let me know what he does, where he goes. You know where to get me. My cell phone is always on."

Fabio Trento took the brochure He was used to working with Conti, both in New York and elsewhere. "Sure thing, Bruno," he said. "I'm ready for anything."

Conti shook his head. "No physical stuff: not yet anyway. Just follow him wherever he goes." He passed an envelope to Fabio. "Here's ten thousand dollars. If you need more for expenses, let me know. You can put it on your credit card. I'll pay it."

"Okay, Bruno." Trento slowly got to his feet. "I better get to the twenty-second floor to keep an eye on this guy."

When Alan left his office at three o'clock to catch the flight to Boston, a slim man with dark stubble followed him into the elevator. Alan carried a case with him. He waved a taxi forward to take him to Toronto's Pearson Airport. Fabio Trento took the next taxi and followed Alan. He bought a ticket to Boston, after he noticed that Alan had checked in for that flight. When they had disembarked in Boston he saw Alan meet Kate and go to Northwestern's departure gate. He took note of the flight and rapidly purchased a ticket. He was seated three rows behind when the flight took off for Amsterdam. Before leaving Boston, he managed to phone Conti. "Bruno, I'm about to board a Northwestern flight to Nice, via Amsterdam. Alan Bruce is on the flight with a young woman. Quite a looker."

"Damn," Conti thought. Why is Bruce going to Nice? He would have to let Varley know. It might be important.

"Good, Fabio. Watch them carefully and call me when you get to Nice. I want to know what they're up to."

Trento was seated three rows behind the couple as the plane left Logan airport. He saw Alan turn to speak to Kate, but couldn't hear what they said.

Alan held Kate's hand as he told her about Varley's phone call and the visit from Conti.

"They're getting desperate," Kate said.

"Sure looks like it." Alan shook his head. "I really don't like to be threatened. It just shows how desperate they seem to be. They want the original Alfonso letter to verify the casket and the hair. But why?" He rubbed his chin. "I can only think it is to verify their provenance."

"Why is it so important to them?" Kate asked.

"Well, of course it must be because they plan to do something with the hair."

"Cloning?"

"Yes, that has to be it."

Kate swivelled in her seat, her knees brushing against Alan's. "And we are going to clone also, just to thwart them?"

"Yes, I think so. Maybe I'm being silly about all this, but it's all I can think of at present."

"So when we see Dr. Vacca, what do we say?"

Alan rubbed his chin again. "Well, first of all I want to know if it's possible to use the hair, or its DNA for cloning. That's the first step. If it is, then I'll need to find an egg donor and a surrogate. If it's not, then I can relax. For then I'll know that Ford and Varley won't succeed. I can go back to being a lawyer, and your husband-to-be."

Kate laughed and held his hand. "OK. That seems clear enough. We'll talk to Dr. Vacca and take it from there. If necessary, I'll donate some eggs." She laughed. "My God, I feel like a broody hen saying that!" She bit her lip and laughed, pushing back some hair that had fallen over her left eye. "Broody hen! I've never said that in years. My Scottish grandmother used to say it. What I mean is, I'm prepared to help, Alan." Alan leaned over and kissed her.

Three rows back, Fabio Trento watched, and wondered about what he would do in Nice.

CHAPTER 27

On arrival in Nice, Alan found a taxi to take them to the Hotel Welcome in Villefranche. Fabio Trento followed and lingered outside the hotel, while Alan and Kate checked in. Ten minutes later he entered, walked through the small lobby and approached the receptionist at the front desk. No, he did not have a reservation, but he needed a room. He booked for five nights, just to be safe and took the stairs to his room. While signing in, he had glanced at the reservation card the receptionist had lying on the desk in front of her. It was Alan Bruce's, and he was in room 32. Fabio requested a room on the third floor, and accepted the key to room 34, right next door to that of Alan and Kate.

In his room he phoned Conti in New York. There was no reply, so he left a message to let Conti know where he was, and went downstairs to the lobby, where he picked up a magazine and sat in a corner chair to observe the passing human traffic. Three laughing young French women passed by, and he watched admiringly as they swayed down the front steps. Time enough for that later, he thought. For now, he had to concentrate on Alan Bruce's movements.

In room 32, Kate sat on the edge of the bed. She stretched and lay down. "Lord but I'm tired," she said. "That was a long journey."

Alan yawned. "Yes, I wouldn't want to do that every day." He stretched out beside Kate, put an arm round her and promptly fell asleep. Kate looked at his face, relaxed in sleep. She watched his breathing become slower as he slipped into a deep sleep, then yawned and followed his example.

Two hours later Alan's cell phone rang. He had left it in his briefcase, which sat on top of a small table beside the balcony. He groaned and mistakenly reached for the phone on the bed-side table and sleepily said, "Hello." There was no reply, just a dial tone. He shook his head and realised that the ringing was coming from his cell phone across the room. He got up and reached it on its last ring. It was Hamish McColl, the Bank of Scotland manager in Edinburgh.

"Sir Alan, this is Hamish McColl. I'm sorry to disturb you, but I need to speak to you urgently. Your office in Toronto gave me your number. I hope you don't mind."

"No, of course not, Mr. McColl. What can I do for you?"

McColl coughed. "Well, it's slightly embarrassing, Sir Alan."

Alan interrupted. "Please call me Alan, or Mr Bruce."

"Really? The baronetcy you hold is an ancient one."

"I know, but it doesn't cut any ice in Canada, so I prefer to be called Mr Bruce, or Alan—as you wish."

"Right then, Alan. The reason I am calling is that we have been approached by the Lothians and Borders police, investigating an alleged murder in Melrose. They want to examine a manuscript they believe we have in our safety deposit vaults. They believe it belongs to you."

"Why do they want to do that? What does it have to do with me?"

"That I don't know, but there is an Inspector Peter Dawson, who wants to see the alleged manuscript. Of course, I told him that it is not possible to open a safety deposit box without your consent. He acknowledged that, but said that if you don't agree he will obtain a court order."

"Can he do that?" Alan asked.

"I believe so. However since you are on this side of the pond, so to speak, I wondered if you might want to come to Edinburgh at your convenience to sort this out. The bank doesn't want to become involved between the police and a customer. But we may be compelled to open the safety deposit box, if we receive a legal order."

Alan looked out of the window and saw the tenders approaching the harbour from a large white cruise liner moored in the bay. It was so tranquil, but in Edinburgh events were developing that he had to control. He made up his mind.

"Tell Inspector Dawson that I'll try to be in Edinburgh tomorrow. I need to check on flights, but I assume I can meet him at the bank late tomorrow morning."

"Thank you, Alan," McColl replied. "I'll let him know."

Kate stirred in the bed. She stretched lazily and opened an eye. "What's going on?" she asked.

Alan told her of his conversation with Hamish McColl. "So, I think I should go over to Edinburgh tomorrow. It's probably nothing, and I should be back the following day."

"What do you want me to do?" Kate asked. "Come with you, or stay here?"

"Probably best that you stay here. If Dr. Vacca calls, you can tell her what we want to discuss. I'll leave the locket with you. If she can't extract useable DNA, then we know that the cloning won't be possible and I—we—can relax about Ford and Varley."

Kate looked at him and lay back on the bed with her chestnut hair outlined against the pale blue pillow. She closed her eyes. "Meanwhile," she said huskily, "why don't you come back to bed?"

Alan rose early the next morning and got a taxi he had booked the previous evening. His KLM flight left Nice at 6:10 a.m. and, with one stop, he was in Edinburgh just after 10:00 a.m.. He took a taxi to the Bank of Scotland's offices on the Mound, between Princes Street and Edinburgh Castle. Having established a flight time, after his talk with Hamish MacColl the previous afternoon, he had alerted Cameron Learmonth, his grandfather Jock's lawyer, and now his own Scottish lawyer. He decided to meet him at McColl's office.

Arriving at the Bank's headquarters on the Mound, he was taken immediately to Hamish McColl's office. Cameron Learmonth was already there. Not unexpectedly, as movers and shakers in Edinburgh's fairly narrow elite society, the two knew each other.

"Yes," Cameron Learmonth said, "Hamish and I often golf together at Muirfield."

Alan declined the offer of tea, which McColl and Learmonth sipped. He wanted to get right to the point. "Mr. McColl," he said, "I flew here this morning from Nice to try to establish just what is going on."

McColl put down his teacup. "Well, Mr Bruce, I did explain it over the phone, and I've also alerted Cameron here to the issue."

Learmonth nodded. "It's not unusual, Alan, for the police to try to establish proof of ownership: at least I think that's what they're trying to do."

Alan was exasperated. "Proof of ownership? What proof do they need? Yes, there is a manuscript in a safety deposit box. The box was my grandfather's, as you know, and I am his heir. So when I inherited his estate, the content of that box also became my property."

"That's true," Cameron Learmonth agreed: "but as I understand it, the police want to know how an ancient manuscript, which the media are now fancifully calling the Alfonso letter, came to be there?"

"It had to have been put there by my grandfather. It was there when I opened the box."

McColl and Learmonth looked at each other before McColl coughed and said, "I believe you. However, I'm sure that Inspector Dawson will try to get confirmation of that. Was anyone with you when you opened the box, by any chance?"

Alan thought for as moment before replying. "Why, yes. I remember it well. Dr. Kate Harris, a family friend then, and now my fiancée, was there. She can confirm that the letter was there."

"Good," Cameron Learmonth said. He looked at McColl. "That being the case, Hamish, providing Alan agrees, we can talk to Inspector Dawson.

"Right, then," McColl said, "my secretary will show you to a room just along the hallway. You can meet him there."

Alan followed Learmonth and the secretary into a small conference room. The window looked out over Princes Street Gardens, a delightful sight normally, but the sound of passing traffic from the Mound was a distraction.

Inspector Dawson stood to greet them. He provided a complete contrast to the blue pinstriped suits worn by the Edinburgh lawyer and banker. He wore a casual grey herring-bone tweed jacket, and dark grey trousers. Alan smiled as he noted the contrast. Cameron Learmonth took the initiative.

"Inspector Dawson, I am Cameron Learmonth, Sir Alan Bruce's solicitor. I am here to help with your enquiries, for I understand, that is the intent of this meeting."

Dawson looked at Learmonth. "I see. I didn't think Sir Alan would need a solicitor. Not yet anyway."

"That's good, Inspector. Why don't you get to the point?" Cameron interrupted.

"Fine," Dawson said. He shrugged and took out a pen and placed it on a pad lying on the conference table.

"Well, here's the issue. As Sir Alan knows, we've been investigating an act of vandalism at Melrose Abbey. At the same time as that was discovered, a dead body, the body of a guide at the Abbey, was found some distance away in the latrine pit as it turns out. He appears to have slipped and banged his head before falling into the water at the bottom of pit. We're not sure yet if it was an accident, or something more. However, since then, I have been told by Sir Alan that he alleges that a silver casket containing alleged hair from Jesus Christ, was stolen from the plinth at the Abbey. He's told me that his grandfather buried the casket beside the heart of Robert the Bruce in 1998. We've all seen the reports in the media that Jackson Ford, that evangelist fellow from the States, says he now has such a casket. And Sir Alan has told me that he has the original of a letter purporting to provide proof of the provenance of a casket answering such a description."

"Yes, yes," Learmonth interrupted, waving a hand disdainfully. "We've all read these stories. What does that have to do with Sir Alan?"

Alan looked at Dawson. He felt the policeman was getting to the point.

"Quite simply, Mr Learmonth, the point here is that we have just recovered some tools—to be precise, a pick axe, a sledgehammer, a small hammer, and a chisel—from a river outside Melrose. We believe these tools may have been used in the vandalism at Melrose Abbey."

"And what does that have to do with me?" Alan asked.

"Probably nothing, sir, but we have to eliminate potential leads. You see we have some fingerprints on the tools."

Alan snorted derisively. "And you think they might be mine, is that it?"

"As I've said, sir, we have to eliminate all possibilities."

"OK, but what has that got to do with the Alfonso letter?"

Dawson smirked. "Well, sir, it's been suggested to me—not that I believe such a thing of course—that you might have smashed the plinth and removed the casket, and that the letter might also have been there."

Alan threw up his hands in disbelief. "That's preposterous. The letter was in Sir Jock's safety deposit box. And I don't think I've ever been in Melrose, certainly not in the last five or ten years. Perhaps my parents took me there when I was younger, I can't remember, but I certainly haven't been there recently—and that I definitely do remember."

Learmonth frowned and said, "These are fairly serious allegations, Inspector. I really do caution you to proceed carefully."

Dawson nodded. "Oh I will, I will, Mr Learmonth." He gazed at Alan. "We can put this to rest, I believe, if two things occur."

"And they are?" Learmonth enquired.

"Well firstly, I would like to take Sir Alan's fingerprints. That should establish whether or not the prints on the tools are his. Secondly, we will need a sworn notarised statement from Dr. Harris concerning the events at the bank, when Sir Alan first opened the safety deposit box."

Learmonth raised a hand to object, but Alan waved it aside. "It's OK, Cameron. He can take my prints—I have nothing to hide. And I'll make sure that Dr. Harris provides a notarised statement within the next week."

"Excellent. I can take your prints right now, if you agree."

Alan did, and Dawson took the prints before raising an eyebrow. "Now, about the manuscript …?"

Hamish McColl led Learmonth, Alan, and Inspector Dawson to the bank's vaults, and inserted the bank's key in box A238. Alan took his key from a key fob and opened the box. At the bottom, as he had left it, lay the envelope with the original of the Alfonso letter.

"That's where I found it. I suspect that my grandfather must have put it there."

Inspector Dawson looked at the ancient parchment, an edge of which peeked out above the envelope in which it was contained. He pulled it out, and frowned. "This seems to be in Latin, if I'm correct," he said.

"Correct, Inspector. Is that a problem?" Alan asked.

"Well since I can't read Latin, I'm not likely to be able to confirm the mention of a silver box, am I?" Dawson replied.

"If it will help, Inspector, I can translate for you." Cameron Learmonth took the parchment and began to read it quietly, his finger tracing the words. "Ah, yes, here it is. The letter states, and here I quote '… with the heart of King Robert I am also sending you a Blessed silver casket in which …'" he coughed. "Well that's what is appropriate. It refers to the casket, Inspector. Will that satisfy you?" Learmonth blinked as he said this. He had not divulged that the words following "in which …" had been "… will be found locks of hair from our Saviour Jesus Christ." Astounding if true, he thought, while waiting for the Inspector's response.

Inspector Dawson thought for a moment, then nodded his head and said, "Mr. Learmonth, I will take your word for it. Thank you."

Cameron Learmonth drove Alan to Edinburgh Airport to catch his return flight to Nice. The KLM flight left at 4:30 p.m. so with luck he would be in Villefranche around 11:00 p.m.. He called the Welcome Hotel to let Kate know, but there was no reply from room 32. Where was she? he wondered.

CHAPTER 28

Conti phoned Varley after his meeting in Toronto with Alan Bruce. He told him that Bruce had not been persuaded to sell the Alfonso manuscript. He continued. "One of my guys, Fabio Trento, is now following him. Fabio phoned me. They're on their way to Nice, France."

"What?" Varley shouted. "Keep on top of this. Tell Fabio to let you know where he goes. Then call me immediately."

Varley slammed the phone down. Nice: that meant Villefranche. Bruce was on his way to meet Dr. Vacca. He must prevent that. He thought for a moment. Last time he'd spoken to Dr. Vacca, she had told him that Grace was pregnant, and that she wanted confirmation of the receipt in her bank account at Coutts in London of the second five hundred thousand dollars. Varley looked at his personal directory and rang his bank manager, confirming that the transfer had taken place one day earlier. Next, he looked for Dr. Vacca's number and dialled long-distance. When a man answered, Varley said he wanted to speak to Dr. Vacca.

In a few moments she came to the phone.

"This is Mark Varley. How is Grace? Is everything well?"

Sophia Vacca sensed the anxiety in Varley's voice. "Yes, she is fine; a little seasick though, as we ran into a gale last night and the ship was rocking quite violently. I've seen her this morning, and she is recovering from the nausea. It's not usually a problem, but with a new early pregnancy I want to keep her for a few days longer. I should be in the harbour in Villefranche on Friday. If you are there, you can collect her then."

"Great, that is good news," Varley replied. "Are you sure the nausea will not disrupt the pregnancy?"

"Mr Varley, I am a physician. I deal with facts. At present she is well. I can't predict the future."

"Okay, thank you. I will be in Villefranche on Friday."

Varley stared at the phone. Vacca had already hung up on him. He shook his head. Doctors had no idea how to deal with customers. He rose from the desk and stood by the window in his office. It looked out over the parking lot, but Varley didn't see the cars parked there, or those passing along the highway. He was deep in thought. He really needed the original Alfonso manuscript to credentialise the casket and hair. As he lit a cigarette and paced up and down his office, deep in thought, an idea came to him. He looked at his telephone directory, found the name he was looking for, and dialled the New York number of Investment Bankers Group. David Kennedy, a partner of the firm answered. Varley spent half an hour telling Kennedy what he wanted him to do.

* * * *

In Villefranche, Fabio Trento was confused. He had risen early, took his coffee into the lobby and sat there apparently engrossed in a magazine. At 9:00 a.m. he saw the woman who had been with Alan Bruce appear, wearing jeans and a smart silk blouse, and watched as she passed by. No sign of Bruce though. He picked up a house phone and dialled room 32, but there was no reply. Bruce was not there. Trento walked over to the front desk and said, "Excuse me, I was supposed to meet Mr Alan Bruce for breakfast, and he hasn't appeared. I rang his room, room 32, but there's no reply. Have you seen him?"

"Oui, Monsieur. Mr. Bruce left very early this morning. I believe he was going to Edinburgh in Scotland. He must have forgotten his meeting with you."

Trento was stunned: he was supposed to follow Bruce; he had let Bruno down, and Bruno was not the sort of person who liked to be disappointed. "Will he be back?" he asked.

"Oui, monsieur. He has reserved his room for two more days," she replied.

On impulse, Trento decided to follow Kate, whose trim figure he saw walking along the quayside beyond the hotel.

Kate walked slowly along the waterfront enjoying the warm sun on her back and the sight of the busy harbour. Yachts of various sizes came and went, and there was a bustle as tourists descended from the cruise ship's tenders beside the small red-roofed harbour building. She stopped and decided to look at the Cocteau Museum. Trento lingered outside, casually smoking a cigarette.

An hour later, Kate emerged, crossed the cobbled road and selected a table at a waterfront café, beneath a blue and white striped umbrella. She ordered coffee, took a magazine from her bag and relaxed.

Across the road Trento watched. She wasn't going anywhere soon, he thought, turning his back to Kate and facing the Mediterranean. He rang Conti to tell him that Bruce had gone to Edinburgh. Conti was furious. He cursed Trento for his carelessness before calming down. "Fabio, listen to me, listen carefully," he said, "you've let me down once. Don't let it happen again. Stay with the woman. Bruce will return to her, I'm sure. Let me know when he does."

* * * *

Alan's cellphone rang as he sat in the departure lounge at Edinburgh airport.

"Alan, it's Cameron Learmonth. You haven't left, then?"

"No, my flight's delayed for an hour."

"Good. The reason I'm calling is that it seems your electronics company in Dumbarton, Bruce Electronics, is in play."

"What do you mean?"

"Well, an American group called Investment Bankers Group—not an original name, I think you'll agree—has sent me an offer. They want to buy a majority share in the business."

"Really? I haven't had time yet to think what to do with it."

"Well, it was sort of a hobby of Jock's. He wanted to bring employment to the area and with the good management he installed, he developed a profitable little business."

"I see. What do you advise, Cameron?"

"Well it seems that a partner in IBG, that's what they call themselves, is in London and wondered if he might meet you there to discuss their offer."

"Cameron, I haven't seen any offer. How can I discuss it?"

"I've been faxed a copy. They sent it to the Bruce Electronics office in Dumbarton for your attention, and they quite rightly sent it to me as the company's solicitor."

Alan thought for a moment, then said: "Tell you what, Cameron, since I'm in Edinburgh, why don't you ask him to fly up from London? We could meet in your office, and that would be a test of how serious the IBG firm are."

Cameron Learmonth laughed. "Capital idea, Alan. If you cancel your flight I'll send someone to collect you. I'll book you into the Caledonian Hilton for tonight and we'll try to meet Mr. Kennedy tomorrow."

When he reached the hotel on Princes Street, Alan rang the Hotel Welcome in Villefranche. He told Kate that he would be a day late in returning. She was disappointed but understood. Kate had one question for him. "If Dr. Vacca calls, what do you want me to do?"

"Hmm," Alan murmured, buying time to think. "If she does, Kate, show her the hair in the locket I left with you. See if she thinks she can extract DNA that might be used if we decide to try cloning. If so ..." he paused in thought.

"Are you still there?" Kate asked anxiously.

"Yes. Sorry Kate, I was thinking."

"I wondered what the lack of sound meant," she laughed.

"Okay, fair enough Kate. If Dr. Vacca says the hair might be usable, tell her I will get back to her when we have a donor and a surrogate."

Kate bit her lip. Alan had forgotten that she had talked of donating eggs. "Well OK," she said. "Take care Alan, I love you. Come back as soon as you can."

"Love you too, Kate. I'll catch the first plane from Edinburgh after I meet with the investment banker. Bye."

Next day Alan walked along Princes Street and went north to Charlotte Square and down the steep hill to Cameron Learmonth's office. When he was shown into Learmonth's private office he found Hamish McColl sitting there.

"Hope you don't mind, Alan," the old lawyer said. "I asked Hamish to join us as he has lots of experience with such matters from a financial viewpoint, and Jock always trusted his advice."

"No, that's a good idea," Alan replied.

They sat around an oval conference table in Learmonth's office. A grandfather clock ticked quietly in a corner, while several paintings of Highland scenes were artfully arranged on the walls. Learmonth passed a file to Alan and Hamish. It was the offer from IBG. They examined it carefully for five minutes. Hamish finally sat back.

"It looks fairly reasonable, Alan. They're offering four pounds fifty a share for a controlling interest. Book value is only four pounds, so that's better than a 12 percent premium."

Alan clenched his teeth. "Is that enough? Doesn't really sound like they are all that keen."

Learmonth tapped a finger on the table. "Well, we won't know what flexibility there is unless we speak to him, will we? Don't worry, Alan. Between Hamish and myself, we'll test the waters."

"Right," Alan agreed. "Why don't we ask him to join us?"

David Kennedy was shown in and greeted the group with a pleasant, warm smile. He was of medium height, with short dark hair and was in his early thirties.

Cameron Learmonth took the initiative after the introduction.

"Mr Kennedy," he said, "thank you for coming here on such short notice. It was convenient for Sir Alan here," he pointed to Alan who sat quietly assessing David Kennedy's demeanour, "as he was already in Edinburgh. Mr McColl is the Chief Executive of the Bank of Scotland and our financial adviser. I am Sir Alan's solicitor," He looked at the offer on the table. "On behalf of Bruce Electronics, we have looked carefully at your offer. Frankly, Mr Kennedy, it is well below our expectations."

"What did you expect?" Kennedy retorted.

"Well since your offer appeared out of the blue, so to speak," McColl answered, "we were a bit surprised. But since then, I've done some research and the 12 percent premium you've offered us is—I hate to use the word—derisory."

Kennedy frowned. "It seems fair to us under the circumstances."

"Really?" Alan asked. "What are the circumstances you're referring to?"

Kennedy looked down at the table for a moment before raising his head. He stared at Alan. "Perhaps it would be better to speak privately about that with you."

"I don't see why. Mr Learmonth and Mr. McColl are my advisers. They should hear what you have to say."

Kennedy tapped his pen on the table, its clicking noise, as he did so, in counterpoint to the ticking of the grandfather clock. He licked his lips and looked at the three men. "Okay, then, if that's what you want. IBG is interested in your company, Bruce Electronics. Frankly, we would probably want to restructure it to improve profitability. That's why we think our offer is reasonable. It's an investment for us. We are always looking for investment opportunities, and while we were researching Bruce Electronics we learned that you, Sir Alan, might have another property that would interest as an investment opportunity."

"And what would that be?" Alan asked, suspicion arising in his mind.

"Well, we've learned that you might have an ancient letter that would be a very attractive acquisition for us. As an investment of course."

"So you've been following all the media attention about what they are calling the Jesus casket?" Alan asked.

"Of course," Kennedy nodded his head. "Of course we have. So, we could sweeten the deal for Bruce Electronics—quite substantially, in fact—if you are also prepared to sell us the original of Alfonso's letter."

Alan's face darkened in anger. He threw his pen on the table.

"So that's it? Who put you up to this? Mark Varley? Jackson Ford? I smell a rat. Which of them is it?"

Kennedy shook his head. "IBG is the interested party."

Alan stood. "I think this meeting is ended," he said.

Kennedy frowned, closed his case and stood. "I'm sorry you feel that way," he said. "It is a good offer."

When he had left, Alan told McColl and Learmonth about the threat he had received from Bruno Conti in his Toronto office. "It's plain to see that the Jackson Ford people are desperate to get the Alfonso letter. He turned to McColl. "Hamish, please make sure that the safety deposit box is secure. I don't know what they will do next to get the letter."

Cameron Learmonth stroked his chin and smiled. "Alan, there could be an answer." He outlined what he had in mind.

CHAPTER 29

"Trouble, Mark?" Jackson Ford looked up as Varley walked into his office.

Varley's face was grim. He shook his head. "Not really, I guess." His face relaxed slightly. "More like good news and bad news."

Ford shrugged. "I see. Well, let's get the bad news out of the way."

Varley's face relaxed even more, and the hint of a smile flickered across his face. "Well, Jackson, on reflection, it is not really bad news. More like not good news. The fact is that we haven't yet managed to get the original of the Alfonso letter. Alan Bruce won't sell. I've tried a few approaches, but he is digging in his heels."

"But he admits to having the original?" Ford asked.

Varley nodded agreement.

"In that case, sooner or later he will have to produce it. The world will demand it."

"The good news is that we are being overwhelmed with calls, e-mails, and pledges—and we are now $32 million ahead of contribution targets for the year. Everyone wants to see the Jesus Casket; the name given by the media seems to have stuck! Also, your TV services are being watched by millions now."

Ford smiled, and raised his arm in the air. "Praise be to God!"

"And, Jackson, I almost forgot the most important thing I wanted you to know. Grace is pregnant! Dr Vacca called to let me know. I'm going to France in the next few days to bring her back to Montgomery."

Ford clapped his hands and beamed with satisfaction. "It is the Lord's will!" he exclaimed.

They discussed the arrangements for Grace's return. She would be taken to a plantation house, outside Montgomery, which was owned by a retired physician friend of Ford's. There she would be looked after for the duration of her pregnancy with an on-site nurse and security guards. No chances would be taken. The pregnancy would be monitored, and the birth would take place in the best obstetric department in Montgomery, at Jackson Hospital.

"That really is excellent news you've given me, Mark." Ford glanced at his watch, and was surprised at the time. "Goodness: it's ten o'clock. I'm due at the Governor's Mansion in half an hour. Can you come with me, Mark? It could be important. He seems very anxious to talk to me."

They were greeted at the door to the Governor's Mansion by Malloy's executive assistant, who led them to the Governor's Board room. She poured coffee before Mike Malloy entered with a broad smile. They shook hands, and Malloy poured a coffee for himself from a silver pot standing on a side table.

"Jackson and Mark, thank you for coming this morning. I'm sure you are both very busy, and I fully appreciate your spending the time with me." He sipped his coffee, then gazed at the preacher. "Jackson, what I wanted to discuss is the plan for the shrine, or museum, we talked about. Time is passing, and I just don't know what is happening."

Varley interjected before Ford could speak. "We've been very busy with the Crusade's work Governor, we haven't been able to make any arrangements so far."

"That's truly disappointing Mark." The Governor frowned, and turned to Ford who blinked several times, not sure how to react. "Jackson, I think you know that I'm in a tough fight for re-election. You've sparked a lot of interest worldwide in what you said about the casket. Everyone wants to see it. When we last spoke, we agreed—at least I thought we had—that we would build a structure, a shrine if you like, to house it along with other religious artefacts. That would be a great tourist attraction for Montgomery—indeed for all Alabama—and it would create jobs." He tapped his finger on the boardroom table before continuing. "I really need to do something Jackson. I've supported you and your Crusade publicly, now I need your help."

Jackson looked anxiously at Varley. "What can we do Mark?"

Varley had been thinking as Malloy spoke. They needed his political help, perhaps more in the future than now, and it would be calamitous if he were to be defeated in the election, for a new incumbent might not be so helpful. He looked at the Governor.

"Mike, I have an idea. We could announce our intention to build a shrine for the casket, and open an architectural competition, which you would help judge. And why not have a ground breaking ceremony next month? We have lots of land adjacent to the church for it. You would be the chief guest. You could make a speech, with lots of publicity and that might help with your re-election."

Malloy chuckled and slapped his hand on the table. "Son of a gun! Great idea, Mark. We'll do it. Are you happy with this, Jackson."

"Of course, it's a great idea."

"Fine. Well, I'll ask Hank Rogers, my chief of staff, to coordinate the arrangements with Mark."

The next day Varley left for France, but not before he had started making arrangements for the groundbreaking ceremony. His staff began to make detailed plans.

When he finally reached Villefranche and checked into the Welcome Hotel a message was waiting for him at the front desk. Dr. Vacca wanted him to call when he arrived. He went to his room, and dialled the number he had been given. Stefano Donadoni answered.

"Mr Varley, good to hear from you," he said in response to Varley's enquiry. "This is Dr Stefano Donadoni, Dr Vacca's colleague. You remember, we met recently? At present we are about twelve hours' sailing time from Villefranche. Why don't you meet me at the harbour tomorrow morning at eleven o'clock?"

Varley agreed and put down the phone. Conti had told him he had an associate in the hotel, a guy by the name of Fabio Trento, whom he had never met. He rang reception and asked to be connected to Trento's room. Although it was now almost midnight he was not there.

Varley left a message and stretched out on the bed to sleep. Early next morning, his phone rang. It was Trento.

"Mr Varley, I got your message. Bruno told me about you, but I didn't know you were going to be here in France," he finished somewhat apologetically.

Angrily, Varley asked, "Where were you last night Trento? I thought you were supposed to be watching that girl."

"Yes, I was. I followed her all day. She went to her room at ten o'clock. I sat in the lobby for an hour, then went to a café outside, had a beer and watched the entrance to the hotel until 1:00 a.m.. Then I went to bed. She didn't leave."

"OK. See me in my room, room 44."

Trento appeared a few minutes later. He had nothing significant to report. Kate had spent the previous day exploring the old town, wandering in and out of shops and stopping at a waterfront restaurant for a late dinner. And, no, he had not seen Alan Bruce. Varley told Trento to keep following Kate, and to call his room if Alan Bruce appeared.

At 11:00 a.m. Varley stood on the jetty at the harbour. Ten minutes later, a small boat arrived. On its side he saw the words 'Tender to Nova Wisp'. The lone person on board tied up and jumped on to the jetty. Varley approached him.

"Mr Varley, good to see you again," said Stefano Donadoni. "Dr.Vacca is waiting on board the Nova Wisp." They hopped into the boat and Donadoni manoeuvred it out of the harbour and sped towards the Nova Wisp at anchor some 150 yards out in the bay. Once they were on board, Donadoni led him to Dr Vacca's state room, which also served as her office. Sophia Vacca wore a white medical coat over a grey silk dress. She rose from behind her desk as Varley entered.

"Mr Varley," she said, "we have been successful in initiating a pregnancy with Miss Christopherson. Her health is good, all the blood work is positive, and I think we must now let events follow their course." A knowing smile flickered for a second across her face. "Naturally, this is far from a normal pregnancy."

"Because of the cloning?" Varley asked.

"Yes. I am making history with what we've managed to do, extracting usable DNA from the hair. It's like a miracle." She gave a knowing smile. "But that's what you hoped for, isn't it? A miracle. A clone from the hair of Jesus?'

Varley blinked several times before replying. "Yes, we did hope for a miracle. But what do you mean about the clone being that of Jesus?"

Sophia Vacca raised her shoulders expressively and gave a short laugh. "Come, come, Mr. Varley. With all the publicity in the media about a Jesus casket and hair in it, and given that your Crusade for Christ has the casket, what could you possibly expect me to think?"

Varley was prepared for this. Before leaving Montgomery he had contacted the Crusade's attorneys who had drawn up a confidentiality agreement with Dr. Vacca.

"Dr. Vacca, you are, of course, correct. We do believe the hair is that of Jesus, so if Grace's pregnancy goes to term, we should indeed have a clone of Jesus."

Uncharacteristically Sophia Vacca clapped her hands.

"So! I am correct! My name will be made in medical and scientific circles, when I write my paper describing the process and the results."

"You can't do that, Dr. Vacca." Varley raised his voice. "We can't allow that. Not yet, not until at least the baby has been born."

Sophia Vacca stuck out her chin defiantly. "And why should I not publish?" she asked.

"Because we need to control the release of the news. It's important for our work. So, I need you to sign a confidentiality agreement." Varley said.

"Pah!" She waved a hand dismissively. "You should have thought of that earlier."

"You're right, I omitted that in our negotiations, but now I need you to sign this agreement." He held it out to her.

She threw it on her desk. "Too late!"

Varley reached over and held her wrist. "I don't think so," he said. "Dr. Vacca, we have paid you very well for the cloning. I congratulate you on its success. In time, after the child is born, you will be free to publicise your research, and the results. Who knows, you may yet get the Nobel prize in medicine. But until then, we do not want you to say anything to anyone."

Sophia Vacca pulled her hand away from Varley's grasp. She blinked, and ran her tongue over her dry lips. After a moment, she shrugged. "Very well, but it will cost you. Time is money for me."

Varley smiled like a cat about to pounce. Within ten minutes, they'd agreed on a fee of twenty-five thousand dollars, and Sophia Vacca signed the confidentiality agreement. She added a clause giving her sole control over publicising and taking credit for her work after Grace's baby was born.

Two hours later, Donadoni took Grace and Varley back to Villefranche harbour. Varley carried Grace's case and led her to the Hotel Welcome. There, he saw her into her room before taking the elevator to the ground floor. A smile flickered across his face. The confidentiality agreement was signed, and the thought of another twenty-five thousand dollar payment to Dr. Vacca did not trouble him, not with all the money pouring into the Crusade. As he left the hotel and walked along the waterfront, where he intended to relax with a drink and a good Cuban cigar, he saw Grace open the balcony doors from her room and sit down on the balcony. She was glowing and healthy. Varley's world was in good shape. He walked on.

Grace felt the warm sun on her face and stretched lazily like a cat. She put on her sunglasses, stood and spread her arms towards the sun. Her left-hand caught the leg of her sunglasses and they fell from her face. Grace looked down, expecting to see them lying smashed on the road below. Instead, a face, a woman's face, smiled at her from the room below, room 32. She held a pair of sunglasses in her hand.

"I guess these must be yours," Kate Harris said, smiling up at her.

CHAPTER 30

Alan looked at Learmonth with a growing appreciation of the old lawyer's perception and skills. He chuckled. "Donate the Alfonso letter to a museum? On the face of it, that's probably what I should do in the long run. It certainly is an important historic document, but to do it now …" he shook his head. "To do it now would only validate the casket. That's what the Crusade and Ford want, and I don't feel I should help them."

Cameron Learmonth watched the younger man wrestling with a decision. "Of course, Alan, I understand completely, but there could be a condition attached to your donation to a museum, say the British Museum in London or the Smithsonian in Washington."

"A condition?" Alan asked. He looked at Learmonth expectantly.

"Yes, a condition. Here is what I suggest."

Alan listened carefully and laughed with appreciation. "Cameron, you are a genius," he said.

* * * *

Back in Villefranche, Kate held a pair of sunglasses in her hand. They had fallen from the balcony above. "Are these yours?" she asked the dark haired woman, who gazed down at her.

"Yes," Grace Christopherson replied, "I guess I knocked them off my face when I stretched. This sun is wonderful."

Kate looked up at Grace. "Do you want me to throw them up?" she asked.

"No, don't do that. I'll come down and get them. Which room are you in?"

"Room 32. I'll let you in. Just knock."

Across the road, Trento watched Kate speak to Grace. He didn't know who Grace was, but knew he should tell Varley about anyone Kate encountered.

Grace knocked on room 32 and Kate opened the door. She held out the sunglasses. "Here you are. Lucky I managed to catch them."

Grace took the glasses and put them on top of her head. "Thank you." Then, reacting to Kate's voice she said, "you're American aren't you?"

"Yes, from Boston. I'm Kate Harris."

"I'm Grace Christopherson, from Montgomery."

"Are you on holiday?" Kate asked.

"Not really. I can't talk about it."

"Oh? OK, well enjoy yourself." Kate smiled and closed the door.

Grace returned to her room. An hour later, Varley knocked on her door. When Grace opened it he said, "Grace, we need to leave right now. We can catch a plane in an hour's time. We'll stop in Paris for a day—let you see the sights—and then we'll fly back to Montgomery before the weekend."

Grace looked down shyly. "Fine, Mr Varley. It won't take me long to pack. I'll meet you downstairs in the lobby in fifteen minutes."

Varley went back to his room, furious at what Trento had told him. He'd seen Grace speak to Kate on the balcony. Varley decided immediately to get Grace away before Kate, and by inference, Alan Bruce, could ask questions that might give the game away.

The taxi taking Varley and Grace to Nice stopped at the top of the hill leading from the old town to the main road to Nice. They had to wait for a break in the traffic flow. As their taxi turned left towards Nice airport, another taxi made a right turn to go downhill to the Hotel Welcome. Alan Bruce gave a casual glance at the occupants of the other taxi: a man and a young woman. He frowned. He was almost certain that the man was Mark Varley.

Kate was delighted to see Alan. They kissed passionately and held each other close.

"I should go away more often," Alan said, releasing her from his grasp.

"Not if you want to keep me," Kate laughed.

"OK: noted," he said before changing the subject. "Have you heard from Dr. Vacca?"

"Not yet."

"OK. Well, it's a lovely day. Why don't we explore the countryside around Villefranche?" Alan rang the front desk and asked the receptionist to get a taxi.

When he went downstairs, a black Mercedes taxi sat outside the hotel's front door.

"*Ou venez-vous, monsieur?"* the driver asked.

"Well, if you speak English, please take us for a picturesque drive. There must be lots of places to see around here."

"Oui, monsieur. I speak a little English. I take you to St. Paul de Vence." He drove them past the hillside villages of Eze and Vence, and within half an hour he slowed as they came to a large outcrop of rock. He pointed. "*Voila! St. Paul de Vence.*"

The village sat on a rocky outcrop shaped like a boat, narrow at both ends and bulging in the middle.

The driver said, "Is the most beautiful village in the world."

"OK," said Alan, "Let's see it." He told the driver to wait for them for up to three hours in the parking lot, then he and Kate slowly walked up the hillside and entered through what appeared to have been the gateway to an old stone fort. Inside, they were enchanted by the sight of elegant fountains leisurely spraying water in the air. Thick green vines covered the stone walls of the old buildings on either side. The streets were filled with displays of flowers growing profusely in painted wooden window boxes. They walked into shop after shop, amazed at the number of artists whose works were displayed, showing what had often been referred to by painters, such as Picasso and Matisse, as the exceptional light of Provence.

They stopped for lunch at La Colombe d'Or, a hotel with an exquisite restaurant. Afterwards they slowly made their way back down the hillside. They came to an old church with ochre coloured walls and a curved roof covered in red tiles. It was L'Eglise La Collegiate, or the Collegiate Church.

They went inside, hand-in-hand. It was cooler than in the heat outside, and the light of the hot Provence sun was filtered through the small windows so that, by contrast with the brightness outside, the church appeared to be in shade. They paused, admiring the beauty of the church. Ahead lay the altar, covered in flowers. Beyond, two arched windows allowed rays of light to shine in, relieving the gloom. Hand-in-hand they walked slowly down the centre aisle. As they did, Kate sensed the presence of the thousands of worshippers who, over many centuries, must have sought solace, and who had surely offered praise and thanks for their blessings. As she slowly moved forward, she felt a warmth suffuse her body. She felt enveloped in a feeling of love and understanding. It was like nothing she had experienced in her life. She felt herself in the presence of something, something wonderful, something she could not explain. They advanced to the altar and stood together in front of the black iron railing which lay before it. Neither spoke. To speak would have broken the sense of awe which filled their beings. They were in the presence of something beyond their imagination or experience.

They stood in silence for ten minutes, basking in the feeling of love that enveloped their whole being. Alan softly squeezed Kate's hand. It was an epochal moment in their lives.

Eventually, reluctantly, they made their way outside, where Alan turned to Kate. "Did you feel what I felt in there? A sense of love and warmth, of a presence, if you like: something bigger than ourselves?"

Kate looked back at the church, and shook her head. "Yes, it was wonderful. I've never experienced anything like it. I can't explain it. If I were more religious, I might find an easy answer. However, I am a scientist, and the chance of us both experiencing exactly the same feelings, at the same time, are extremely remote. It definitely was something else." She bit her lip pensively. "You know, it's what I imagine it might be like being in the presence of God."

"I'm not particularly religious either," Alan replied. "But something happened in that church: for sure it did."

Returning to Villefranche they had a leisurely dinner, sitting outside under a large striped umbrella at one of the restaurants on the waterfront. At their hotel, Dr. Vacca had left a message asking Kate to be at the harbour at ten o'clock the following morning.

"I'll go with you," Alan said. "We both need to speak to her." He looked at her with an inquiring gaze. "Are you still willing to be the egg donor?"

She nodded, "I've been thinking Alan, especially since what happened at the Collegiate Church in St. Paul de Vence today. If we don't have a surrogate, I think I'd be willing to consider it."

"You can't be serious, Kate!"

"I think I am. But first we need to speak to Dr. Vacca to see if I would be suitable."

Alan raised his voice. "But what about us Kate? It wouldn't be my baby if you carry it!"

"Well maybe that's what we should do. I mean, I'd love to have your baby. I'm 34 now, and as the women's magazines say, my clock is ticking. I don't really think that cloning is the right thing to do, although I know that you want to thwart Varley."

Alan blushed and licked his lips. He gazed down at the table. "Well, I'm not even sure if that would be possible, Kate. I did mean to tell you later, but …" he drummed his fingers on the table before continuing, "… but now is as good a time as any I suppose."

Kate looked concerned. "You're not ill, are you?" she asked.

"No, just a little damaged."

Kate raised her eyebrows and waited for him to continue.

"You see, Kate," he looked down and pointed at his crotch, "my little guys are not very good swimmers."

Kate guffawed. "You mean your sperm have low motility?"

Alan forced a smile. "If that's the technical term, yes."

Kate was anxious. "And just how did you find out, Alan?"

"Well, it happened because of an injury on the football field. I was the quarterback for the U of T team and I was hit," he grimaced, "really hard in the testicles."

Kate smiled and put a hand to her mouth to suppress a laugh.

Alan was very serious. "It's not funny Kate! It was really painful. I was swollen for about ten days, then the doctor ran tests and discovered I'd been damaged. My little guys couldn't swim in a straight line."

Kate reached over and held his hand with tears in her eyes. "Don't worry, Alan, I still love you. These things can often be corrected."

That night they slept soundly in each other's arms. Kate could not forget the feelings of love and bliss and happiness that she had encountered earlier that day in St. Paul de Vence. Did it mean something for her? Although brought up as an Anglican, she did not go to church often. But now, doubt crept into her mind about the meaning of what she had experienced in that old church. Tomorrow, she would decide what to do, once she had spoken to Dr. Vacca.

CHAPTER 31

Varley and Grace were met at the airport by two security guards in a black stretch limousine. They collected their bags, and were driven to an old plantation on the outskirts of Montgomery. It was owned by Dr Jerry Van Papen, an old friend of Jackson Ford's, and one of his strongest supporters. The limousine drove up a long winding road flanked with oak trees. Varley and Grace got out at the front door of the Plantation House, a graceful white building, with pillars at the front supporting a second level veranda, which ran along the entire front of the building.

Jackson Ford and Jerry Van Papen waited to greet them. Ford held out his hands and grasped Grace in an embrace.

"Welcome, Grace. You are blessed."

Van Papen, a distinguished figure with erect posture and closely cropped white hair shook her hand.

"Miss Christopherson, welcome to my home. It will be yours for the next while, and I will make sure you're looked after during your time with us." Van Papen's wife, Emily, appeared and led Grace into the house while the security guards carried her bags into the front hall. Ford looked at Varley.

"So, it was successful?"

Varley nodded in agreement.

"Good. Grace looks well. Jerry and Emily will look after her and we have a security group to provide protection. She must be secure. She is carrying the future of our world."

Inside the Plantation House, Emily led Grace along a corridor filled with antique furniture from the colonial period, a mixture of walnut and mahogany tables and sideboards on which large vases of yellow roses and pink carnations sat. Several large mirrors reflected the flowers, whose bright colours enlivened the pale walls. Grace followed Emily to a bedroom at the end of the corridor. When the door opened, Grace's eyes widened, and she looked around. The room was large, with a queen sized bed covered with a patterned bed cover. Four chairs, covered with a delicate floral pattern, were set near a large window which looked out over endless acres of the plantation grounds, grounds on which cotton had been grown many years before, but which now lay fallow.

Grace followed Emily on to the room's balcony, and looked in amazement at the green fields, which stretched into the distance. Grace caught the smell of newly-cut grass

"This is lovely, Emily," Grace said with a smile.

"Well, make yourself at home, Grace. I'm going downstairs now. Join me when you have freshened up, and we'll have a coffee and a chat."

Emily went down and turned right into a large living room, again filled with antiques and with an eclectic array of furniture. Varley, Jackson Ford, and her husband were drinking coffee. They stood as she entered.

"Grace is settling in. She and I will have a chat, but in the meantime I'll leave you gentlemen to complete your discussion."

When Emily left, Ford said, "Mark, I've been telling Jerry the whole story. He needs to know so that he can help protect Grace."

"Fine, Jackson, I'm sure Grace will be safe here, especially with the security firm we've arranged. I assume that is OK with you, Jerry?"

"Of course," Van Papen said. "We will do anything to help Jackson and his Crusade."

Varley excused himself, saying he was tired after the long journey, and promised to meet Jackson Ford early the following morning.

The next day, Varley, refreshed after a good night's sleep, met with his staff in the Crusade's conference room to review the arrangements for the groundbreaking ceremony for the shrine. They had been in constant touch with Governor Malloy's staff, and the ceremony could take place in about two weeks' time. Varley was satisfied and gave his approval.

He returned to his office and picked up a letter on his desk. It was from the Alabama Institute he had asked to date the hair in the casket. His eyebrows raised as he read it:

Dear Mr Varley,

We have now radio carbon dated the samples of hair you gave us.

There is a mix of hair, not all from the same time period.

Most of the specimen hair has been dated as approximately two thousand years old.

However, we found a few strands which are of much more recent times. We calculate that these are from the twentieth century, and are approximately 80 years old ...

"Damn it!" he shouted and threw the letter away. There must be a mistake. However, the main thing was that he now had independent proof that at least some of the hair in the casket was of the right age for his purposes. He decided to contact the Institute and get them to revise their letter to suit his needs. Meanwhile, he would keep this information to himself. Jackson Ford did not need any additional distraction.

He went to see Ford, who looked anxious. He had been phoned by Cindy Ritcey of CNN, who wanted his comments on a statement issued earlier that day by the Vatican. Ford had declined to comment until he saw the statement Ritcey had faxed to him. He handed it to Varley who read it carefully.

Statement from the Vatican

The Holy Father has observed with growing concern the publicity that is being given to the so-called Jesus casket.

There is simply no proof of the provenance of this casket. Furthermore, the suggestion that it contains hair from the body of our Lord Jesus Christ is basically absurd. Over the ages there have been many stories about relics of the Saviour, including drops of his blood, and tears of St. Peter's all carefully enclosed in caskets that those foolish enough to buy might wear on their body. Sadly, even the faithful can be gullible.

Undoubtedly, the casket referred to in the media reports may be ancient. That does not make it a relic of Jesus Christ. The assertion that this casket contains hair from our Lord is absurd. There is no historic or religious record of any such hair having been obtained.

Moreover, the Holy Father wishes to express his repugnance at any suggestion of attempting to create a clone using that hair. Cloning is a violation of human dignity. In 1987, the Vatican's Instruction on Respect for Human Life stated that there should be a legal prohibition of human cloning. We are glad to see that such prohibitions have been imposed in most, if not yet all, countries.

God made man. This was his will, and we mortals disobey God's intentions at our peril.

Varley tossed the statement on to Ford's desk. "We can't be too surprised at what the Vatican says, Jackson. The casket of hair wasn't found by the Catholic Church, so they have no reason to try to accept it."

Ford frowned. "I agree Mark, but we are, to some extent, walking on thin ice. Without the original Alfonso letter, it could be made to look as if we have made the whole thing up." He lifted his hand to his head and rubbed is eyes. "We are really taking a lot of risks without that letter, and without knowing how the casket came to us. You can see that Mark, can't you?"

"The provenance is real, Jackson. The English copy I was given by Sir Jock Bruce is a faithful translation of the original letter. The casket was supposed to have been buried in Melrose Abbey with King Robert's heart, but it wasn't, as we now know. However, what we have is real, although it is a translation. There's no doubt the original letter exists. It's a pity we don't yet have it: Bruce won't sell it, and I haven't yet found a way to get it. It's been dated, so I don't see that there can be any argument with that."

Varley blinked a few times. He was getting quite expert at his story regarding the casket. Ford need never know how he had indeed retrieved it from Melrose Abbey. He picked up the Vatican's statement and looked at it again. "What do you want me to do about Cindy Ritcey, Jackson? Would you like me to talk to her?"

Ford pondered the question for a moment. He was at his best in a formal service, where he controlled events. An interview was more demanding, particularly one in which he might—would—be criticised by CNN's reporter. "Yes, Mark, I think it would be best if you talk to her. But before then let's work on our own statement."

Two hours later, Mark Varley sat in a conference room in the church's office building. Cindy Ritcey sat opposite; and a cameraman had set up lights to record the interview.

"Ready, Mr. Varley?" she asked.

He nodded his agreement.

Cindy looked at the camera. "This is Cindy Ritcey of CNN. I'm with Mark Varley of Jackson Ford's Crusade for Christ."

The camera caught Mark's face before returning to the reporter.

"Mr Varley," she began, "today, the Vatican issued a statement. Have you seen it?"

"Yes, I read it a short time ago, after you faxed it to us."

"And how do you respond?"

"Well, Cindy, we have also issued a statement. Here's a copy. He leant over and handed a sheet of paper to her before continuing. "Would you like me to read it?"

Cindy Ritcey nodded assent. Varley looked at the camera and said.

"Statement from the Crusade for Christ: We have read a statement today from the Vatican, and wish to respond in the spirit of Christian love. The casket we have is of proven provenance. Its age has been accurately determined by scientific means, and the hair it contains is two thousand years old—again a matter of scientific fact. The provenance is provided by the letter from King AlfonsoXI of Leon and Castile in Spain. The copy of that letter we have is an English translation of the original, which is believed to be in the possession of Alan Bruce, the heir to Sir Jock Bruce, who gave us the copy of the English translation. To clarify the provenance of the casket, we now ask Mr. Bruce to produce the original Alfonso letter. With regard to cloning, there are different religious, moral, and ethical views, as pointed out in the President's report on that subject in 1997. We ask for understanding as we pray for guidance about the future disposition of the casket and the hair."

Cindy Ritcey took over. "Mr Varley, we have heard all this before. What precisely are you doing with the casket, and it is there any truth about cloning?"

Mark Varley was used to dealing with the media. He had said all he wanted to say in the Crusade's statement. He smiled and looked at the reporter.

"Cindy, if you read our statement again, you will see that it covers all the important points. There's nothing I'm going to add. Thank you." With that Varley rose and walked from the conference room, leaving Cindy Ritcey to sum up and sign off her report.

Ford nodded with satisfaction when Mark Varley went to his office to tell him about the CNN interview. "Well done, Mark. The reference to Alan Bruce having to produce the original Alfonso letter will switch media attention to him for a while."

Varley's phone rang as he entered his office. It was Bruno Conti. He had heard from Fabio Trento in Villefranche. That evening—it was now evening in France—Trento had seen Alan Bruce and the young brown haired woman speaking to a man who had sailed into the harbour. Trento noted the name of the small boat: it was Tender to Nova Wisp.

When Varley heard this he lost his temper. "Damn it, Bruno! What are they doing?"

"What do you mean, Mark?" Conti asked.

Varley was silent. He did not want Conti to know too much. He trusted him only so far, but he was aware that Conti was a mercenary, and would probably sell his soul to the highest bidder.

"I don't mean anything at all," Varley replied, "only that your guy Trento has to keep on their trail. Let me know what they do. Call me any time, day or night."

Varley slammed the phone down. He needed to cover the bases to avoid Bruce getting to know what Dr. Vacca was doing on Nova Wisp.

On the third ring, Sophia Vacca answered his call.

"Dr. Vacca? This is Mark Varley."

"Yes." she said, waiting for more.

"I just wanted to remind you of our confidentiality agreement and …"

She interrupted. "It will be in place as soon as my bank advises me that the twenty-five thousand dollars has been paid into my account."

"Oh it will be. In fact it should be there by now. Check on it, will you? However, it is very important, very important indeed, that you observe the confidentiality agreement."

There was silence from Dr. Vacca so he asked, "Are you still there Dr. Vacca?"

"Yes," she answered in a soft voice.

"Well, I just want to tell you that I am a very reasonable man. I believe in the sanctity of contracts, such as the confidentiality agreement."

"That is no problem for me," she responded.

"I'm sure it isn't, but, …" he paused for effect, "… but I have been known to react quite severely if anyone breaches a contract, if you get my meaning?"

There was a gasp at the other end of the line. Varley smiled as Sophia Vacca said in a small quiet voice, "I understand you, Mr. Varley. Completely."

"Very well, in that case, I believe a man called Alan Bruce, along with a woman, is coming to see you, why is that?"

"Mr Varley, I cannot breach patient confidentiality. You should know that."

"Yes I do. However, I have two requests—probably demands, if you like. The first is that you should not give him any information about Grace Christopherson, and cloning."

"That is no problem. Patient information is confidential."

"Right. My second point is that I want you to tell me what Bruce wants from you."

"As I've said, Mr. Varley, that is impossible. Such information is confidential."

"We'll see about that, Dr. Vacca," Varley growled down the phone. He hung up, satisfied that he had given Sophia Vacca something to think about. He would come back to that point with her at a later date, once Bruce had left Nova Wisp.

He lit a cigarette and smiled with satisfaction. Things were falling into place. Grace was pregnant, and was secure in the Plantation House. He had succeeded, he felt, in transferring media attention to Alan Bruce. One way or another, Dr. Vacca was probably going to tell him what Bruce was up to. Plans for the ground breaking ceremony for the shrine were moving ahead. Most importantly, Trento was keeping a close watch on Alan Bruce's movements. He would react to that once Conti got back to him.

CHAPTER 32

Alan and Kate met Stefano Donadoni at eleven o'clock the next morning. He was waiting with a tender when they reached the harbour. Donadoni had moored at the end of the jetty, away from the wash of the orange roofed tenders, which sailed back and forth across the bay, disgorging cruise ship passengers who were en route for a day in Provence.

Donadoni helped Kate to get into the small craft, gave them a smile and gunned the outboard engine as he left the harbour and headed across the bay to Nova Wisp. He moored alongside, and Kate and Alan stepped on to the platform at the stern of the ship, while sailors helped Donadoni to bring the tender on board. Donadoni pointed forward in the ship. "Please," he said. "This way."

They followed him along the teak deck and Donadoni knocked at a state room door before opening it. Sophia Vacca, wearing a white medical coat, rose from her desk. She held out her hand to Kate. "You are Dr. Harris, I presume?"

Kate shook her hand. "Yes, and this is my fiancé, Alan Bruce."

Dr. Vacca looked at him appraisingly, and shook his hand. She pointed to chairs in front of her desk. "Please sit down," she said. "Dr. Harris, I believe you wanted to consult me about arranging for a cloned child?"

Kate looked at Alan before replying, "Yes, that's why we contacted you."

Vacca nodded her head. "I see. Well, I need more information." She took a pen from the desk, opened a folder and looked at Kate. "Who is going to donate the eggs?"

"I am," Kate said.

"And the surrogate mother: has she been identified? I'll need to examine her, you know," Vacca continued. "Ethically, I can't accept anyone who does not meet my criteria." She looked at Kate. "Do you know the name of the surrogate?"

There was silence for a minute. Kate pursed her lips; it was decision time for her. Finally she raised her head. "Yes I know the surrogate mother. It's the same as the egg donor: me. That is, if cloning is possible."

Vacca placed her pen on the desk. "You are donating eggs and carrying the child?" She looked at Kate. "If you and Mr. Bruce wanted to have a baby there are more conventional ways of doing so, as I'm sure you are aware."

Kate did not intend to be patronised. "Of course," she snapped. "That is not the issue. Alan has problems with low sperm motility, but we could probably deal with that in a different way at some time ..."

"Let me speak, Kate," Alan interrupted. Dr. Vacca, the truth is that we want to clone an historic figure. We have his hair, and we would like to know if it is possible to clone him, with Kate as the mother."

Sophia Vacca sat silently for a moment, her face whitening with anger. She threw her pen on the desk with a loud noise.

"Are you fools?" she said. "What are you talking about? Are you motivated by the media talk about the Jesus casket? My God, this is unreal."

Dr. Vacca slumped back in her chair, her mind racing. It was one thing to clone from the hair that Varley had given her. That had resulted in a successful pregnancy; and in a few months, she would be able to reap the prestige of having been the first to develop a cloned human. Was her future success going to be compromised by others who wanted to do the same from specimens of hair, skin or blood from the past?

Kate sensed the turmoil in Dr. Vacca and leaned forward with her right hand on the desk.

"Dr. Vacca, this is really very important to us for many reasons," she said. "I sense that you have reservations. I understand why, believe me, so if it is not something you wish to do, perhaps we should speak to Dr. Antinori or Dr. Zavos."

Sophia Vacca frowned. She had already achieved a cloned child. In time she would reveal her methodology and gain fame and prestige, perhaps even the Nobel prize in medicine. If she could replicate the feat her methodology would be proven; it would not be a fluke, a statistical aberration. Why should she allow Antinori, Zanos, or anyone else the chance to upstage her? She made up her mind. "Very well, Dr. Harris, I'll consider proceeding." Vacca picked up her pen.

"Now who is it you want to clone?" She smiled. "I don't do Hitlers or Stalins."

"No, it's nothing like that, I assure you," said Kate with a quiet smile.

"Very well. And what material do you have that will help me extract the DNA, for I'd assume you don't have live sperm?"

Alan took the gold locket from his pocket and carefully opened it to show a lock of hair inside. Vacca looked at it and laughed. "Mamma mia! Hair!" She wiped a tear from her eyes and looked at Kate. "Hair?" she said inquiringly. "Are you serious?"

"Very serious," Kate nodded.

Vacca gave a deep sigh. "Very well, I will need to examine it to see if I can extract usable DNA." She paused before asking, "and how old is the hair?"

Alan and Kate looked at each other for a moment. "It's reputed to be two thousand years old," Alan replied softly. "It has been carbon dated."

Sophia Vacca threw her hands in the air. "Two thousand years! Are you trying to clone Jesus?"

There was silence, before Alan said, "Would it trouble you, if we were?"

Vacca leant forward, her left hand supporting her head, while she thought. Kate watched, knowing the conflicts that might be passing through the other woman's mind. Eventually Sophia Vacca looked up.

"I'm not a deeply religious person, but I'm sure that Jesus would perhaps make a difference in our troubled world. It's not my place to judge that. I'm a physician and a researcher. I guess that if you believe in God, he will not allow us to do anything against his will." She smiled. "That sounds like a copout, I know." She shrugged her shoulders. "I can't judge the religious reaction, or what the moralists will say. All I can do is exercise my skill, and if it results in a clone, then so be it."

Kate looked at Vacca for a moment, then nodded acceptance.

"Thank you, Dr Vacca."

"Hold on," Vacca replied, "this is a costly procedure. I can't agree to proceed until an advance payment has been lodged in my bank in London."

"What is your fee, Dr. Vacca?" Alan asked.

Sophia Vacca thought quickly. She had charged one million dollars to Varley and the Crusade and then had made a profit of four hundred thousand dollars over actual costs, including the full rental of Nova Wisp for six months. Her fixed costs were basically covered, so she could afford to be more reasonable with these young people, for they were not a corporation, such as Varley represented. She decided, and said, "I'll need one hundred thousand dollars as an advance and another one hundred thousand dollars once a successful pregnancy results, as well as full rights to publicise the results when a child is born."

"I agree to your financial terms, Dr. Vacca," Alan said, smiling. "If I can use a phone, when you give me details of your bank account, I'll arrange for an electronic transfer of one hundred thousand dollars." Alan scratched his nose. "But I'm also a lawyer, so I'll need to see the legal agreement about publicity before I agree to that."

"Pah! Legal agreements? We have a simple concept and you people always wrap it up in convoluted language."

"To you, perhaps," Alan replied. "To me, the language used is the essence of the agreement, and must be clear to everyone."

"Oh, OK. I'll get my lawyer to send you something. Meantime, when I have been advised by my bank that the money is in my account, I will begin to examine the hair and also Dr. Harris. I'll need to check her suitability."

"Of course, Alan said. "Now if I can have the details of your bank account, may I use your phone to call my bank?"

It took only a few minutes for Alan to speak to Hamish McColl at the Bank of Scotland in Edinburgh and make the arrangements to transfer one hundred thousand dollars to Dr. Vacca's account at Coutts Bank in London. He put down the phone. "It's done," he said. "The money is now in your account."

"You won't mind if I confirm that," she replied, and rang her bank in London. After a brief conversation she nodded, put down the phone and turned to Alan and Kate. "It is done. Now, Dr. Harris, I intend to sail at 6:00 p.m.. I need to do my work in international waters. Dr Donadoni will take you back to Villefranche. You should return with clothes for the next two weeks."

Kate looked at Alan. "And what about Alan?"

Vacca shook her head. "Only you. He would just get in the way. Besides, I can't accommodate more than one person on Nova Wisp."

Kate took Alan's hand. "Is that OK, Alan?"

He squeezed her hand. "I guess, though not what I expected." He looked at her with concern. "Will you be okay?"

She nodded her head. "Yes, but I'll need to take some vacation to cover my absence. I'll call Harvard when we get back to the hotel."

Donadoni dropped them at the harbour and said he would return at five o'clock to collect Kate.

Back in their room at the Welcome Hotel, Alan hugged Kate. He kissed her, and stroked her back. "Are you sure this is OK?" he asked, his eyes searching for a clue to her true feelings.

Kate had tears in her eyes. "Oh, I think, so." She sobbed, and put her head on his chest. "Oh, Alan, I just don't know what to think."

He held her close. "Well, we don't need to do it."

"I know, I know!" Kate wiped tears from her eyes. "Now we are at the decision point I'm getting cold feet. But," she gave a little smile, "you know it might be best to go ahead. We've talked our way through it before. And after our experience at St. Paul de Vence—I can't forget that experience in the old church—I'm really beginning to feel we should go ahead."

Alan was emotional too. His voice was husky as he replied. "Like you Kate, I have been troubled with this. I've had my doubts, despite my earlier decision to try to thwart Varley and his gang. But now," the tension visibly relaxed in his face, "now, I feel more comfortable and I agree. Let's do it"

They held each other close, then slowly moved to the bed. Their love-making was an emotional release for both of them. Afterwards, Kate went to the bathroom, and carefully withdrew a package from her make-up bag. She placed some material in it, sealed the package, and placed it in a separate section of her handbag. She looked at the thermometer in her room: 23 degrees Celsius, so the material might survive for a day.

Kate had no difficulty in arranging two weeks vacation. She packed her bags and, Alan by her side, met Donadoni on the pier at 5:00 p.m.. Alan gave her a last kiss and waved as the craft set off into the bay.

Fabio Trento watched from a corner of the harbour. When Alan looked round at him, he casually lit a cigarette and strolled off, speaking into a cell phone as he walked towards a waterfront restaurant for a beer. Alan looked at him and frowned. He was sure he'd seen Trento before.

* * * *

In New York, Bruno Conti listened to Trento's report. He told Trento to keep following Alan Bruce. Then he called Mark Varley in Montgomery. Varley listened intently, but with growing anger, as he learned that the young woman who had been with Alan Bruce had gone back to Nova Wisp. He told Conti to go to Villefranche so that he would be there when she returned to the mainland.

* * * *

The Nova Wisp sailed promptly at 6:00 p.m.. Kate had been taken to a spacious state room with a large bed and its own sitting area. Dr. Vacca visited her and said she and Dr. Donadoni would be busy that evening testing the hair, so she would not be able to see her until the following day. Dr. Vacca rose to leave.

"Please sit down, Dr. Vacca," Kate said. "There's something I need to ask you." Kate produced a small plastic pouch containing a whitish viscous fluid. She placed it on the coffee table beside her chair. "I'm sure you'll not be surprised to learn that I have been struggling with the whole idea of cloning. In one respect, I'm inclined to proceed, if it proves possible, though not as convinced as Alan, my fiancé. But before I make a final decision, I would like you to examine this specimen."

Sophia Vacca's eyes opened wide. "What is it?"

Kate blushed slightly. "It's Alan's semen. I collected some, so I could have it tested."

"Do you think he has some disease?"

"No, that's not it. I want to know if the sperm is viable." Suddenly, in a rush, Kate blurted out her concerns. "Alan suffered a blunt trauma to his testicles when he played football. He told me his sperm has low motility. I'd like to know if that is the case. Will he be able to father a child for me?"

Sophia Vacca looked sympathetically at the confused young woman sitting across from her. "I understand. I'll ask Stefano to test it right away, before you make a decision about cloning. I am a specialist in reproductive medicine, you know. Cloning is not my only skill." She looked down, concentrating on a thought that flitted through her mind. "How old is the semen?"

"A few hours only. And it's been kept at room temperature or better, as far as I can judge."

Sophia Vacca cradled her head in her left hand, deep in thought. "If it's only a few hours old, it's probably still viable. I seem to recall one study that said that more than 25 percent of sperm were moving after twelve hours in a test tube at room temperature. So, after only a few hours, I imagine that the odds of their still being viable are rather good. I'll ask Stefano to test the sample and I'll let you know the results when he's done so."

An hour later, Dr. Vacca knocked on Kate's stateroom door. "May I come in?" she asked.

When they were seated, Vacca said, "Well, I'm afraid Stefano doesn't have very good news about your fiancé's sperm. Although it's not impossible, it is unlikely that the sperm will ever be able to produce a natural pregnancy."

Tears rolled down Kate's face. "It's that bad?"

"I've seen worse."

"Is there anything you can do with the sperm?" Kate was anxious to know if Dr. Vacca's statement provided any hope. "I need to know before I make a final decision."

Dr. Vacca smiled: she understood Kate's predicament. "Let me speak again to Stefano. He did say there was one thing we might try. Also, Kate, Stefano now thinks he can sequence the DNA from the hair you gave me, so you'll need to let me know what you want to do."

Two hours later, Dr. Vacca returned and spoke at length to Kate. The decision was now hers. Kate bit her lip as she thought through the consequences of what Dr. Vacca had told her, and she wondered how Alan would really react to what she was about to do. All the way through, she thought, he had really been a bit flippant about the whole cloning thing.

Sophia Vacca listened carefully, as Kate gave her decision. "Well," she said, "if that's what you want, Kate, I need to move quickly." She took Kate into the examination room, where Stefano Donadoni waited with the ultrasound machine. The medical team worked with practised speed, and within thirty minutes they had finished locating the follicular fluid and had extracted several eggs from Kate.

Donadoni took responsibiilty for the fertilisation of the eggs, which would be left to incubate over night.

"Kate," Dr.Vacca said, "would you mind going to my office? I'll be along in a few minutes."

Kate left the two doctors and came out on deck. She blinked in the bright sunlight, unsure of her directions. A passing sailor asked if she needed anything. "Just the way to Dr. Vacca's office," she said. He led her to the door. Kate knocked and entered. There was no one in the room. Not knowing what she should do, Kate sat in the chair facing the desk. A yellow folder was open, and naturally Kate glanced at it from her chair. She had always been able to read upside-down words, as she put it, a skill she had developed as a child. The name on the folder caught her attention: it was Grace Christopherson. Kate's eyes opened in surprise. That was the name of the woman whose sunglasses she had caught when they fell onto her balcony at the Welcome Hotel. So, Miss Christopherson was a patient of Dr. Vacca. Interesting, Kate thought, then gasped. What had Grace said? Ah, yes! She was from Montgomery, and that was where the Jackson Ford Crusade was based. Kate had to phone Alan. This was where Grace and the Crusade had come for the cloning attempt. No wonder Sophia Vacca had reacted the way she did when Alan had produced the locket!

Kate turned in her chair as the door opened and Sophia Vacca entered. Vacca looked at the yellow folder and closed it. She stared suspiciously at Kate and said, "One of my egg donors. Not suitable, I'm afraid."

Kate smiled. She did not believe Vacca.

Kate returned to her cabin and picked up the telephone to call Alan. It took time to make a satellite connection. Then, when Alan's phone finally rang, he wasn't there.

Kate left a message. "Alan, it's Kate. I have important news. Call me as soon as you can."

CHAPTER 33

The next two weeks passed quickly for Mark Varley. He had regular meetings with Governor Malloy's staff about the arrangements for the ground breaking ceremony for the Saviour Shrine, as Jackson Ford had decided to call the building in which the silver casket and the remaining hair—that which had not been used by Dr. Vacca—would be displayed. Ford was enthused about the opportunity to have a building in which the religious artefacts would be displayed, along with other art and objects testifying to the Christian faith. While Varley acknowledged these benefits, he had also investigated other revenue-earning opportunities to use the vacant land near the church. He was looking at the development of hotels, to accommodate the large numbers of tourists who were expected to visit the shrine. Although he was already extremely wealthy from the success of the Crusade, abetted by the massive public interest in the Jesus casket, he was driven by his alpha male nature to do more. Varley smiled: everything was progressing. Today, the ground breaking ceremony would attract even more attention and publicity for the Crusade, and undoubtedly even more pledges to help Jackson Ford's work.

* * * *

The sun cast long shadows from the church over the site of the ground breaking ceremony. Stands had been erected to accommodate the thousands who turned up to watch. At two o'clock, Governor Malloy and Jackson Ford emerged from the church accompanied by the blue-gowned choir, who followed in columns of four—more than one hundred choristers in all.

Malloy looked every part the Governor in his dark blue suit. He waved to the crowd and smiled as the cameras caught his politician's quiet, confident, grin.

Jackson Ford was, as always, a distinguished figure. His white robe, matched with his thick white hair, gave him an ethereal appearance. He looked solemn, and clasped his hands together as if in prayer, as he slowly walked towards the platform from which he and Governor Malloy were to speak. He stopped for a moment at the stairs leading to the platform and whispered to Governor Malloy, "Mike, as we agreed, after I give the opening prayer and we have the choir lead us in singing Amazing Grace ..." (very appropriate, he thought, thinking of the pregnant Grace Christopherson, who would be watching the ceremony on the plasma TV set in her room at the Plantation House) "... I will call on you to speak."

"Fine, Jackson," Malloy replied, "I have some interesting news, direct from the President. It should help you."

Ford raised an eyebrow. Trust a politician to try to steal the limelight. He walked to the microphone, set up at a lectern on the platform, raised his hands and waited for the noise in the crowd to abate. Satisfied, he smiled.

"Welcome, friends, to this important ceremony. Before we begin, please join me in prayer." He watched as people bowed their heads. "Gracious God, grant us your blessing on our humble attempts to glorify your name, through our human efforts to praise you. Bless our endeavours as we begin to develop a suitable place to present proof of our faith. In Jesus' name, Amen."

At a signal from the choirmaster, the choir began to sing the well-known words to "Amazing Grace." The crowd joined in; and the beauty and strength of the music and words brought tears to many eyes.

As the final note ended, Jackson Ford stepped forward to the lectern.

"This is an important day for all of us," he began. "Today, we will break ground for the new Saviour Shrine in which we will display the casket—the casket in which we discovered hair belonging to our Saviour Jesus Christ. But there will be even more, as you will learn from our distinguished guest, my dear friend Governor Mike Malloy." Ford started to clap his hands, and the crowd also applauded as Malloy stepped to the lectern. Malloy shook Ford's hand and glanced over his audience.

"My friends," he began, "this is a great day for the city of Montgomery, the great State of Alabama, the United States, and indeed the whole world. Today we will break ground for the new shrine that the Reverend Jackson Ford referred to." He glanced over the crowd. "Not only will the shrine display the casket, it will also accommodate many treasures from the Smithsonian Institute." Reporters present, including CNN's CindyRitcey, sat up at this point. This was news, a real slant that they could put on the reporting of the ceremony. Malloy smiled as he assessed the reaction.

"Yes, my friends, only this morning the President called me to give his agreement to my request that various works of religious art and religious artefacts housed in the Smithsonian in Washington, would be loaned to the shrine here in Montgomery, and various pieces would be rotated between the Smithsonian and our Montgomery shrine for periods of time. So, my friends, what begins today in Montgomery is the start of a place that will display the wonders of the Christian faith for all to see."

Malloy smiled broadly, and waved a hand in the air. "Now I wouldn't be a politician, if I didn't also emphasise that this shrine will attract tourists to Alabama. That will create jobs, lots of jobs. Indeed, the Reverend Ford has agreed that I can tell you that his Crusade is already in discussions with major hotel chains, who are anxious to begin planning for new hotels on the site. That will create jobs and ongoing employment of people in hotels, as well in the construction of the shrine and hotels. It's all good news, believe me. Now, one final point. The media has already noted that while Jackson Ford has the casket containing Jesus' hair, the provenance of the casket is dependent—only to an extent mind you—on the so-called Alfonso letter. What the Reverend Ford has is an English translation, undoubtedly accurate as we know. However, the original letter is believed to be in the hands of Mr. Alan Bruce, a Canadian who is the heir to the late Scot, Sir Jock Bruce. I sincerely ask Mr. Bruce, in a spirit of co-operation, to allow the original Alfonso letter also to be displayed here. That would help complete the value of the shrine's religious and historical objects."

Governor Malloy turned to Ford. "And now I will ask the Reverend Jackson Ford to join me in breaking ground for the new shrine."

Ford and the Governor descended the steps from the platform and each were given a silver shovel, inscribed with their names and the date, along with an inscription stating these shovels were used by Governor Mike Malloy and the Reverend Jackson Ford to break ground for the new Saviour Shrine in Montgomery, Alabama. With cameras flashing, Ford and Mike Malloy picked up the shovels, pushed them into the ground and each turned a sod to mark the location of the new shrine. The audience applauded and Ford returned to the lectern on the platform. There, he gave a closing prayer, before he and the Governor, followed by the choristers, slowly walked back to the church building.

Once inside, Ford took the Governor into his office, where Mark Varley joined them.

"Thank you, Mike," he said. "Your mention of Alan Bruce and the Alfonso letter will put pressure on him. It will help if we can get that original letter."

"Of course, Jackson," Mike Malloy nodded, "that will also help tourism, and that creates jobs, not a bad thing for my re-election." He pointed his finger at Ford. "And if you can get the hotel chains to begin building before the election, it would be even better." He thought for a moment. "Tell you what, Jackson, let me know the chains you are talking to, and I'll phone their chairmen myself. I want construction to start as soon as possible."

Mark Varley jumped in. "I'll get that for you right away, Governor. Like you, we don't want any delays, and, personally, thank you for mentioning the Alfonso letter."

Varley left Ford and the governor in discussion about the selection of architects who were politically suitable. He returned to his office and checked his voice mail. The first message was from Bruno Conti, who was now in Villefranche. He listened as Conti's message played.

"Hi, Mark, this is Bruno. I've some news for you about Alan Bruce and his girlfriend. Call me when you can."

CHAPTER 34

The phone rang in Kate's suite on board Nova Wisp. It was Alan, returning her call.

"Kate," he said, "how are you?"

"Fine, darling. Listen, I have important news for you. The 'others' have been here, and the cloning has worked."

"The others?" Alan asked, before the penny dropped. "Okay, got you. So we know what to expect."

"I guess so. It just makes my decision a bit more meaningful, if you follow."

"I do," Alan said. "Listen, Kate, it's up to you. I know we reached a decision to go ahead, and I still think it's correct, but if you have any doubts—any doubts at all—we'll abandon it."

Kate felt the tears come into her eyes. With a free hand she took a tissue, wiped her eyes and sighed, "Oh, Alan, I'm a bit confused."

"Well, darling, don't do anything. I'll fly out tonight and join you."

Kate laughed. "OK, Superman, where are you going to find me? I'm on a ship, in the middle of the Mediterranean."

"Slipped my mind," Alan chuckled, "but seriously, you can ask Dr. Vacca to take you back to shore. I'll still pay her full fee."

"That's very generous, Alan, but I think I should sleep on it."

"Whatever you want is fine with me. I miss you darling."

"And I miss you, Alan. I'll call you tomorrow. Goodnight darling." Kate put the phone down. She slept soundly that night. Her conversation with Alan had helped her to air her doubts.

Kate saw little of Dr. Vacca over the next two days, and took advantage of the balmy weather to bask in the sun as the Nova Wisp slowly sailed to the south.

Kate sat in a lounger at the ship's bows. She stretched out, feeling the warmth of the sun on her face. It relaxed her, and the tension she had felt about making a decision melted away. An hour later, Kate woke from a restful sleep to find Stefano Donadoni standing by her side. She sat up. Donadoni smiled and said. "Dr.Harris, you have slept soundly?"

"Why yes," Kate replied. "I guess the warmth of the sun relaxed me."

"Good, good," Donadoni said, sitting down on a chair beside her. "Dr. Vacca and I are now ready for you. We should be ready to begin within the next hour." He looked at Kate for a moment, then stood up. He gave a short bow, and said, "Now, please excuse me. I have to meet with Dr Vacca."

Kate stretched languidly on the chair, and a smile slowly spread over her face. A short time later, Dr. Vacca selected the egg that had been fertilised and which now was what Vacca called a "healthy embryo" of six to eight cells. Kate was taken into the operating room and it was inserted into her uterus through a catheter. She was told to remain in bed for three days and Donadoni took charge of ensuring that she had regular meals and was comfortable. Eventually, Dr. Vacca's tests showed that an early pregnancy had been achieved.

That night, Kate phoned Alan at his office in Toronto, where it was mid-afternoon. His secretary put the call through, and Kate wept as she heard his voice.

"Alan," she said, "I'm pregnant."

"Wonderful," he replied. "That's great news, darling. How are you feeling?"

"Confused, happy, and sad at the same time. We're returning to Villefranche and should be anchored in the Bay in two days' time. Can you please be there to meet me?"

"Of course, Kate. I'll get my secretary to book flights when I get off the phone. Do you want to go to Boston or Toronto?"

"I don't care. I just want to be with you."

Alan thought for a moment. "Let's make it Boston. And darling, while we are there let's get married."

"Married? That takes time to arrange."

"Well, we probably have a week. I'm sure between you and your mother you'll be able to arrange something."

"You're an idiot, Alan Bruce! It takes much longer!"

"Perhaps, but I really don't want to wait a moment longer, and I don't care whether it's a quiet ceremony or a big wedding. I just want you to be Mrs. Alan

Bruce—or, if you like, Lady Bruce when we are in the UK—just as soon as possible."

"Lady Bruce? It has a nice ring to it. However, I don't really care what I'm called just as long as you love me."

"That I do, deeply."

Alan heard Kate sigh before she said, "OK, Alan, I'll call Mom and see what can be arranged. Make sure that you are there to meet me in Villefranche."

"I will darling, good night."

Two days later, Alan checked into the Hotel Welcome. There was no sign of Kate, so he assumed that the Nova Wisp had not yet moored in the bay. He left his luggage in his room and walked down to the harbour. As he turned the corner to the jetty where tenders arrived, he saw a dark haired man looking at him for a moment, before studiously turning away. Alan had seen that face before, but where? Then it came to him: the man had been at the Hotel Welcome last time Alan had been in Villefranche. Perhaps he was local; but again, Alan had a feeling that there was more to it. He resolved to watch for the man and to speak to him if he felt that he was being followed.

There was a flurry of action as three tenders arrived in quick succession from the Celebrity Cruise Lines' ship "Millennium." Passengers stepped ashore and were directed towards guides who would lead them to buses, which would take them to Nice, Monte Carlo, and into the hillside villages of Eze and St. Paul de Vence.

Alan felt a tug on his arm. He turned and Kate hugged him tightly.

"Alan," she said in a husky voice, "it's so good to see you."

He kissed her passionately, oblivious of the cruise ship passengers jostling past. "Kate, my darling," he said, "you look wonderful. Glowing is the word."

"I am," Kate said, squeezing his arm. "I feel wonderful." Kate turned as Dr. Donadoni walked past. "Thank you Stefano. It was good knowing you."

The Italian spread his hands wide apart and smiled.

"It was my pleasure, Dr. Harris. Keep well," he said, and walked away towards the seafront restaurants. Alan looked at him as he strode away, and he frowned, as he saw the man he had caught staring at him turn to follow Dr. Donadoni. Another stockily-built man, whose face also seemed familiar to Alan, fell in behind, and spoke to Donadoni's follower. Like lions stalking their prey, they purposefully followed Stefano Donadoni as he crossed the road towards a seafront bar.

Back in their room at the hotel Kate told Alan that she had been in constant touch with her mother about arranging a quiet wedding. "Mom was anxious to ask why, was it because you made me pregnant? I told her that you wouldn't do such a thing." Kate blinked rapidly before saying, "Alan, there's something I need to tell you."

Alan looked concerned. "What is it darling? You're not ill?"

"No: in fact I've never felt better. You see, my love, I am pregnant, and it is with your child."

Alan looked at her in disbelief. "But how can that be? I was told I was infertile." His face beamed. "Is it true, Kate? Did Dr Vacca manage a miracle?"

"Something like that. Dr Donadoni was able to stimulate some of your sperm to fertilise one of my eggs." She held out her arms to Alan. "I'm going to have your baby, not a clone."

Alan grasped her tightly round the waist and kissed her. "Are you sure? How can that be?"

Kate bit her lip. "Well, after we made love at the Welcome Hotel—you know, just before I left to see Dr.Vacca—I saved some of your semen, and Dr. Donadoni was able to use it for *in vitro* fertilisation"

"And that worked?"

"Of course! Dr Donadoni worked a miracle, I think, for your sperm were really not too active."

Alan blinked at the unexpected news of his fertility, something he had not expected. Was Kate being honest with him, he wondered? He shook his head dismissing the thought.

"That's great: wonderful!" He calmed down as he thought about Varley. "I think we should still let Varley think it's a clone. I don't want to take any pressure off until he returns the casket.

"Whatever you want, Alan."

"And now, about our wedding: do we have a date?"

"Yes, two weeks from now. I'll be about four weeks' pregnant, but it shouldn't show."

CHAPTER 35

Varley dialled the phone and Conti answered after two rings.

"Bruno, it's Mark. What do you have for me?"

"Hi, Mark. Well, quite a lot. Let's start at the beginning. Yesterday, that woman we were watching returned to the hotel from the Nova Wisp. She is there right now. Alan Bruce arrived this morning, so me and Trento are watching their movements.

Varley grunted. "OK. What else?"

"Quite a lot," Conti continued. "After the tender dropped the woman at the pier in Villefranche, the sailor who was driving it got off and went to a local restaurant for a drink."

"So?"

"So, we followed him. Got into a little discussion, which continued outside in an alleyway. We wanted to know what had been going on aboard the Nova Wisp. Well, it took a little bit of persuasion," Conti laughed, "just a little, and then the guy—he's a Dr. Donadoni—spilled the beans."

"What did he say?" Varley enquired, anxious to know if Donadoni had said anything about Grace Christopherson.

"Say?" Conti asked. "He said a lot, not that it all made sense to me, but it might to you. He said that the woman's name was Kate Harris. She was a patient of Dr. Sophia Vacca on board the Nova Wisp. Vacca seems to be an expert in cloning, and Harris wanted her to help clone a child."

"Did she—Vacca I mean: did she succeed?" Varley asked, his anxiety growing.

"I guess so, Donadoni said she was pregnant.Mind you, he was a bit confused after we had finished with him. He told a weird story about how he had helped to develop a clone involving DNA from some ancient hair that was two thousand years old. Can you believe it?"

Yes, Varley could believe it, but it was not something he wanted Conti to know, at least, not just yet. He contented himself by saying, "Yeah, that is a weird story." He had a thought. "What did you do with Donadoni?"

There was a harsh laugh from Conti before he replied.

"Do? Well, me and Trento smashed his face for telling us stories. Then we left him lying in the alley. I think he'll live."

"For your sake, Bruno, I hope that is right," Varley said. "Keep me in touch with what Bruce gets up to." He hung up, and lit a cigarette while he pondered the information Conti had given him. So Alan Bruce's girlfriend Kate Harris was pregnant. She was carrying a clone, derived from DNA extracted from hair that was two thousand years old. It had to have come from the same source as the hair in the Jesus casket, but how? Varley frowned, deep in thought. It must have been Sir Jock Bruce's doing. The gold locket that Varley's bug had heard Sir Jock mention to Alan Bruce, had to have been the source of the hair that Dr. Vacca must have used. Sir Jock had likely kept back some hair from the casket, and now Alan Bruce had it. But why would Bruce want a clone of Jesus? Varley took a last deep puff of a cigarette, stubbed it out in a glass ashtray on his desk and lit another.

The answer came to him. Alan Bruce wanted another clone to destroy the Crusade's claim to have cloned Jesus. Jesus, as the Bible pointed out, was God's only son. It would be inconceivable that there could be two of them; and any attempts by the Crusade to prove that their clone was, in fact, Jesus, would be mocked. There couldn't be two Jesuses. If that happened, the Crusade would become a laughing stock, and all Varley's work and planning would have been for nothing. He must talk to Jackson Ford. Varley stubbed out his cigarette and walked down the corridor to Ford's office and entered.

Ford sat in an armchair, his fingers steepled under his chin as if in prayer. He looked up as Varley entered. "What's the matter, Mark?" he asked.

Varley sat down opposite him and recounted the story Conti had told him, while omitting the fact that the information had been extracted from Dr. Donadoni through very persuasive physical means.

"So, Jackson, the upshot is that we may have a second Jesus."

Ford blinked. "Would that be so bad for the world?" he asked ingenuously.

"Well the point could be debated, I guess." Varley replied. "However, the fact is that if there is a second clone, we will look foolish, and all the good work of your Crusade will be mocked, not to mention the viability of the Saviour Shrine," he added.

Ford wrinkled his forehead in thought. He stood by the window beyond his desk and looked out at the site of the ground breaking ceremony held earlier that day. Crews were busy dismantling the stands that had been erected to accommodate the crowds. He gave a deep sigh.

"Yes, Mark I see what you're saying. It would look foolish and could destroy all we have worked for." His face brightened as a thought entered his mind. "But we don't know for sure that either pregnancy will go to term and that a child will be born. So isn't it wise to wait—wait and observe what happens with Grace, and what happens with that other young woman? I assume that since Grace was Dr. Vacca's first patient she would give birth before the other woman and …"

Varley interrupted. "And if everything is fine, and Grace bears the Jesus clone we can deal with the other woman. We can't have two Jesuses."

Ford gave a brief frown. "I don't really want to think about that, Mark. If necessary, we will cross that bridge when we reach it. For now we will pray that Grace keeps well and that she bears a healthy child."

Varley give a quick nod of assent. "OK, Jackson, that works for me. But I'm going to have people keep a close watch on Alan Bruce and this woman, Kate Harris. I want them followed. I want to know what they do. I want to know where to find them, if we need to take action."

CHAPTER 36

The wedding in Boston was not the large event that Beth had always visualised for her youngest daughter. There were only fifty guests, mainly family and close friends. Kate wore a silk dress in ivory. Alan wore the Bruce tartan kilt and traditional dinner jacket and black tie. The ceremony in St Augustine's Episcopal Church was traditional, and afterwards the reception was held at the Harris family home, where a large marquee had been erected in the grounds. Alan and Kate spent their wedding night in the Harris home, before leaving next morning for Toronto.

Bruno Conti, wearing dark glasses and a hat as a simple disguise, had watched the wedding ceremony from the rear of the church. He spoke to an elderly couple as they left following the wedding service and, with a few deft questions, he established that the Bruces were leaving the next day for Toronto. He phoned Fabio Trento and told him to book the first Air Canada flight to Toronto for the next day. He was then to wait at Toronto's Pearson Airport for arrivals from Boston, in the event that the Bruces were not on that first flight. Then Trento was to follow them, and call Conti. Varley did not want to lose contact with the Bruces.

The next morning, Kate and Alan said goodbye to Kate's parents and sisters, and caught an Air Canada flight to Toronto. There, Alan collected their luggage, and as he and Kate passed through Customs and into the Arrivals area he saw the face of the man he had seen watching him in Villefranche—the same man he had seen following Stefano Donadoni, when he met Kate on her arrival from the Nova Wisp.

"Kate, hold on to the cart for a minute." He pushed his way through the crowd and grabbed Trento's arm. "Who are you? Why are you following me?"

Startled, Trento took a step back. "Whaddaya mean? Let go."

"You were in Villefranche. I remember you now. You were in the lobby of the Welcome Hotel and pretended to read when I passed by a few weeks ago. Then, more recently, you were watching me at the harbour there. What are you up to?"

People around began to stare. Kate wheeled the trolley over to him. "Darling what's the matter?" she asked.

Alan said. "This guy …" turning to face Kate, and as he did so, Trento pulled his arm free and disappeared into the crowd. Annoyed, Alan pushed through the people around him only to see the back of Trento as he left the airport arrivals area, and stepped into a waiting limousine.

"Damn!" Alan said. "That guy is up to no good."

"Don't worry, Alan," Kate said. "It may just be a coincidence."

Alan and Kate spent that night in his apartment. The next day they planned to go to Alan's cottage for a week's honeymoon. Before leaving Toronto, Alan decided to drop into his office at Commerce Court to check on a few files he had left his associates to work on. He parked his car in the underground lot and took the elevator to his office. Exiting the elevator, he saw a number of TV camera crews outside his office. Lights flashed as he approached. Voices were raised as reporters threw questions at him. Alan hesitated, what on earth was going on, he thought? A young man with an English accent stood in front of him, microphone in hand.

"Mr Bruce," he began, "I am Simon Locksley of BBC Newsworld. Would you like to comment on Alabama Governor Mike Malloy's suggestion that you donate the original King Alfonso letter to the new Saviour Shrine in Montgomery?"

Alan blinked. He had not known of Malloy's comment.

"I cannot really say anything. I haven't seen, read, or heard of what he has proposed."

"Well," Locksley continued, "essentially, he's asking you to donate the original document, so that it can be alongside the Jesus casket in a new shrine, or museum, if you like, that they intend to build in Montgomery."

Alan's lips tightened in a thin line.

"They have a nerve suggesting that. The casket belongs in Scotland. That's where they got it, by some unusual means, and that is where it should be. So, here is my proposal. Return the casket to Scotland and I will donate the Alfonso letter to be alongside it in the Royal Museum of Scotland in Edinburgh. I think that's fair and reasonable."

Locksley continued, "So your answer to Governor Malloy is a 'no'?"

"You've got it!" Alan smiled and pushed through the TV crews to enter his office.

Later that day, Alan drove Kate north from Toronto, for about two hours past Peterborough and Bobcaygeon, where he turned west for five miles before making a sharp right-hand turn down a dirt road. Tall stands of pine trees glowered over the road. A bend took them past a beaver pond, before Alan turned right down a steep hill where the waters of a deep blue lake glistened in the afternoon sun.

Kate gasped as she saw Alan's cottage. It was L-shaped with a steep roof. Wall to wall windows looked down towards a small jetty by the lake, beside which a twenty-six-foot powerboat bobbed in gentle waves. Across the lake she saw a steep series of hills covered with pine and maple trees. "This is wonderful," Kate said. "Did you design this?"

"No, Mum and Dad found the spot and put a lot of love into its design. It's very quiet here. There are only twenty cottages on the lake." He grabbed her round the waist with one arm, and placing the other under her legs, he lifted her up. He kissed her.

"Well, my bride, shall we begin our formal honeymoon?" With that, he carried her into the cottage, and walked through the large great room, with floor to ceiling windows, which gave a spectacular view over the lake to the thickly wooded hills beyond. He placed her gently into a king-sized bed in the master bedroom.

Kate lay back and spread her arms wide, luxuriating in the comfort of the bed. "Isn't this the time to pop the champagne?" she asked.

Alan laughed. "I'll put it on ice," then added, with a glint in his eye, "I hope that's the only thing I have to put on ice."

Back in Toronto, Trento watched the TV news and saw Alan Bruce's interview. Ten minutes later his phone rang and Conti spoke to him. Varley had also seen the TV reports and wanted to know where Bruce and Kate were; Trento was given the task of finding out. Not being particularly subtle, Trento took the direct approach by phoning Alan Bruce's office and asking to see him. Donna, Alan's secretary, said he was on vacation at his cottage and inadvertently let slip the location: Cavendish Lake.

Trento had no idea of the geography of Ontario, but after a few minutes with a map he found Cavendish Lake, west of Bobcaygeon, wherever that was, and called Conti.

"Go there," Conti said. "Be discreet, but keep an eye on them. If necessary, I'll come up to Canada and be with you."

Trento rented a car and set off for Cavendish Lake. He had difficulty in finding the cut-off that Alan had taken earlier, but after a few unsuccessful attempts, he found the road and drove down past two cottages with the owners' names showing on large wooden signs at the start of their driveways. The third cottage, remote from the others, had a sign showing "Bruce's Castle."

Trento stopped the car and walked slowly down the hill. Lights were shining from the windows and he could hear a CD playing soft jazz. As he watched, he saw a woman enter the main room and sit down in an armchair facing a log fire. It was Kate Harris; but there was no sign of Alan Bruce.

He moved closer. A voice behind said, "Who the hell are you?"

He turned to see Alan Bruce facing him with a baseball bat in his hand. Alan leaned forward as he recognised Trento.

"You again," he growled. "Okay, this time I want answers."

Trento kicked out hitting Alan on the knee. He fell, and Trento turned to run. Alan hurled the baseball bat and hit Trento's knee, which buckled as he fell to the ground in agony. Alan limped over. He stood menacingly above Trento, picked up the bat and held it in his hand.

"Right," he said, "now I need some answers before I start breaking bones."

Trento sat up, trying to figure out how he might escape from this predicament. He had a knife in a sheath attached to his left leg. "Help me up," he said, trying to distract Alan as he pulled the knife from the sheath. Alan glimpsed the flash of metal and brought the baseball bat down on Trento's arm. The bone broke with a resounding crack, and Trento fell back in agony. "You bastard," he cried. "I'll get even with you for that!"

"Perhaps," Alan said, standing over him with his bat held ready for another swing. "But now, little man, you are going to tell me who is employing you."

Over the next twenty minutes, Trento told all he knew. He had been employed by Bruno Conti to follow Alan and Kate, and to let Conti know where they were. He said he knew nothing about any connection with Mark Varley, Jackson Ford, or the Crusade. Alan was almost sure of that after he had applied some pressure on Trento's broken arm. But since he knew that Conti worked for Varley, it was obvious that Varley was behind the surveillance. Alan led Trento to his car, which was parked in the bushes at the end of his driveway. He pushed Trento into the driver's seat.

"Tell Conti, and whoever is behind him, that I won't be pushed around. And don't come near me or my wife again, or I'll do even more damage to you next time."

Alan watched as Trento gingerly, with only one usable arm, attempted to reverse the car to return to the main road. "By the way Trento," he said, "next time you come into cottage country, remember that noise travels a long way. I heard you coming a long way off, and you didn't even put out the car lights. Stick to city crime."

When Alan returned to the cottage, Kate was standing anxiously by the porch.

"What was that, Alan?" she asked anxiously.

"I think Varley and his gang must know something. They seem to have people following us. We'll need to be careful." Inside the cottage, Alan opened a bottle of chablis and poured a glass. Kate declined. "That's a no-no now. I really shouldn't have taken that glass of champagne earlier, but that will be the last for a while." Alan was frowning.

"Lighten up, Alan," Kate said. "There's been no damage to us."

He put his glass down. "Not yet," he said. "But I intend to stop Varley and his crew."

"How do you propose to do that?"

Alan scratched his chin as he thought; then he found an answer.

"I'll let them know that if they don't stop following us, I'll leak the name of Grace Christopherson to the media."

Kate and Alan had a wonderful week at the cottage. They swam and took the boat for long sails down the lake, exploring small bays where they would anchor, swim, and make love later in the small cabin. One time, Alan caught two large lake trout and barbecued an unforgettable meal under the stars. Together, alone, for a glorious week, they were like children discovering the surprises and joys of Christmas morning.

At the end of the week they returned to Toronto. Kate left for Boston to wind up her teaching duties before arranging an extended maternity leave. Alan returned to his office where mail awaited him. One letter was from Dr. Vacca. He read it with growing dismay.

Dear Mr. Bruce,

I regret to advise you that my colleague, Dr. Stefano Donadoni, has been seriously assaulted by two American men. They beat him up, and forced him to divulge that I had treated Dr.Harris, and that she was now preg- nant. Please understand that under normal circumstances neither Dr Donadoni nor I would have revealed the name of Dr. Harris. I apologise for the fact that these criminals have extorted the information from Dr Donadoni, who remains in hospital suffering from multiple fractures.

Under these circumstances, I thought you should be made aware of the situation, which I trust will not present you with a problem.

Please understand that I have preserved patient confidentiality regarding Dr. Harris; and I know that you will understand that Dr. Donadoni revealed the information only under extreme duress.

Yours sincerely,

Dr. Sophia Vacca.

Alan threw the letter down on his desk. Right, he thought: I can play tough too. He asked his secretary, Donna, to get a number for him. When it rang he spoke to Simon Locksley of BBC Newsworld.

"Mr Locksley," he said, "I have some interesting information for you."

CHAPTER 37

The phone rang as Mark Varley returned to his office. It was Bruno Conti, who sounded angry.

"Mark," Conti said, "It's Bruno. Some news for you. Fabio Trento followed Bruce and his wife to a cottage in Ontario. He was doing as I asked, keeping a watch on them. But that bastard Bruce broke his arm."

"What?" Varley shouted. "I told you to watch them, not to be involved. I didn't want any contact with them. Not yet anyway."

"I know, I know," Conti replied. "Fabio made a mistake. It was dark, and he was in the bushes watching their cottage when Bruce came up behind him. They had a struggle and Bruce hit him with a baseball bat."

"Damn!" Varley said. "Fabio is a fool. Do you still need him?"

"Well, he's not going to be any use for seven or eight weeks, until the fracture heals. But then, yeah, I need him. He's good at the physical stuff, and I guess we might need his muscle at some point."

Varley thought for a moment before replying.

"OK Bruno. But I don't want any more slip ups."

"You still want us to watch Bruce?" There was silence on the line and Conti said, "Mark? Are you still there?"

"Yes, I'm here, just thinking." Varley ran a few scenarios through his mind before deciding that he did not need a continuous watch on Bruce. Nothing much would be gained by that. When a child was likely to be born, about seven months from now for Grace and probably a few weeks later for Kate Bruce, he would reinstate the surveillance. Aloud he said, "Bruno, I think we can put the watch on hold for a few months. I'll contact you when we need to restart."

"Fine with me: you know where to find me."

Varley lit a cigarette and stood by his office window, overlooking the site where the shrine and several new hotels would soon begin construction. Remembering Governor Malloy's request for the names of the hotel chairmen he had been in contact with, he opened his door to speak to his secretary who could provide the contact details.

She looked flustered. "Mr. Varley," she said, "we're getting a lot of telephone calls from news media. They're asking questions about Grace Christopherson."

"What?" Varley's blood pressure rose and his face turned red. "Who is calling you?"

"It's easier to say who's not. We've already had calls from CNN, ABC, Fox, BBC, etc."

"Okay, I'll deal with it. Are there media waiting?"

"Yes, quite a few camera crews and reporters are in the parking lot."

"OK. Please call Governor Malloy's office and give them the names and contact numbers for the hotel chairmen I've been speaking to." Varley went back into his office, pondering his next steps. First, he decided he needed to speak to Jackson Ford.

"You look like you've seen a ghost, Mark," Ford said as Varley walked in without knocking.

"Something like that," Varley replied. He then told Ford what he had learned.

Ford slumped in his chair, despondent. "How can we deal with this?" he asked.

Varley walked to Ford's window, deep in thought. He turned and sat down opposite the preacher. "Jackson, we need to think our way carefully through this. I don't know how the media got Grace's name and whether they know about the cloning. If so, it could only have come from Dr. Vacca." Another thought crossed his mind. "Wait a minute! There could be another explanation. Alan Bruce's girlfriend, now his wife, was on Nova Wisp a few days after Grace. Perhaps she discovered Grace's name and Bruce has given it to the media to cause us problems."

Varley crossed to Ford's desk and picked up the phone. He rang his secretary and asked for Sophia Vacca's phone number before dialling her.

"Hello, this is Dr. Vacca," he heard on the other end.

"Dr. Vacca, this is Mark Varley. I'm very concerned. The media here are asking questions about Grace Christopherson. Have you or any of your staff given her name to any reporter?"

"Of course not!" Vacca snapped back. "Patient information is confidential. Neither I nor any of my staff would resort to such a breach."

"Thank you, Dr. Vacca. That's reassuring." Mark Varley put the phone down. It had to have been Alan Bruce's work. He turned to Jackson Ford who raised an eyebrow, questioningly. "It must have been Alan Bruce. He's the one who must have told the media."

Ford leaned forward. "Now what?"

"Well, we could say that Bruce's wife is also carrying a clone, but that defeats our purpose. Or we could deny any knowledge of Grace, but the media will probably keep snooping until they find her, though I think she's pretty safe at the Van Papen's Plantation."

Varley lit a cigarette. He knew that Ford disapproved of smoking, but he needed to relieve his tension. He took a deep draw on the cigarette, exhaled a puff of blue smoke from his nostrils.

"Tell you what, Jackson, I'll inform the media that Grace used to work here, but has left. I'll also say that a woman somewhere in Europe is carrying a clone of Jesus. That should keep them busy for a while."

"Will they buy that?" Ford asked anxiously.

"I don't know. It will make some headlines and set reporters scurrying. They'll want to know our involvement, but I'll stonewall. No comment will be my approach."

An hour later, Varley entered a conference room in the church's office building. It was filled with reporters and TV crews. He went to a platform, looked down on the crowded room and said, "I'm Mark Varley, CEO of the Crusade for Christ. I understand some of you have been making enquiries about Miss Grace Christopherson, an employee of the Crusade ..."

He was interrupted by Cindy Ritcey of CNN. "Yes, we have. Where is she?"

"In a moment, Miss Ritcey, if you don't mind. Please allow me to speak, then I'll take a few questions." He continued, "As I said, Miss Christopherson is an employee of ours. She is on a leave of absence, and is not working here at the moment. We expect she will return in a short time. Now, I'll take a few questions."

Simon Locksley of BBC Newsworld jumped in. From the information Alan Bruce had given him, he had just broken the story in a report in the BBC Newsworld programme. "Mr. Varley, it has been suggested to me that Miss Christopherson is pregnant and is carrying a clone of Jesus Christ. Can you confirm that?"

"Certainly not. We do not divulge personal information, but Simon, you're on the wrong track. Yes, we have succeeded in cloning, but the surrogate mother is in Europe, in a location I cannot divulge, for obvious reasons."

The media sensed a huge story and pressed for more information, with Cindy Ritcey leading the way. Everyone wanted to speak. Varley raised his hand for silence. Then he pointed to Cindy.

"So," she began, "you're telling us that you have cloned Jesus, that the surrogate mother is in Europe, and that it has nothing to do with Grace Christopherson ..."

Varley interrupted before she could say more. "I think you've answered your own question."

Cindy Ritcey was not going to be deflected so easily.

"Okay, then, when is the clone due to arrive. Can you at least tell us that?"

"In about seven months' time I expect," Varley smiled. "By then the Saviour Shrine and the hotels we are building on this campus will be ready. I invite you all to come for the opening ceremony." With that, Varley turned and left the room, leaving behind reporters who felt they had been thrown only a few crumbs; but the more astute realised that the big news was the successful cloning, even though the surrogate mother's name or location had not been divulged. Still, the name of Grace Christopherson would help with speculation, which was likely to continue over the next six months.

Varley returned to his office and phoned Jerry Van Papen to confirm that Grace was well and secure. He advised Van Papen to let Grace know that the media had her name and that the Reverend Ford wished her to remain at the plantation, where he would visit her to provide counselling and prayer.

* * * *

The next seven months passed quickly for Ford and Varley. Construction of the shrine and two hotels moved ahead—money being no object. A date for the formal dedication of the shrine was set. Both the Crusade and Governor Malloy were delighted with the quick progress. Malloy was especially pleased for the jobs that were being created, as a result of which his re-election seemed to be a formality, judging by the opinion polls.

Ford was becoming less and less concerned with worldly matters. He was completely absorbed by the Saviour Shrine, and frequently rehearsed the dedication ceremony in the privacy of his office. What a great day it would be, he thought. He would display the casket, and also, if his prayers were fulfilled, the actual clone of Jesus. He could hardly wait!

Grace, meanwhile, was content at the Plantation House. Never had so much attention been given to her. Ford visited regularly. The Van Papens looked after her like a well-loved daughter; and she glowed with health in the pregnancy. Although to some extent she was a prisoner at the plantation, she did not mind. She was going to bear the clone of Jesus, a blessing that her simple mind welcomed. Grace was now thirty-eight weeks pregnant, and felt ready to burst. The baby was strong and kicking. The doctors who visited her were pleased with the progress of her pregnancy. It was normal, they said.

She went into labour late at night, and called for Emily Van Papen. Emily was prepared and called for an ambulance to take Grace to hospital, where the on-call obstetrician was wakened to help with the delivery.

Grace was taken straight to the delivery room as her contractions were coming at regular intervals, only minutes apart. Before long, her waters burst and she felt tremendous pressure in her back as the baby began to descend. The medical and nursing staff monitored the progress, which went normally at first. However, the baby's pulse rate began to drop, and the obstetrician knew something was wrong. He decided to perform a caesarean, and a nurse rang the operating room. to get it ready. But before the staff could transfer Grace, the doctor shook his head. There was no pulse from the baby.

"Damn it!" he said, and decided to do the Caesarean on the spot. He told the anaesthetist to give Grace another epidural. "Don't worry Grace," he said, "the baby is going to be OK, but I need to get him out quickly."

Grace sobbed as the epidural began to take effect anaesthetising her lower abdominal area.

The obstetrician grew anxious. "I think we have an umbilical cord prolapse," he said. He knew that the baby's head was probably squashing the cord, cutting off oxygen, which could lead to brain damage. He got Grace into a knee-elbow position, and reached inside her vagina. He found the baby's head and tried to push it back into the uterus, but it was blocked by the cord. "Damn," he said, "the cord is cutting off the baby's blood supply and oxygen."

He picked up a scalpel, quickly made a transverse cut just above the edge of the bladder and proceeded to explore for the baby. After a few minutes he lifted it out. It did not breathe. "Quick," he cried, "we need resuscitation."

It didn't work. The baby was dead.

"No! Grace screamed. "It can't be! Jesus can't be dead!" She burst into tears.

The obstetrician looked at the anaesthetist will deep sorrow in his eyes. He shook his head. There was no more he could do.

The Van Papens had alerted Ford and Varley to the fact that Grace had gone into labour, and they were in the waiting room when the obstetrician arrived. He shook his head.

"Gentlemen, I'm sorry. Grace's baby didn't make it. The umbilical cord was wrapped around its neck, choking off the blood supply and oxygen. We did everything we could, including an emergency Caesarean, but it was too late." He looked distraught as took his glasses off and rubbed his eyes. "It's almost as if the baby had been strangled, the way the cord was round his neck."

Ford wept. It was not to be. However, he asked, "And Grace, will she be OK?"

"Yes," The doctor nodded, "she's a strong young woman. She'll recover physically. What it will do to her emotionally and psychologically, I don't know. We'll give her every support, of course, through our counselling services."

Ford and Varley thanked the doctor and went to see Grace. Ford hugged her.

"You did everything right, Grace. I'm proud of you. It was not to be. It was God's will and we must accept it."

Varley, of course, did not accept that this was the end. Kate Bruce was pregnant so there was still a chance that a viable infant might be born. He would have to find a way to get the baby, despite the obvious complication of kidnapping that might arise. He decided to sleep on the problem.

The next morning he was at the church office by 8:00 a.m.. Ford had not yet arrived; however, Varley had already decided on a plan of action. He rang Alan Bruce's office in Toronto and learned that he was out of the country. Pleading urgency for an important legal matter, he discovered that Bruce and his wife were in Scotland, at Bruce House in Dumbarton. He rang Bruno Conti in New York. A grumpy Conti answered his call. He had been out late the previous night, had drunk too much, and had a severe hangover. "Yeah, what is it?" he said.

"Bruno, this is Mark Varley. I need you to sober up, quickly. We need to catch a plane to Scotland tonight. Get Fabio Trento as well: we're going to need help in dealing with Alan Bruce."

Conti yawned then a smile crossed his face. "Bruce? Fabio will love dealing with him. I'll call him right now. Can you get your secretary to arrange the flights? I guess you'll come through New York?"

"Yeah. That makes sense. I'll be in touch later."

Varley hung up and went out of his office to give instructions to his secretary. In view of the need for speed and confidentiality, assuming they managed to kidnap Kate, Varley told his secretary to charter a jet. It left Montgomery at noon and flew to New York, refuelling and picking up Bruno Conti and Fabio Trento. After an eight-hour flight they landed in Scotland at Prestwick Airport, south of Glasgow. That airfield dealt with charters and was likely to be less concerned with bureaucratic paperwork than Glasgow's international airport. Nevertheless, they still had to pass through Immigration Control. The bright young Scottish officer smiled and took their passports. As she swiped Conti's, a window flashed on the screen. The police were interested in knowing about Conti's movement should he return to the UK, and Inspector Peter Dawson of the Lothians and Borders police was to be notified. She handed the passport back to Conti.

"Where will you be staying, Mr Conti?" she asked.

Varley interrupted. "We're going fishing. Hope to catch something interesting."

"I see," she said and took his passport. Again a warning notice flashed on the screen.

Inspector Dawson was going to be busy, she thought. "Here you are, Mr. Varley," handing the passport to him, "I still need to know where you're going to be staying."

"At Cameron House on Loch Lomond," Varley blurted out, with the first location that came into his mind.

Trento's passport did not prompt any warning, so with that the three men left Immigration and went to the car rental area, where Varley collected the keys for a large BMW and got directions which would take him to the Glasgow area, where he would use the Erskine Bridge to cross the River Clyde to the north shore. From there it would be a short ten-minute drive to Bruce House.

* * * *

In Edinburgh, Inspector Peter Dawson frowned as the names of Varley and Conti came up on his computer screen. The message had come in ten hours earlier, while he had been out of his office attending a "must-be-there" meeting with senior police officials. So, Varley and Conti were going to Cameron House apparently, and had arrived on a privately chartered jet. He tapped his pen on his desk, pondering what all this meant. He picked up his phone and spoke to detective Malcolm Wright, a former Scottish rugby star and still a very fit athlete. "Malcolm," he said, "can you call Cameron House on Loch Lomond and see if they have any reservations for a Mark Varley or a Bruno Conti?"

The answer came back five minutes later. There were no reservations in these names. Dawson scratched his nose. Something strange was going on, but what? He went back in his mind over the Varley and Conti connection. It had all arisen because of the vandalisation of the Bruce plinth at Melrose Abbey—not to mention the still unsolved murder of Andy McPhee. Dawson tapped his pen on his desk as he thought. Then it came to him. Early in his enquiries, Varley had denied knowing Conti! That had to have been a lie! But why were they back in

Scotland? As he thought, he remembered that Alan Bruce had tried to convince him that Varley might be behind the incidents at Melrose. He knew that the Bruce estate was near Loch Lomond. Could Varley and Conti be on the way there? But why would they want to see Alan Bruce? Dawson got the phone number for Bruce House. Jamie Robb answered his call and listened to his request. "Right you are, Inspector," he said, "hold on for a bit and I'll get Sir Alan for you."

A new voice came on the line. "How can I help you Inspector?"

"That I don't really know, Sir Alan. I've just been alerted to the fact that two individuals we might want to question in connection with the incident at Melrose Abbey last year have arrived in Scotland from America."

"Really? How does that affect me?"

"I was hoping you might help me answer that," Dawson replied.

"I'd be glad to help. What are their names?"

"Mark Varley and Bruno Conti."

"What?" Alan shouted. "Varley and Conti? Inspector they are trouble. I'm sure they must be on the way here. I think we need help."

"Right you are sir. I'm on my way and I'll also alert the Strathclyde police."

Alan put the phone down and went to look for Kate. He found her sitting in an armchair, by the double bay window that looked south over the River Clyde, far downhill. She was nearly at term: her body clearly showing that her pregnancy was near its end. "What's the matter, Alan?" she asked, seeing the anxiety in his face.

"Bad news, I'm afraid. Inspector Dawson has just phoned me. It seems that Mark Varley and Bruno Conti have arrived from America, and I suspect they may be on the way here."

"But why?"

"Don't know for sure, but you know that I gave their surrogate mother's name, Grace Christopherson, to the BBC. And you'll remember that a few nights ago we saw that brief clip on the BBC about Varley's news conference in Montgomery, in which he again denied that Grace was carrying the clone. Perhaps he's found out that I gave the name to the BBC and wants some sort of revenge." A darker thought, crossed Alan's mind and he frowned.

"What's the matter, darling?" Kate saw the anxiety on his face and touched his arm.

"Damn!" Alan said. "Varley obviously believes you are carrying a clone of Jesus. Maybe he wants to make sure that your baby doesn't survive. He won't want two clones of Jesus!"

"Don't say that, Alan." Kate put her hand to her mouth. "Surely nothing can happen. Not now. Not after almost nine months carrying the baby."

Alan put his arms round her, and kissed her cheek. "Don't worry darling, I'll get Jamie to help me make the place secure, and by the way, Inspector Dawson and the police should be here soon."

CHAPTER 38

Darkness was falling as Varley and his colleagues turned right, off the main road from Glasgow and drove up the Dumbuck Brae towards Bruce House. They had spent the day at a small hotel outside Glasgow, resting for the night's work ahead. All going well, they expected to be back at Prestwick Airport in the early hours of the morning. The pilots had been told to expect a 3:00 a.m. takeoff for Montgomery.

A full moon, partially obscured by clouds, began to appear in the sky, outlining the craggy hills above Dumbarton. The grey stone tower of Bruce House stood out in the moonlight above the old stone walls of the baronial mansion. A ripple of light twinkled across the lily pond to the south of the house. In the overwhelming silence of the lonely hillside estate the only sound was a soft wind that hushed through the bushes.

Varley stopped as he reached the stone pillars at the entrance to the Bruce House estate. Fifty yards ahead, he saw a thick stand of rhododendron bushes, an ideal place to conceal the car. He pulled in, making sure that the car was not easily seen. They got out and Varley gave instructions

"I'll go to the front door and deal with whoever answers. Bruno and Fabio—you go round to the back of the house. You're sure to find another way in. Deal with whoever you meet, then join me at the front of the house. Remember, all we want is the pregnant woman. Everyone else is disposable."

Conti smiled. "Waste them, you mean?"

Varley normally detested violence, but if there were any surviving witnesses to the kidnapping his plan would be thwarted. He had now gone too far to let anything stand in the way of his grand scheme. It must appear that the cloned child was the one that the Crusade had initiated.

"Yeah, I guess that's what I mean, but we have to make it look like an accident." Varley considered how an accident might be contrived. A solution came to him. On his last trip to Bruce House he'd seen a stone bridge just to the west of the house. It spanned a waterfall that tumbled down the hillside into a stream about one hundred feet below the bridge, an excellent place for an accident he thought.

"There is a stone bridge just a few yards beyond the house. It has a rock-filled stream about one hundred feet below. That might be a good place for an accident."

Trento smiled. He could hardly wait to get his revenge on Alan Bruce. Varley watched Conti and Trento creep through the bushes and disappear down the hillside towards the rear of Bruce House. With a final shrug of determination he walked boldly towards the massive wooden front door of Bruce House, past the two stone lions guarding the entranceway.

While Varley rang the doorbell, Conti and Trento went silently down the hill. The garden to the rear of the house was in shadow as the moon went behind some dark clouds. They reached a door, which Conti tried. It was locked: no problem, he had picked locks before. In a minute he heard a click as the lock was sprung and he pushed the door open. It led into a small entrance hall off the kitchen. He looked around. No sign of anyone. He signalled Trento to follow him. Varley had mentioned that on his last visit there had been an elderly housekeeper and a man who seemed to be Sir Jock's gardener-handyman. But he didn't know if they lived in the house. No problem, Conti thought. Between Trento and himself they could deal with any opposition.

Gingerly, Conti opened the kitchen door. It led into a hallway, across which he assumed lay the dining room. At the end of the corridor he saw the back of Alan Bruce, who opened the front door where Varley's face appeared.

"Fabio," he motioned the younger man forward and whispered, "try to get behind Bruce and deal with him. I'll look for the others."

Trento grinned. Time for revenge on the bastard who had broken his arm.

Varley had stood patiently as the doorbell rang. It seemed to echo hollowly within the large mansion before Alan Bruce opened the door. He gazed at Varley, astonished at his bold effrontery in making such a direct approach.

"Varley! What the hell are you doing here?" he said.

"Mr Bruce, good to meet you again. I think there is a situation of mutual interest that we should discuss."

"Mutual interest?" Alan chuckled. "My God, Varley, you have a nerve. I can't think of any mutuality of interest, unless you have come here to return the casket you stole."

Varley smiled benevolently. "Well, Alan, I guess that's something we might discuss. May I come in?"

Alan was not taken in by Varley's apparent reasonableness.

"No, you can't. In fact, I think I should let the police know that you are here."

"I wouldn't do that," Varley said and pushed forward. He was no match for Alan who held him and pushed him back. "Get out, Varley," he shouted.

Alan felt a tap on his shoulder. He turned and saw Fabio Trento smiling at him, just before Trento hit him on the head with a cosh. Alan slumped to the ground and Trento went to hit him again.

"I wouldnae dae that mister," said a voice behind Trento. It was Jamie. He pointed a loaded shot gun at Trento. "Pick Sir Alan up," he ordered Varley, still keeping the gun aimed at Trento.

Alan groaned as Varley started to pull him to his feet. While Jamie's attention was distracted, Trento moved quickly, pushed Varley to one side and got behind Alan. "Now you old fart," he said to Jamie, "what are you going to do? If you pull the trigger you'll kill your boss."

Jamie hesitated. "Aye, but I'll also get you bastards!" he growled defiantly. "Now, before I shoot, release Sir Alan."

Trento was not fooled. He'd been in tight situations before in New York. Being threatened with a gun was nothing new for him, particularly as he saw Conti appear from a doorway down the hall. Alan, although dazed, also saw Conti.

"Look out Jamie!" he shouted.

Jamie turned, and Trento hit Alan again on the wrist: he yelled in pain. Jamie swung back. "You bastard!" he shouted, cocking the gun. But he had forgotten Conti, who ran forward and hit the old man on the head with a poker. Jamie dropped like a stone.

Alan was now surrounded by the three intruders. His head ached, and it felt as if Trento had broken his wrist.

Varley pushed a finger against Alan's chest. "Okay, Bruce. No more games. Where is she?"

"Who?" Alan asked.

Trento punched him in the stomach and Alan groaned and dropped to his knees.

"Your wife," Varley said.

"Here I am!" Kate appeared at the first floor landing in the central stairway. "What do you want?" She looked in dismay at Alan who was obviously in pain, and then noticed Jamie, lying unconscious. As fast as she could, she ran to her room, locking the door behind her. She dialled 999 for the police, but there was no sound. Conti had already cut the telephone lines.

Downstairs, Varley told Conti and Trento to take Alan and Jamie and dump the bodies off the stone bridge. He began to climb the stairs to Kate's bedroom.

Inspector Dawson and his men had been delayed by a bad accident on the M8 between Edinburgh and Glasgow. They also had difficulty in finding the correct cut off from the Glasgow road, which would lead them to Dumbuck Brae, the road leading to Bruce House. As a result, Dawson was about twenty minutes behind Varley.

The police car quietly entered the Bruce estate. Detective Malcolm Wright, who was driving, slowed as he saw the outline of a car hidden among some bushes. He stopped the car and got out. It was a silver BMW, with no sign of any occupants. He noted the car's registration number and called Strathclyde police to check it out. Within a minute the answer came back. It was a rental from Prestwick Airport, and the renter was Mark Varley.

Dawson nodded when he heard the news. "Let the air out of the tyres, "he ordered. "They can't get away with flat tyres."

A few seconds later they approached Bruce House, and Wright stopped the car at a bend in the road beyond which the castle-like tower of the mansion was clear in the moonlight.

"We walk from here," Dawson said.

The four policemen went forward cautiously and dropped to the ground behind bushes as the front door of Bruce House opened. A shaft of light emerged, and in its glow, Dawson saw four men appear. Trento was dragging Jamie, his hand under his shoulders, while Jamie's feet bumped along the path. Alan Bruce, who appeared in some pain, was walking in front of Bruno Conti, who kept squeezing on Alan's injured wrist while keeping an arm around Alan's neck.

With hand signals, Dawson motioned his men to move forward, silently. They crept along behind the bushes that led to the old stone bridge. They could now hear the distant sound of rushing water cascading down the hillside and splashing into the rock-strewn stream below the bridge.

Conti and Trento had now reached the bridge. On it there were four curved abutments, or viewing places, where, in normal times, visitors could stand and watch the waterfall below. But the times were not normal. Conti stood with his arm around Alan's neck. Dawson was now close enough to hear Conti say,

"Fabio, we'll toss the old guy over first. That way Bruce will have some idea of what lies in store for him."

"Wait a minute!" Alan shouted. "Why are you doing this? If it's money, I can pay more."

Conti shook his head. "It's not about money. We're well paid. It's revenge. Varley is annoyed at you for upsetting his plans for the Crusade and their Saviour Shrine. But there's something else too; I don't know what exactly, but I suspect it's to do with all that talk of cloning Jesus."

Alan snorted, "And that's reason enough to kill us?"

"I guess so," Conti said signalling Trento to pick up Jamie. Fabio Trento bent and began to lift Jamie from the ground.

There was the sound of rushing feet on the bridge as Inspector Dawson and his men ran forward.

"Police!" he shouted. "Stand back from the edge of the bridge! Release these people!"

Conti looked round in dismay and let go of Alan. Trento was more defiant and began to hoist Jamie over the edge. Alan ran forward and kicked Trento viciously in the groin. Trento groaned in agony and released Jamie, who was caught just in time by Detective Wright. He looked admiringly at Alan. "Nice kick," he said "Right in the goolies!"

"He deserved it, and more!" Alan growled, starting to run towards Bruce House with Inspector Dawson following. "There's one more, Inspector," Alan gasped as he ran, "Mark Varley is alone in Bruce House with my wife."

Kate stood by the dressing table in her bedroom. She picked up scissors, the only instrument she could find to try to defend herself. Varley had stopped knocking at the door, and she heard a click as he picked the lock and pushed the door open.

"Get out!" she cried, pointing to the door.

"Mrs Bruce," Varley said, smiling patronisingly, "there's no need to be unreasonable. I won't harm you."

"What are you doing here? Where is my husband?"

"He's fine, Mrs Bruce," Varley said, trying to calm her. "Now, I'd like you to come with me. You'll be safe, I assure you."

"I don't believe you!" Kate cried.

"No matter, Mrs. Bruce. However, I do need you to come with me." Varley moved forward holding out his hand to her.

Kate stabbed his hand with the scissors. Varley grunted in pain as blood squirted from the back of his hand.

"You bitch!" Varley shouted. He slapped her face. Kate screamed.

At the front entrance, Alan and Inspector Dawson heard her cry and rushed towards the stairs leading to the first floor bedroom.

"Sorry Mrs. Bruce," they heard Varley say, "I didn't mean to hit you." He paused, wiping blood from his hand. "You see, Mrs. Bruce, I really do need you to come with me. We need your child when it is born. It will fulfil our dream of cloning Jesus.

"What happened to Grace Christopherson? Hasn't her child been born?"

Varley shook his head. "Sadly, it died in childbirth. Jackson Ford said it was God's will. Perhaps it was, but we have a second chance with your baby. Perhaps that's God's will too."

"You're mad!" Kate shouted.

Varley shook his head. "No, I'm just a perfectionist. When I first heard of the casket that Sir Jock had buried at Melrose, I had to get it. I also wanted the Alfonso letter, but he wouldn't give it to me. So I had to take the English translation he had here at Bruce House"

"Take?" Kate asked, trying to keep Varley talking. She was sure that Alan or Jamie would appear soon to get rid of him.

"Yes, take," Varley replied. "The old bastard wouldn't give it to me. In fact, he slapped my face and told me to get out. Well, no one gets away with hitting me, as I'm afraid you've found out. I punched him, and he collapsed."

Kate's eyes opened wide. "So you killed him?"

"No, I hit him. One punch to the chest. If he had a heart attack—well," Varley smiled, "maybe that was also God's will."

"That's contemptible. You really are mad!" Kate said, moving back from him and trying to find a means to avoid him coming closer.

"Well, that's your opinion. But now, Mrs. Bruce, I really do need you to come with me."

Kate shook her head. "Not until you tell me how you got hold of the casket."

"Mrs Bruce," Varley sighed, "you really are becoming tiresome. OK, if you must know, I smashed the plinth at Melrose Abbey and removed the casket. The guide had told me it was there, and unfortunately," Varley smiled, "he met with a little accident."

Inspector Dawson had waited quietly outside the bedroom door while Varley boasted about his accomplishments. He threw the door open.

"Police! Mr. Varley, I am placing you under arrest."

Varley started to run. He pushed past Dawson, but Alan, who was waiting outside, tripped him up. Varley fell to the floor with a crash and instantly Alan jumped on top of him to stop him getting away.

"Varley," he growled, "I should kill you for threatening my wife, and for killing my grandad."

"But you won't," Inspector Dawson said, touching his shoulder and asking him to rise. "Sir Alan, we'll take care of Varley and his crew. We've heard enough to put them away for a lifetime."

Before the police left with the three Americans in a wagon dispatched by Strathclyde police, they summoned an ambulance to take Jamie and Alan to hospital to get treatment for their injuries. Jamie had a concussion and Alan's wrist had been broken, as he'd suspected. He also had a large bump on his head. The police called British Telecom to restore the telephone line, and a police car was sent to fetch Mrs Doig, who had spent the night at her sister's house nearby. She would be company for Kate until Alan returned from hospital. Inspector Dawson also arranged for two policemen to stand guard outside, although he did not expect any more trouble.

Kate lay in her bed exhausted from the night's events. She was glad to know that Varley would not bother them again. Soon, with God's will—she was now able to smile at Varley's frequent use of the phrase—she would hold her own child.

* * * *

A few miles away, at the Vale of Leven Hospital, Alan held out his arm as the nurse wrapped a plaster cast around his fractured wrist. He gave a quick laugh, surprising the nurse.

"People don't usually laugh at this point," she said.

"Oh, it's nothing to do with the cast," Alan replied. He smiled as he again thought about Varley's confession. When the story became public, Ford would not be able to retain the casket, and his grandiose plans for the Saviour Shrine would crumble. There would be no casket, and no clone. What a satisfying ending. "Thank you," he said.

"You're welcome." the nurse said, smiling.

But the "thank you" wasn't meant for her.

CHAPTER 39

In the months following Sir Jock's death, it emerged that Alan was going to be a very wealthy man. Jock's investments exceeded what his old lawyer, Cameron Learmonth, had anticipated. Alan was left with the knowledge that he need never work again. Nevertheless, he maintained his law practice in Toronto, but made his two associates full partners and brought in several young lawyers to help. Alan became the rainmaker, bringing in business, but leaving the detailed legal work to his colleagues.

Kate grew to enjoy Toronto, and together they bought a large house in a leafy area only ten minutes from the downtown core of the city. Kate left Harvard and secured a teaching position at the University of Toronto. However, Alan decided that he would maintain Bruce House in recognition of his grandfather Jock's wishes, and also to preserve the Bruce name and history.

As Kate's pregnancy developed, they had to reach a decision about where the baby should be born. Alan announced that he thought the child should be born in Scotland. Kate didn't mind, just so long as she was well looked after and the baby was born safely. She had gone through regular checkups in Toronto and knew that everything was normal.

Through contacts in Toronto, Alan had arranged a referral for Kate to see Dr. Donald Walker, reckoned to be the top obstetrician in Scotland. A week before the incident with Varley and his men, Kate had seen Dr. Walker at The Queen Mother's Hospital in Glasgow. Walker was a tall, distinguished looking Scot, with dark grey hair and glasses. He examined Kate and told her that he estimated she was almost due. As Kate was a private patient, he told her that he would be called whenever she presented at the hospital, and would personally supervise the birth.

Four days after Varley had been arrested, Alan was nursing a cast on his fractured wrist, which limited his manual ability. However, when Kate told him that she was experiencing labour pains, he said he would drive her to The Queen Mother's Hospital in the West End of Glasgow, about twelve miles away.

"Don't panic, Alan," Kate smiled. "You can't drive with that wrist. I'll get Jamie to take us."

"Well, OK, but I'm coming with you."

Kate felt the labour pains coming closer together as she reached the hospital. A nurse appeared with a wheelchair and Kate was taken away. Jamie went to park the car, and Alan was directed to the waiting room. Dr. Walker was one of the old school, and believed fathers should not be present, since they were often a distraction.

Five hours later, Dr. Walker appeared and smiled at Alan. "Congratulations, Sir Alan." He gave a broad smile. "Your baby is waiting, and," he added, "Kate is fine. She is a strong healthy woman and will be a great mother."

"Thank you," Alan said, and followed the doctor into the room where Kate proudly hugged a small bundle. Alan leaned over and kissed her.

"How are you darling?" he asked.

"Great, everything considered," she replied.

"And how is he?" Alan pointed to the baby.

"He? You mean she, don't you?"

"She?" Alan raised an eyebrow.

"Yes, she. It's a girl!"

"So it's really not a clone?"

"Didn't you believe me, Alan Bruce?"

"Well, of course." Alan shook his head. "But I guess there was always a little doubt in my mind."

"Don't have any doubts, darling. Can't you see? Paula has the Bruce nose and eyes." Kate pushed back some hair that had fallen over her face. "She's ours." A mischievous smile flickered across her face, and she said: "Unless you seriously want to believe that God has sent us his daughter!"

Epilogue

Six weeks later, Kate, Alan, and their daughter sat in Cameron Learmonth's office in Albyn Place in Edinburgh. The lawyer had phoned Alan a week before to remind him that he had a letter from Sir Jock, a letter which Jock had directed should be opened on the first anniversary of his death.

Alan and Kate could hardly believe that twelve months had passed since Jock's death. So much had happened in that time, so many surprises and twists of fate. But they were safe now, and baby Paula was proving to be a delightful child. She seemed bright and healthy, and her eyes sparkled with innate intelligence.

"Alan and Kate, it's good to see you again, not to mention your bonny wee daughter," the old lawyer smiled.

Kate comforted Paula as Cameron Learmonth continued. "You both certainly have had an exciting time from what I hear. That American—Varley, isn't it?—deserves to spend the rest of his life in jail. And if I were to believe that he had a hand in killing my old friend Jock ... why, I think even I might be tempted to violence."

Alan nodded in agreement. "I know how you feel, Cameron. Now, I suppose you want to give me Grandad's letter."

"Of course," Learmonth agreed. He reached into his desk drawer and produced a file. Opening it, he extracted an envelope on which, in Sir Jock's bold handwriting, were written the words: "For my grandson, Alan Bruce."

Cameron Learmonth handed the envelope to Alan.

"Please make yourselves comfortable here in my office. You may want to sit over there." He pointed to an oblong mahogany conference table near a large bay window overlooking Charlotte Square. "If you'll excuse me for a few minutes, I need to speak to one of my partners. Please ring my secretary in the meantime, if you need any help."

When Learmonth left, Alan held the envelope in his hand, deep in thought. What had Jock wanted to say to him, he wondered?

Kate looked at him and raised an eyebrow. "Well, aren't you going to open it?" she asked. Baby Paula murmured sleepily in her arms as she held her close.

"I guess I should," Alan said. He picked up a letter opener from Learmonth's desk and returned to the conference table, sitting close to Kate. He slit the envelope, and removed a letter and, with Kate peering over his shoulder, read his grandfather's words.

My dear Alan,

By the time you read this I shall have been dead for a year. Strange to write that: like most people, I have felt myself fairly invulnerable, and to write about death is somehow to accept one's frailties. However, I am now 83, and have been given only a few months to live so, like it or not, I have to acknowledge that my life has come to an end.

I've had a good life and wonderful wife and son, and you, Alan—a grandson whose love I have cherished. I have watched your career with interest and I'm proud of you. You bear the Bruce name with honour and dignity.

I'm grateful that we have been able to see each other quite regularly, despite the three thousand miles between our homes. In that regard, I do hope you will accept Bruce House as yours, and that you will maintain the tradition of occupying it with a wife and children in the years to come.

There is only one matter that now concerns me, and that is the recent attempt by an American by the name of Varley to acquire the casket that I buried beside the heart of our ancestor King Robert the Bruce at Melrose Abbey. I've met the man and I do not like the cut of his jib at all. Given his involvement with that evangelist, Jackson Ford, I sense that his interest in the casket is because of the hair—the hair of Jesus—that it contains. That is why I have phoned to alert you to that interest, for I believe he has some nefarious purpose in mind, should he acquire the hair, not that that is likely; but I've learned over my lifetime never to discount the possibility that some people are prepared to go to any lengths to acquire property.

Having phoned you earlier today, I am glad to know that you will be here tomorrow, for that will allow me time to tell you all I know about the casket and its provenance. It's real. I have no doubts about that.

I'm glad that I was able to rectify the omission of our ancestors by burying the casket, with the hair, alongside Bruce's heart and so—centuries later—fulfilling the request of King Alfonso. However, here I must confess to being a little bit devious. It must be something in our Bruce genes! I did not place all the hair in the casket. I decided one night—perhaps after too many malt whiskies—that I should retain some. But where to keep it? The answer came to me.

My late wife Molly had a gold locket in which she had kept a lock of her lustrous black hair. It was really lovely. She had strong black hair, with a distinct curl. (But here I digress. Forgive an old man!) So, I decided to place some hair from Jesus in the locket, and to find another place to keep your grandmother's hair. I recall taking Molly's hair from the locket and placing it on my desk. Then I took some hair from the casket that King Alfonso had given us in the fourteenth century and also placed it on my desk.

I smile now as I recall the scene. There was a roaring fire in the library. The sky was dark outside and thunder growled and rumbled in the distance. I rose from my desk to refill my glass and returned, a little shakily, I now admit, to my desk. As I sat down, my left hand inadvertently hit the two sets of hair and it all fell to the floor. I bent and retrieved what I could find—all of it, I'm now sure as I write this. I placed the hair in two piles, and put some of the hair from the casket in the locket, and replaced the rest in the casket. That is what is now buried beside Bruce's heart.

Your grandmother Molly's hair is now in my safety deposit box in Edinburgh. I'm fairly sure that all the hair in the gold locket I wear around my neck is that of Jesus. But quite honestly, as I think back, perhaps some of it is Molly's.

In any event, I'll tell you more when I see you.

In case anything happens to me, or I'm just forgetful, I intend to send this letter to my dear friend and our family lawyer, Cameron Learmonth in Edinburgh. I'll instruct him to give it to you one year after my death, by which time I hope I shall be looking down on you with pride.

Your loving Grandad,

Jock Bruce.

Alan's eyes filled with tears as he put the letter down on the desk. Jock had been his sole relative before Kate. There was silence, broken only by the soft tick of the grandfather clock in Cameron Learmonth's office. He turned to Kate, who shook her head sympathetically, sensing the emotions going though Alan's mind. She reached out and held his hand.

"God, I miss him!" he said.

"I know, he was a wonderful man. I could have fallen for him if he'd been a bit younger, or if I had been of his generation."

"He would have loved to have known that," Alan said, casually wiping a tear from his eye.

Kate gazed at him, hoping he'd seen what she had noted in Jock's letter. "Jock gave you a message," she said.

"Yes? I'm still trying to figure it out."

"Oh, I think I've got it," she said with a knowing smile.

"What?"

"From Jock's letter, there is an intriguing possibility."

"Tell me," Alan said, becoming impatient at Kate's teasing look.

"It's easy, really," Kate laughed, and looked at him with love in her eyes. She reached out and put an arm around him. "Darling, what Jock was saying; what his message is," she paused and shook her head in wonderment, "what his letter says," she wiped her eyes which were filling with tears.

"What is it, darling?"

Kate bit her lip wondering how to put it to Alan. She looked up, gazed at him with love in her eyes.

"Don't you see, Alan, if Dr Vacca had used the hair in the locket, Paula could have been the clone of your grandmother, Molly!"

Alan smiled momentarily, then a frown swept across his face as an errant thought chiselled into his mind.

THE END

978-0-595-45458-7
0-595-45458-5

Printed in the United States
86276LV00003B/19-36/A

9 780595 454587